Praise for Be

"Bogard has created a transformative story of murder and intrigue, paradise found and paradise lost, and a woman trying to find the truth within herself. *Beach of the Dead* entertains with its descriptive writing and interesting characters. ... The unique storyline captures and holds the reader's attention from the opening murder to the climactic finish."

— *American Writing Awards*

"... a fantastic continuation of the story...*Beach of the Dead* is a great experience to take pause and think about acceptance, what matters most in life, and how much the truth really can set one free."

— *Diane Lunsford for Feathered Quill Reviews*

"...Grabbed my attention right from the start, and the book kept getting better. ... Bogard expresses [trauma] eloquently without compromising her character or the integrity of her story. ... Highly recommend... Its ending left me with a feeling of empowerment."

— ☆ ☆ ☆ ☆ ☆ *Justine Reyes for Readers' Favorite*

"Bogard presents a deeply personal look at love, friendship, human connection, regret, and redemption in her compelling second installment in the Heartland Trilogy, 1986. Readers will devour this one and eagerly await the final installment in the trilogy. A stunner."

— ☆ ☆ ☆ ☆ ☆ *Bookview*

Beach of the Dead

A NOVEL

CYNTHIA J. BOGARD

atmosphere press

To Maggie, who posed the question,
and to Martha, who provided the answers

1

Pine Hill Station, Texas
March 1986

My first purchase in my new life as a fugitive was a pair of scissors. A smaller one than the standard-issue office model I'd used as a murder weapon just an hour before. But still.

There was blood on the sky-blue sweater, the one Ma had given me for Christmas. Not much, but it would leave a small oblong stain on the cuff. It was dried now, no use washing it off. Evidence I should dump as quickly as possible. Those were my first thoughts — regrets about a ridiculous sweater — as I hurried through the bone-chilling rain toward the bus station, my soaked sneakers making squishing sounds with each footfall.

Get rid of the evidence but keep the sweater, I decided, as I began to make out the Greyhound sign in the blinding torrent. It was the only one I had with me, and it might be cold in Mexico, at least in the mountains.

So, after checking the schedule and buying a one-way ticket, I used the time until the bus left to buy a pair of scissors, a traveler's sewing kit, a navy-blue workman's bandana, and a map of Mexico at the pharmacy next to the bus station.

An overnight bus to El Paso was leaving in forty-five minutes.

The chances they would be looking for me this soon, at that crossing, were remote. It was across the state from Pine Hill Station, Texas, where I'd been a graduate student in history until an hour ago when I had murdered my professor and graduate advisor. And lover. That life was over now, which hurt, because, more than anything, I loved school.

His wife was away for the weekend, wouldn't be home until Monday afternoon, he'd told me earlier, frantically patching together an excuse for why he had staked out my place, standing for hours in the inadequately sheltering bus stop across from my apartment in the frigid downpour. He'd looked so forlorn and bedraggled when he accosted me in the alley behind my house, begging for an explanation as to why I had ended our affair, that I stupidly, oh so stupidly, agreed to meet him later at his office on campus. Saturday night. I was confident that not even a janitor would enter Johnny's office and find his body until Monday evening. With any luck, I'd be over the border heading south by then.

The pharmacy had a private, self-enclosed bathroom. After making my purchases, I locked myself in and used the scissors to cut off my shoulder-blade-length blond hair until it was about an inch long all over my head. I flushed my locks down the toilet. It wasn't the greatest haircut, but it would do. I cut off the bloodied cuff of my sweater and the other one to match, unraveled each of the sleeve ends a bit so they wouldn't block up the john, and flushed those down, too.

Glancing at myself in the bathroom mirror, I realized how much I looked like Ma with my hair the length she had worn it when my father was alive. I remember vividly the morning she came downstairs without her beautiful head of thick, long, blond hair — hair that my father used to grab her by right before throwing her to the floor, kicking her while I watched, terrified, from under the kitchen table. Her shorn head was rewarded with a punch to the gut, but even as an eight-year-old, I understood that she had won that morning by literally cutting off one of the ways he had controlled her.

I fished my plain brown baseball cap from my backpack. I pulled it down over my uneven new hairdo and was satisfied with my anonymous and androgenous look. Brown raincoat, brown cap, blue jeans, wet sneakers — I could be anyone on this stormy night.

I returned to the station early enough to get a window seat on the bus six rows from the front. The bus was half full, evenly split between white kids heading to Mexico for spring break and Mexican-looking folks heading home or to visit relatives south of the border. No one sat next to me. I breathed a sigh of relief. The bus wouldn't stop again until Austin. I had time to think.

My mind tended toward rational thought, a quality I had put to effective use in these past minutes. In the seconds after the murder, I had attempted to make Johnny's office — the scene of the crime — look like a robbery. He had five rare Roman coins and a small vial made of ancient glass in his office. I pocketed them on my way out. I zipped up his pants to hide evidence of his attempted rape of me. I wiped all my prints off his desk and the scissors handle, but strategically left them on the smaller desk I used as his office assistant. And I pocketed the photo of Jenny, the reason for my crime.

I didn't like to think about the lapse in judgment that had put me on the lam, nor my initial decision after I'd returned home a murderer, to turn on the gas heater valve, crawl under the covers, and let my life ebb away. Jenny, my inspiring angel, had made me turn off the gas at the last minute, visiting me in a vision as the gas fumes wafted around me.

Fortuitously, I had cashed my work check to pay the rent on my near-campus studio apartment. Once I'd decided to head for Mexico instead of die, I grabbed the $300 in rent money from the desk drawer and hurriedly threw what I thought I would need into my backpack. Time would tell if I had packed adequately.

While we bus passengers sat in the dark, waiting to leave,

I took my new bandana out of the front pocket of my backpack stuffed under the seat in front of me, and surreptitiously removed the coins and the thumb-sized vial from my raincoat pocket. I wrapped these objects carefully in the bandana and tied it into a little ball, burrowed down to the bottom of my backpack, and placed the tied-up bandana gently between my socks and underwear.

My hands were steady, my heart beat regularly in my chest. About my recent actions, I felt nothing, nothing at all, a reaction I recognized as akin to what I had felt when I'd discovered my forty-year-old father dead on the sofa six years before. Shock, the women at the funeral insisted. That's why she hasn't cried. But it hadn't been shock then. Wasn't now. I didn't like to think about why I'd felt nothing. Was I soulless?

The Greyhound began rolling forward. But the bus driver, airbrakes hissing, stopped abruptly, opened the double doors, and said, "Well, come along, this bus is leaving."

A slight, dark-haired man about my height bounded into the bus with a small, faded orange backpack and took the empty seat next to mine. After realizing his thoroughly soaked red jacket was dampening the seat, he stood up, took it off, and put it in the overhead bin. His shirt, which wasn't too wet, was a vivid orange and brown paisley, with a wide collar. I thought those had gone out with the seventies.

"Hola, hello." He flashed a quick smile.

"Hi." Damn. Better not to talk with anyone so they couldn't ID me. But he was the friendly type. I could see that already.

"You go all the way to El Paso?" he asked, in Spanish-accented English.

"Uh-huh."

"Continuing on to México?" He pronounced it Meheco.

"Yes."

"Got your visa already?"

"I thought I could pick one up at the border." I hadn't thought about the issue of a visa, nor knew I needed one. Never been out of the country before.

"That is indeed the case." He spoke English with a formality that indicated it was a second language. "For the right price."

"I have to pay a bribe?" I couldn't help but blurt out. Must I commit bribery now as well?

"It is your good fortune, señorita, I have seated myself next to you. More good fortune, I have a cousin who works in the visa office in Ciudad Juárez, where americanos crossing in El Paso need to get a visa."

"I don't have much money," I said, truthfully enough. "How much would it cost to get you to help me with the visa?"

At that, my seatmate laughed. "It is my cousin who takes money for visas, not me. All I ask is that you be my American friend for this journey. I hope to practice my English with you." My seatmate beamed at me. He had a beautiful smile.

Great, just what I needed, a talkative man sitting next to me for the eighteen hours we'd be stuck together. On the other hand, if he could get me a visa...

"Me llamo Alejandro Jiménez, but in America I am Alex. And you, señorita?"

Name. One more item I hadn't bothered to think about during my, by now, two-hour stint as a criminal fugitive. Jenny, after the young woman in the photo? Not a promising idea. Likewise, I rejected Ma's name, Helen.

"Anna," I said finally. It had been my great-grandmother's name. Far enough removed from my own soon-to-be-former name, Jane, but a bit of my past, nonetheless. She had died before I was born, so I only knew her from two sepia photographs Ma kept in the cedar chest. But she was a link to my past I thought I could hold on to.

"And why do you travel to my country, señorita Ana? Business? Pleasure?"

"Ah...I need to get away for a while," I said truthfully. "Maybe for a long while."

"Me too. I must leave America for a small time. The law is looking for me. Don't worry, I won't hurt you!" He laughed.

2

Heading South

"Do not be alarmed, señorita. I am not a bandito. It is only because of a party. We were dancing under the disco ball. The music was loud."

"Why would that make the law look for you?" Surely, he must have done something more serious — slugged someone, or slit them with a switchblade? Wait. *I* was the stabber in row six.

"I hope this does not offend you, señorita Ana." Alex turned toward me with doubt in his eyes. "But I swore to my soul that I would be who I am when I can. I like boys. I am gay, as you say in America. And others like me too were having a party, and it was — how you say — raided by the policía. In Texas, it is not legal to like boys. I ran for my life but my boyfriend — I have an American boyfriend from Texas — su nombre es Luke — wasn't as fast as me and the policía banged his head with their stick and put him in the patrol car and off he went. I, myself, ran for the bus station. As I am a very lucky man, this bus going to El Paso stopped for me. And here I am."

"I didn't know that it was illegal," I said honestly. An image of my favorite professor at my former history graduate program, Maddie Haystead, flashed into my mind. Johnny, the man I had killed, had accused her of this very thing. Was she in danger of being tarred a criminal, too?

"I hear in New York, in California, it is okay to be who I am. But not in Texas." Alex looked down. "I hope Luke is not suffering in jail. He knows I will head back to México if there is trouble. But I wish I could tell him I was okay. And find out how he is."

"I could call the police station when we get to Austin and ask after him for you. The schedule says we stop for an hour there," I said, before thinking better of it. I was unused to being a fugitive, that was the problem. I was used to being a kind person when I was able. That would have to change too, sadly. Alex beamed a smile at me. He was quite handsome.

"Señorita Ana, it would be so great a gift... Shall we make a trade? I get you a visa and you produce this phone call for me in Austin. Luke and I have a plan. If we have trouble, we find a girl to call the police station. She says she is our sister — Juanita, if it is me who is taken, Jane — Jane is the name we use if it is Luke. Will you do this for me?"

The coincidence — that one of their codewords for concern in a time of trouble had been my name until a few minutes ago — sealed the deal for me. Logic told me no one would be looking for me until long after the bus left Austin. Helping someone unfairly made a criminal was one last act of charity, of normalcy, I could offer before I left my country forever for the unknown travails ahead. I nodded. "Sure. No problem."

"Muchas gracias, señorita Ana. Also, because you are going to México, shall I learn you español as you improve my English?"

"I don't speak Spanish at all, so, yes, that would be wonderful." Alex was proving to be a most useful seatmate.

We chatted amiably for a time; he providing me with words and simple sentences in his language, and I offering different word choices and correcting grammar mistakes in aid of his mostly fluent English.

The bus screeched to a halt. We had arrived in Austin.

"Here is the number of Pine Hill Station policía, señorita Ana. We carry it with us always. He is Luke Campbell. You say you are Jane Campbell, okay?"

I called. After a long wait and many words of pleading to tell Luke that his sister Jane had called, the officer on the other end finally admitted that my "brother" had been charged with public lewdness, fined, and released a few minutes ago. When I asked if he would have to go to court, the officer hung up on me.

"They let him go! He will be safe now." Alex was jubilant.

"Will you return to Pine Hill Station?"

"No, I will go to visit mi mamá for this month. Where will you go to in my country? ¿A dónde vas en México?"

I said the first place that came into my head, from a memory from the one real social event I'd been invited to since arriving in Texas. A dinner with Maddie Haystead, my former history professor, during which she told me of her adventures during graduate school, including a memorable winter break spent at a Mexican idyll. "Zipolite," I answered, recalling the name of the place she had spoken of enthusiastically. "I hear you can live on the beach cheaply there."

"Ah, I know it. Zipolite — the beach of the dead."

I looked at him in horror. "The beach of the dead?"

3

South Texas/The Border
with Mexico

Upon seeing my face, my good-looking seat mate laughed again, an easy, joyful sound that would have been infectious in other circumstances. "No, señorita Ana, it is not because of piratas — the men of the sea who attack other ships..."

"Pirates."

"Yes, pirates. No pirates in Zipolite. But there is a kind of water under the sea, that if you get stuck in it, will pull you out into the ocean. These poor people can never return to the shore. They die in the sea. A gringo meets this fate some years, I am sorry to say. The people who live in Zipolite, they know where is the bad water and how to avoid it. But tourists... Long ago, the Aztec people named this place 'beach of the dead' — Zipolite." My face must have stopped looking so alarmed because Alex laughed again. "Do not swim in the sea in Zipolite and it is no problema."

"Thank you. Good advice." I tried to smile but felt increasingly exhausted. The night's events were catching up with me.

"I see it is time for you to sleep, so I am quiet now, señorita Ana."

I dozed a bit after that, surprisingly; I usually can't sleep in public. But my body had been shot through with adrenaline for hours now and had reached its limit. When I woke an unknown time later, Alex was softly snoring in the seat next to me. It had been a rough night for him, too, what with the police raid and his boyfriend's arrest. It was wrong that we were both defined as criminals — me, for the worst crime imaginable, him, for being himself.

It was definitely my strong farmgirl arm, hardened by years of chopping wood for our stove, that so forcefully and accurately planted the pair of red-handled scissors deeply into Johnny's back. Any court of law would find me guilty. Though I could have claimed self-defense — he was trying to force himself on me at that moment — it was an unpersuasive argument. There was no evidence in that room now indicating that was his intent. There was also the inconvenient fact that we had been lovers for the six months before my arm did what it did. Who was I to persuade a jury that after six months of allowing him to do what he wanted with my body, I had suddenly changed my mind? It seemed unbelievable, even to me. Yes, it was my body that had committed this heinous act. But Jenny was there with me, her spirit animating my typically passive and fearful self. We acted together. Jenny pulled the rage from the dark place where I had buried it, mixed it with her own, and together we found the power to do what my arm did. Deep inside, I did not feel solely responsible.

Nor could I muster any self-reproach for what my arm, my body, did. Instead, I felt like a grievous wrong was now redressed, a grievous harm was, in a small way, rectified.

It seemed a small price for me to pay. Jenny was free of him forever.

Suddenly, the scene came back to me, vivid, technicolor. My brown raincoat dripping onto the plush Persian carpet, my jeans soaked and stuck to my legs. My hand in my coat pocket, wrapped around Jenny's high school graduation photo like a talisman. Repeating the mantra under my breath, "for Jenny, for Jenny, for Jenny." For Jenny, I'd confront him with the evil he'd done. I would make him comprehend the soul-destroying violation he perpetrated on his daughter. On both of us. But by the time I'd entered the history building, my will had frozen in my chest and I'd stood before him, quaking in fear, silent as ever. I had managed to take the photo from my pocket and thrust it in his face. He had frantically backpedaled once he'd realized that I had concluded that the only reason he wanted me was because I looked so much like his daughter. "What middle-aged man doesn't secretly want to make it with his beautiful daughter?" he'd said, obnoxiously, by way of explanation. He'd gone on to unconvincingly insist that it was me, only me, that he loved. He was pitiful to me in that moment.

It might have ended then, with me merely walking away, home to nurse my shame and humiliation. But when he realized I had not accepted his ridiculous attempt at an excuse, he'd grabbed me, had forced his lips on mine, had backed me up against the desk, had unzipped his pants, had wanted to continue to force himself on his daughter's stand-in. Me. Jenny came to me then, inhabited me. No more mere lookalikes, we seemed forged into one person, both unspeakably scarred, one (Jenny) with a righteous anger.

No recall of exactly what happened next, but the result was clear enough. His last word, a gasped "Jenny," convinced me that he had understood. His death mask made the check for a pulse I did unnecessary, but I clearly recall kneeling next to him to do it. I zipped up his pants, pocketed his Roman coins and tiny ancient vial, made sure my prints had been wiped off the scissors, the desk, the zipper. And walked back out into the freezing rain.

It was early morning now, judging from the pre-dawn gray outside my dusty window. While the bus lumbered through West Texas — Abilene, Coahoma, Odessa, Toyah, and the rocks, dirt, and junipers in between — I retrieved my sewing kit from the pack, carefully took off my sweater so I wouldn't awaken Alex, and tried to sew hems on the quick-to-unravel knit sleeves of my newly three-quarter-sleeved blue sweater. It wasn't raining in West Texas. Indeed, it looked like it had never rained. It was warm enough that I folded my sweater into my backpack when I'd tied the last knot and cut the thread.

My watch told me it wouldn't be long now until the border crossing, when I'd leave my country behind forever. Besides Ma, I had precious little to hold me here. No one else I really knew or cared about. Now that I had abandoned my history graduate program, no future to work toward and look forward to, either. I acknowledged these facts without emotion. Perhaps my feelings had seeped out of me permanently, staining the Persian rug in Johnny's office along with his blood.

Out the dusty window, I could see we were coming into a city. Sure enough, the bus driver announced, "El Paso, final stop. First stop in El Paso, Puente Libre, second stop Greyhound Station."

Alex woke with a start at the driver's announcement. "Good morning, señorita Ana. We will get out at the Puente Libre and walk into my country in a few momentos. Many people do this every day. It is no problema."

"I'm with you, then."

"Do not worry, I do this trip many times. As it is morning, my cousin will be at the visa office."

The bus stopped and most of the passengers disembarked. To one side of us was a massive building labeled "U.S. Customs and Border Control." But Alex pointed straight ahead to a many-laned road, with a pedestrian walkway next to the lanes of cars and trucks.

"This is Puente Libre — the free bridge," he explained. "When we pass here, I have no worries. I will help you now, so you also have no worries."

With that, we got in line with the many others who wished to go to Mexico. We walked over the bridge and over the Rio

Grande. No one gave us a second glance as we passed from being fugitives from justice to being just a Mexican citizen and a tourist from America.

Alex took a moment to stop at the restroom to change from his disco outfit to a denim shirt. "It is best to look like everyone else here. Especially when we go to visit Héctor, my cousin. He is not friendly to boys who like boys. I always take this shirt with me. In case it is time to look like a macho hombre!" He grinned and I couldn't help but smile back at him.

The American students who were with us on the bus were shedding their jackets and lining up in front of the small dun-colored building at the end of the bridge that served as the Mexican visa office. Alex motioned for me to stand on the shady side of the building. He politely cut in front of everyone and disappeared inside. He returned with a small, burly man with graying hair. Alex and the man walked quickly into the alleyway behind the building. I followed.

"This is my cousin, Héctor, señorita Ana." To Héctor he said, "Señorita Ana needs a special visa."

"Thirty dollars, señorita, for a special visa," Héctor said quietly in heavily accented English. "On this visa, any name can go. And it is for one year, not three months like tourist visa."

Though it was a decent portion of all the money I had with me, I quickly nodded. Héctor removed an official-looking document and a pen from a small leather zip pouch he carried under one arm. He handed both to me. "Fill quickly, please."

I had no problem coming up with a fictitious address in Michigan where I supposedly lived and rapidly filled in the other required information, using the back of my backpack as a table. But at the top of the document was the space for a name. I printed my new name, Anna. Alex saw me hesitating over a last name.

"How about Jiménez? Maybe we are marido y mujer!" He grinned. "Who is to know?" He started spelling his name for me. I wrote the letters. "It has an accent, here in the middle," he pointed and indicated the accent's direction with a hand motion. "And in Spanish, Ana has one N only and you must say it ahna," he added. I scratched out the first name and printed "Ana." Héctor chuckled and slapped Alex on the back. I got the money from my pack, handed it to Héctor, and he disappeared around the corner.

I went to the restroom behind the visa office. I balled my raincoat into as small a lump as I could make it and stuffed it, too, into my backpack after removing a clean blue t-shirt and changing into it. I used my new pair of scissors to cut my driver's license into small pieces and flushed them down the toilet. "Goodbye, Jane Meyer," I said aloud as the bits disappeared down the drain. "I'm not sure I ever really knew you."

Seeing my serious expression when I returned to where he stood waiting, Alex smiled his beautiful smile. "Do not worry, señorita Ana. How I live, many times we need new names. I could see in your eyes that it was the same with you. Welcome to México, Ana Jiménez!"

4

Heading South to Mexico City

Alex would travel with me as far as Oaxaca, he informed me, as that was where his mother lived. "Mi papá died long ago. Mi mamá, she must take care of six sons. I am the baby, so she is old now, gray of hair. She lives with my brother Manuel and his wife Gabriela. But you will meet them, señorita Ana, because you will get off the train in Oaxaca with me. Believe me, you will need a good sleep in a bed by then!"

We would take the train, Alex told me, because on the bus they would ask for papers. "It is a good paper Héctor gave you, but better if you do not show it to the policía. On the train, only the peasants go, so no policía. It is a long ride, but only a little money. Yes, for you, the train is better. And for me, because I have little money."

I wondered how Alex seemed to know that I was not just some American wanting to get away from it all, but of course, I didn't ask. I wondered why he was so willing to help a strange girl from the north with a bad haircut. The answer to that question, at least, was shortly forthcoming.

We exchanged American dollars at the train station, and with our newly acquired pesos we bought third-class tickets on a rickety old train with wooden benches for two. Even though I was only of average height for an American woman, the rows were impossibly close together. Alex and I both had to either put our knees sideways to fit in the seat, or, if we were trying to doze, rest our tailbones on the hard bench, bend our knees, and lean our shins on the back of the row in front of us. It was uncomfortable when it wasn't excruciating, as the train, screeching steel wheels on steel rails, lumbered slowly through the dry terrain of a state Alex told me was named Chihuahua, "like the tiny dogs, señorita, it is here where they were born!"

To Mexico City, it took three days.

"Please, señorita Ana, drink a small bit of this," Alex said to me when my stash of granola bars had run out at the end of the first day. "And I will buy us tortillas and elote. And we will not become sick in our stomachs." He handed me a familiar pink liquid in a triangular bottle. "It is a trick I learned from an old American boyfriend — an archeologist. It is fortunate I meet him because I go to America, I come here, I go there. In both places, I was sick in my stomach before this trick."

Having visited the lavatory on this train and hoping never to do so again, I took a swig of the familiar remedy for an upset stomach. At the next stop — and the old train seemed to stop at every cluster of shacks and adobe houses, no matter how small — Alex hopped off, and quickly bought two cans of what turned out to be pineapple juice, a stack of tortillas, a lime, and two ears of roasted corn dripping with a creamy orange sauce that an elderly Indian woman had efficiently wrapped in old newspaper. After taking out a jackknife and slicing the lime in two, Alex used the blade to slice the corn kernels off the cob. He scooped kernels and the sauce from the newspaper into a tortilla and squeezed a lime over the corn before rolling it closed. The sauce turned out to be mayonnaise with a smoky pepper sauce mixed in. I found the corn-filled tortillas tasty, which was convenient, as that turned out to be the mainstay of our diet as the train trudged on through the mostly rural landscape.

Alex and I settled into a pattern. We'd talk for a while, then he would doze while I read. The hours plodded by. My dog-eared copy of *Jane Eyre* got another enjoyable read-through. Alex asked me to tell him the story of it and I tried to render the familiar tale in detail. When I finished, Alex asked, "When Jane said yes to Mr. Rochester, when after many bad moments, they became marido y mujer, were you happy? Was it a good ending for you?"

"Oh yes," I said. "They both so deserved a happy marriage."

Mostly, we kept our conversation light, sharing words to describe the passing scenery, practicing phrases and new words in each other's languages. With three days of intense instruction, I was becoming confident of basic phrases and vocabulary. It helped that I had taken Latin as an undergrad.

I didn't sleep much. I didn't think much. Every time a thought about my past, especially my recent past, threatened to break into my consciousness, I struck up a conversation with Alex or reread a favorite passage of *Jane Eyre*. For now, I had to focus on the road ahead.

Finally, we came upon the outskirts of Mexico City, mile after mile of shacks to the horizon. A few were made from adobe with corrugated tin roofs. Most were made from construction scraps and plastic sheets. All of them looked completely insufficient for sheltering a family. Everywhere, people in scruffy pants or skirts and American cast-off t-shirts were going about the business of daily life. When the train slowed, young men ran alongside, yelling to those passengers who paid attention that they had food or newspapers or hats or children's toys or innumerable other items for sale for a few pesos.

"No one should live like una cucaracha," Alex said, dismayed. I remembered the word from a song learned in elementary school. "I feel shame to show you this part of my country, señorita Ana. In the countryside, there are poor campesinos, but they have fresh air, it is clean, they have animals and gardens, and every person knows every person. But here..."

We both stared out the window at the endless squalor for a time. Off in the distance, I could see a cloud of smog hanging over the city, and even in the train, the air seemed to be getting thicker.

"In a small time, we reach the station in the city. I speak to you now of something very important. I will ask this very important favor and you will tell me before we reach Oaxaca if you can do this for me."

I looked up at him sharply. We were in his country, not mine. Everyone spoke his language, not mine. What favor could he be thinking of? I had come to genuinely like Alex these past few days. He was kind and helpful and didn't ask a lot of questions. I hoped my impression of him would not change when he asked me for this favor.

Alex looked straight ahead when he spoke. "I am twenty-six. For many years now, my mother and my brothers are asking me, Alejandro, when will you settle down? When will you take a wife? When will you have children? Every year, these questions are louder and louder. I love my mother and my brothers. Every one of them has a wife and bebés. I cannot tell them I like boys. My brothers, they would hate me. They would tell me to go away and never come back. My mother, her heart would stop beating and she would die. I think and think and only two answers to this problem can I find. One is that I never see them again. I go off to America. I never come back. But I love mi mamá. I love mis hermanos, my brothers. So, I ask you the other answer."

Alex was sitting next to the aisle, and he now stood up. He turned to me and smiled his beautiful smile. He got down on one knee. "Señorita Ana, will you marry me?"

5

Mexico City to Oaxaca

I looked in vain for some indication that this was a joke. Instead, I saw his face grow serious. I saw him fumble in his jeans pocket and pull out an unadorned golden ring. He reached to hand it to me. The old women in the seat across from us were beaming at me and nodding. "Muy guapo," they were saying, pointing to Alex and indicating with their hands that they were speaking of his face. Very handsome. Yes, he was.

I opened my mouth to say something. Possibly, I would have said, "But you hardly know me," or, "But you're gay," or, "But I'm a murderer and a fugitive." No, not that. But when I opened my mouth, I found I couldn't catch my breath enough to say anything. Instead, I started wheezing, gasping, and panting rapidly. I was breathing in, but not out. There was not enough air in the train car, though all the windows were open. The faces of the old women, mixed in with Alex's face, started swirling around me. I broke out in a sweat. I thought I might faint or vomit.

"Oh, señorita Ana, I see I have upset you greatly. I am sorry. Please, put your head like this." He was sitting on the filthy train floor, his head between his knees. I tried to follow his direction. I most definitely did not want to faint in a strange country. It did help a bit to put my head down. But there was something wrong with the air. I could not get enough of it. The train screeched to a halt. The old women were giggling and pointing at the gringa with the baseball hat pulled low. They were saying something to Alex, and he was smiling and shrugging. Alex was taking my backpack now and his. He was urging me up from the bench, grabbing my arm and pulling. I was gasping and everything spun around me. But I had to get up and off the train. Eventually, he was able to pull me to a stand, take me by the arm, and muscle me down the aisle and down the two steps off the train and onto the platform.

Fortunately, two men vacated a bench in front of our train car just as I was stumbling onto the platform. "You sit here." Alex put down the backpacks, lifted each of my legs in turn, and slipped one strap from each of them under my foot. "For safety – there are many banditos in the station. I will come back with a drink. You wait here." And with that, he disappeared into the throng.

The air smelled of diesel fumes and garbage. There was not enough of it. Panic started to rise in me. Though a warm breeze blew around the giant station building, I was shivering and sweating, both at once. And I simply could not breathe. It occurred to me that Mexico City was in the mountains and that I had never been in mountains in my life. The air *was* thinner than I was used to. In, out. In, out. I thought about my lungs, the polluted, thin air, the potential backpack thieves Alex had warned me about – anything to keep me from thinking about his unexpected proposal. He returned with two open bottles of guava-flavored soda.

"Here, my sick friend, drink. Drink, and then we will find the train to Oaxaca."

Guava soda was wondrous, unlike any flavor I had tasted before. It helped to focus on what my mouth was experiencing. And not to not think. I finished my bottle, and Alex placed it in the crates for empties that littered the station. He grabbed my arm and pulled me to my feet, had me lift one foot after the other to free the backpack straps, and slung the two bags over one shoulder while guiding me forward.

"Come, we must go to find our track. The train will leave very soon. I have the tickets. You can give me pesos for your ticket after we sit." Alex had grown very business-like, not at all the charming companion of the last three days.

"I'm sorry," I tried, but Alex waved my apology away. "Later, we talk. Now, we walk."

I meekly let him weave me through the crush of other travelers, mostly people I took for Mexicans or Indians of some kind, though there were tourists, too. I breathed in, out, in, out, and stumbled along until we came to our track. The train was there, doors open, and we entered the car we had been assigned and found our seats. This was a first-class car, Alex told me.

"When I go home, I go first-class from México City to Oaxaca because the stationmaster in Oaxaca is my uncle. I want my family to think I find success in America. Also, we can sleep in these seats, as they are muy comfortable."

"How many more hours to Oaxaca?" My voice was quavery, and I sounded almost desperate. I wondered if I would be able to breathe long enough to get there.

"Only this night more, señorita Ana. In Oaxaca, the air is clean and cool, not like here. You will be well again. You close your eyes and sleep now. We will talk later."

I did as he suggested almost instantly. I was roused minutes later, as the train lumbered past the endless sea of shacks and the conductor came to take our tickets. When I next awoke, dawn had broken. All outside our window was lush and jungly. The air was clean and a bit humid. Most importantly, there seemed to be more oxygen in it. In, out, in, out. It was easier to breathe.

"You feel better, señorita Ana? There is more air because we are going down. And no smoke from tail of car or factory

23

here in the jungle. Only green and muy hermosa." We both looked appreciatively out the window.

"Okay. Now I tell more to you. If on the paper, I had a wife, mi mamá, my brothers, they would quit asking, when Alejandro, when will you take the wife? And if I signed this paper with an American girl, it would be very good because my family do not speak English so they will not make the questions or ask to meet your mother and father. Mi mamá will say, 'My baby boy, he marry an American!' And they will be happy, and I will be happy because they think I have an American wife. I will only kiss you once, when the padre says we are marido y mujer at the church. I promise, only one kiss! We will be friends only, señorita Ana. This way is good for me, and it is good for you. I see the way you fill out the visa paper. I think you are one who wants to be someone else. So, why not señora Jiménez?" He was nodding and smiling his beautiful smile. "Am I mistaken, my American friend?"

"No, you are not mistaken, but..." I didn't know how to proceed. I could not tell him my new status as a fugitive. I only half believed it myself. And for him, it was not safe to know. Wasn't there a law against harboring a fugitive, never mind marrying one? Even in Mexico? He was a nice person. He deserved better. And yet...

"Okay, okay, I see you are not ready. Did you sleep enough to go on?" I nodded. "So, we do this. I will go to Oaxaca. I will help you find the bus to Puerto Ángel, the village next to Zipolite. In three weeks, I will come to Zipolite. You think if you want to be señora Jiménez. I will ask you again. But," he looked at me earnestly but also with a twitch of a smile, "can I say I have an American girlfriend when I see mi mamá?"

I nodded. "You can tell her that. I am your friend, and I am a girl. And please, Alex, call me Ana — not señorita Ana."

Alex laughed and gave me a quick hug. "Thank you, Ana, my beautiful girlfriend!"

Three weeks to think. I hadn't been doing much of that

these past few days, even though I had so much to think about. I wasn't sure I wanted to be alone to think. I wasn't sure I wanted to go on to Zipolite alone. I wasn't sure I wanted to go on at all. It was only a vision of Jenny that had prevented me from the natural, comforting, moral choice of turning on the gas after I killed Jenny's father and letting my life ebb away as I breathed propane in, out, in, out. Going on had only brought further moral quandaries. And this was only day five in my new life as someone not named Jane Meyer. "Isn't there a bus to Zipolite?"

"No, Ana, the only way to get to Zipolite is to walk."

6

Oaxaca to Puerto Ángel

Oaxaca, the little I saw of it, was charming, human-sized in a way that Mexico City had not been, and very green, my lungs filling with blissful humid air. I focused on breathing deeply, in, out, in, out. It was 700 meters lower than Mexico City, Alex told me, which made all the difference in the world to my lungs. We stopped briefly to say hello to Alex's distinguished-looking uncle, the station master. Alex introduced me as "señorita Ana, mi amiga americana" — his American girlfriend. "Ella no habla español," he continued, and I tried to smile sheepishly beneath the brim of my protective hat.

"Bienvenida, señorita," said Alex's uncle, who smiled and gave a little bow to me.

Fortunately, a young mother, her child wailing in her arms, her ticket waving frantically in the station-master's face, demanded his attention, and he turned to help her. "Adiós, mi tío," Alex waved and led me away.

We walked the short distance to the bus station and Alex took some pesos from me and bought me a one-way ticket to Puerto Ángel. He pointed to where a rickety and brightly painted blue bus was taking on passengers.

"When you get to Puerto Ángel, the bus will stop at the

plaza, and there will be a small place outside for fruit drinks. A friend go there and he told me this. I hope it is the same now. Buy a drink from the woman there and ask her for the road to Zipolite. It is easy. She will show you the right road and you walk until you find Zipolite. Another woman there will find you a hut and food. Remember, mi amiga, do not swim there! There are other beaches. I will visit my family and come for you after three weeks. Okay, Ana? In three weeks, you give me your answer."

I nodded, suddenly too tired to care what I might encounter at the end of this interminable journey. "Thank you, Alex. You have been a lifesaver for me. I don't know how I would have made it this far without your help."

"No fue nada, I am happy to meet you." He smiled his perfect smile at me. "I hope you like Zipolite." He hugged me, turned, and walked away. I watched his figure receding, alarm bells ringing in my ears. What if I never saw him again? What if he did come to find me and I had to decide what to do with his proposal? There was a sinking feeling in the pit of my stomach. I was truly on my own now.

This bus, like the first train we had taken, was a local peasant run, which meant it stopped often and the seats were impossibly close together. The rearview mirror next to the elderly driver was festooned with medallions of various saints. When I breathed in, my nose tickled with the sting of black-red peppers the driver had hanging in a braid from the windshield's left edge. I found an end seat so my knees could remain in the aisle, next to a sepia-skinned elderly woman who had a basket full of vegetables on her lap. When she smiled shyly at me, I could see she had a missing tooth right in front. Across from me were two other women who had been to the market in Oaxaca, too. The one closest to me showed me what was wrapped in the newspaper in her lap. It was a large lizard — an iguana, I guessed — and I started at the unexpected sight. All three of the women laughed at me, the ignorant gringa. The one who had the lizard on her lap rubbed her stomach and said, "Muy deliciosa." I tried to smile back.

The bus lurched forward. I attempted to keep myself from bumping out of my seat on the rough dirt road and my knees from hitting the woman or the dead iguana across the aisle. At one stop, an elderly man got on with a live goat; fortunately, he only rode to the next village as the pitiful thing wouldn't stop bleating in fear. After a couple of hours, during which we stopped at every modest cluster of adobe houses, most of the locals had gotten off with their baskets and string bags and I had a row to myself. The scenery continued to be verdant jungle punctuated occasionally by a farm or small village cut out of the forest. We were winding down the mountains on a road that sometimes seemed not wide enough for the bus as the driver navigated past farmers on horseback or sitting atop a donkey cart, or the occasional car. The road lurched steeply downhill, and we zagged through hairpins, one impossibly tight turn after another, with the bus on the outside of the dry mud track, not a guardrail in sight. Beautiful views of deep ravines passed by as we hurtled along, but I shut my eyes rather than look at them. I could feel blisters rising on my palms as I gripped the rusting bar on the back of the seat ahead of mine. I would have prayed if I thought it would do any good.

Eventually, the road straightened out to hills rather than mountains. The jungle gave way to farmland. We rounded a corner, and there it was, the sapphire Pacific. I had never seen an ocean before. Somehow the vastness of the horizon, so limitless, so unfathomable, scared me to the depths of my being. How could I find my way in all this infinitude? Panic welled up in me; I could feel it tingling at the ends of my fingers. The bus coasted to a stop.

For my benefit, the driver called out, "Puerto Ángel," and everyone gathered their things and began to file out. Though there was a bit of a breeze blowing through the bus window, it was quite hot here. I broke into a sweat. On one of the mountain village stops, I had taken off my sneakers — by this time thoroughly filthy, though dry — tied their laces together, and looped them over one of my backpack straps. I had gotten out my plain, deep brown, flat-soled sandals — embarrassingly out of style in my former life as a Texan graduate student but perfect for this use — and strapped them on. But I had nothing to replace the filthy jeans I had worn throughout my flight except a clean pair of jeans, which I could tell already would be unbearable. I was so thirsty I thought I might faint. I exited the bus and found myself standing in the dry red dirt of a large open space, bordered by a few adobe buildings interspersed with rough wood stalls with thatched roofs.

I spied the modest fruit drink stand Alex had mentioned — Margarita's, it said, in carved letters on a sign nailed to the front. Open on four sides, a thatch canopy covered the shop. There were counters all around each side, with a motley collection of bar stools pushed up against them. A blender stood on a card table in the center of the shop along with baskets filled with fruits of all kinds, some of which I didn't recognize. A blue cooler was lodged under the table, possibly filled with ice. A yellow electric cord ran from the blender to a shop at the edge of the plaza. Most importantly, a black-haired, stout woman in her forties in a red t-shirt and patterned skirt was talking and laughing with her one male customer as she expertly chopped fruit and whirred it in the blender. Margarita, it must be her.

"Hola, turista, what's your pleasure?" she smiled at me after taking some pesos from the man, who walked away with his plastic cup of fruit smoothie. Her English was un-accented American.

"Something with guava?"

"You are as white as death. Sit, and I will make you my special guava banana orange smoothie, just for fresh-off-the-bus turistas like you."

I sat. I propped my chin in my hands and leaned on the wooden bar top. I was glad for the noise of the blender. Otherwise, I might have fallen asleep right at the juice stand.

She brought me a large glass full of an orange-pink mixture. It was the best thing I'd ever tasted, and I sucked it down as if I hadn't had anything to drink in days, which was close to true. She came over with her still half-full-pitcher and I indicated a refill. After I drank that at a more leisurely pace, she said, "You'll be wanting the road to Zipolite, I take it?" I nodded. "Do you have a skirt? It is a long walk to be wearing jeans."

"No, I didn't realize it would be so hot." Sweat appeared on my upper lip as I spoke.

"See the clothes over there under the umbrella?" She pointed to a thatched umbrella. There was a sheet under it on which assorted items of clothing were displayed. "The tourists leave clothes here when they get back on the bus to go north. I wash them and sell them to new tourists for a few pesos. Go have a look."

I walked the few feet to the used clothing display. There were shorts, skirts, dresses, and blouses. Some were American castoffs; others were made in Mexico. A turquoise Speedo swimsuit looked like it might fit me. I decided on a turquoise and pink skirt from India, and a pink blouse. Wanting to buy something local, I also chose a white cotton shift that had orange and red embroidered flowers on the bodice. I brought my selections back to the bar and asked Margarita for a tally for the drinks and clothes. It was surprisingly reasonable.

"There is the baño. Put on your skirt and I will show you the road."

The little outhouse made from palm fronds was tidy and clean and I changed into my swimsuit and skirt, put on the pink shirt, rolled up the back, and tied the front at the waist. I turned my jeans inside out to be washed sometime later and crammed them in my backpack. I put on the sunglasses I had grabbed from my distant room in Texas at the last minute. I lowered my brown baseball cap over my bad haircut.

"No." Margarita decreed when I came out of the baño. "You

must have a new hat, a hat for a girl." She rummaged through a bag under the bar. "This is what you need." It was a pink, floppy hat that looked like it was from a decade ago — and it was faded — but it went well with my pink shirt and patterned skirt. "No charge," she smiled as I exchanged it for my brown baseball cap. "Just a promise to return for a smoothie in a few days. I'll give you a better haircut, too. Now, come, I will show you how to get to Zipolite."

Margarita walked past a building across the street from her smoothie stand and disappeared into the jungle beyond. I grabbed my stuffed backpack and ran to catch up. I followed as she made her way down a narrow path leading toward the sea. When the ocean was visible, she paused and turned to me. "Walk until the end of this path. Look to your right. You will see a small wooden sign. The sign will say 'Zipolite' and will have an arrow pointing. Just stay on that road for one-half hour, and you will see Zipolite — the beach of the dead. You know you cannot swim there?"

"Yes, I was told."

The woman stuck out her hand. "I am Margarita. If you have any problem, you come see me."

"J — Ana," I said. "Ana," I said again.

She smiled and turned back up the path, leaving me to walk through the jungle alone and find a little sign that would finally, finally, get me to Zipolite. Fear surged through me as my sandals took one step after the other toward my new life as a fugitive in a place completely foreign to me.

7

Puerto Ángel to Zipolite

I would never have seen the sign if Margarita had not told me to be on the lookout. It was a foot long and half that high, hand-lettered and weathered, just black paint on a bleached-gray board with an arrow pointing to a short trail that led to a narrow, rutted road partially shaded by windblown tropical trees I had never seen before. I walked, my sandals causing little puffs of dry dirt to rise from the road and turn my feet brown. I was glad of the shade offered by the floppy hat, glad of the calf-length skirt shading my white legs, glad of the shirt I had rolled to the elbows shading my Midwestern white shoulders. When there was a gap in the trees, the sun bore down on me with an intensity new to me. There was no one else on the road and I immediately guessed the reason — it was the hottest part of the day. Any sensible person would be napping in the shade or having a cooling drink under a thatched umbrella somewhere.

Part of the story of Zipolite from that October dinner with Maddie Haystead came unbidden into my mind. "Our hut was in the hills above the beach. We had a beautiful view of the water from our hammocks, but we could also see the road from Puerto Ángel. So we had a bird's eye view of the only horror of Zipolite."

"What was it?" I had asked, wide-eyed, expecting violence or tragedy. It turned out to be both.

"The turtle truck. Every day during our siesta it would chug on by, as wide as the road, an old green dump truck on the way to Puerto Escondido, where rumor had it, there was a turtle factory. Huge sea turtles, perhaps a dozen of them, gasping for air, piled on top of one another, off to be made into soup or glasses frames or who knows what. I never got used to that sight. It brought tears to my eyes every time it went by. It was the only sad thing about that beautiful place." When Maddie had told me, I'd seen the decade-old memory cast a shadow over her face.

It was siesta time right now. Would my first view of Zipolite be a truckful of soon-to-be-slaughtered sea turtles gasping for air as they dried in the sun? I didn't think I could take a sight so cruel in the best of times, and surely it would be intolerable when I was this near to completely breaking down.

But no turtle truck, nor any other sign of humanity, marred my trudge to paradise.

As Margarita had promised, it was a half an hour later when the road gave way to a stick hut with a thatched roof. And I could see more huts nestled among the green on the hillside to the right of me. On the left was a long, caramel-colored beach stretching to some rocky outcroppings, beyond which was the seemingly innocuous Pacific, as placid right at that moment as its name implied. A nearby open-air pavilion on the beach had a plank floor and crude tables and benches under a thatched roof held up by rough poles of tree trunks. In the middle were shelves holding tin plates and cups, a couple of prep tables, and two charcoal grills made from halved tin barrels. Not a soul was visible at first, though on further inspection, I could see a half-dozen people in front of the hillside huts, rocking gently in colorful hammocks under thatched overhangs.

I stopped, looking for someone, anyone, who could point

me to a place to buy something for my parched throat. I had never experienced such heat, such dryness. I felt faint and wondered if it would be okay to sit on one of the benches at what seemed to be an outdoor restaurant. I started to walk over to the nearest bench when a door creaked open from the hut on the hill side of the road. It was nestled in the shelter of banana trees, their huge clusters of green fruit unmistakable even to my uninitiated eyes. A woman with a gray streak in her long black hair emerged. She was wearing a simple blouse and skirt, both in bright yellow. In her hand, she held a small open Coca-Cola in its unmistakable green bottle.

"Seet," she said, gesturing to the bench nearest me. She put the bottle in front of me. "¿Autobús Puerto Ángel?" She pointed from where I had come. I nodded as I gratefully gulped. "¿Otras turistas?" She asked, and I shook my head no. "¿Cabaña sola para ti?" She waved at the huts above us on the hill and I felt confident enough in my understanding that I nodded vigorously. She went back to the hut and returned with a battered monthly calendar in Spanish. She pointed to a square that I presumed must be today's date, though I had lost track. We traced the weeks left in March and went through two in April until we were both confident that I was indicating a month's stay. On the last blank page of the calendar were random figures written by different hands in black and blue ink. She pointed to the one that said $10. "Por un mes," she said, indicating the four weeks we had outlined. I fished in my backpack for the bill, grateful that she accepted dollars and that she had asked for so few.

"¿Cuánto?" I asked and pointed to the cola, but she shook her head and smiled.

"No hay problema." She returned to the hut with the calendar and my empty bottle and returned with a combination lock and a short length of chain.

I followed her up a narrow path to a row of huts made of sticks lashed together with rope. Each of the five had a thatched overhang bolstered by wooden pillars with two hammocks attached. She took me to the second one. She pushed open the stick door after showing me how to wind the chain through the door and doorframe, and the dirty piece of paper that said 9, 2, 7 on it, my combination. Inside the windowless enclosure were two crudely built wooden chairs with thatch seats and an open-sided, 18-inch wooden box set on its side with a shelf midway down that could serve as a nightstand or a small table. A half-burned candle sat on it in a terracotta holder. An army cot with a light cotton blanket folded on it stood against one uneven wall. And that was all. She motioned me to follow her and pointed to a cubicle made from thatch at the end of the path. "Baño. Nosotros comemos cuando el Sol está más bajo," she continued pointing to the benches and tables below. Seeing my blank stare, she added, "Comida," and made the universal sign for eating. She pointed to the sun overhead and repeated, "Cuando el Sol está más bajo" and lowered her arm to the horizon.

"Entiendo, I understand," I repeated the word Alex had taught me. "Ahora, siesta." I pointed to the hammock. "Muchas gracias, señora." It was the most Spanish I had used so far.

"Hasta luego." She waved and took off down the trail back to the hut under the banana trees.

Now, I was truly alone. I looked around at the primitive huts on the hillside. Zipolite had sounded like such a paradise from Maddie's description. Had it changed since she had been here? To me, it seemed like an impoverished tiny village, albeit with a spectacular view. But then, I didn't deserve paradise, did I?

I put my backpack on the cot in the stuffy hut and took my sandals off next to the hammock. I spent a few minutes figuring out how to get into a hammock and lie down. On the third try, I managed to get both head and feet positioned properly, balanced so that the hammock didn't swing wildly or threaten to disgorge me. I noticed a short piece of rope just within reach tied to one of the sticks comprising the hut. It was a cradle-rocking rope. I reached for it and pulled. The hammock moved back and forth, just enough to send me gently rocking. There was shade from my thatched overhang. There was a small breeze with a hint of salt air in it. There was a hammock with a cradle-rocking rope. I was here, safe. It was enough for now. I closed my eyes and left the world behind for a while. It was the best nap of my life.

8

Zipolite

"Hey, new lady, it's time for happy hour!" I was startled awake from my deep, dreamless siesta by an attractive bearded man in a straw fedora. His accent was Midwestern and he looked to be about forty.

"Sorry, you're probably still recovering from that terrifying bus ride to Puerto Ángel, right?" A female voice belonged to someone I couldn't see. "Frank, we should have let her sleep."

"Nah, best if you dive into the lifestyle right from the start," Frank replied. He offered me a hand, not to shake but to help me get out of the hammock. Graceful entrances and exits from my new sleeping mode would take practice.

"I'm Kathy and this is Frank," a skinny, very bronzed woman in oversized sunglasses and a sombrero of gigantic proportions told me as I struggled to my feet. She was wearing a cotton shift with embroidered flowers identical to the one I had bought from Margarita. "And Frank's right. Best to get into our ways right away."

"I'm...Ana. Thanks for inviting me." Happy hour. I'd never been to one in my life. My stomach fluttered in fear. Would I be able to fake it, act like I'd done this all my life? What would I possibly talk about with them? Conversation, especially with

37

strangers, terrified me. But I couldn't see how I could possibly get out of going with them.

"Frank's been coming here since the sixties. He knows what he's talking about." Kathy added.

"This is the seventeenth winter I've spent here. Of course, like everything, it was better in the '60s." He grinned. "Fortunately, 'beach of the dead' isn't that great of an advertisement, which has helped keep Zipolite, Zipolite. And of course, the road sucks, though I hear they have plans to grade and pave it in the next few years. That will be the end of this place, that's for sure. Smoke?" He offered me what could only be a marijuana cigarette that was lit and half-smoked.

"No, thanks," I mumbled. I had never seen one before, and had certainly never been offered one. Wasn't marijuana illegal in Mexico? I didn't need to commit another crime.

I went to grab my backpack, but Kathy said, "All you need is sunglasses and your hat. Madre Hermosa keeps a tab. Beer and liquor are the same price as soda pop. She comes by to collect once in a while."

"Better use the combo lock, though," Frank added. "And stash your cash and valuables in a baggie in a 'sand bank,' by which I mean a hole that only you know about. In the old days, we shared our dope, and nobody cared about money. But now... Well, there have been a few thefts this season, all of them by newcomers."

"But in the old days," Kathy chimed in, "there weren't any outhouses — everyone just went where they went. Win some, lose some."

Maddie, who had been here in the toilet-less "old days," thought this was paradise?

Frank and Kathy were wending their way down the hill toward the cluster of rough benches and tables I'd seen on my way in. A dozen people were already sitting there, drinking beer and soda. More were plodding down the track toward the place, festooned in colorful swimsuits, hats, and skirts, towels slung around their necks. Frank and Kathy headed toward the table with the best view of the water. It seemed to be reserved for them, and the others, already drinking, talking, and smoking, raised arms in greeting or said, "Hey, you guys, how's it going?"

"Buenas tardes, Madre Hermosa," Frank addressed the woman in yellow who had rented me my hut.

"That means beautiful mother, Ana. And Madre is certainly that to all of us," explained Kathy.

"Tres cervezas, por favor," Frank continued, giving her a peck on the cheek, which caused her to smile broadly and reply, "Hola, Francis." A skinny dark-skinned boy in cutoffs and a dusty red t-shirt brought our beers to the table and uncapped them expertly using the table edge as an opener. I had limited experience with beer and didn't think I liked it. I knew I couldn't afford to get tipsy in front of these strangers, no matter how nice they seemed. But thirst was raging in me again and the beer looked cold. I smiled my gracias, and when the boy gave me the bottle, I couldn't resist rubbing its wet, icy exterior against my cheek.

"Juan Carlos," Frank said to the boy, "¿Tenemos abulón esta noche?"

"Si, señor Frank," the boy replied. "We have many abalone tonight."

"Good boy!" Frank beamed at his English pupil and the boy laughed and scampered off.

"You are in for a treat, Ana. I take it you have never had abalone?"

"Ah...I'm not even sure what it is."

Kathy grabbed an ashtray from the next table, a large shell with lustrous, many-colored mother-of-pearl lining its interior, way too lovely to be an ashtray. "There is a large abalone colony just offshore. They live in these. They are hard to harvest because of the famous riptide around here. It's almost like the abalone knew the tide would protect them. Only the most skillful divers, like Juan Carlos, have the skills to harvest them. They are muy expensive in the States, and only the high-end restaurants have them. Here, they are just the same price as any dinner. Just you wait, Ana."

"Juan Carlos is a seafood diver? He looks about eleven."

"He's thirteen," Frank replied. "But he's been diving for years already. It's a village tradition, lucky for us. Most luscious food in the sea if you ask me."

"I'll try it," I said. Was the food why Maddie had spoken about this place in such glowing terms?

"How'd you find out about Zipolite, Ana? We've noticed it's usually word of mouth," Kathy asked after we'd sipped our beers for a few minutes. I tilted my head to catch the breeze from the sea. Way high up, a black silhouette of thin, long wings with a crook in them that looked like a pterodactyl circled overhead. Kathy followed my gaze. "Frigate," she said. She was waiting for my answer.

"My friend Maddie told me about a trip she'd taken here long ago. She thought it was paradise on earth, so I thought I should check it out."

"Wait, Maddie? Is she small and slim with lots of curly brown hair? Likes to tell stories and asks lots of questions?" Frank was suddenly animated.

A chill ran through me. Frank had told me he'd been coming here for years. What was I thinking? I was the worst fugitive ever. Had I blown my cover already? The third sentence I'd spoken in the place? But what could I do now? I nodded.

"Remember her, Kath? Maddie and the Amazons, we called them. She came here with these four other statuesque dykes. One was like six feet tall and the Black one had a gorgeous bod and this great belly laugh. Maddie was tiny compared to the rest of them, but she was always out in front, walking like she had somewhere to go quick. We decided she must be the empress, and the rest were her Praetorian Guard. They were all smart as hell — in graduate school in Madtown, wasn't it

Kath? But those ladies liked to party! That must have been, what? — '73 or '74 — great years down here. Such a groovy bunch of ladies. Great poker players, too, especially Thorpe. How's Maddie doing after all these years?"

I was panicking now. I couldn't tell them where I knew her from, the scene of the crime. Quickly, I improvised. "I really don't know her very well. I went out to dinner with her and a big group at this conference a couple of years ago. She mentioned this place, and the name stuck in my mind."

Like a saint from heaven, Juan Carlos returned to our table. "Tres más — three more?" He asked, and we nodded. He left to fetch them from the cooler next to the tin drum grills.

A guy with a scruffy reddish beard appeared at the table. "Tell me it ain't true, you two. You headed back to el Norte? And who's this new chick you're sitting with?"

"Yeah, we gotta make this art fair in San Antonio next week," Frank said. I suddenly noticed that both he and Kathy were wearing necklaces that featured seashells.

"Did you make these? They're beautiful." It was true. The shells on Kathy's were of two kinds, and both were purple. And Frank wore something that looked like a spiral shell sliced in half on a leather thong around his neck. But I wouldn't have said anything except that they offered a way to change the subject from Maddie.

"I'm Ana," I said to the bearded guy, as if I'd had the name all my life. A red bandana was tied around his head and his shoulder-length blond hair stuck out in dreadlocks from beneath it. He looked for all the world like a pirate, contrary to what Alex had told me about Zipolite.

"Welcome," he said. "I'm Andy and my ol' lady over there is Linda. We'll see ya at the party later." He sauntered back to a table filled with laughing people.

Kathy answered my question. "Frank's been making jewelry out of the shells of Zipolite since the '60s. That's why he originally started coming here — he heard about the collecting opportunities here. Nice, huh?" She looked over at Frank fondly. "Not much of a living, but hey, we're free."

The moment had passed. They were leaving soon, they said. Hopefully, it wouldn't come up again. Next time, I'd say a nameless guy I met in Oaxaca told me about this place.

The grilled abalone we had later atop a plate of beans and rice was the most indescribable, delectable thing I'd ever eaten — buttery, crunchy, the very essence of the sea.

9

Zipolite

The moon was so bright you could play cards by it.

After dinner, after the moon became a silvery beacon in the starry sky, a battery-powered boombox appeared, the tables were moved to the edge of the plank patio we'd been sitting on, and dancing, mostly to classic rock songs, commenced. At the tables, decks of cards came out, and poker games formed using seashells for chips. Madre Hermosa produced a bottle of mezcal from her hut. She began pouring what Kathy called mezcalitas — mezcal and fresh squeezed orange juice.

"Madre only lets us drink after the moon comes up," Frank said, with a twinkle in his eye. "Otherwise, we'd all be drunkards by now. If anybody has too much on a night, she gives you an early morning tongue-lashing in Spanish, real loud, calls you every nasty name she can think of. Wakes the whole place so everyone knows your sin. She shuns you for a day. Since she controls all the food around here, you wouldn't believe how well that works. None of the regulars ever get drunk. The newbies only get drunk once. Consider yourself warned, Ana!" He laughed. I could see how much he admired Zipolite's "beautiful mother," as everyone called her.

I begged off the mezcalitas but did have a taste of Kathy's

drink. A smoky orange burned all the way down. I begged off the poker game, too. And the dancing. I didn't drink, play cards, smoke marijuana, or even dance. My previous life as a near-hermit student of history hadn't prepared me for life in this community. But, as they say, it beat the alternative.

It was interesting to see what other people's social lives were like, fly-on-the-wall style, from my perch at the edge of the patio. Because my father made Ma and me stay home every evening, especially during my high school years, I'd never been to a school dance or a prom. I hadn't gone to social events in college, either, just commuted to my classes, then home to the farm and Ma every evening. My solitary habits became ingrained. Never had a date. Well, a normal date with a boy my age. I had been to a seedy hotel bar (and room) with Johnny four times, before he'd decided to instead come up to my studio apartment for our "dates." I shook my head. That life seemed too distant to claim as mine anymore.

I had to wait until someone in my hut row left the party, as I had no flashlight to help me find my hut or open my combination lock. It was Linda, the pirate's "ol' lady" who decided on an early night. She walked me to my hut, waiting while I fumbled with the combination lock, 9, 2, 7.

"We're going up to swim and wash clothes at the falls tomorrow. Come on along. After breakfast," she clarified.

"Thanks. That sounds great. Thanks for walking me up. I've got to get a flashlight, that's for sure."

"Go see Margarita for that," Linda advised. "You met her in Puerto Ángel?"

"Yes, she pointed me in the right direction."

"She's good at that." Linda laughed from the moonlit trail. "Good night."

I changed to the cotton shift, with narrow shafts of light from the high-in-the-sky-moon coming through the spaces between the sticks my hut was made of. I tried to lie on the army cot with the hut door closed but found it airless and hot.

I could hear unknown creatures scurrying about. I tried sleeping with the door open, but no breeze reached me no matter how I placed my cot. I finally took my thin blanket, went outside, and crawled into the hammock. The night was alive with insect noises exotic to my northern ears. But the thatch overhang shaded my head from the moon's glare. The breeze was light but steady and cooling. I thought about safety for a second but decided it didn't matter. My life had been marked by rape, murder, and attempted suicide up until now, so what else could happen? And, if it did, did I care?

I used my cradle-rocking rope to get the hammock to sway gently and looked out at the blue-black sea. I could hear a little lap, lap as small waves hit the beach. The moon's reflection made a shimmering river of sparkling silver to the horizon. I tried counting my blessings instead of worrying when I couldn't sleep, an old habit Ma had gotten me into doing before bed when I was a child and my father had done something particularly scary to her that day. She'd even sing the Bing Crosby song.

Worried. I was that all right. I hadn't had a decent night's sleep since the night before I had done what I had done. That was five or six days ago. I didn't have a plan. I didn't have an alibi. I was proving to be clueless as a fugitive, though possibly that was related to not having slept in a week. I was lucky I wasn't psychotic by now, or at least I hoped I wasn't. First blessing: I hadn't gone nuts. Second blessing: Alex, and all the help, all the companionship I'd gotten from him. And my first, and no doubt only, marriage proposal. Third blessing: Margarita, her lovely guava drink, her used clothing shop. She had remade me without knowing it into a colorful-skirt-wearing, hippie-like, innocent-looking tourist. Fourth blessing: Zipolite. I had made it here. The people seemed friendly, open, unlike what I had mostly experienced in Texas these past few months. It was beautiful; I was beginning to appreciate — and I hadn't even explored it yet. The food was nothing short of wonderful. I didn't have to make it myself. But the crowning glory of Zipolite was Madre Hermosa. She'd taken care of me, a stranger. She'd fed me, housed me, trusted me to pay her later for my drinks and food. She deserved her own blessing. What was I up to? The fifth blessing. Tears started forming in the corners of my eyes, tears for the pragmatic kindness of Madre Hermosa, who watched over us and fed and housed us here in this tiny place outside of the real world.

In the wakeful sleep I drifted into after thinking of these blessings, I saw Maddie, her slim frame clad in a long golden dress, her wild curls blowing about her face. She was standing on the beach, her back to the azure sea. Behind her, straight as arrows and tall, were four Amazons, holding bronze shields in one hand, spears in the other. "Let me teach you to play poker," said the dark-skinned one, who broke into an uproarious belly laugh.

"Ana, wake up, it's time to go shelling." It was Kathy, gently touching my arm. "With the full moon last night, there's sure to be a bountiful haul. Wait 'til you see what Mother Nature has left us."

Dawn was breaking, a cool breeze swept up from the sea, and a bit of dew glistened on the tropical bushes that surrounded my hut.

"The tide is out, now's the time. Let us show you the best place," Kathy urged. "It's not far."

I rolled from my hammock, buckled on my sandals, and followed Kathy down the hill. I didn't stop to think that I was wearing nothing but a cotton shift, the same one I had slept in. Lacking any other plan, I was stuck in Zipolite for now and I'd better go see what it was all about. Frank greeted me with a tip of his hat and the three of us set out on my first full day in paradise.

10

Zipolite

I left my sandals above the tideline as Kathy had done. It was the first time I had ever walked on a beach barefoot; the caramel-colored, silt-fine sand felt wondrously cool on the soles of my feet. The tide had neatly washed up that night's shells into a two-foot band at the high tide mark. We walked above and below it, eyes down, peering for perfect specimens. At first, they all looked perfect to me, so many shapes and colors had nature made as homes for her creatures. Frank brought over a handful of examples and named them: dove, olive, auger, scallop, cockle, murex, harp. Most were small, just the size for jewelry, but every now and again, a large shell appeared that hadn't been pummeled by the surf.

Two-foot waves rolled along the beach, casting a spray as they dissipated. The cool morning air left a faint taste of salt on my tongue. I breathed in, out. I stopped to look out at the white-tipped blue-gray expanse. I felt the ocean's comforting rhythm in the squish of sand below my feet. Above, the black slash of a frigate soared high. I looked down at the band of tumbled shells, each an intricate work of art. Step, stare, stoop, step, stare, stoop. I soon had a collection of my own. I gave most of the jewelry-sized shells I found to Kathy and kept a few for myself, including a scallop large enough for a soap dish. Mesmerized by their variety and awed by how much there was to learn, I was sad that the experts, Frank and Kathy, were leaving Zipolite. It was a delightful hour, cool and colorful. "Off this beach, you can swim safely," Frank told me. "Just avoid those rocks there if there are waves. It's shallow, and there are sea urchins on top of the rocks."

We walked back around the corner, past the cluster of rock formations that bounded Zipolite on one end, back along the dirt track to Madre Hermosa's restaurant. People were beginning to gather around tables that had been put back into their daytime configuration. With a gadget mounted to her worktable, a blond woman squeezed oranges as quickly as a woman with long red braids could slice them. Linda, the woman who had walked me to my hut last night, was filling tin mugs from a giant tin coffee pot, and another woman brought trays of them to the tables. Two men stood in front of iron griddles placed on the charcoal grills. One cracked eggs onto one of them; the man at the other griddle was slapping corn tortillas on it and stirring a large pot of salsa and a second one of black beans.

"Madre used to get up to feed us breakfast, but about a decade ago we finally put a stop to that," Frank informed me as we reclaimed our spots at the best-view table. "There are so many trusted old-timers here that we told her we'd get ourselves breakfast and she could sleep in, walk into Puerto Ángel, do her laundry or whatever else she wanted to do. We do lunch this way, too, everybody pitching in. There's a sign-up sheet hanging on the hut wall over there — just pick a job and make sure you show up for it. Hey, Andy, it's huevos rancheros again, huh?"

Andy, the pirate, was the guy putting tortillas on the griddle, I saw, now that he had turned around. He laughed.

"That's what we have every morning," Kathy said.

"Ana, good morning," Andy nodded at me. Linda turned

around from filling mugs with coffee. "Don't forget, we'll go to the falls later. Bring your laundry and soap and a towel."

I smiled and nodded. I had laundry but no towel. And only a tiny bar of soap that I'd taken from the motel Johnny and I had stayed at. Kathy anticipated this. "Ana, you can have my towel and laundry soap. We're leaving this morning and we never take that kind of thing with us back to the States."

"Thanks so much, Kathy. You sure?" She nodded.

"Around here, we take care of each other, don't we Linda?"

Linda smiled her agreement. "That's why Andy and I can't quit this place. We spend six months a year here — six months in paradise for a couple hundred dollars. You're not going to find a deal like that many other places on this godforsaken planet."

I was beginning to understand. It wasn't the stunning view or the warm weather or the sapphire sea or even the well-prepared, if simple, food that made Maddie refer to this place as paradise. It was how people were to one another on top of all the natural beauty. Kind. Generous. In it together. I hadn't had much of that in my life. It was always me and Ma against the world. The world being mostly HIM. Now Ma had found friends, had started dating. I had started graduate school, but my solitary habits had remained. Nothing had changed in my life when I'd moved to Texas. Except for Johnny.

The eggs almost made me cry because they tasted so much like the fresh-laid ones we had at the farm in Iowa. On the hill side of the track, chickens were scratching in the dust, clucking softly. "Besides laying the most delicious eggs on earth, the girls keep la cucaracha in check," said Andy, noticing my gaze. He sat down at our table when he'd warmed sufficient tortillas for the 50 or so people who had shown up for breakfast.

Kathy gave me other gifts besides the towel and laundry soap. Two books of matches and a candle stub, a small length of rope to use for a clothesline. Most importantly, she gave me a canteen. "Linda will show you where to fill it. When you leave, just pass it on to another newbie. This one has been around so long, we passed it on, and so did everyone else, and years later, we got it back. It happened again this year.

"You take care, now, Ana. We'll see ya around the bend," Frank said, and Kathy gave me a brief hug. After the four old friends said their goodbyes, Frank and Kathy took off, each with a small backpack, walking the track back to Puerto Ángel to catch the bus to Oaxaca.

After more coffee and a spate of washing breakfast dishes, Linda, Andy, and I started off on a small footrail heading inland. The path ran next to a stream that emptied into the Pacific at the Puerto Ángel side of Zipolite. A short distance up the trail, we were in the jungle, with humid warm air and the smell of patchouli all around. A thousand plants I didn't know the names of lined the well-worn path, each vivid green in its own way. After twenty minutes of walking, Kathy stopped to show me a stream of water gurgling out of a rock wall covered in ferns. "This is our water fountain," she said, with awe in her voice. "The purest water on the planet, right from a spring." We paused to fill our canteens. Another ten-minute climb beyond the rock ledge water fountain, the trail made a sharp right turn. I drew in my breath in surprise.

We were on the far side of a large green-blue pool, fed by a glorious waterfall 100 feet high. Around the base of the pool lay a scattering of huge stone slabs flat enough for sunbathing or drying one's laundry. About a dozen people, dwarfed by the towering waterfall, were already there, splashing in the pool, swimming, or washing their hair or laundry. Not one had a stitch of clothes on.

11

Zipolite

"Bet you never did your laundry in the Garden of Eden before!" Andy said while stripping off his t-shirt and shorts. He wasn't wearing any underwear.

I looked away, but not soon enough.

"I think she's new to nudism," Linda observed unnecessarily, as I flushed to my roots. "Don't worry, hon, that was me at your age, too. But don't clothes seem unnecessary in a place this perfect? Besides, it's practical to do all your wash while you're up here. Andy, let's leave the poor thing alone while she gets used to it."

Andy called out to someone nearer the falls and strolled off, Linda behind him.

They were right, of course, and the longer I stood there, the only one dressed, the more I stood out. I saw a couple swimming in the pool and decided to try nude swimming at least. I unbuckled my sandals, pulled off my Mexican shift, and lowered myself quickly into the surprisingly cool water from one of the rock slabs. The water was deep, but one thing I had learned, despite the constraints of my childhood, was how to swim. The Jacobsons, the neighboring farm family Ma left me with in the summers when school was out and I was too young to stay on my own, had a swimming hole on their land. The older Jacobson kids taught the younger ones and me how to dive and swim underwater and dog-paddle and crawl on the surface.

I dove beneath the surface of the pool to see how deep it was. It felt wonderful to swim naked, the refreshingly cool water rippling over my skin. After a time crawl stroking around the pool, diving as deep as I was able but not finding the bottom, I felt comfortable enough in my own skin to get out of the pool and start washing myself and my clothes. It helped that I was across the pond from the other nudists.

I washed all the clothes in my backpack and the Mexican shift, too. The filthy jeans and socks I'd worn on my trip down here felt like foreign objects to me now. The sky-blue sweater with its hacked-off sleeves seemed to belong to someone else, as indeed it did. It belonged to Jane. Increasingly, I was becoming Ana-with-one-N, assisted by the completely new way to live I had accidentally discovered.

"We've got some fruit and shade over by the waterfall — come and join us," someone said behind me as I was soaping down my useless blue jeans. I jumped, lost in memories of the person I used to be.

"You should get out of the sun soon. I can see you're new," she said to my pale backside. "I'm Lily," she said as I turned around, face to face with a naked female for the first time since the shower room in high school.

There was nothing to do but rinse my jeans in the pool, spread them on the rock slab to dry, and follow Lily back to where the others were peeling and cutting oranges, bananas, and other fruits that I learned were guavas and papayas, under an old purple blanket that had been made into a canopy with some found sticks serving as tent poles. Bowling-ball-sized rocks on a ledge on the rock wall anchored the other end of the blanket. As we approached, the sound of the waterfall grew louder, but not too loud to drown out conversation. The makeshift sunshade was close enough to the falls that droplets from the downpour splashed the blanket and kept the area underneath naturally air-conditioned.

It was the first waterfall I had ever seen. The wonder of the waterfall — a cascade spilling over pale brown shale festooned with ferns, falling from high above us into the blue-green pool — helped me forget my own nakedness and that of the people around me. We sat cross-legged on the damp rock slab with a woven rush mat on top of it beneath the purple overhang, chatting and sharing fruit and a marijuana cigarette that I passed on without partaking. I listened to their easy banter and answered questions others asked with the lies I had hastily developed back in Ciudad Juárez.

"Here. I hardly use it anymore, I've been here so long," said Lily, throwing me a mostly full bottle of tanning lotion. She was as bronzed as Kathy had been, so I just said thanks. "Put some on before you walk back. The sun gets brutal in about an hour."

Most everyone went into the pool for a final dip after we threw our fruit peelings and seeds into the jungle. There were papaya trees growing all around us, Lily told me, pointing at a skinny trunk with a cluster of fruits and leaves at the top. "We've planted these over the years, just by eating fruit here and leaving the seeds. Cool, huh?"

In the water, I dove deep, but once again, I couldn't get to the bottom. I did see shimmering schools of tiny silver fish flash by though, and when I surfaced near my laundry, I scared up a blue heron that had been hunting them. My clothes, even the jeans, had dried on the rocks in what seemed like minutes. I stowed them in my pack and wriggled the now-fresh-smelling shift over my still-wet body.

"Wow, thanks for taking me here," I said to Andy and Linda as they waited for me to finish packing up and strap on my sandals. "This is the most beautiful place I've ever been."

"Agreed," Andy said. "That's part of why we keep coming

back, year after year."

"We came here first when we were in college twenty years ago," Linda said. "And just made it a habit. We were supposed to get normal jobs, buy a house, and have kids. But we chose Zipolite instead and the rest of that suburban stuff be damned."

"No regrets," concluded Andy. "Though it might be all over soon if they put in that road the government's been threatening."

We walked past the water fountain in the rock and filled our canteens again. Back at Madre Hermosa's, people were dishing out rice and beans from a couple of big cauldrons on the charcoal grill.

After lunch, we took to our hammocks for siesta while the sun was high and hot. In the later afternoon, Lily stopped by to see if I wanted to swim in the sea. "Swimsuits mandatory," she told me. "Madre Hermosa insists on bathing suits wherever the village kids might go."

"I thought Madre Hermosa and Juan Carlos were the only locals here."

"The villagers keep to themselves, though Madre Hermosa's cousin Regina helps her out sometimes and three or four boys swim at the shell beach when they get home from school in Puerto Ángel. And go diving for our dinner. The men keep boats they take out for fishing in the early morning. You can see them poking out from those trees on the beach over there." She pointed to the Puerto Ángel side of the beach. "Fishing was good this morning; we're having grouper for dinner." At my blank look she added, "That's a fish — a delicious fish. You sure are green, aren't you?" Lily added with a smile.

"I'm from the Midwest," I said.

Lily laughed. "Gotcha."

"Where's the village, though? I haven't seen it at all."

"Ah. That path to the waterfall? About ten minutes from the beginning, there's another path branching off. That leads to the village. It's in the jungle and everyone who lives there is Zapotec, people who have lived in these parts for over a thousand years. The older ones only speak their language, not even Spanish, I've heard. We gringos never go there unless we're invited. It's interesting, if you get a chance."

We walked down the track, past the riptide beach of Zipolite, and around the corner to what I heard Lily call the "shell beach" — the place where I had been early in the morning to collect shells with Frank and Kathy. The Pacific had grown calm in the afternoon heat.

My first time swimming in the ocean. I tentatively waded in, the sand beneath my feet firmer than the silt bottom of the swimming hole of my childhood. With the air above so hot, I'd expected the ocean to be warm; instead, it shocked me with its numbing chill. Lily, already calling to me from 20 feet out, her toes visible as she paddled leisurely on her back, encouraged me to wade forward. Knees, thighs, the icy thrill that hit my crotch as it, too, became submerged. At waist high, I took a breath and dove forward, swam toward Lily, and surfaced. Rubbing salt-stung eyes and lips with already-cold-shriveled fingers, I couldn't help but grin. I floated effortlessly.

Lily smiled and pointed toward the outcropping that separated the shell beach from the dangerous riptide beach. I followed her steady stroke toward the rocks. Soon, she had her face down in the water. I followed her lead, put my head in the sea, and opened my stinging eyes. A pint-sized underwater forest grew on a dark ledge a few feet below me in shades of purple, green, and red. Corals, these must be corals. Small fish, intricately patterned in yellows, blues, oranges, and black and white, scooted around the intricate branches of the coral. I drew an involuntary breath of wonder, popped up from the water, and coughed up seawater. But I was enchanted; I could return to this delightful scene whenever I wanted!

"Pretty sweet little village of life," Lily said when I'd stopped choking. I smiled in agreement. We put our faces back in the water to look upon the ever-changing scene again, until my eyes could no longer take the salt. Floated leisurely on our backs back to shore. Spread our towels in the warmth of the sand and lay our chilled selves down to let the sun warm and dry us. My mind quieted. All was simple, obvious. I breathed deeply of the salted air. In, out.

Lily was in her late thirties, with carrot-colored curly hair and freckles. She worked as a secretary for a car dealership in San Antonio and she and the other secretary had gotten the owner to let them spell each other for a month while the other took vacation. The other secretary went on a cruise for a week and then drove to see her mother in Phoenix, Lily told me. Lily came here, and had done so every year since she was first introduced to the place by a boyfriend long ago.

"A lot of folks seem to come back year after year."

"Zipolite grows on you. You'll see. When I'm not here, I dream of it."

Later, we wandered up to where everyone was gathering for dinner. We had grilled grouper with lime squirted on top, fried starchy bananas called plantains, and of course, as much beans and rice as we wanted — I was already calling the staple frijoles y arroz like everyone else. Madre Hermosa's younger cousin, Regina, was at the grill tonight while Madre was plating generous portions and passing them to Juan Carlos, who distributed them to the people gathered at the dozen tables.

"Thank you, Juan Carlos. I know you want to practice, so I will be happy to speak with you in English."

He smiled shyly at me. "Thank you, señorita. I am sorry, but what is your name?"

"Ana."

"It will be good to speak English to you, señorita Ana!" He smiled and turned to get more plates to deliver to the other diners.

Like yesterday's meal, the fish was scrumptious. Like yesterday, the after-dinner drinking, dancing, and card playing proceeded. Madre Hermosa made drinks — tonight's featured rum and pineapple.

I had signed up for evening dishwashing. Regina showed me where to find the stacks of simple cotton towels and where to put what I dried — tin cups, tin plates, utensils. It took almost no time at all. Linda motioned for me to come over to their table and have a drink and I asked Madre for "un trago pequeño," Linda supplying the word for drink — trago — for me. I imbibed my pint-sized rum and pineapple drink because I had to try to be Ana now and get comfortable with the natives — both the Zapotec people and those drawn here more recently. Like last night, Linda walked me back to my hut.

So, the pattern of daily life in Zipolite was revealed to me, with its pleasant rhythms of sun and water, eating and sleeping. So much natural beauty and mellow, gentle people. I could feast on these calming rituals, the healing effects of this magical place. There was one dark element of Zipolite, however — one I could not control and one that might ruin this for me and for others, too. That dark element was me.

12

Zipolite

"Federales! Federales!" It was Andy, yelling loudly. The word wasn't one I recognized, but the panic in his voice was clear enough. Dawn light, which was not when most people got up around here, I already knew. When I raised my head from my hammock though, I could see hammocks up and down the hill, disgorging Americans in a flurry

Some ran into their huts, others quickly headed down the slope to the restaurant. I heard an unfamiliar engine noise. I looked out to sea just in time to see an official-looking boat painted in army olive emerging past the clump of palms that bordered the Puerto Ángel side of the beach. The boat was pulling close to shore and a dozen men scrambled over the lip of the craft and into the knee-high water. The men had on uniforms of some sort. And they had guns.

The moment I registered that these were uniformed officials with guns, my heartbeat doubled. Had I been found out so soon? Were they coming for me?

The men were moving quickly now, and they were headed toward our cluster of stick huts. If I waited much longer, the path to the beach and the people gathering there would be blocked. I grabbed my backpack, my floppy hat, and sunglasses to hide my face and scrambled down the sandy path, my bare feet stinging as my soles hit a patch of gravel. I gritted my teeth and kept going. In my haste, I hadn't locked my hut.

I wasn't fast enough. As I rounded the last jag in the path, just yards before it hit the beach, I stubbed my bare toe on a rock and stumbled forward. As my knees skidded and burned in the sand and gravel and I struggled to get back on my feet, two soldiers appeared smack in front of me. They were both pointing rifles.

"Backpack," one of them yelled in English, and waved his gun at my pack. He took one hand off his gun and made an unmistakable gesture — give it to me, now! I cowered under my hat and sunglasses, took the backpack off my shoulder, and handed it to him. He pawed through the main opening and found nothing of interest. All my clothes were back in my hut, arranged on the cot. All I'd left in the backpack was *Jane Eyre*, which I thought I might read from if I found sitting at the restaurant alone uncomfortable.

Everything of worth, my small stack of twenties and the ancient coins and glass vial, was in my open-to-the-world hut. Fortunately, these valuables were buried in a baggie in a couple of inches of sand underneath the small wooden box that served as coffee table and nightstand. I silently thanked Frank, who had told me to devise a sand bank. The soldier unzipped the small front compartment of the backpack. Besides my hairbrush, it held my fraudulent visa and the remnants of the dollars I had changed into pesos at the train station a million years ago in Ciudad Juárez. The soldier took the paper pesos and the nearly worthless centavos coins from the small compartment, unceremoniously threw my backpack at me, shoved me aside, and continued up the path. What the two men hadn't done, I sighed with relief, was examine my visa or make me take off my hat and sunglasses for a better view of my fugitive face. I forced myself not to run to the restaurant a few dozen steps away.

Andy and Linda and a couple of other people whose names I didn't know, were busy getting breakfast together. They loaded the tin drums with dried wood and cactus skeletons, measured out coffee and water in the fire-blackened coffee pot, retrieved the pans of salsa and beans from the cooler, and began to set the tables. It was a good hour before the village usually began this ritual.

"What's going on, Linda?" I asked, keeping my voice low as the dozen soldiers could be seen, Madre Hermosa with them now, going hut by hut. She opened the combination locks with a gun pointed at her, and they spent a couple of minutes in each hut before moving to the next one.

"The monthly drug bust, probably," Linda replied quietly. "But with Federales, you never know."

"Yeah, that's why we're making breakfast for them," Andy chimed in from in front of the tin drum grill that was burning nicely now. "Usually, that works. They go through our stuff, supposedly looking for drugs, but they'll take anything that strikes their fancy. If we're nice to them, they typically haul out what they took and you can 'buy' it back — you know, give them a bribe. I've never seen them show up this late in the season, though. With so few folks here, the pickings will be slim. That probably means they'll haul someone away to the jail in Puerto Ángel. Probably James, the old pothead. Wouldn't be the first time, either."

"Jail?" I echoed, an unmistakable note of terror in my voice.

"Unless they are really in a bad mood, when they take someone away, they tell us what his bail is. We take up a collection and go to Puerto Ángel to pay it. Usually, they let him come back here." Linda looked at me with concern. "Did you have a lot of cash in your pack? I saw them going through it."

"Five dollars' worth of pesos. Frank told me about burying my valuables right away when I arrived. I'm sure glad he did — I would have never thought of that myself."

We heard Madre Hermosa, her voice raised, talking to

several of the soldiers. She was standing in front of one of the huts, shaking her head, arms crossed over her chest.

Andy cocked his head, listening to Madre on the hill above us. "She's saying that someone is sick in there and they can't go in. Very sick," he translated. "She's saying they will find nothing in there anyways. She's inviting them to breakfast, instead."

With that, Andy turned toward the now sizzling grill and cracked some eggs on it. Linda placed our pots of coffee, beans, and salsa on the other stove to warm. We could hear Madre continue to talk to the soldiers.

"She's saying she only has good, clean tourists here and that we are poor."

The soldiers were coming down the paths from the huts now, their boots clomping loudly, disturbing the quiet of the morning. Madre Hermosa hurried in front of them, entered her hut under the banana trees, and returned with a couple of packages of cigarettes and books of matches. She handed several cigarettes and a book of matches to each of the dozen eager soldiers. With a sweep of her arm, she invited them to sit for breakfast. As they smoked under the thatch roof of the restaurant, we hurried to squeeze oranges for juice, slap down mugs of coffee, and get them plates of eggs, beans, and salsa as quickly as we could.

The men were apparently happy with these gifts, and the few pesos they had managed to find in the huts they'd entered. The only item of any worth they invited us to buy back was the canteen Frank and Kathy had given me. As I was fresh out of pesos, Linda bought it back from the teenaged soldier, taking several peso notes from a little leather purse that was tied around her waist. Madre Hermosa, meanwhile, made a point to ask each of the soldiers about their parents, offering to pray for their good health. Andy said Madre was the reason that most times, no one was taken away from Zipolite to the jail in Puerto Ángel.

"She lets them search a few huts so they can say they've accomplished their mission to the superior officer but then wins them over with breakfast and her concern for their parents," Linda explained. "Today, she was able to talk them out of opening James' hut. No doubt, they would have found some joints lying around. He's such a stoner that no matter how often we tell him to hide his stash, he never manages to get around to it."

"Remember that one dude, though?" Andy asked the small group of us that gathered around a table after the Federales had left. "They frog-marched him outta here and made a point to show all of us a giant plastic bag of dope, hash, and even some 'ludes that he'd brought with him from the States. We heard he got disappeared into one of the hideous prisons they have here. Never heard from him again." Andy looked at me, his serious expression a contrast to his usual jovial demeanor.

"Just make sure not to do anything dumb, Ana. They can take you away for anything they want to."

Too late for that.

A short time later, when the sun had risen but was not yet hot, I walked the beach alone for a time, trying to tell myself that the Federales were unlikely to be on the lookout for an American fugitive. Even if they had found me out, wouldn't they extradite me back to Texas? But the incident had scared me to my core.

13

Puerto Ángel and Zipolite

At mid-morning, I walked to Puerto Ángel with three Americans heading back to the States. They were grateful for Andy's warning, a scruffy guy told me. It had given him time to hide the money he needed to get back to Chicago, where he was headed. The place would begin to empty out in the weeks to come, his girlfriend told me. Only a dozen or so stayed on through the sweltering summer months.

"Could you give me a haircut this morning, Margarita?" I asked, after ordering something with guava in it at her drink stand.

"Just sit tight until the bus leaves," she told me as she handed me the drink and left to fill the orders of people waiting for the bus to Oaxaca.

Puerto Ángel was bustling today. It was market day, the departing tourists told me, and farmers from the countryside had come to town by donkey cart, on the bus, or in aging pickup trucks loaded with fruits, vegetables, and animals. The vendors had small spaces marked off in the dirt. They spread blankets and unloaded baskets of bananas, papayas, tomatoes, onions, and a thousand varieties of peppers in greens, yellows, and reds. Vegetables and fruits I'd never seen before were stacked in attractive piles. Other vendors sold woven handmade baskets, embroidered blouses, and colorful, intricate weavings of animals and flowers.

At the tiny bank, I changed forty dollars into pesos from my dwindling pile of twenties. My remaining funds might last me three months more if I was careful. I didn't know what I would do after that, nor where I would go. But for now, I felt safe and anonymous. That was the best someone like me could hope for — to be safe for now.

After the bus left, the people who could afford a smoothie also subsided. Margarita dragged one of her brightly painted bar stools under a coconut tree near her shop, told me to perch on it, and proceeded to efficiently give me a short but even-all-over clip with the pair of scissors she drew from her apron pocket. "It's a boy's haircut, but I didn't have much to work with. And it will grow," was her pronouncement as she looked me over. "Promise me you'll never try to cut it yourself again." She smiled.

"Were you a hairdresser back in the States?" It seemed a reasonable question, given her perfect American English and her proficiency with a pair of scissors.

"In Houston," she said. "My parents brought me to the States when I was five. Papá worked as a landscaper; Mamá cleaned offices. I lived there until I was thirty, going to hair-dressing school and eventually cutting hair for a high-end salon, saving my tips, all so I could get enough together to come back here with my folks, help them remodel their place, and start my smoothie stand. They were heartsick for Puerto Ángel for twenty-five years! But they wanted a better life than they could have as campesinos here, and a better life for me. We three all got what we wanted in the end. They live back in the house I was born in, just a mile up the road, but fixed up with electricity and plumbing from my Texas savings. They're happy now. And I have my business, which I love. But they sure had to work hard and be homesick long before they were able to get back to this little piece of heaven."

I almost said, "I'm liking Mexico better than I liked Texas." But I thought better of it. Margarita would ask me where I lived in Texas, and what would I say? So, instead, I said, "It's so great that you have this place. It nearly saved my life when I got off the bus and there you were with a guava smoothie! And you cut hair too!" I smiled at her, my face muscles feeling like they were in an unusual position. Smiling. It had been a while.

"Like I said, you need something, I have it or can get it." Margarita smiled back.

"Let's test that. You have a pocketknife and a flashlight to sell me?"

"Sure do — with batteries, no less."

I put the floppy pink hat she'd given me a day or two ago — was that all it was? — back on my head, put my sunglasses back on my face, and became anonymous again. I followed her over to her little shop of used clothes under the thatch umbrella and, in a covered woven basket on the edge of the blanket, she found me a flashlight, batteries, and a pocketknife. I gave her pesos worth about $10, thanked her, and strolled over to the street market.

At one farmer's blanket, I bought a bunch of tiny bananas and a half-dozen guavas that I could peel with my new knife. At another, I bought a proper bar of soap and a large plastic bottle in which to store washing-up water. I headed back to Zipolite by myself. There were no newcomers to the little paradise this morning.

The day continued as the one before, with the usual lunch and usual siesta and later afternoon hours on the shell beach with Lily. I kept my legs covered by my aqua skirt and my shoulders by the pink blouse when I could. But I was getting sunburned nevertheless, especially the tops of my feet, which I hadn't thought to lotion until it was too late. I swam out to the corals again to watch the myriad nameless small fish dart around, keeping my eyes open until they began to sting.

Later, we walked to the restaurant for cervezas before dinner. Talk about the end of the season drifted around me as we ate our dinner. Tonight, it was grilled scallops with a vegetable that looked like a pear but tasted a bit like a cucumber.

"Chayote," Lily informed me. "And aren't these the best scallops you ever tasted?"

"Absolutely," I agreed. I didn't tell her they were the only scallops I had ever eaten.

Juan Carlos came over to see if we needed additional drinks. A donkey cart had made the trip to Puerto Ángel and back with provisions today, including ice and guava soda. I gladly ordered a second.

"Did you dive for the scallops?" I asked Juan Carlos in English.

"Callos de hacha," he replied, pointing to the scallops. Callos was a tough word to wrap my tongue around and Juan Carlos grinned at my efforts.

"Yes, señorita Ana, I and my friend Pedro went down into the sea for them this afternoon." He pointed to an area offshore that was in the no-go riptide area for gringos.

"How do you dive there safely? I thought that there are dangerous tides that can wash you out to sea."

"We take three people always," Juan Carlos nodded. "Two divers and one to sit on the One Rock and watch in case we are catched — caught — in the riptide. If that happens, Pedro's papá and the other fishermen come out in their boats to look for us. Once it happened to Pedro, but me, never. I take care."

"Can you know where the riptide is and how to avoid it?"

"Yes. If you swim out over that way," he pointed to the left side of playa Zipolite, "on the left side of the One Rock, there is no danger. But the scallops, also the abalone, are in the riptide area. Sometimes, the riptide is not so strong, and that is when we go diving for the callos de hacha and abulón. Like before, when the sea is flat. This is when we go. No las olas," he added, to increase my vocabulary. "No waves. Can you dive, señorita

Ana?" When I nodded, he added. "Someday, I will take you with me. It is so beautiful under the sea there."

"Muchas gracias. I would like that very much."

With a shy smile, he turned toward the cooler to fetch more drinks for the other diners.

"You're bold," Lily said to me after Juan Carlos left. "I would never risk it. I've been hearing about gringos dying in these waters ever since I started coming here. Once, six years ago, an American man drowned the day before I arrived. Cast a shadow over the whole season that year."

When it grew dark, we moved the benches and tables to their evening positions. The boombox played hits from the '60s and '70s and a handful of people danced. The card games started, and the alcohol came out. Without my asking, Madre Hermosa made me a guava soda with a splash of mezcal in it. The smoky flavor mixed with the pear-strawberry flavor of the guava was sublime. I had found my drink.

"Deliciosa." Madre Hermosa smiled at me. She had noticed my preference for guava, as she noticed everything that went on in Zipolite.

I sat with Lily for a time. We sipped our drinks and looked out at the moon, risen above the hills now and shimmering across the water. It was the third night of the full moon, my third night in Zipolite. It seemed a lifetime ago that I had lived in Texas, longer still since I had lived with Ma on the farm in Iowa.

I said goodnight to Lily and headed off to sleep. For the first time, I was able to climb the path to my hut overlooking the sea and click open my combination lock by myself, aided by my new flashlight. The breeze was gentle and just a bit cool — once again, perfect sleeping weather. I was growing used to sleeping outside in my hammock, the light cotton blanket that came with the hut spread over me, a pull on my cradle-rocking rope to lull me to sleep. My first two nights here, I had slept deeply and except for a brief dream about Maddie, dreamless-ly, recovering, no doubt, from the adrenaline-fueled flight and grueling days of travel I'd endured to get here. I settled in, hoping for another night of peaceful slumber under the stars and moonlight. But my subconscious had other plans.

14

Zipolite

In my dream, I saw the eyes again — Jenny's eyes staring out of the darkness. I hadn't known there was a Jenny until Johnny's wallet had inadvertently slipped out of his pocket into the cushion of the chair in my apartment. He'd told me about his wife, Liz, but had never mentioned having a teenaged daughter. When I found the wallet and discovered the photo, I understood why. We were identical: pretty blonds with blue eyes. I saw immediately that we looked alike enough to be twins. When I turned it over, I learned her name. "To Daddy, your Jenny," it said.

The photo explained much about my relationship with Johnny. It explained why Johnny once said to me, "I know you," when we were nearly strangers. Why he said, "You've come back to me," when I hadn't left. Why he said he loved me when he barely knew me. Why he insisted on calling me "Janey" — a name that, once I knew about Jenny, sounded remarkably like "Jenny" in his Texan accent.

The night I found Jenny's photo I had a nightmare about Jenny's eyes being just like mine. Just like my haunted, secret-keeping, wounded eyes. Eyes that had witnessed, over and over, the hideous violation of a father's sacred bond of love for a daughter made instead into something perverse and shameful. When I woke, I was convinced, and remained convinced, that Jenny and I shared this most soul-crushing secret, the defilement of daughter by father. Her eyes hid the same shameful secret as mine, a shame that nothing could heal. A horror that Johnny was trying to continue by substituting me for Jenny.

I tried to avoid him and that worked for a few weeks. But his wife Liz went to visit Jenny in Wisconsin, where she was now a student, leaving him free to stalk me and cajole me into seeing him in his office. In a moment of weakness, of sympathy, for the bedraggled figure shivering in the dark in a March downpour, I had gone.

This time, in the dream about the eyes, the eyes in a dark void — Jenny's eyes, my eyes, no matter, they were the same eyes — this time, the eyes had a voice attached to them. It was a female voice, but I couldn't tell whose. Possibly, it was Jenny's voice. Or Maddie's, the voice that had lured me to this improbable community. Or, it was my own voice, but a decisive, firm version of my usual hesitant tones.

The voice said, "You must cleanse yourself of all that is death."

When I woke on high alert, drenched in sweat, those words echoing in my mind, I saw the moon had set and the sun had not yet risen. It was growing light, but not quite dawn. The sea was dead calm.

I knew exactly what the words meant, what I must do. I was carrying death with me, carrying Johnny with me in the guise of his prized antiquities, the Roman coins and the ancient glass vial. I had taken the coins and vial in those moments after I had killed him, thinking to make it look like a robbery gone wrong instead of whatever kind of crime I had instead committed. I had kept them, thinking the evidence safer with me, thinking I could pawn them or sell them when my meager funds started to run out. The dream had revealed to me that instead of resources, these relics of my relationship with Johnny, of my brief life as a graduate student studying ancient Rome, were weights around my neck, making it impossible for me to move on or even survive what I had done. I had to dispose of them, this instant. And what better place than in the sea of Zipolite, offshore of the beach of the dead?

Juan Carlos had explained that the lone rock sticking out of the water off the beach of Zipolite on the Puerto Ángel side — the One Rock, he had called it — was out of range of the riptide. He'd said that if the sea was calm, it meant the riptide had subsided. It was the calmest I had seen the sea since arriving here. It was early, so no one would see me go. I would drop the coins and fill the vial with sea water so that it would sink, too. The water was deep there. Juan Carlos and his friends dove to eight or nine meters to get the abalone, he told me. I would drop the coins over the abalone colony where no one would ever find them. Or if local divers did some day, they wouldn't know where they had come from. They would be a curiosity, nothing more. I would be free of all that is death. I could go on as Ana and Jane would be no more.

I got out of the hammock, went into my hut, slipped off my Mexican shift, and slipped on my aqua Speedo. I dug into the sand under my night table and retrieved the large navy bandana I had wrapped around the treasures I took from Johnny's office. I tied a knot to secure the coins and tied the bandana around my waist. Once I had rolled it properly, the vial fit snugly into the folds. That way, my hands would be free for the swim out there. Sandals on, I made my way down the path to the beach. It was light enough not to need the flashlight but dark enough not to need sunglasses or hat. All was quiet in the village of hut-dwelling Americans and there was no sign of any of the Zapotecs, either. If I swam quickly, I could be back before anyone had noticed I'd gone.

I left my sandals above the high tide mark. The still sea was cold, but I entered quickly and quietly, and, when the sandy bottom gave way, I efficiently stroked my way out toward the lonely rock that marked the border between where the sea was safe and where it was not. In minutes, I was at the One Rock, which had a small ledge that I hoisted myself up on. The sea remained calm. I undid the knot around my waist, undid the knot into which I had tied the coins, and carefully uncoiled the bandana to retrieve the vial. I retied it around my waist. I would swim just a few strokes toward where Juan had said the abalone colony was, drop my treasures over it, and return to the far side of the rock and swim to shore. It would take only a minute.

It was an awkward swim, the remnants of ancient Rome and of my life in Texas in my hands, making a good stroke harder. But I was soon over the colony — the water was so clear I could see its dark mass down below. One by one, I dropped the coins and dipped my head under water to watch them drift downward. I floated for a moment and filled the vial with water so it would sink too. I opened my hand and the vial, too, started its journey to the sea floor.

I took a deep breath and dove down to watch it drift to its new home in the abalone colony. The vial suddenly jerked away from its destination. A moment later, a strong, cold, current swept me up too and both of us were pulled rapidly away from the abalone colony, away from the shore. I fought for the surface; I was running out of breath. When I finally reached it and gasped, choking on sea water but managing to fill my lungs with air, I looked for the lonely rock. It was nowhere in sight. And the shore was far, far away and growing ever more distant.

The tide that had given Zipolite its name had come for me.

15

The Pacific Ocean

Keep breathing, keep afloat. That's all there was to do. Caught in a current too strong to fight that was dragging me toward the vast emptiness of the Pacific. It pulled me west from Zipolite — how far, I had no way of telling. The rapidly receding shoreline became an indistinct line of tawny sand with a band of green above it. Nothing big enough to give me a landmark. Not that it mattered.

I had told no one where I was going. The only evidence I had left on the sand above the high tide mark was a plain pair of leather sandals that could belong to anyone. Juan Carlos told me that his fellow young diver, Pedro, had been swept out to sea on this current but was rescued. The boys always dove in pairs with a sentry left behind on the One Rock, he said. Presumably, the lookout boy had alerted someone on shore. Presumably, a boat was sent to look for Pedro. And had found him. No one had served as a lookout for me. No boat would be sent to scour the sea for a bobbing blond head with a boy's haircut.

This was it.

No sense struggling for the shore against impossible odds, though it didn't seem right to help matters along by taking seawater into my lungs, either. I would let nature take its course, though I hoped that didn't involve getting eaten by sharks. I had heard drowning wasn't so bad a death; would that be my fate? Or hypothermia? The sea was much colder than I imagined it would be, and the further I got from shore, the colder it was becoming.

I had taken a human life, even if it had been the life of so vile a man as Johnny. So there was justice in this odd, inhuman execution I would soon be facing. My life was of little matter to anyone but myself. No one would miss me. Few would even notice I was gone. I had no friends to mourn me, no relatives either, except for Ma. I had ended any relationship with her the night I killed Johnny. My father's cruel control had kept my life a tiny thing, confined mostly to the farm. Ma and I had both had to hurry home when her time at work, mine at school, finished for the day. He demanded to know where we were at all times. So, except for my childhood years, I had no ability to make friends, no afternoons chatting and gossiping with them like other girls did.

When I was little, I used to pray to grow fast so that I could protect Ma from his beatings, rapes, and humiliations. I did grow up enough to sort of protect her, but not with fists flying at him, the way I had imagined as a child. Instead, I had become a convenient repository for all the rage his failed life had ignited in him. After he started regularly raping me the summer I turned twelve, he hadn't come at Ma as frequently as he had before. It was my one worthy decision, to never tell her what he did to me. She had suffered enough under his hands.

Ironically, my prayers were answered just as I stopped believing in God. I had prayed to be big so that I could protect Ma. And I did become the outlet for his darkness, though it seemed an unholy answer to that prayer. I also had prayed for his death for years, until I felt abandoned by God and had taken to wishing on evening stars instead. But one day, when I was seventeen, I came home from school to find him dead, of a heart attack, they said. Another prayer answered.

I suppose most people in my situation — about to die — would find it an occasion for confession and prayer, or a plea for a miracle. But it was too late to turn to God now, after I had committed the most horrific of crimes. We had poor timing, God and me — my too hasty turn from prayer, his tardy beneficence.

"You must cleanse yourself of all that is death," the dream had spoken in a woman's voice. Jane Meyer's life had been all about death. Hadn't my father killed me a little every time he violated me, every time I witnessed what he did to Ma? Hadn't Johnny, too, now that I knew what perversity lay behind our affair? Now they were both dead, possibly by my prayers in one case, definitely by my hand in the other. Jane's life had been about nothing but death. Goodbye for good now, Jane. Death had her/me by the throat.

Out of the corner of my eye, I saw a large, dark form approaching. It was a bit below the surface and the sea around me was just choppy enough so that I couldn't distinguish what manner of creature this might be. About ten feet in front of me, it surfaced. Though I had never seen one before, it was easy enough to identify. It was a huge sea turtle. She seemed to be looking at me. I half realized that the current had bypassed us or dissipated, or we were floating above it. But what we weren't doing was continuing a headlong rush into the open sea. We were floating and looking at each other. She came closer, and turned around so I could see the whole of her green-brown shell. Right on the top, there was a scar about a foot long. Remarkably (or I was hallucinating), the scar was in the shape of a "J."

She must have taken a new breath for she put her head under the sea and started to swim toward the far away shore. I had the crazy idea to follow her. I had nothing better to do than wait for death to claim me. The current that had swept me out this far was no longer.

It was the longest swim of my life, but the sea was buoyant, the huge turtle, motivating. She headed resolutely toward a shore that was gradually taking on definition. She flapped her front flippers as if they were the wings of a bird in flight, raising them together over her head and stroking downward, propelling herself slowly toward the green and tawny slash of land. Her back flippers she used for navigation, I noticed, to correct her pitch or direction. She was a leisurely swimmer, so by alternating dog-paddle and crawl and using my legs to kick when I could muster the energy, I was able to keep pace with her. Stroke, stroke, glide, stroke, stroke, glide, we two unlikely swim partners made our way toward the shallows and safety. Just when I thought my arms couldn't take another stroke, we drew close enough to the beach that I could see the palm trees waving in the breeze. Suddenly, the sea turtle dove and disappeared.

"Thank you," I whispered hoarsely to the turtle, as her back flippers maneuvered her away from me.

I gathered what small reserves I had left and took the fifteen or so strokes until I felt sand under my feet. I stumbled onto the deserted beach and collapsed under a small stand of palm trees.

Minutes, hours, or days later, I heard a voice from far away say in accented English, "You are from the beach of the dead, no?" Someone lifted my head and put a canteen to my lips.

16

On the Beach

"You were saved by Santa Juanita, were you not? As I was myself some years ago."

The voice was soft and masculine. It spoke with reverence. I was too exhausted to open my eyes to see who it belonged to.

"Señorita, please drink. You make the long swim to el océano Pacífico, I think." Someone held my head up, and I felt the press of metal on my lips. I swallowed blissful mouthfuls of fresh water. The owner of the voice had put a straw hat over my head to shade my eyes from the sun, which now beat mercilessly down on me. My swimsuit was dry, completely dry. How long had I laid here?

"Señorita, please, out of the sun. You are too white. You will burn. Please, sit. I will help you to the trees."

The voice was insistent. My mind was still floating in the endless sea.

But my skin was hot. The voice was right. I was burning. No good to die from burning mere hours after I had avoided drowning.

I cracked open my eyes and peered at him from under the straw hat. Dark eyes set in a weathered face were looking at me with concern. Graying mustache, graying stubble beard, his black, chin-length hair fluttered in the breeze from the sea.

"Please, sit. I help you to where the sun is not."

I sat. He reached for one of my arms and pulled me to my feet. I staggered but he put my arm around his neck and dragged me a dozen feet to where the shade from the palm trees had traveled while I lay here on the beach. When he put me down, he propped my back up against the trunk. Wordlessly, he put the canteen to my lips and, again, I felt the cool unsalted liquid slide down my throat. My head lolled; it seemed too heavy for my neck to support.

"Gracias," I croaked to this Mexican man who had saved my life almost as much as the sea turtle.

"I must ask you a strange question, señorita. Did a very large, very old sea turtle show you to this place?"

My head jerked up. "Yes," I said with astonishment. In a raspy, salt-dried voice, I managed to continue, "I thought I would..." — I had a tough time with the word — "...die...out there. But a turtle..." I couldn't finish. My mind, my body, were still rushing out to the cold blue depths.

"Did she have a mark? On the shell?" the man continued urgently. "Like this?" I could hear him scraping the sand near me. "Look, señorita. Like this?"

I cracked my eyes open again and looked down. Near my left hand, he had drawn a large "J" in the sand. "Yes," I whispered again, incredulous. "Huh?" I gasped. Was I dreaming? But I heard the waves lapping at the shore. I felt the warm sand and the scratchy palm fronds beneath my body. When I tilted my head upward, I saw blue sky. Not dreaming. Not dead.

"Ah, it is true. Bless the Holy Mother." The man was saying to himself in wonder as he crossed himself. "Santa Juanita, she bring you here."

"What?" It seemed neither my mind nor my mouth was capable of more than a word or two.

"This turtle, I call her Santa Juanita. She come for the lettuce I leave. And found you."

Lettuce? "Have you..." — I searched my foggy brain for the word — "...tamed her?"

"Oh no, señorita. This no one can do. Look. Do you see that square out in the sea?"

I squinted in the direction his arm was pointing and nodded.

"I tie lettuce to that small platform. Santa Juanita, she love lettuce. And she knows that when the moon is full, I put lettuce. Look now, you see her head above the water."

"Yes. I see her. But why..." — I paused to find strength to continue — "...do you feed her?"

"I feed her this time of year to see that she is well. Why do I do this? Because ten years ago, she save my life as she save you this morning."

"I owe you both for my life," I said, still hardly believing that I was alive. This man with his strange story of a saintly turtle was not helping to reorient me to reality. "Thank you. Please put out lettuce for me for Santa Juanita," I croaked. I tried to smile, and my salt-dried lips split open.

"Here, eat." He handed me a quarter of an orange and I bit into it with a raw hunger, split lips be damned. I'd never tasted anything so sweet. I listened to the waves murmuring at the shore. I squinted at the bright blue sky. I felt the juice of this sweet orange run down my chin.

"She save my life," the stranger/savior was saying, "but she also give me a new life."

"What do you mean?" I looked at him, sitting cross-legged a dozen feet from me, his unruly hair wandering around his head as the wind found it. He wiped his sweating forehead with a red bandana — I was wearing his hat, I realized, but I didn't have the energy to lift it from my head and give it back to him.

He wordlessly put the canteen up to my lips again. This time my left arm was recovered enough to take it from him and hold it to my own lips.

"She tell me there was a better life for me. Now I live this life. Now, I am saint of sea turtles. To honor Santa Juanita."

I wasn't sure what he was talking about, but it sounded nice, peaceful. I struggled to find my voice again. This time, one word followed another, and sentences passed my sore lips in the raw whisper the salt sea had given me. "I am glad to hear this. I heard only one terrible story about Zipolite before I came here. It was that there was a truck that drove over the road that goes past Zipolite every day and that the truck was full of big, beautiful sea turtles, taking their last breaths, on their way to Puerto Escondido to be slaughtered for soup or eyeglasses frames. My friend said it made her sad every day to see this."

"I was the driver of that truck."

17

On the Beach

"What?" I said, wondering if I needed to reevaluate this man who was my savior.

He looked at me with a great sadness, a feeling I instantly and profoundly recognized as the mainstay of the last half of my life. I nodded, in solidarity, and to encourage him to say more as I struggled to overcome the state of hopeless exhaustion that had taken hold of me. In my weak, near-drowned state, I could no longer keep it all inside. Shame, anger, sadness broke over me like the waves in the nearby Pacific. I felt I might suffocate under their immense, cold weight. I tried to focus instead on this man who seemed to both kill sea turtles and worship them.

"My brother and me, we know where the turtles like to eat the seagrass. So, we put nets in this place. It is a place between Puerto Ángel and Zipolite, not too far from the land. It was easy to catch the turtles. We needed only a small boat to get them, one by one, back to shore and onto the old truck. Some were dead. Sea turtles need air to breathe, and they would die in the net. But some were alive when we put them in the truck. It was easy work, putting turtles in the truck, making the drive to Puerto Escondido, to the factory. The only hard thing was the very bad road."

I saw the net in my mind's eye, the turtles frantically try-ing to escape — and failing. I saw the stinking open-backed truck that Maddie had described to me making its rickety way over the rutted road past the stick huts, sullying the idyll that was Zipolite with the death of these old, wise creatures. A tear escaped my right eye and traveled down my cheek.

The windblown man reached out and patted my hand, try-ing to comfort me. His eyes looked teary, too, and his words were filled with sorrow.

"We never think about their lives, I am sorry to say. We never think, if we take turtles many times, soon there would be no more. We think only about the money and the easy work.

"One Sunday morning ten years ago, I go to Mass in Puerto Ángel. I visit the widow in the village behind Zipolite beach — she is now my wife. I think to row out to the One Rock to see the abulón colony. I think to take them from the sea, also. More easy money, that is all I think. I know about the fast riv-er under the sea, of course, everybody here know about this. But I think I will put my anchor next to the One Rock and tie another rope around my middle. I will dive to see the abulón, I will be safe, I think. I am a proud man. I think I know the sea very well."

From the depths of my near-drowned brain, a word strug-gled to form in my mouth. "Hubris," I whispered, leaning forward toward him as he handed me the canteen once again. It was a concept I had studied in an ancient Greek literature class I had taken in my former life. When he looked at me, his eyes a question mark, I took a deep breath and tried to clear my throat. "When you think you are so good, or good at something, or so strong, you can do no wrong." I struggled to make my thick, salted tongue form the words. "In books, bad things happen to people with hubris because they have too much pride — they are arrogant." This small display of intellect completely exhausted me, and I slumped back against the palm trunk.

My companion smiled. "Yes, I had this...hubris. It is a good word for the young man I was. I go from my boat into the sea. The rope is around my middle and tied to my boat. The other rope has the anchor for the boat and it is down on the bottom of the sea. I think I am very smart, very safe, this way. I dive down under the water. I see the beautiful colony of abulón that I dream I take for good money. But I did not tie the rope so well around my middle. When the river came for me, the rope was no more. The undersea river catch me and pull me out to sea. It is the same for you, señorita, no?"

"Yes, just there, just above the abalone colony." I remembered how the Roman coins I dropped fluttered down to rest among the living mountain of abalone clustered together far below me in the sea, in the seconds before the current took me.

His eyes got a far-away look in them and I knew he was reliving his version of what I had just experienced. "I am taken out to el océano Pacífico. I think my life is over, I think I never marry the widow Verónica, the woman I love. When all hope is gone, the undersea river let me go. But I am far away from the land, and I am no good to swim far."

He paused and searched my face. Again, I nodded in solidarity. "I, too, was far from shore when the current let me go."

"But instead of death, el milagro — the miracle," he continued earnestly. "A green turtle, very old, she swim close to me so I grab her shell. She must swim to the playa, and nothing, not even when a man grab her shell, will stop her. It was the time of laying eggs, and nothing stop a sea turtle from her playa when it is her time. So, Santa Juanita, she swim with me, my hands on her shell, all the way to this playa, until I could stand up in the water.

"I sit on the sand. I try to find my breath, and I think: Why does the Holy Mother bring this miracle on me?"

"Did you figure it out?"

"Yes, the old turtle, she tell me. She give me el momento de la verdad — the moment of truth. As I sit in the sand, waiting to get my body to move to find fresh water, I see her. Even though she is very tired after she swim me to the playa, Santa Juanita, she dig a hole with her back feet, a big hole for her eggs. Her life, I see, is about life. My life, I also see, is about death, the death of her kind, the kind of life that save my life. El momento de la verdad: I must cleanse myself of all that is death."

"What did you say?" I gasped. Surely I was hallucinating now. But my companion repeated the very words I had heard in my dream — was that only a few hours ago? A lifetime had gone by since the dream.

"I must cleanse myself of all that is death," he said again.

"I dreamed those very words last night," I found myself admitting to this stranger, in a voice that did not seem my own. "That dream is the reason I went out to the One Rock and the reason I got caught in the current."

"Ah, Santa Juanita, she visit you in the night. Not the turtle, but she who after I name the turtle. Like me, it is time for you to find el momento de la verdad."

"I am not a believer," I said, in response to the bizarre turn this already strange conversation had taken.

"It does not matter to the Blessed Virgin what you believe," he replied with conviction. "Santa Juanita is the name of fondness we in México gave to the Mother of God when she bring a young girl back to life long ago. When we are in mortal danger, we pray to her. I am dying in the sea, so I am praying to Santa Juanita when I see the turtle! I call the old turtle Santa Juanita, after the Holy Mother, who come to me as a sea turtle in my hour of need.

"When she bring me to the playa, I was not so tired as you, I think, because Santa Juanita, she do the swimming. While she make the hole for her eggs, I use the knife in my pocket to make the mark on her back. Because I know this turtle save my life. If I see this turtle again, I want to know it is Santa Juanita. But also, I see in my head, in my heart, that it is a sin to kill the sea turtle for money. The Holy Mother make me see this. So, no more net. No more we take the turtles to Puerto Escondido. I tell my brother of this miracle and he agree. No more.

"Now, my life is to save sea turtles. To guard the playa when Santa Juanita and her sisters come here to put their eggs. I keep away the birds and the small animals of the jungle. There is el patrón americano who lives in Mazunte. He pay me to do this work. So, it is my life, now, to be the saint of the sea turtles."

"That is a wonderful story. I am glad you found your true calling."

My companion smiled his thanks, but his face grew serious again. He leaned toward me and looked into my eyes.

"But is your soul in mortal danger, like my soul, señorita? Is this why you go into the sea in Zipolite, the beach of the dead?"

I didn't know how to answer this question. I wasn't sure I had a soul. Or if I had once had one, if it had died long ago on the hard floor of the farmhouse on a hot summer's morning the August I turned twelve. But it felt important to say something honest to this man who had helped to save me.

"Like you, my life has been all about death," I said slowly, thinking it over. "When I had the dream, I knew the words I heard were correct, that I must cleanse myself of all that is death. I knew that cleansing myself involved going into the sea in Zipolite, even though I knew about the riptide there. It might be that, like you, I had to nearly die to be reborn, to find my moment of truth. It might be that Santa Juanita has enabled me to start a new life, now." I wasn't sure I believed in Santa Juanita, the Virgin Mary. But Santa Juanita, the sea turtle, was real beyond dispute. And she had motivated me to save my own life. For what purpose, I had no idea.

Then, he said the strangest thing of all.

"I need someone to help me with the sea turtles, señorita. Santa Juanita bring you to me to do this job."

18

Mazunte

"Eat this. We must walk to Mazunte." The world-weary man pulled another orange from a string bag I hadn't realized he had, quickly cut it in fourths with a jack-knife he drew from his pants' pocket, and gave me a wedge. The juice stung my split lips, but it also revived me.

After we had shared a third orange, I told him, "I think I am strong enough to walk now."

"The American holy sisters who teach me English when I am a boy are yelling at me from heaven right now, señorita, because I do not introduce myself," he said, looking up at the sky as he pulled me to my feet. We started walking west on the sandy beach. Me, barefoot in my used aqua Speedo, the bandana still around my waist reminding me of my brush with death, his straw hat shading my head. He, in a faded blue shirt and dirty jeans, bareheaded because of his kindness. He carried his sandals in one hand, in deference to my bare feet.

"My Christian name is José Maria Jesús Garcia. My father tell me he name me after the words my mother scream when she give birth to me." He smiled over at me. "But even as a boy, I think there is too much — hubris," he tried the word slowly, "in three first names. I honor my father and my mother who name me, but I am José, only. And you, señorita?"

I hesitated not a moment. "Ana. Ana Jiménez." For the first time, the name seemed like mine.

"A mexicana name for a young lady who does not look mexicana."

"I had to cleanse myself of all that is death." I tried to smile but it hurt my split lips too much.

José looked over appreciatively. "Yes, names may hold many memories of death. Sometimes, it is good to start over completely, even the name."

"My great-grandmother was named Anna," I said slowly, thinking the idea out while I spoke. "She came to America to start over, to start a new life. I wonder if I took her name because I, too, need to start a new life in a new country."

José smiled over at me. "Do you like turtles, señorita Ana?"

"I never saw a sea turtle in my life until Santa Juanita appeared in front of me this morning." Was it only this morning? "But I have always loved all animals, all of nature." I said this with passion that surprised me. "That's why I had hoped I would never see the turtle truck my friend told me about. I knew it would horrify me." Walking in nature, observing the life around me, had been my secret solace in those dark years while my father was alive. I'd never told anyone of my love of nature before. But I felt compelled to share with José. I owed him honesty for saving my life. At least as much as I could share without telling him about what I had done. Was that a bit more than a week ago?

"Turtle trucks are no more. Do not worry. There are not enough turtles for the factory. It is closed. Now, it is me and el patrón. We work so there are more turtles. It is a deep regret in my life, señorita Ana, that I take the life of so many turtles. But, in these years, when I am saving turtles, I make sure that thousands go to the sea safely. Each year, when Santa Juanita's children break from their eggs, I mark each baby with her mark, so I will know her children from all other turtles. In a few years, the first I marked will be old enough to come back to the playa where they were born, the playa Santa Juanita bring you to. When baby turtles grow up, they put their eggs on the same playa. El patrón and me, we start a hospital for turtles. But someday, we will make a center for the American tourists. Now, we do research on sea turtles. So, I need ayudante." At my blank look, he added, "Someone to help me with turtle research."

"Would I be paid?" I hated to be so crass, but the small stack of twenties buried back at my hut would not last forever.

"I will ask el patrón, but I believe the answer is yes. He would be happy to have una ayudante americana. He is from Texas."

Texas! Did he follow the news there? Would he see a wanted poster of my former self? For a moment, I had hoped I had found the beginnings of a new future for myself. But working for a Texan?

"Does...does your patrón work side by side with you?" I had to know more about this mysterious Texan.

José laughed. "Never. We are partners because he has money, and I can do the work. We have a small building in Mazunte with tanks for injured sea turtles. I find them on the playa. I try to make health for the sea turtles. If I can make health for them, I free them. El patrón, he pay for the turtle hospital and for me. One or two times in the year, he visits the turtle hospital. He stay all the time in his big house or he go to fish in his big boat."

"Is there a place for me to live in Mazunte?" I tried in vain to imagine my new circumstances.

"I need una ayudante to stay in Zipolite, not Mazunte. The turtles, they swim back and forth, Zipolite, Mazunte, Zipolite. For people, the underwater river is a way to be lost in the sea. A way to die in the sea. But for the turtles, it is a highway to go to Mazunte to eat the grasses in the sea. There are playas where the turtles put eggs that are close to Zipolite. So, I will work in Mazunte. My ayudante will work in Zipolite. This is best."

He talked on, expanding on his dream of how an assistant from America could help him. Could I write letters to American universities to find what research had been done on sea turtles? If any books had been written about them? Margarita in Puerto Ángel had a typewriter, José said. "You know her?" I nodded. And it would be wonderful to count how many sea turtles came to the seagrass forest between Puerto Ángel and Zipolite. Was I a good swimmer? Could I dive? Could I keep records? By the time we started to see evidence of human habitation, José was confident that I would make a wonderful assistant.

I found myself warming to the work. He would get me a snorkel, mask, and fins, he said, and a record book to record everything I did and saw both in the sea and on the beaches I would be assigned to patrol. I could read books or scientific articles on sea turtles if any had been written and summarize them for him, and start to collect a small library for the future sea turtle center the patrón had promised to finance. I would become an expert on Pacific Mexico's sea turtles, he told me. It all sounded fine to me, if unexpected. But I focused on the two qualities of the job that seemed most important: I could stay in Zipolite, far away from the Texan patrón, and he would pay me enough to live there.

We left the beach and headed inland on a small path. I could see the thatch of roofs now and buildings made from adobe and painted. At a modest one of these buildings with a wooden door, shutters, and screened windows, José paused. "This is my home. Please come in and meet my wife, Verónica. You are very hungry, no? We eat now. Verónica will give you clothes. We talk about when you start the work with the turtles. Santa Juanita found for me la ayudante perfecta! Verónica, please, this is señorita Ana. She was in the turtle highway. Santa Juanita find her. She bring her to the playa where I was, too." José spoke in English.

Verónica looked up from the pot she had been stirring in

the outdoor kitchen in the garden behind the small house. I started. She looked just like Madre Hermosa! Even the gray streak in her hair was the same.

Verónica smiled. "You think I am Madre Hermosa," she said in heavily accented English. "I am her twin sister, Verónica. Bienvenida, señorita."

She spoke to José, who translated. "My wife will tell Madre you are safe. She find your sandals on the beach. She is worried you are lost in the sea."

"Gracias. I didn't realize there were any telephones in Zipolite."

"No teléfonos, señorita. Madre Hermosa — her name is Gloria, but I, too, and even Verónica, call her Madre Hermosa — and my wife, they can make the think talk when it is needed.

"Come to the bedroom. Verónica will find you a skirt and a blouse. We will eat tamales. Verónica say she feel this morning we will have a guest for lunch, so she make many of them."

19

Mazunte and Zipolite

Verónica insisted I take a siesta before walking the three and a half miles back to Zipolite. She had offered a bed for the night, but I felt a strong urge to go "home" to my modest hut. After her lunch of tamales filled with roasted squash and herbs, I thought I could make it, but, with the sun high in the sky, I agreed to a nap. Taking a siesta in a double bed seemed so foreign, even though her simple guest room had a cool breeze blowing through the shutters. Already, I had become accustomed to my hammock. But I did fall into a dreamless sleep. I *was* exhausted from my near-death morning and long swim. The next thing I knew, José was shaking my shoulder gently, saying, "Ana, mi hija, if you are to walk before dark, you must leave now."

Verónica had packed a small paper bag with provisions exotic to my Iowan diet — dried pineapple, mango, fig, and two bottles of guava soda. When I remarked, "Thank you, guava is my favorite," she nodded and smiled.

"I know."

I didn't dare to ask her how she knew. Was the communicative connection between the twin sisters able to transmit such details?

"I will see you in three days, señorita Ana," José was saying. "And show you the boat you will use to go to the seagrass forest."

"A boat? I don't know how to drive a boat."

José laughed. "It is a small rowboat. We will row out together to the forest. By the time we return to la playa, you will know all there is to know about the boat."

Verónica had provided me with a bright blue skirt, a pullover short-sleeved white blouse, and flip-flops for the walk home. She said I could keep these items if I liked, thus increasing my Zipolite wardrobe by a third.

"You have been so kind," I said to Verónica. To José, I said, "How can I ever thank you, José? I would not have survived without your help. And now you offer me a job, too? Are you sure? Wouldn't someone educated in marine biology be a better choice?"

José smiled and did a little bow. "I did not choose you, señorita Ana. Santa Juanita bring you to me. As she is all-wise, you must be the one I need." He would not be shaken from this belief, however mistaken I thought it must be.

"If you see a hurt turtle on the beach as you walk, put water on its back, look carefully to know where it is, and tell Madre Hermosa. I will come. Otherwise, in three days, I will come for huevos rancheros at the restaurant of Madre Hermosa. I see you at breakfast, mija. Adiós, Ana. Go with God," he translated the ancient word.

I waved and walked southeast along the shore. There were beaches and shallow coves, all of them deserted, all of them lovely, between Mazunte and Zipolite. I saw no turtles nor any humans, only the frigate birds soaring high above me with their otherworldly wings.

"Ana Jiménez." I spoke the words, trying them on to see if they could fit. "Ana Jiménez, sea turtle protector. Ana Jiménez, sea turtle expert. Ana Jiménez of Zipolite." The words sounded completely foreign. But so did "Jane Meyer, murderer." My past made me the scarred, scared young woman who accepted a scholarship to study history in the foreign land of Pine Hill Station, Texas. Possibly, that plan to remake my life was always doomed, even without making the disastrous decision to become my advisor's lover. Even without killing him.

The people I had met since fleeing America had been so kind to me, starting with Alex who gave me a new identity with paperwork to prove it and a chance to legitimize myself further by marrying him. Margarita, who completely changed the way I looked to the rest of the world. In the last ten years, I had never worn colorful clothes or even skirts. Madre Hermosa, who quietly watched over me and fed and sheltered me. And now José and Verónica...

Was this the life I was supposed to lead? I couldn't bring myself to believe I was the recipient of divine intervention — it was the coincidence of running into a hungry sea turtle. But still, fate or luck or happy accident had resulted in me walking toward "home" along a pristine coast in tropical Mexico when I might have been drowned in the sea or captured, tried, and sent to prison. This was a gift I should take very, very, seriously. Resolved to embrace my blessings, I walked determinedly on the rugged track in the growing darkness toward my new home, my new life.

In the distance, I could hear '60s music from the boombox.

The waning moon had barely made itself evident over the eastern hills. Someone was walking toward me in the dim light. Juan Carlos.

"Hola, señorita Ana. Mamá told me to come to meet you. She saved dinner for you. Tonight, we have a soup from many sea creatures. Muy deliciosa."

I was no longer surprised that my homecoming had been known in advance by Madre Hermosa.

"Hola, Juan Carlos. Thank you for coming to meet me. José

and Verónica are your aunt and uncle, aren't they?"

"Yes, it is like I have two madres, because tía Verónica look just like mi mamá! And tío José is a very nice man. He will come for breakfast in a few days!"

There must be something in the air. Everyone knew everything immediately, even though there was no electricity for a telephone in the little village. "Your tía and tío," I tried out the new words for aunt and uncle, "called me 'mi hija' and 'mija.' What do they mean, Juan Carlos?"

"Both mean, 'my daughter,' señorita Ana. It means you have a place here." Juan Carlos tapped his heart.

I felt a surprising clench in my chest at these words. "Mi hija, mija," I repeated the words in a whisper and shook my head at the wonder of it.

"Are we cousins?" I smiled over at him.

He giggled. "I would like you for la prima, a cousin, señorita Ana." His face grew serious. "But first I must say I am sorry. So sorry. It was my fault, your voyage on the turtle highway."

"What do you mean, Juan Carlos?"

"I told you that it was no problema, this highway, when the waters are calm, when there are no waves, no olas del mar. But I did not tell you the most important part. Also, the tide must be low. When you went for your swim early, the tide was not low. This is why the turtle highway — the riptide — took you away. I am very sorry!" The boy looked grief-stricken.

"I made the decision to go in the sea, even though I knew about the current. You did not make me go. It is not your problem, no problema," I emphasized, patting his arm, making sure his eyes caught mine in the waning light. "Besides, I think I had to be taken by the current to learn to embrace this place, my life here, all the nice people here. Like you. You have nothing to be sorry for, Juan Carlos, nothing at all."

Juan Carlos looked over at me, a shy smile lighting up his face. "Will you be my cousin — mi prima — señorita Ana? I never had a girl cousin with short yellow hair before!"

"And I have never had a master diver for a cousin before!" I smiled back.

Juan Carlos took my hand, and we walked toward the flickering candlelight of Madre Hermosa's restaurant and bar. She had set a bowl of seafood soup and a guava soda on the table with the best view.

"Bienvenida, señorita Ana." She gave me a brief hug and a brief smile.

Next to the table sat my leather sandals.

20

Zipolite

"We haven't met, yet. I'm Steven." A black-haired stranger tapped me on the shoulder as I was putting away the last of the tin plates from dinner. Behind me, I could hear wood scraping wood as people shifted the tables and benches to the evening configuration.

"Oh," I replied, startled by the unexpected touch. "Hi. I'm Ana." I tried to smile, but my split lips prevented it. Instead, I grimaced.

"Ouch, that must have hurt," Steven replied, noticing my injured lips. "That happened to me, my first year in Zipolite. Sun and salt water can be tough on the tender spots." He smiled. "Out in the ocean too long?"

Yeah, you might say that. So long it was almost permanent. "Guess so," I responded neutrally. I wasn't ready, and never would be ready, to tell the other turistas in Zipolite about my experience in the riptide.

"Come sit with me over there, so we can get to know each other a bit." It felt like a command. Was I being picked up? "It's mezcalitas, tonight. I'll get you one."

I looked around frantically for Lily, Linda and Andy, or even Juan Carlos. But I didn't see any of the few people I had talked with since I'd arrived.

You live here, now, I coached myself silently. You've got to try to fit in, be friendly.

"Thanks," was all I could manage.

We retrieved a couple drinks from Regina, who was the designated bartender that evening. Even Madre Hermosa had abandoned me. I followed Steven to a solitary bench at the far side of the plank patio, far away from the boombox, the dancing, the poker playing. He motioned me to sit facing the ocean. Had he moved the bench here? I never noticed one set so separately from the others before. Had he planned this?

The moon had only begun to rise beyond the mountains behind us, so it was nearly dark. The usual evening breeze from offshore hadn't yet made itself known, so the air was still quite warm. Not knowing what else to do, I pretended to sip my drink.

"Your first time?" Steven turned to me. I started at the question, and he laughed. "In Zipolite, I mean, Ana."

"Ah, yes. I've been here about ten days now."

"This is my third season. Sure beats winters in Iowa. That's where I'm from."

Iowa! Panic crept into my throat. "Ah, where in Iowa?" I croaked.

"Just finished at the U in Iowa City in December. Grew up in Des Moines, but I don't want to move back there. I need some space from my folks. Not sure what's next, so I came here to think. Zipolite's good for that. You?"

Iowa City? The same school I had graduated from less than a year ago? Had we been in some of the same classes? I wracked my brain, searching frantically for the right response. What backstory had I told other people here? After a frantic few seconds, I realized only Frank and Kathy had asked me a question that led to my past. And they were gone.

"Mmmichigan," I finally managed, remembering what address I put on my fraudulent visa. "A small town there. Just finished school at Ann Arbor," I stumbled on, mimicking the structure of what he had said. Surely, we'd had no classes together in Iowa City. Surely, if we had, he wouldn't remember me, a shy girl who always left right after class and rarely spoke to anyone. A girl with long hair in baggy jeans. Not a girl with a buzz cut in a colorful skirt. Whose name was Ana, not Jane.

I looked at his profile in the near-dark, trying to decide if I'd ever seen it, seen him before. I'd gone out of my way not to look at people all through college. So unsurprisingly, he didn't seem familiar.

"You come here to think about what's next, too?" he said after a small silence. "I majored in economics, but I didn't like it much. Trying to please the ol' man, now that I think about it. I shoulda majored in journalism or creative writing. That's what I actually like. Funny how you don't realize what you want until it's too late to get it. Did you like your major?"

I scoured my brain, trying to think of what to say. "I majored in history," I finally admitted honestly. "I liked it, but I don't know what to do with it." It seemed safest to put myself in the same post-graduating quandary as he seemed to be in. Part of me wished I could relax into this conversation and act like a normal young woman meeting a guy for the first time and striking up a conversation. But all my senses were on high alert, like there was danger lurking in the shadows. I was supposed to think of a question to ask now, to move this duet along. He seemed nearly my age, and nearly my status in life. Even in this dim light, I could see that he wasn't bad looking; tall, slim, a boyish grin, dark hair, thick and curly. Boyfriend material, or at least someone good for a few nights' romance. I tried to drum up some interest in this man, in our hesitant interaction, from my tattered reserves. But I could dredge up nothing. I felt nothing, except a supreme unease. Was it because I was still exhausted physically from my long swim? Was it because I was still deadened emotionally from my catastrophic act? Had my relationship with Johnny and its perverse rituals ruined me for other men?

Steven broke into my reverie. "Moon's almost up. Walk on the beach for a bit?"

"Thanks, but I'm real tired. I think I'll turn in early tonight."

"Can I walk you up to your hut?"

"I'm okay. Thanks, though."

"Some other night when you're more rested?"

"Ah, I'm just not ready, yet," I found myself saying. It was true, in a way.

"Hurt bad by somebody?"

"I can't talk about it." Another truth. Johnny had hurt me, degraded me, reduced me to nothing but a cheap copy of what, of who, he really wanted. Because of what my father had already ruined in me, I had thought myself incapable of being hurt further. I'd been wrong about that.

Steven was getting to his feet now. "Well. Guess I'll move along. 'Night, Ana."

He walked off to join the others.

I retrieved my flashlight from the kitchen shelf where I'd left it earlier and walked slowly up the hill to my hut, the noises of conversation, laughter, music, receding behind me.

Why, Jenny? I silently asked the image of her I conjured after I crawled into my hammock and tugged on the cradle-rocking rope a bit. *Why did you come to me in a vision, make me get up and turn off the gas, when I was so close to solving the problem of my sorry life?* I looked to the stars for an answer but saw only the constancy of the constellations. I listened for an answer but heard only the chirping jungle insects and the sounds of a party I would never be part of. I stared at the sky until the waning moon was high in the heavens, but no vision, no voice appeared.

21

Zipolite

Two more days passed. I walked the beaches seeking injured turtles and trying on my new identity: Ana, Ana. I didn't see any turtles. But Ana Jiménez started to feel familiar, at least a bit.

"Good morning, Ana. It is good to see you again. Are you well?"

"Buenos días, José. Estoy bien, gracias." I sat down across the table from the older man. Today, his hair was neatly combed, his white shirt pressed. The straw hat he had shaded me with lay beside him on the wooden bench. I had worn my swimsuit and put on the blue wrap-around skirt over it.

"I have talked with el patrón, and he welcome you to the turtle project. He will pay Madre Hermosa for your hut and your food, and he will give you this, every week for one month." He drew three American twenty-dollar bills from a wallet he took from his pants pocket. "After one month, we will talk about if we will continue with you and you with us. Please say yes, Ana. It is the will of the Virgin!"

I smiled and nodded my assent. "Who am I to fight the Blessed Virgin?"

After the usual breakfast, we walked to the scattering of

rowboats pulled up onto the sand that Lily had pointed out to me a day or two ago. "This is your boat, Ana," he said, pointing to a small craft painted bright blue. Across the back of the little craft was the word "*La Tortuga*" — turtle. "You put it into the sea, please, so I can see if you are strong."

If there was anything I was talented at, it was surprising people with the strength of my arms. I flipped the craft over and pulled the small wooden boat to the shore without too much effort by grasping the "bow" as José instructed me to call it. He said it was easier to pull it to the water's edge when the tide was all the way out, as it was now, or all the way in. It was easier to pull it on dry sand than wet, he told me.

"I don't know how to row," I admitted sheepishly. "I've never been in a boat before." I had decided, in the days between my rescue and now, that no matter what, I would try to be honest with José. I owed him that much. He looked at me as if I had three heads. But all he said was, "It is simple, mija. Sit here," he pointed to the middle seat of the boat, "and I will tell you what to do." He showed me how to step to the middle with one foot before putting the other one in so as not to rock the boat in the knee-high water.

He gave a little push, got in, and sat on the rear plank seat. He instructed me to take the wooden oars from the bottom one by one and lock the metal pin near the center on each into its ring on the sides of the boat. Only then should I put the paddle end of the oar into the water. I felt the water push back against the paddle as I took a few tentative strokes, correcting my position and my stroke as my patient teacher instructed. When I wrapped my hands around them, I noticed that the oar handles had been polished by many years of use. It was easier to row than I had expected. It was a comforting motion — pulling both oars simultaneously — and rewarding, too, as the boat glided across the top of the sea. I learned to go straight, turn right or left, even back up, without too much difficulty.

"You were born for this boat, I think!" José said with satisfaction, as he indicated the direction to the seagrass forest a small distance offshore. There was a red buoy marking the spot. For a moment, I was mesmerized by the ocean, so deceptively placid this morning, so attractively blue and clear. Respect for its hidden power, though, was fixed in my bones now, forever.

When we arrived, he showed me the iron ring embedded in the red anchor buoy and how to tie the bow rope to it. He had placed the buoy here many years ago when he caught turtles and brought them to shore in this very same boat.

"Go into the sea now, and find the turtles," he ordered me with a smile. He described how to get out of the boat by falling backward into the water from the craft's middle, and for the first time since "the cleansing," as I had named it to myself, I was in the chilling sea. My heart was steady; I felt curiosity, nothing more. I silently thanked the older kids from the farm next door, who had taught me to swim and dive in their farm's swimming hole all those years ago. It was harder to dive in the buoyant saltwater, but easier to float. In contrast to the swimming hole, the sea seemed always in motion.

Below me was a dark, greenish mass. I took a deep breath and swam downward toward it. As José had called it, it was a forest of seagrass, emerald spikes up to a yard long, waving in the sea current. And scattered throughout it were sea turtles. I counted five of them before I had to come up for a breath, though none were the size of Santa Juanita. They were unafraid and slowly swam among the grasses, taking mouthfuls when they saw an appealing plant. But it was hard to see clearly as I squinted in the salty sea.

José motioned for me to return to the boat and showed me the two-rung rope ladder hanging off the end that I could use to hoist myself back into the small craft. I pressed my palms to my eyes — the salt water made them sting.

"Tell me what you see and then we will go to Puerto Ángel. We find a mask, snorkel, and the flippers and speak with Margarita."

I tried to be as precise as possible within the limits of my vision, telling him the number of turtles, estimating their sizes, and the color and shape of their shells.

"You do this well, Ana. I show you how to put it in the book. Now, please row back. Please bring the boat back onto the sand so I know you can do this."

I did as he asked. By the time we reached shore, my swimsuit was dry. I pulled the boat back up past the high tide mark and tied the bow rope around a tree trunk for good measure. He picked up the small satchel he had brought with him. I put on my skirt and blouse over the dry suit. Then we walked the half-hour to Puerto Ángel, José telling me about the habits of sea turtles and me asking questions. I hadn't spoken so much since I had been a graduate student in Maddie's research methods class.

When we arrived at Margarita's, she kissed José warmly, greeted me by name, and made us each a smoothie. As we sat at the bar sipping our drinks, José got the ledger out of his satchel and showed me the meticulous records he had kept for the past ten years. The turtle count at their favorite feeding places, the number injured and what had happened to them, estimates of the number of egg-laying turtles, eggs hatched, tiny turtles who had made it to the sea. Then he gave me an identical blank book, and I copied the layout of his pages. "Make the writing as soon as you can after you see what you see," he said. "Exactly what you see. Especially, look for any turtles with Santa Juanita's mark."

Margarita came over with a snorkel and mask and handed them to me. "This will help with your eyes," she said. She showed me how to put it on and told me how to clear the lens by wetting it, then spitting on the inside of it, then rinsing it in the sea. "It's a time-tested method," she smiled. She then had me try on some blue fins. She nodded in satisfaction at how they fit.

"El patrón will pay for this," José added.

The two spoke rapidly in Spanish for a moment and I thought I discerned the words "teléfono" and "Oaxaca."

Margarita translated. "I called the library in Oaxaca and asked the librarian to research the addresses of American universities with marine biology departments. We will start in California. When the addresses arrive, you will come with me to my home, Ana, and use my typewriter to write them to ask them for any books or papers written about sea turtles. Or any experts among the professors."

"We will find many informations about sea turtles so we know them," José added. "For the center we will someday have in Mazunte."

"I will do my best," I promised these two people, who had both, in their way, taken me under their wing. "Thank you for giving me this chance."

All three of us looked up as the bus from Oaxaca screeched to a halt a few yards from Margarita's.

A scattering of men and women from the mountain villages got off with their string bags and their baskets and strolled toward the bank or the small cluster of shops that surrounded the dusty plaza. Last to emerge from the bus was a broad-shouldered, sturdy white woman with ear-length brown hair, who looked distinctly American, somehow.

She hoisted a large backpack to her shoulders and began to make her way to Margarita's, looking as exhausted as I must have looked when I got off this same bus a bit more than a week ago.

Margarita got off her bench and walked purposefully over to the woman. She took her backpack off her back and placed it on the ground. "Thorpe? Is it you?"

The woman broke into a wide smile, and tears came quickly to her eyes.

"Oh Margarita, how I have dreamed of you and your smoothies!" Then she threw her arms around Margarita and the two hugged for a long time. Margarita put her arm around the woman and walked with her to where we were sitting at the bar.

"Surely Frank has told you about the Amazons who came here one year." She looked at me and I nodded. How could I forget the five women Frank had described as "Maddie and the Amazons" after I stupidly admitted that I knew Maddie. I remembered he'd said they were lesbian graduate students. It was the moment when I'd almost blown my cover. "Well, this is one of them," Margarita continued, "come back to the nest! Ana, José, meet my dear friend Thorpe."

22

Puerto Ángel and Zipolite

I somehow managed to smile and nod at the exhausted woman, but my brain had gone to red alert. The Amazons! She must know, and could still be close friends with, Maddie! I silently thanked fate that Frank and Kathy, with whom I had been way too honest about how I knew of Zipolite, had left a day or two before.

"A shame, you just missed Frank and Kathy," Margarita was saying as she walked back to where the woman had dropped her backpack, hoisted it onto her own shoulders, walked back to the bar, and deposited the pack next to its owner. "They left a couple of days ago to catch an art fair in San Antonio."

"Damn," Thorpe said. "I knew I'd miss some of the regulars if I came this late in the season, but I couldn't get away until now."

"What do you have in this backpack, my sweet?" Margarita said. "Rocks?"

"Books," the woman called Thorpe replied. "Can't tell if I've found something new if I don't have my reference books with me."

"Thorpe spends her time in tropical jungles, looking for useful plants," Margarita explained to José and me. "Where have you been this time, hon?"

"Corcovado, in Costa Rica," Thorpe replied as she slumped onto a bar stool and put her head down facing us on the bar. "Most pristine rainforest left in Central America. Please hurry with my drink, or I might just die here and now."

Margarita cut up some watermelon and whirred it in her blender with lime juice and ice. She poured it into a large glass and brought it over to her thirsty friend.

"Now, that's a friend for you," Thorpe smiled as she gulped. "Someone who remembers what you like to drink without even asking."

We let Thorpe rehydrate in silence for a while. "José and Ana study our sea turtles — and work to save them," Margarita told Thorpe.

"Are you marine biologists?" Thorpe asked.

José laughed. "No, but we try to save turtles, and we collect informations about them. Ana is new to this job. She will look for turtles in the seagrass forest between Puerto Ángel and Zipolite. I look in Mazunte, where there is another forest. We have un patrón — an American who lives in Mazunte, Mr. Nathan Nelson."

"Interesting. I know someone at UCLA who would love to look at your data."

"Is it so?" José beamed. "We want to write to universities to find sea turtle scientists."

"Mañana, I'll help. Today, siesta is about all I'm good for," Thorpe smiled at José. She turned to me. I hadn't spoken a word to her, yet.

"You're staying in Zipolite? Ah...I didn't catch your name."

"Ana-with-one-N," I said with more authority than I was feeling at that moment. "And yes, I'll be staying for some time, I think, helping José."

"Great," Thorpe replied. "I know most of the Americans leave this time of year, so it's good to know there will be someone to drink with at night!"

"Thorpe comes here every other year or so," Margarita chimed in. "When she needs some civilization, she says." Margarita smiled. "For Thorpe, a stick hut to call your own, a baño, and Madre Hermosa's cooking is the definition of luxury."

"Better than the Ritz," Thorpe agreed. "But really, I come for the magic. There's something about this place that undoes all the damage the world can do."

I found myself nodding along with that.

José insisted on carrying Thorpe's backpack along the rutted road from Margarita's to Zipolite.

"Can I carry your books?" I asked, like an old-fashioned high-school boy walking his girl home from school. Thorpe nodded. She looked too road-weary to do it herself. I removed the drawstring bag of books from the zippered midsection of her framed hiking pack. Books. How I missed them! There was a visceral pleasure in the weight of them, five thick reference books straining against the dirty yellow stuff sack. Here, I had only my worn copy of *Jane Eyre*, my equally worn copy of *Meditations* by Marcus Aurelius, and a paperback I hadn't yet read, *Contact*, by astronomer Carl Sagan. How could I sustain my life without books? A sigh escaped me.

"Are those too heavy?" my tired fellow hiker asked.

"No, I'm happy to carry them. I miss books, is all. Normally, I have two or three going, always. But here..." I drifted off.

"I have a few books, mija," José said. "But, alas, they are in Spanish."

"I'm like you," Thorpe said. "Always reading, always wanting to read more. When I'm traveling, when I'm in the jungle, it's my books I miss most. I'm not sure what that says about me. Major loner, I guess." She smiled ruefully.

"Never be sorry for loving books," José replied. "They make us human."

"True," replied Thorpe. "They allow us to grow, as individuals, as a society. We can improve upon what has gone before.

We don't have to start from zero every generation. Because those who have gone before us have left us books." Thorpe's face came alive with these thoughts.

José smiled. "Three lovers of books are walking the road to Zipolite."

"Where there are almost no books," Thorpe added.

We all three chuckled over that.

A half hour later, we strolled into the village. Madre Hermosa emerged from her hut under the banana trees and came to meet us. "Hola, Angelina. Bienvenida a casa," she beamed at Thorpe and hugged her tight.

Thorpe smiled through her tiredness. "Es bueno estar en casa, muy bueno."

The two friends continued in a rapid Spanish I had no hope of following.

I had signed up for lunch duty, so I excused myself to take a quick dip in the sea to get a bit of the road dust off me. I changed into the shift with the embroidered flowers, put the brown baseball hat on my head to shade my eyes, and headed back down the hill to get the rice cooking and heat up the beans someone had made yesterday. Lily was already there, setting the tables and restocking the coolers with beer and soda.

"My last day." She smiled sadly at me.

"Wish you were staying, Lily. I'll miss you."

"I heard Thorpe came in this morning. Get to know her. She's got this great sense of humor — hmmm, 'wry' is the right word. She'll keep you laughing when I'm gone." Lily gave me a little hug. "I'll miss you, too, Ana. Are you sure you'll be staying on?"

I wasn't sure of anything, I wished I could have replied. Being that I was a fugitive from justice for the most serious of crimes. Even though that seemed like a different life, nothing to do with Ana, the quiet girl with the buzz cut who was now going to study sea turtles for a while. I hadn't told Lily — or any of the remaining Americans in Zipolite — about almost drowning and being saved by a sea turtle. I told myself it was a story no one would believe, but in truth, I was ashamed of how stupidly I behaved. Did I go there hoping to drown? I wasn't sure what strange motivations had compelled me to go into the sea that early morning. I told Lily only that I had met a man who saved sea turtles, that he had needed an assistant, and that he had hired me for the job. "Yeah," I replied finally. "I need to make some money, and this sounds like a job I'll like."

"Hopefully, you'll still be here when I come back next year."

People were drifting in for lunch and we two started getting them their drinks, their plates of beans and rice and the grilled plantains left over from breakfast that Lily had reheated. Our village of ex-patriates was shrinking rapidly. People were gradually melting away, going back to their lives and jobs in the States.

I looked around for Thorpe, our one newcomer. But she had disappeared.

23

Zipolite

Thorpe was as good as her word

After an early swim to the rock-ledge reef and a brief scour of the beach for shells, Lily and I were having coffee at the best-view table while a couple of men cooked up the morning's huevos rancheros. It was a pristine morning, with a breeze from the ocean and not a cloud in the sky. Frigates circled high above us; closer in, a trail of seagulls followed one of the small fishing boats, a solitary oarsman rowing his bird-announced way back to shore. "Better to see the turtles late in the morning, when the sun shine through the water," José had informed me. Thus instructed, I would row myself out to the seagrass forest after breakfast, anxious to try the mask and fins that José had bought for me in Puerto Ángel.

Suddenly, Lily jumped up and started running toward the hill. "Dammit," she yelled, "why didn't you stop by yesterday?" Lily flung her hat in the air and flung her arms around Thorpe, who had just wandered down the trail from the huts on the hill.

"Please, no affectionate gestures before I have my coffee." Thorpe smiled at Lily. "No telling what I'd do."

Lily gave her backside a friendly swat, took her hand, and

led her to our table. As Lily opened her mouth to introduce us, Thorpe said, "'Morning, Ana. What a day, huh?"

"Wait, you two know each other already?"

"She carried my books on the walk here yesterday," Thorpe explained, as Lily reached to fill a tin cup with our full-bodied, hint-of-smoke, stovetop-cooked coffee. Thorpe sat and lifted her head to sniff the breeze. She had beautiful skin, smooth and flawless, with a natural subtle rosiness to her cheeks. Her chestnut brown hair was cut straight across at ear length, and she kept trying to push it behind her ears, but the wind was having none of that. I offered her the brown baseball cap I'd put on that morning. She pulled it over her unruly hair and mouthed a sheepish thanks. The sun wasn't high enough for me to need a sunshade and I sure didn't need it to keep my inch-long hair out of my eyes.

"Nice buzz. Looks like Margarita's work. Once I'm settled, that's where I'm headed for the same treatment. Never could cut my own hair."

Lily handed Thorpe a coffee and we three sipped in silence for a moment, our eyes turned to the cerulean sea. Andy sauntered over to our table. "Hey, Thorpe, you had enough coffee to talk, yet?" He smiled and gave her shoulder a squeeze. "Soon as I saw you coming down the hill this morning, I said to Dylan, 'Now, we'll get some first-rate poker played around here.'" Andy grinned. "The usual for you three ladies?" When we nodded, he went off and returned with plates of beans, tortillas, eggs, and hot salsa. "Save a spot at the A table for you tonight, Thorpe?" She smiled with genuine pleasure and nodded.

"Count on it. Been dreaming about all the ways I'm gonna rob you and the gang blind."

"Welcome back!" Andy grinned and went off to field more breakfast orders.

"Too bad they don't play for real money," Lily told me as we scooped our beans and salsa into warm tortillas. "Thorpe could quit her day job tomorrow and just live on her poker earnings. She's got the best poker face I've ever seen and nerves of steel. How's the hunt, anyway?" She asked, turning toward Thorpe, who was nodding in pleasure as she chewed her bean-filled tortilla.

"Believe it or not, I may have found something interesting in the wilds of Costa Rica. Needs testing, of course. I sent samples to a lab in the States. If it is what I think it might be, I need to think through the implications for a bit. No place better to think than Zipolite, so here I am."

"She's always so mysterious about her work," Lily said to me. "Cuz of patents and such that might come of the stuff she finds in the jungle. Not sure I understand what she does except tramp around in the woods, but it sounds interesting!"

We finished our breakfasts slowly, trying to make the moment last.

"Time to get on the bus and go back to Texas," Lily said, finally, and rose from the table. "I can't believe this is it. I haven't seen you in forever, Thorpe, and now I have to leave already. Life's not fair!"

Thorpe gave Lily a big hug. "We'll meet again, Tiger Lily, you can bet on it."

Lily wiped a couple of tears from her cheeks and gave me a hug, too. "Hope you see lots of turtles, Ana. And that you'll still be here when I get back." I hugged back in silent assent, but I didn't say anything. I didn't want to promise. I could be in a Texas prison by next year.

Lily picked up her framed backpack, settled it on her shoulders, and started on the trek to Puerto Ángel, waving a goodbye as she walked away.

"Lily's one of those heart-of-gold gals, isn't she?" Thorpe said as we watched her walk off toward Puerto Ángel.

"She took me under her wing, and I needed it. Still figuring this place out."

"When you figure it out, let me know, huh? I always wonder how this place can even exist."

I turned to walk back up to my hut. "I've got to get going. It's time for my maiden solo voyage out to the seagrass forest. Hope I can work the boat the way José showed me."

"Would you mind some company?" Thorpe asked. "I could look at your methods and field notes and see if I have any suggestions. And we could talk about that UCLA colleague I mentioned yesterday."

"Thanks, that would be great. Do you know how to maneuver a rowboat?"

"Sure. I grew up on a lake, so I was learning to manage a boat when other kids were learning to ride a bike."

We went back to our respective huts to brush our teeth and get our gear and set off for the five-minute walk to the rowboats. They were all back on the beach by now, as fishing was best in the pre-dawn hours or early evening. Thorpe expertly flipped the boat right-side up after I untied it, and we dragged it down to the water. "I'll row, you save it for diving." I didn't argue, thinking I could observe her experienced stroke and learn something. "Where are we going?" I pointed to a red buoy made tiny by the distance. Thorpe climbed in and I gave the small craft a push and joined her. Thorpe rowed. Dip, pull, dip, pull, we cut an all but silent path through the water.

"Feels good. I've been traveling for days to get here, all squished up in plane or bus seats." She had well-toned arms, used to lifting or carrying, and her legs too, were nothing but muscle. She looked exactly how I had pictured Amazons; solid, strong. If Maddie's other friends had bodies like hers, it was no wonder they'd gotten that nickname long ago. I wanted to know more about Maddie, about Thorpe's relationship with her, but, of course, that topic was taboo. I decided to ask her about her work instead.

"Lily said something about hunting for useful plants? I don't understand how that could be a job."

Thorpe snorted. "I work for a pharmaceutical company in their deep research division. Searching the earth for plants that have efficacious properties so that the company can develop drugs from them. When I started, I was naïve enough to think that if I found useful plants somewhere, it would inspire people to save the rainforest. Environmentalists still talk like that. But the drug company tends to take plants I've found, identify their salient properties, and synthesize them in a lab. Once that's done, no need for the plant itself or the rainforest I found it in. I thought I was embarking on a career devoted to conservation, and instead, I have become a roving witness to the worst environmental destruction the world has ever known."

"That sounds depressing. Maybe you need a new job."

"Can't make it in a lab, the only other thing I'm cut out for. The politics drive me crazy, and I tend to tell everyone just where they can go with their plots and competitive ways. I'm better in the jungle, wandering around, camping out or staying at rangers' stations, never too long in the same place. Been doing that for eight years since getting my PhD in tropical horticulture in '78. I'm thirty-three. Eventually, I'll have to give up sleeping on the ground, but it works for now."

"Sounds lonely, though."

"Sometimes. Sometimes lonely is better than the alternative, I've found."

"True." I could tell Thorpe had a tale or two that fit that storyline. I wondered what her story was but didn't dare to ask. Then she'd ask me for my story, and what would I say?

Thorpe continued to row toward the undersea forest.

"I see one," I said, pointing to the little head poking above the water. Thorpe had to instruct me on the best way to put on flippers and remind me of how to get the mask to be clear of fog yet fit snugly.

"You do know how to swim, huh?"

I nodded and flushed but saw her smiling. She had a little gap between her two front teeth, which somehow made her seem young and boyish. "I'm new at practically everything around here. Never been to the ocean before. Never lived in a stick hut, or without electricity. Never drank mezcal or tasted guava. A total gringa. But I do know how to swim. Watch me!" I fell backward off the rim of the small boat with a splash, righted myself, and put on my fins. I spit in, rinsed, and sealed my mask, took a deep breath, and disappeared from Thorpe's view. I dove deep enough to almost touch the tips of the sea-grass forest. There were three turtles there, two greens and a leatherback, which I identified by remembering the photos José had given me. I watched them for a minute, trying to estimate their sizes, before I had to paddle to the surface to get a breath. It was amazing how easy it was to see and swim with mask and flippers.

Thorpe motioned me over to the side of the boat. "Describe what you saw in as much detail as possible," she commanded, as I bobbed a half dozen feet from the boat. I told her what I had seen. She recorded what she called "your first observational data" into my data notebook. I dove again, noted the original three turtles, and saw two new ones had arrived. Surfaced again to describe my "findings," as she called them. Another dive, another surfacing. Thorpe suggested I proceed clockwise around the perimeter of the forest, which helped prevent counting the same turtle twice. This took me farther from the boat so I had to develop a way of remembering what I saw each dive. The turtles were on the young side, judging by their size.

"Okay, spill as much as you can, as logically as you can," Thorpe said, once I had taken off my flippers while floating in the sea and thrown them into the boat, put the mask on top of my head, and hoisted myself back into the boat using the rope ladder. Because it was new to me or because my livelihood depended on it, my memory of each of the segments and the turtle life therein was sound. "Precise observational memory, Ana. You have a good start on the basics of field biology."

Thorpe had me row on the way back and corrected my technique, so that by the time we reached shore, I was confident in my ability to handle the little boat — at least in calm seas. Back at Madre Hermosa's we shared a beer and Thorpe augmented the data template I'd copied from José. "Keep it for a few months, type up a summary, and send it to my buddy Clare at UCLA. She'll love to see how the population is beginning to recover from the wholesale slaughter days. And I'm sure she'll be happy to send you a bibliography of other work being done on the species." She got up from the table. "Okay, I feel a siesta coming on. Hope to see you at the poker table later!"

I managed to get a muchas gracias in, to which she replied, "De nada," and gave me a brief smile before strolling away toward her hut.

24

Zipolite

I helped move the tables and benches into their evening configuration after taking my turn doing dishes. There was a palpable buzz among the usual card players — Thorpe was back! The men were competing to see who would get to lose to Thorpe her first night back. I asked Andy, "Why are you convinced you'll lose before the game even starts?"

He just looked at me. "Just you wait, Ana. You've never seen anything like it in your life."

I looked up and saw Thorpe ambling down the hill in the near darkness. "Primero come, Angelina," said Madre Hermosa, shepherding her to a table and setting down a plate of grilled abalone and the usual frijoles y arroz. She also set a cola next to her plate. "No bebas mezcal, Angelina," she smiled. "O será un desastre."

"Damn right, Madre. If I drink, I lose," Thorpe agreed amiably. I wondered why Madre called her Angelina. "Ana, I have a fucked-up favor to ask you." Thorpe looked up at me as I passed by putting the tin plates away. "But I hope you won't mind."

"What?"

"Poker players are like baseball players, by which I mean

we're a superstitious lot. When I first started playing poker with my dad and his friends around our kitchen table on Friday nights, I used to rub my little brother Bobby's head for luck before the game started. He had a blond crew cut just like yours. So, I was wondering..." Even by candlelight, I could see that Thorpe was blushing furiously but trying to act like it was nothing.

I laughed — a sound so unfamiliar I hardly recognized my own voice. "I'm glad this haircut is good for something." I bent my head towards her.

"Ah...it has to be right before the first deal," Thorpe said solemnly.

"Okay. I'm kind of curious about what the guys have been saying about your poker skills, anyways."

"Really, Ana? You okay with this weirdness of mine? Seriously? You won't be embarrassed in front of the guys?"

"Believe me. I'm way past being embarrassed by any of them. We've seen each other naked, you know." I smiled at my small joke and rushed to clarify before she got the wrong impression. "Up at the falls, I mean."

Thorpe smiled. "You're a pal."

While the men sorted out who would get slaughtered by Thorpe tonight, Thorpe and I took our places around the poker table. I sat next to Thorpe on the bench, facing the water. Dylan got out a well-used deck of cards with a red pattern on the back and ceremoniously handed them to Thorpe. Madre Hermosa brought sodas for all the players. No mezcal tonight.

"Now," Thorpe said. I leaned toward her, and she rustled my little spikes vigorously. "Ana's my good luck charm," she explained to the group gathered 'round.

"Now, why didn't I think of that?" Andy grinned.

Thorpe started doing some fancy shuffling. If she could play as well as she shuffled, the men would be massacred.

They were.

The waning moon was emerging over the mountains and

the candles were burned down to stubs when Thorpe cleaned out Andy, the last of the men to have anything to lose.

"I think I'll open a shell shop." Thorpe eyed her foot-high pile of shells and grinned wickedly as the men groaned. But they loved it, and her, I could tell.

I didn't know a thing about card games, but I could see she was an expert at deciding when to bet and when not to. I now knew exactly what the term "poker face" meant — she had a flawless ability to keep a straight face, even while kidding and cajoling. She had no "tell" — a term I heard bandied about that meant a signal on one's face or body that revealed if someone held a good hand or a poor one and was bluffing.

"Come-on, Thorpe, let's play one last hand," Dylan implored.

"Only if we play for real stakes this time."

"Such as?"

"Each bet is one KP duty promise."

"That's steep, Thorpe."

"You wanna play or not?"

"Yeah, I got to see you do your thing one more time," agreed Andy.

"Winner deals." Steven handed her the cards.

Thorpe displayed the deck one way, then the other with an expert hand. She shuffled with a faster-than-the-eye-can-see magician's rapidity, banged the cards in front of me to cut, and snapped a deal around the table. The others folded almost immediately, but Andy had a good hand.

Betting proceeded until Andy and Thorpe had each promised the other a week of duties.

"Damn you, Thorpe, I'll have no time to relax if I keep this up. I fold! But I gotta see everyone's cards. Just this once."

"Yours first," Thorpe nodded, now that her week of no kitchen duties was assured.

Andy had a straight, which Thorpe explained to me was five cards in sequential order.

Steven turned up his cards — he had three sevens.

Dylan turned up his cards — he had a pair of sixes.

Bill turned up his cards — he had two pair, fours and eights.

"Nice evening, gentlemen." Thorpe started to rise from our bench.

"No you don't, lady. Let's see 'em."

She gave a sly look and turned over her cards. A pair of twos was all she had.

"And that," Andy declared, "is how you play poker."

"I got breakfast tortilla grill duty tomorrow, Andy. Just saying."

Andy groaned but I could see he really didn't mind losing to Thorpe.

"I'll get you back tomorrow. 'Night, ladies." He tipped an imaginary hat to us and took off up the hill to his hut with Linda. She'd left hours ago, as had all the others, including Madre Hermosa. Dylan, Steven, and Bill all mumbled good nights and sauntered off to their respective huts.

Thorpe pocketed the deck, scraped the shells into a plastic bag she'd brought for this purpose, and blew out the candles. "I'll divvy them up again, tomorrow. And I'll only make Andy do one shift. I don't care about winnings — it's the game that gets me."

We walked up the hill, my flashlight bobbing up and down as we made our way.

"How come you win so often?" I asked quietly, as we came to the hammocks hanging from my front porch. The waning gibbous moon had risen over the hill behind us and was shining onto my hut. We could see each other quite clearly.

Thorpe looked at me for a long moment.

"I'm willing to take risks," she said.

Then she kissed me full on the mouth, turned, and went on her way.

25

Zipolite

Eventually, I realized I had put my fingertips to my lips, as if touching where she'd touched me would help me know how to feel. I'd been standing there for some minutes; Thorpe was long gone, and the moon was higher in the sky than it had been when she'd kissed me.

Kissed me. I'd read about it in novels, how kissing could feel, how it could cause a body to shiver or grow suddenly warm, or a heart to clench in a mix of pain and delight. I remembered it being described as a melting feeling — as if the one kissed was made of wax or butter.

I had thought myself incapable of such feelings. Until now.

The handful of times I'd been kissed before...I didn't like to remember them.

The first time he'd been bruising, violent, as was all touching by my father starting that summer when he first came at me. He'd only pressed his lips on mine once, that first time...

Then there was Johnny. He'd only kissed me at the very beginning of our relationship before we had settled into the routine he preferred — one where he demanded that I "keep still" as he quickly did what he did. Those early kisses had always felt perfunctory, placating, like something he did on the way to doing what he wanted. I suddenly remembered: he had pressed his lips on mine that last night. It was right before he'd unzipped his pants and tried to rape me.

My first kiss had produced only shame. Johnny's had evoked nothing in me, but since I thought myself ruined by my father, I hadn't expected anything else.

But this...

It had shocked me, this surprise answer to an innocent question about her poker-playing acumen. Not just the kiss itself, though it had been entirely unexpected. It was my body's response that had stunned, scared...intrigued me. *My* heart clenched; *my* core felt a frisson of...something. So, Jane wasn't dead inside? Hadn't been emotionally snuffed out by the only two people to have ever touched her intimately? Or was this Ana, awakening to her new life after her near death like a prince-kissed Sleeping Beauty?

Thorpe had kissed Ana, I reminded myself; she knew nothing of Jane and never would. These feelings must belong to Ana. Could Ana be capable of feelings that had been extinguished in Jane? Like the wild Eve Black enjoying her nights out at the bar while the timid Eve White cowered in her housewife's role? What was that old black-and-white Joanne Woodward movie I'd seen on TV as a teen? *The Three Faces of Eve*, that was it. But that woman had been crazy, had been in dire need of a psychiatrist to sort things out, to get at the truth of her life. I was merely a killer trying to escape the consequences of her actions by taking on a new identity that I didn't always recognize. Since I couldn't tell anyone what I'd done, there was no one to help me find the path forward. No one but me.

I quietly walked up to the baño, the moon now high enough for me to see the path before me. The night, as it always was here, was alive with the chirping of insects and rustling of the larger nocturnal creatures like coatis, possums, and armadillos that made Zipolite their home. When I returned to my hut, I climbed into my hammock and pulled the rocking rope gently. I looked out at the sea. Gentle waves refracted the dimming moonlight.

Ana, the hastily chosen persona I had projected to Alex the night of my flight, could be anyone she wanted to be, couldn't she? She could be outgoing to Jane's enduring shyness, she could be funny to Jane's over-seriousness, she could be confident to Jane's stumbling awkwardness.

To Jane's passive acceptance of men, despite everything they'd done to her, could Ana be attracted to a woman?

The reaction my body had to this surprise kiss served as a clue. Ana, the woman I was trying hard to become, had reacted to that kiss with something her body had never felt before.

I remembered Jane's reaction to the time when Johnny told me that Maddie was a lesbian — a "dyke" he had called her, with contempt in his voice. The evening before I had been her guest for dinner, a sumptuous meal that had ended with homemade cheesecake. She had wrapped two pieces for me to take home afterward, improbably asserting that her narrow hips would suffer if I didn't help her eat the leftovers. The next evening, I shared the gift with Johnny. When he'd found out who had made it, he'd grudgingly admitted that even lesbians could make great cheesecake. He had warned me to stay away from her, projecting his own motivations to start an affair with one of his graduate students (me), onto her. I should be careful, he said. I was "dyke bait." I hadn't guessed she was a lesbian, but when he'd told me, it all made sense. I was intrigued by this news. I wondered what it must feel like to love other women. Despite how Johnny had characterized her (or perhaps because of it), I wasn't repelled. I was interested.

Now I knew that a friend of hers, Thorpe, had been part of a group of five lesbian graduate students that had come to Zipolite ten years ago.

Now, that friend had kissed me in a way I had never been kissed before.

I let the rocking rope fall and hugged myself in the safety

of my hammock. Surprisingly, I fell into a peaceful, dreamless sleep.

I lingered over my morning coffee longer than I needed to, hoping Thorpe would saunter down the hill and take the bench across from mine. But she was nowhere to be seen. Eventually, I started to feel I'd been foolish to take her kiss so seriously. She might have been joking. What had seemed so important to me had meant nothing at all to her.

When the sun was high enough for turtle spotting, I got my gear and headed toward my small craft — *La Tortuga*. My first solo trip as a turtle researcher. The breeze today was light. The water was as placid as it ever had been. A good day for me to take the boat out by myself. I had no trouble getting the boat in the water. I fixed the oars in their locks, put my gear in the bottom, shoved off from the shore, and climbed aboard in one fluid motion. I rowed confidently out to the buoy, looking over my shoulder from time to time and correcting my course when needed. When I pulled alongside the red anchor buoy, I tied the bow rope securely to it, prepped my mask and put it on, made sure I had a secure hold of my flippers, and fell backward into the water. Thorpe had told me it was easier to put flippers on in the buoyant sea, and indeed, they went on without trouble. I adjusted my mask, took a breath, and swam toward the green mass below.

Today, at first, I saw no turtles. Instead, a manta ray, white spots on black, glided beneath me. Almost my size, its water-slicing wings slowly, elegantly, rose and fell, a silhouette against the emerald seagrass. I ventured deeper, closer, and saw its underwing was pure white. A magnificent creature! A small school of hand-sized silver fish scooted among the fronds, and on a bare spot of sand at the edge of the forest, an orange sea star slowly crept along. As I swam clockwise around the edges of the seagrass forest, I saw a huge chestnut and beige fish with a large mouth sitting on the sea floor. Grouper, I recalled from José's description. I came up for air, marveling at the diversity of life that found refuge in the seagrass forest. I would never tire of this ever-changing, always fascinating tableau.

I took another deep breath and down I swam again. For an air-breathing, land-based creature like me, the sea was a foreign and dangerous environment. Yet I found myself comforted by all this life going on with the business of survival with no thoughts of the two-legged creatures above and all their complexities. All my lies, all the terror and error of my life melted away to meaninglessness here as I felt myself becoming part of the undersea community, at least for a moment. A sea turtle appeared in the periphery of my mask, and I turned to watch it. The turtle ambled toward me, using the distinctive birdwing flap I knew by this time was emblematic of its species. As it approached, I saw it was an old, huge green turtle. It dove down toward the waving grasses below us and I clearly saw the scar on its shell. Santa Juanita had come to say hello.

Seawater started to leak into my mask. I made for the surface. By the time I was floating on the surface again gratefully filling my lungs with air, I realized why my mask had failed. I had broken the seal due to contorting my facial muscles. Because I was smiling with joy.

I dived and looked, dived and looked, dived and looked, until I had circumnavigated the forest. I saw thousands of nameless fish, creatures I had never seen before, eight different sea turtles. But I did not see Santa Juanita again.

After jotting my sightings in my researcher's notebook, I rowed back to the shore on the all-but-still sea. I pulled my little boat to its spot under the coconut palms and worked at tying the bow rope around the tree that had shaded the boat for years. I felt a peace, a calmness that I was quite sure I had never felt before. The sea could have been my killer, but thanks to my saviors — turtle and human — it was now my tutor, my solace, my joy. Was this happiness?

A shadow crossed me, and I looked up.

"Buenos días, Ana," a familiar voice spoke from a familiar face with an unfamiliar short haircut. Thorpe smiled her gap-tooth smile. "Wanna head up to the waterfall with me this afternoon?"

26

Zipolite

Though the day was hot, and the sun was high in the sky, I was shivering. I needed no doctor to interpret that symptom — I was scared. But something else hovered on the edge of my conscious mind. Was it curiosity? Anticipation? Or could it be...desire? Desire. I wasn't sure I could identify that feeling correctly. I flashed on Johnny. I wasn't sure I had ever desired him. He had desired me. I'd felt unable to deny him. And I had stupidly thought it would be a relationship I could manage. My worst decision ever.

It was mid-afternoon, when any sensible person living in this climate was taking a siesta, a habit I had quickly adopted myself in the less-than-two weeks I'd been in tropical Mexico. Instead, I was trekking up the well-worn trail through the still, hot jungle toward the waterfall and its deep, clear pool. Thorpe had been right behind me on the path, but she'd stopped to fill her canteen at the trickle of water that came out of the limestone rock face. I kept walking. If I picked up my pace, I could strip and be swimming in the pool before she caught up.

When she'd suggested going to the waterfall in the afternoon, I'd understood her intention. No one went to the falls in the afternoon — not the dwindling numbers of Americans, who typically went after breakfast, nor the villagers, who, Lily had told me, went at dawn. It was obvious, even to someone as ignorant as I was, that Thorpe had chosen the heat of the day so we'd be alone. I was pretty sure it wasn't to talk field biology.

There wasn't a soul in sight when I rounded the corner and the waterfall came into view. Though I was in a hurry to get into the pool, I couldn't help but stop and breathe in the paradisiacal view. It felt so undeserved, all this beauty. The fern-festooned waterfall, the pool that was clear all the way down, the jungle, a tangle of intricately connected plants and animals. The nearby ocean too, the shallows with its many-shaped corals and rainbow-hued fish, the deeper water seagrass forest bursting with movement and life — Zipolite had so easily shared its beauty with me. In my constrained, tiny life, I never considered that I would, that I could, experience such a place. But here I was, surrounded by the healing balm of nature, splendor everywhere I looked. Strangely, I was now enveloped in this nurturing landscape only because I was a murderer and fugitive. How could it be that my death-dealing act was the catalyst for winding up in a place filled with life? I shook my head to try to clear it from such thoughts, pulled my Mexican shift over my head and dropped it on a rock, and dove into the clear aquamarine pool.

The pristine water was instantly refreshing. I swam down, down, down toward the deep blue bottom of the pool. It was still beyond my diver's reach. As I rose to the surface, a school of tiny silver fish shapeshifted around me. They were scattered by a kingfisher diving straight down an arms-length in front of me and, moments later, rising to the surface and taking flight with a hapless fish caught in its beak. I looked back at where the path met the pond. Thorpe was nowhere in sight.

As if a switch had flipped and the pool had become suddenly electrified, a jolt ran through me. It took me a moment to identify what had happened. My earlobe had been gently tugged from behind. She dog-paddled around to face me, our wet heads a hand's width apart. "Lovely," she said quietly and looked up at the jungle, the pool, the falls. "Lovely," she repeated softly, and looked straight into my eyes. Then she touched her lips to mine, briefly, almost imperceptibly. I gasped at the shiver that ran through my core in response. "Come now, Ana," she whispered, and turned to swim toward the waterfall. I gathered myself to follow her.

She emerged from the pool, stretched her arms toward the gushing water nearby and twirled a bit, her face lit with joy, tilted upward to catch the mist from the waterfall. The water crashing into the pond from high above us made conversation difficult. No matter. We were beyond words. Thorpe looked down at me, a half-smile on her lips, and offered her hand to help me out of the water. She looked at me — all of me — a long moment. She opened her arms in an offering of shelter, of safety, of love? I stepped forward tentatively, but willingly, and her strong arms enclosed me. For the first time in my life, I began a kiss.

Later, when I re-entered normal time again, when I came back to earth from wherever my body and spirit had been hovering, when the feeling that I was inside joy had subsided, we were entwined on the woven grass mats under the purple blanket canopy. Thorpe caressed my two-week-old crew cut tenderly. "You're new to all this, huh?" she murmured into the earlobe that had started the whole thing.

"Was it that obvious?"

"Yeah, but in a good way, an incredible way. You were totally there, totally open to it. I was honored to be your first, Ana, honored."

"Jane," I almost corrected, "I'm Jane." At the last moment, I realized where I was, who I was supposed to be and why. I quickly turned my half-utterance into, "Jesus," a word I'd never uttered since I'd stopped praying a decade ago. "It was —

magic..." I stumbled on. "I never knew that I could...that you could...that we could..." I had to quit talking to stifle a sob. Tears were smarting in my eyes. I buried my face in Thorpe's shoulder so she couldn't see. All the dammed-up misery of my life threatened to release itself, obliterating all these fine feelings I had newly experienced. I took deep breaths, fighting for control.

"Hey, now, it's all going to be okay. You'll see." She hugged me close and stroked my back for a long moment. With one graceful movement, she rose from the mat and dove off the rock ledge into the pool. "Come on," she turned toward me as she surfaced. "I can hear a mezcalita calling my name."

I got clumsily to my feet, feeling a bit dizzy and very disoriented, and dove in after her.

27

Zipolite

What followed were the most wonderful days and terrible nights of my life. I spent almost every waking minute with Thorpe. In the early morning, we swam at the shell beach, snorkeling the corals along the rock outcropping, walking the beach for shells, sitting on the sand, the ocean-cooled breeze tickling our faces. It was easy to get her to talk about her work — all I had to do was ask a question about an exotic spot she'd explored. She was a good storyteller: her scenes so vividly rendered I felt I'd been there, her adventures described with self-deprecating humor that had me smiling, even laughing.

As our community's ace poker player, Thorpe was tacitly rewarded with the best-view table. Here, after we returned from the shell beach, we took our coffee and ate our huevos rancheros and did our share of kitchen duties. When the morning sun rose sufficiently, we'd get my gear and head out in *La Tortuga* to spot turtles, Thorpe rowing out to the forest, me diving my circular route around the mass of green fronds. As soon as I emerged from the water and got back into the little rowboat, I wrote up my field notes in my spiral notebook. I rowed back to shore while Thorpe critiqued and offered suggestions to my notetaking. Some days we had lunch; others, we'd take our canteens and walk the deserted beaches, looking for injured turtles. We held hands on these walks, and sometimes stopped to kiss. Sometimes, it became more.

In the mid-afternoon, we would hike up to the falls and deliciously reinvent our first afternoon. I found I could hardly wait for siesta to overtake the village so that we could get away to our patch of Eden. It was as if my body was determined to squeeze all the passion I'd never experienced as a teen or young adult into a few hours. In the aftermath of all these intense, unexpected feelings, waves of delirious joy were my evening companions.

I found myself smiling, even laughing, at moments both opportune and not. When Thorpe touched my arm or brushed a hand through my hair, I shivered and smiled. I laughed when Thorpe employed what Lily had called her wry sense of humor, no matter how subtle or weak the joke. I was giddy. I was higher than any of the stoned hippies who shared this paradise. I was hug-myself-in-disbelief happy.

After dinner, Thorpe became the expert poker player. I was her mascot. She tousled my hair for luck — now, a feeling that caused my core to contract with pleasure. She gave me the cards to cut when she dealt. The men called us "the love birds," but because these long-timers had long been fond of Thorpe, no one bothered us about it. Thorpe would end the game at midnight: "I need some think time."

The men would groan and roll their eyes. "Yeah, right, think time."

But Thorpe seemed unable to be anything other than straight-forward. "Think time," she'd emphasize. She'd walk with me up the hill to my hut, kiss me long, tenderly, and say, "Sleep well, beautiful Ana." She'd turn and disappear up the hill until she came to my hut to fetch me for our morning ritual at the shell beach.

I never slept well.

Left alone in my hammock to think, I panicked. How could I

continue to deceive her? I had done nothing but lie to her, right down to my phony name. When she asked what I'd been doing with my life before Zipolite, I tried to brush it off. "Just living a boring life in the Midwest," I tried first. When she persisted, wanting to know where I'd grown up, what I had done after high school, I made up a more detailed fictional background. I'd put "Hopkins, Michigan" on the visa form I'd filled out because that was the first town not in Iowa that came into my head. The reason I'd written Hopkins was because my great-grand-mother Anna had grown up there and we had Christmas-card cousins I had never met still living there. So, I told her I was a farm girl from Hopkins. I told her I went to school majoring in history at the University of Michigan-Ann Arbor, a place I'd never been to but knew was a large university.

She hadn't asked me my last name yet. I had no idea how I would explain that one — my mom's sailor boyfriend from Mexico? My mom's affair with a foreign exchange student? Or a farm worker? There were exactly zero Mexicans or Mexican Americans in my actual hometown, Hutton, Iowa. I doubted it was any different in Hopkins, Michigan. And there was the problem that I didn't look like half my genes came from anyone with Mexican blood. German, Polish, Norwegian. But Mexican?

I had also made up a story about my time since college. I extended my college years by a semester — a mess-up with the records department at the university necessitated an extra semester, I told her. In my made-up life, I hadn't graduated until December. Kept my waitress job in Ann Arbor for a few months to save money, I said. I decided to take off for the warmth of Mexico as a little post-graduation present to myself, I said. It was horrifying how easily these lies left my lips. When she asked how I heard about Zipolite, I told her a guy I met in Oaxaca mentioned it and said it was cheap to live on the beach here, the lie I had invented after stupidly telling Frank and Kathy that Maddie had recommended it. I figured

Thorpe wouldn't see them again until at least next season and lots could happen in all that time.

Such as my arrest.

During the daylight hours, I was Ana, a young woman drunk on her first love. During the excruciatingly long night, I was confronted with my real self: Jane Meyer, a vile, lying murderer. The first night after love found me, I scrambled out of my hammock in the dimming moonlight and vomited into the nearby bushes. The second night, I wept the night away, terrified that all would be revealed and Thorpe would forever hate me. The third night, I went over and over my faux biography, trying to remember all the details I'd blurted, trying to take them into myself and make them mine. Oh, I wanted the daylight hours so badly. But the price the night exacted was almost more than I could bear.

Thorpe needed "think time," she told me, because of what she had found in the jungle of Costa Rica. "It might be nothing. Probably, it's nothing," she said, but the way she said it made it sound like she believed the opposite. "But in case it's something, I have to be prepared." When I asked her what being "prepared" meant, all she would say was, "In case it's a gamechanger." She abruptly changed the subject. "Besides, have you ever tried two in a hammock? Not the place for cuddling." So, night after night, I was left to what wild fears my imagination could conjure.

I tried telling myself I deserved no better than these dreadful nights, so filled with self-recrimination.

I tried telling myself I deserved some happy days, for hadn't such a large measure of my life been given over to my father's unrelenting violence? His against Ma was the mainstay of my childhood. His against me was the terror of my teen years. After that, years of isolation. Despite going to college, days could go by without speaking to another human being but Ma. So, didn't I deserve this respite?

Not a chance, you murdering, lying, lesbian. Not a chance.

28

Zipolite and Puerto Ángel

One morning, Thorpe did not come for me. I walked to the shell beach alone. She wasn't there. I tried to snorkel, but found the water murky, the colors muted. I walked back to the restaurant, took my turn heating up the pot of salsa and the pot of beans, putting tortillas on the grill. Still no Thorpe. Linda came to make the coffee, Andy to make the eggs. Still no Thorpe. I thought she was supposed to set the tables and plate the food this morning? Linda and I divvied up her duties. Finally, Juan Carlos ran up to me, white shirt, red necktie, and gray slacks, a net bag with his books over his shoulder advertising his destination — the Catholic school in Puerto Ángel.

"Buenos días, Ana. Señorita Angelina, she say she must go to señora Margarita this morning to make the teléfono. She say to tell you, sorry!" He smiled his shy smile.

"Muchas gracias, Juan Carlos," I called to his back as he scampered off down the rough track. Just a phone call, that's all it was. Just a phone call.

I finished breakfast, eating with Linda and Andy, slow-sipped my coffee while the sun rose a bit higher, and traipsed back up to the hut to get my gear. Guess I was taking *La Tortuga* out on my own this morning. A mysterious frisson of —

fear? — made my stomach flutter uncomfortably. I knew how to row, no reason to be afraid, I coached myself — but I knew that wasn't it. It wasn't the sea. It was the phone call. It had broken into our little piece of heaven, an unwanted intruder, tangible, unlike my own midnight terrors, reminding me that the world was going about its business beyond the shelter of Zipolite. A world completely out of my control.

When I finally rowed my little craft to the red buoy against a sizeable wind, I saw the futility of my journey. The sea was choppy today, the seagrass forest disappearing in a sandy murk. There would be no turtle spotting today. I untied the boat from the anchoring buoy and rowed back to the shore in the wind-blown sea, a panic rising in me the closer I came to the beach. I knew, I just knew, I should have dropped what I'd been doing and run with Juan Carlos to Puerto Ángel.

It's a phone call, I chided myself. A phone call, nothing more. I dragged *La Tortuga* to the craft's usual spot, flipped the boat, and tied the bow rope around the old coconut palm. I hurriedly dressed and tucked my flippers and mask under the boat for later retrieval. I pulled my faded floppy hat onto my head, perched my sunglasses on my nose, flung my backpack over one shoulder, and set off at a trot down the road to Puerto Ángel. I was thirsty, but that would have to wait.

My two-mile walk-run-walk seemed to take forever. I grew unaccountably frightened as I grew closer to Puerto Ángel. Only a phone call, only a phone call. I repeated the mantra over and over as I hurried along. But it did not comfort me.

Finally, I emerged into the plaza with Margarita's smoothie stand at its center, the plaza where the old blue bus from and to Oaxaca stopped and started off about this time of day. Noise greeted me — laughing, guffawing, rapid Spanish exchanges. There was someone standing on the steps into the bus, visible from the belt down. Everyone was in a jovial mood, everyone seemed to be laughing. I saw the figure make a little bow and heard applause and laughter from inside the bus. I saw the bus driver's hand shooing the figure off the bus, while he gunned the engine to go.

The figure jumped from the steps of the now slowly rolling bus and started toward Margarita's and me as I hurried forward.

"Señorita Ana? Mi amiga, mi prometida, is it you?" The voice, the questions, stopped me in my tracks. I looked at the figure in astonishment.

Alex, for of course it was Alex, his handsome face aglow with pleased surprise, pointed at me for all the passengers to see. He looked back at the bus, nodded vigorously, smiled, and pointed. I heard excited yells from inside the bus. I saw fingers pointing at me through the open bus windows. Dramatically, he got down on one knee, opened his arms wide and said, "Ana, mi amor, I am here to ask you once again, will you be my bride, mi novia?" I heard cries of delight from inside the bus as it rolled slowly past us and turned onto the road to Oaxaca.

I looked at Alex. I looked at the bus full of people who had witnessed Alex's second proposal of marriage with enthusiastic approval. At the very back of the bus, looking out of the closed rear window was a white face, her mouth hanging open, a look of incredulous shock on her face. Then the bus rolled out of sight.

29

Puerto Ángel

I stood in the plaza, eyes closed, trying to unsee what I had seen, telling myself it was only my imagination, ignoring the handsome man feet from me, saying, "Ana, mi amiga, are you not happy to see me? What is the problema, Ana? Why do you stand like a statue?"

It could not be. But it was. She was gone. But it was worse, way worse than merely gone.

Thorpe spoke fluent Spanish. She'd understood every word Alex had said on the bus, which had no doubt been a charming story about coming to Zipolite to claim his novia americana. She had seen him get off the bus, a delighted smile on his face as he saw that I had come to meet the bus. She had seen him gesturing. Yes, there she is, the woman I was telling you all about, mi novia, my bride, my love, Ana. She had seen him get down on one knee, play the part of the romantic hero, the husband-to-be, as the passengers laughed and cheered, and he had smiled his charming smile. She had seen, had heard, had understood all of it. I was rooted to this spot on the now-empty plaza. My feet no longer knew how to walk. My eyes no longer knew how to focus. Nor could my lips form words, my lungs breathe. My head swam. I thought I might faint or vomit or both at once.

A hand closed on my upper arm. "Ana, come sit down." It was Margarita, suddenly at my side, her voice of reason, her strong hand, urging me to walk with her. "I'll make you something with guava." Something with guava — it had become our little joke by now. "Thorpe left you a note. Come and read it."

To Alex she added in Spanish, "¿Quieres algo de beber, señor?"

To me, "Or is he bothering you, Ana? Should I tell him to get lost?"

Her words broke the hex that had fixed me to the dusty spot in the plaza. I began to walk again, Margarita's hand still around my arm, guiding me the few yards to her many-colored bar stools. I began to breathe again, to form words with breath behind them. "No," I said. "Alex is my friend. Give him a drink."

Alex followed us. He kept his distance. When it came time to pick a stool, he hesitated.

"I am sorry, Alex," I managed finally, and looked at him standing a few feet away from the juice stand, confusion and sorrow setting his mouth in a frown. "So sorry. Not your fault." I turned away, but not soon enough. He saw the tear escape my eye and wander down my cheek.

"Oh, Ana! It is me. It is I who am sorry! I did not mean to... avergonzar..." He looked imploringly at Margarita, who was taking guavas out of one of the fruit baskets and efficiently peeling and chopping them.

"Embarrass," she supplied.

"Yes, embarrass you. I did not think you would meet the bus. I thought only to tell a story to the driver of the bus. But everyone hears my story. They ask me questions about mi novia americana. So, I tell them how beautiful you are, how I will ask you to marry me a second time. I tell a story. Not the truth. Then, there you were, una hermosa novia, a beautiful bride. So, I got down on my knee again...I am so sorry to embarrass you!" Alex — handsome, familiar Alex — looked to me for forgiveness.

"I'm not embarrassed..." I started but found myself at a loss. I motioned for him to sit on the bar stool next to mine.

Margarita, who had been blending my guava smoothie in the background, appeared with a pitcher, two cups, and a piece of paper, frayed on one edge from being torn from a spiral notebook. It was folded in thirds. My fake name, "Ana," was printed in large block letters on the side facing me.

She filled my cup with the guava smoothie.

"Guava okay, for you too?" She asked Alex in English. He nodded. She poured. I unfolded the paper.

Something came up re: my latest find

Off to U.S. East Coast. Back when able

Wait? Please?

Thorpe

"Better, now?" Margarita smiled at me. "Thorpe will be back, Ana. You can bank on that."

Margarita was trying to comfort me, but her faith in Thorpe only made the last few minutes worse. Made my vision of her astonished face in the back bus window worse. Made my days of endless lying to her worse. I put my elbows on the bar, my face in my hands, and started to sob uncontrollably.

"What is it? What is the problema, señora?" I half-heard Alex ask Margarita.

"Looks like she's in love," Margarita replied while pressing a clean bar towel between my elbows.

Neither of them said a word for a while, until my sobs subsided. I gulped for air. I wiped my eyes and nose with the towel. I took a swallow from my drink. I looked at Alex and Margarita helplessly.

"No entiendo," Alex looked to Margarita for an explanation.

Margarita raised a thumb in the direction of the departed bus.

"Señorita Ana, she love someone on the bus to Oaxaca?" He was looking at Margarita, not me, for confirmation. "He hears my story? He sees what I do?" Now Alex was backing off the bar stool in horror. "Ay Dios mío, now Ana will hate me. And I will deserve it. I have ruined her life. And she will not be mi novia. She loves a man going away on a bus. Ay Dios mío."

Alex was about to turn and walk away. His head hung in shame and regret.

Margarita looked at me. "You wanna tell him, hon? Or I will. I don't get this whole situation. You want to tell your hairdresser and bartender Margarita about it?"

Something in her tone roused me. "Alex. Wait. Stop," I managed.

Alex turned. I got off my barstool and walked the few steps to him.

I took his hand in mine. "I have to tell you what has happened to me."

30

Puerto Ángel

Looks like she's in love.

Margarita's words sliced through the part of my brain — or was it my heart? — that was immobilized by grief, by shame, by guilt. Grief at Thorpe's sudden departure. Shame over the very many lies I told her. Guilt that now I'd never be able to do right by her. She was gone.

Looks like she's in love, Margarita said.

Was this how love felt? I'd sobbed more in the past few minutes than in all the years since my childhood abruptly ended with my father's unspeakable act. My heart literally ached, clenching in my chest, threatening to either implode or burst through my ribcage. My breath was coming in panicky gasps. I was dizzy, nauseous, weak. Was this how love felt?

Did I love Thorpe? I felt incapable of answering that question.

I was a stranger to romantic love. My relationship with Johnny hadn't been love. I'd known that since the day I'd consented to his touch. I said yes to it mostly because he seemed to want me so much. I'd never known what it was to be wanted. Since he was married, our relationship would be furtive, part-time, not headed anywhere. At the time, that seemed like just the level of entanglement I could manage. But he never made my heart clench, nor had I felt any passion during our ritualized couplings. I never thought those feelings were possible for me. But Thorpe...

I wasn't even sure of her name. Was it Angelina Thorpe — or was Angelina just Madre's nickname for her? She was ten years my senior and worldly-wise. She'd had lovers before, possibly many of them. She was the same sex as me, which in this world meant only hiding and trouble. But...

Could my body lie just as my voice constantly did? Even to myself? I didn't think so. It didn't feel so. Instead, these past few days were the first time in a long while I inhabited my body, owned its feelings, felt its longings. The first time since I was a little girl riding my bike down the dirt road to the Jacobson's farm, a flicker of breeze mussing my hair. Swimming in their pond, lying on my towel, shivery but satisfied under the summer sun, enfolded by the patch of meadow that surrounded our towels, its grasses and flowers whispering in the warm wind, the air suffused with sweet pea, alyssum, alfalfa, and the buzz of honeybees. How happy I'd felt, living in the moment. How capable my body felt. How all-over alive I'd felt.

Here, at our waterfall paradise, touching Thorpe, being touched by her, I was as fully alive as I'd ever been, as happy as I'd ever been. Was that love?

My eyes were closed. I opened them to see Alex and Margarita looking at me expectantly.

I took a breath and turned to Alex. "The person who left on the bus is a woman, not a man."

Alex looked confused for a moment, then his eyebrows went up and his face became a question. "Ana, is it true? You are like me? Why did you not tell me those many days we sat together on the train and on the bus?"

"I didn't know," I replied, my voice hoarse from crying and raw emotion. "I never thought about it. But when I met Thorpe..." Tears welled up in my eyes again and I put my hands over my face to cover them.

"But this is wonderful!" Alex was back to his usual enthusiastic self. "There is no macho hombre I must fight to win your hand! We will tell your girlfriend of our plan and since she is like me too, she will understand. She will agree. Oh, I am indeed a lucky man to have such a prometida americana!" He beamed over at me, and I couldn't help but offer a weak smile in return.

"Okay, somebody's got to fill me in. Right now." Margarita topped off our drinks and drew her stool up to the bar on the other side from where we sat. "And whatever it is, it better not involve hurting Thorpe. She's a good friend of mine!"

Alex looked at me and I nodded a go-ahead. I was dabbing my eyes with the bar towel again, fear, longing, and maybe-love threatening to start me sobbing again.

"Señora, I am twenty-six and I have no wife," Alex said simply.

Margarita nodded. "In this country, that is a problem."

"I have another problem. I have no wife because I like boys, I am gay. Do not tell mi madre this!" He smiled mournfully.

"Understood. I'm a hairdresser, so I've worked with lots of gay men. I know how hard it is to be gay in America, never mind for a man in a macho culture like this. Got it." She drew her thumb and forefingers across her lips, to zip them into silence.

Alex nodded his thanks.

"I sit with Ana on the bus, to Ciudad Juárez, on the long train to México City, on the long train to Oaxaca. I tell her my problem, that I must marry a girl soon or I must never see mi mamá and brothers again. I ask her to marry me as a friend only, so mi mamá, mis hermanos will stop asking me when, when Alejandro, will you have a wife. But I see Ana is not ready to say yes. So, I put her on the bus to Puerto Ángel and I tell her I will come in three weeks and ask her again. And here I am."

Margarita turned to me. "What's in it for you, Ana? It's no small thing, you know, getting married. I know. I've tried it."

This was news to me. I'd never thought of Margarita having a husband, possibly children. "Oh, I didn't know you were married."

"I was, once upon a time. No more of that for me. But we can talk about that some other time. What's in it for you, Ana?"

I dreaded this question. I didn't want to lie to Margarita. But the truth — or even a part of a truth — was impossible. She was friends with Thorpe. She knew everyone in Zipolite, Zapotecs, Mexicans, and gringos alike. If I told her even a toned-down reason why I was entertaining his proposal, soon, everyone would know I was a liar. So, I tried a partial truth that I hoped would satisfy her.

"Alex was so great to me ever since we got on the bus together," I said, purposefully leaving out the town we'd left together, the one where he was running from the law for being gay and I was running from the law for being a killer. "He helped me get a visa and showed me the ropes the whole way here. I wasn't involved with anyone and I wasn't looking to be. So, I didn't turn him down." I didn't mention the part about needing a new name and how Alex had supplied it for the visa, and how he would, if I married him, legally bestow on me a gift that might help me evade the law. While Margarita bent her head back to empty her glass of the guava smoothie she'd poured herself, I surreptitiously glanced at Alex and was gratified to see him give me the briefest of nods. He was a pal, a dear, no doubt of that.

"A big payback for a few days of help, Ana." Margarita decreed. "But if it's only a paper marriage, I don't suppose Thorpe would mind. If you and she are even a couple. But I think you are. I've known Thorpe for a decade now. There's only one love she ever talked about to me and that was over a long time ago. I've seen her with women here a few times. But I've never seen her smitten like she is with you, Ana."

147

"Señora, do you have a telephone? We must call this girl-friend of Ana, tell her everything, and she will feel okay again." Alex was a considerate man.

"I do, at my parents' house up the way a mile or so. Thing is, though, Thorpe will be on the road for a couple of days at least and she didn't mention exactly where she was going. Some East Coast university — Boston? Baltimore? — where her friend was doing something in a lab to what she found in Corcovado. She sent a sample of it up there before she came here, she said. But she didn't tell me the friend's name or where she worked. Just said she'd be back as soon as she could. And that I should emphasize that to you, Ana. So, I'm telling you. She'll be back."

I nodded. Thorpe's astonished face in the back of the bus appeared in front of me again, as clearly as I saw it the first time. "What am I going to do, Margarita?" I started weeping again. But Margarita reached out her arm, put her hand under my chin and lifted my face so we were eye-level across the bar.

"You'll wait. And have faith in Thorpe, Ana. That's what you'll do."

31

Zipolite

I invited Alex back to Zipolite with me for a few days and he consented.

"Mi mamá, she think she will be at the church on sábado, crying at her baby boy's wedding," Alex said to me when we had walked through the patch of jungle on the edge of the plaza, past the hand-lettered sign to Zipolite, and were making small dirt quakes as our feet hit the bone dry track back to the village. "I did not tell her you would say 'yes,'" Alex insisted. "I say, 'Madrecita, those American girls are very independent, so I cannot promise.' But she say, 'Why would even a gringa turn down such a handsome and charming man as my youngest son?'" Alex turned on his considerable charm as he said this and grinned at me. "I have good news for you, Ana. I go to the place where they give the card to drive a car and I say, 'My American girlfriend, soon to be my wife, she had an accident in the sea. Her passport and her driving card went into the water. Gone. All she has is her visa to México and soon, her licencia de boda. Can she get a mexicana card to drive a car?' And the man, he look over at me a certain way and say, 'This is possible, difficult, but possible.' Ana, this is the way in México we tell someone that for a little money under the table, something can happen. So, now what do you say? Does that help you say yes?"

I flipped the broad brim of my faded pink hat out of the way and stared at him. "You astonish me, Alex. You would make an excellent husband, not just charming and handsome, but thoughtful, too!" I smiled sadly. "It's too bad you don't like girls."

"Too bad for me, too, Ana. If I like girls, I have no worries. But I like boys." He shrugged.

"Will Luke mind if you marry me?" I asked. "Have you ever talked about it?"

"Oh yes, many times. He will be happy if I never again talk to him about my brothers, mi mamá, begging me to marry. He would like to find a girl to marry, too. His father is a holy man..." Alex paused, knowing he didn't have it right but not remembering the correct word.

"A minister?" I guessed.

"Yes, so he has to pretend like me, that he does not find yet the right girl to marry." Alex sighed. "It is difficult to be gay, in México and in Texas, too. But what can we do?"

"Marry lesbians?" I asked and found an impish grin on my face.

"Perfecta!" Alex laughed. "Tell me about your girlfriend, Ana. Is she beautiful like you? Does she make you laugh? Is she good to you?"

I was touched by this. Alex was trying hard to be my friend, to help me with what he correctly perceived was my need to become someone else. He was hoping that would make me more likely to consent to marry him. His strategy was working.

"I haven't known her very long," I admitted. "I'm not even sure I know her full name. She goes by Thorpe. She's older than me, ten years older. She's a scientist who studies rainforest plants. She's a great poker player. I like being with her.

She's strong and, yes, beautiful, and, yes, she makes me laugh and..." I faltered and found myself blushing furiously under my floppy hat.

Intuitive as always, Alex filled in what I could not bring myself to say. "Ah, she is good with the touch. I know this feeling. Luke is very good this way, also. It is muy importante, this part of love, ¿no es así?"

"I didn't know that, until Thorpe touched me that way," I found myself admitting to him. "Yes, muy importante."

We came to Madre Hermosa's hut under the banana tree. She came out to meet us with the customary sodas. I introduced my friend Alex from Oaxaca and the two chatted about how beautiful it was in Oaxaca and here in Zipolite.

"Do you have a hut for Alex, señora? He will be here for two nights." I said these two short sentences in Spanish and both Alex and Madre Hermosa beamed at me approvingly. A tiny price was negotiated. A hut in the row above mine was pointed out and a combination lock and chain produced. Madre indicated that Alex could rely on me to tell him how things worked around here. She nodded her goodbye and disappeared back into the hut. No doubt we'd interrupted her siesta.

"I am needing also the siesta. Will you come for me when it is time for drinking on the beach?"

I walked him up to his hut, made sure he was proficient with a combination lock, and pointed out the baño.

When siesta was over, I walked up to Alex's hut to find him splashing water on his face. The previous tenant had left a jug and Alex had found the raised rainwater cistern next to the baño for washing water.

"Do you play poker?" Andy asked Alex after I'd introduced him to the table of Americans sipping Coronas with lime slices shoved into their bottles. Alex shook his head. "Mi madre would kill me. She believes cards are del diablo — of the devil."

"She's got something there," Andy grinned.

"Do you dance?" Linda asked.

Alex grinned broadly. "I am an excellent dancer. Flamenco, vals, the dancing of México — Jarabe Tapatío, Fandango, Concheros, many more. But I am best at American disco. This is my favorite. I have my dancing shirt with me!" Alex smiled enthusiastically. "Will we make dancing tonight?"

"We will!" said Linda, who I had seen twirling with abandon when the music of her youth was playing. "We may even have some disco music. But before that, I would love to be your partner for flamenco."

"Linda studied dance for years," Andy added. "That would be great to see — I've got two left feet. No matter how hard I try, that kind of dancing is not my thing."

"Fortunately, he's got other talents." Linda grinned wickedly and pecked him on the lips.

After our dinner of grilled shrimp with pico de gallo and the usual frijoles y arroz, I helped Andy and Bill clear the floor for dancing while Linda went to put on a skirt more appropriate for flamenco than the short denim skirt she had on. Alex went back to his hut to put on the disco shirt he was wearing when I first met him. When he returned, I saw he'd combed his hair back, and had on white bell bottoms and white leather shoes along with the orange paisley shirt.

"John Travolta has arrived!" Linda laughed and Alex struck the actor's famous pose — back arched, legs at the ready, arm extended, finger pointing to the sky. I'd never seen the film, but I had seen posters for *Saturday Night Fever* outside the theater in Hutton when, years ago, it had played in our little movie house. Alex was quite a bit more handsome than Travolta, and I could see Linda was charmed. She was wearing a peasant skirt with ruffles and huaraches on her bare feet. "Best I could come up with," she smiled apologetically at her dance partner.

"Perfecta!" Alex bowed formally to his dance partner.

Andy hit "play" on the boombox and music I presumed was flamenco filled the night air.

The two danced like they had been practicing together for years. The dance required stamping out rhythms on the floor, which the two accomplished despite their inadequate footwear. Flamenco was a dance where each partner had solos, back-to-back or twirling around one another, bodies touching, eyes locking on one another with lovers' intensity. We were all in awe of them, none more than Madre Hermosa, who had quit making mezcalitas and was standing at the edge of the dance floor staring at the duo in complete astonishment. We clapped and cheered and yelled for an encore and the two complied, growing even more attuned to one another the second time around.

Linda curtseyed deeply, and Alex returned her gesture with a bow. "Wow. That was incredible, Alex. Where did you study?"

"The same place I learned English." Alex smiled sheepishly. "On the televisión. 'Danzas de España,'" he said in a deep broadcaster voice, "at three in the afternoon on sábado. While all the other boys were in the plaza playing fútbol, I was at my uncle's taberna, watching his television, dancing with my cousin Guadalupe. We thought we would be on TV someday!" Alex smiled his beautiful smile.

"Now, let's see you do Travolta," Linda commanded and chose another tape from a plastic bag next to the boom box. "Can't imagine why this made it all the way to 1986 — it was a Christmas present from my Aunt Fran years ago. I never got around to throwing it out, I guess. *Classics of Disco*," she read and inserted the tape into the box. She gestured to Alex to take the floor and started the music.

Alex struck the Travolta pose as the music started and performed incredible, acrobatic dance moves that I couldn't begin to describe, never mind engage in myself. The whole gang was roaring with approval and clapped enthusiastically as Alex finished a third song and left the stage to give a beaming

Madre Hermosa a big hug. Alex was murmuring something in Spanish in her ear and Madre was smiling and giggling — something I had never seen or heard her do before.

My mouth hurt from smiling, my hands from clapping. I was so proud to have brought Alex to our little community.

Linda put on a slow song — "*Colour My World*, by Chicago," she'd told me the first time I had heard it — grabbed Andy and led him to the floor. "I can't dance, hon," he protested weakly but gave up on it as she wrapped her arms around him and kissed him on the mouth.

"May I have this dance, beautiful Ana?" Alex was at my elbow, all sweetness and gentlemanliness.

"I don't know how to dance," I exclaimed, in a voice that sounded alarmed, as indeed I was.

"It is no matter," Alex replied. "I will lead, you will follow. Come, mi amiga, it is very good to dance. You will like it, I know. In America, I work in a dance studio. I make all the ladies, very young and very old, love dancing. I will do the same with you."

Having no real excuse, I let him lead me onto the dance floor. I looked at Linda for how I should position my body and put my arms around Alex's neck. He led me slowly around our rough-board dance floor, humming the music a little in my ear as we danced. It did feel good, to be part of a man and woman couple in public, the way I had not been with either Johnny or Thorpe, for wildly different reasons. Alex was someone safe to pretend with. Someone safe to be with. It all felt so good. But I kept envisioning Thorpe, face pressed against the back bus window. How betrayed she must feel!

As if he was a mind-reader, when Andy and Linda moved within ear shot, Andy looked at me. "Thorpe's gonna be jealous," he said in a taunting voice, looking me in the eyes. He tried to say it as a joke, but I could see the disapproval in his face. As with Margarita, Thorpe was a friend of his and he felt protective. I blushed, but once again, Alex came to my rescue.

"Do not worry, Andy," he said in a gentle tone. "I know

about Thorpe. Ana is my friend, nothing more."

I smiled my thanks as Andy and Linda moved away. Alex was the best friend, the only friend, I ever had. Everything in my being told me he was offering me a gift that would never come again. I should take it.

32

Zipolite

The morning after the first dance of my life, I walked up to get Alex out of his hammock to go for a morning swim at the shell beach. I brought my mask and snorkel along. He had brought a bathing suit, something for which I was immensely grateful. I told him of Madre's prohibition against nudism on the shell beach. Alex just laughed. "The people of México do not go naked in the sea, Ana. We are all Catholics here," he said, by way of explanation.

Today the wind had calmed, and the sea was clear again. We walked down the track to the shell beach. It was growing warm already and unusually humid. We dropped our towels above the tide line, I put my mask on top of my head, and we waded into the sea. Alex was a competent swimmer. "Would you like to see something special?" I asked as we paddled on our backs in the buoyant water, and Alex nodded his assent. I headed off to the rocky ledge where the corals grew, Alex following me with a steady stroke. I spat into my mask and rinsed it, put it on, and stuck my face in the water. As usual, the ledge was teaming with small, multi-hued fish, and the corals, too, were intense in their golds, oranges, and purples. I put my head up, took my mask off, and handed it to him as we floated near the rocky ledge. "Do what I did," I said, assuming he was new to snorkeling. He was, but he was good at mimicking. He spat into the mask as I had done, rinsed it out, secured the mask to his face and put the snorkel between his lips. He put his face in the water above the ledge where I had been.

"Oh, it is so wonderful in the sea! So colorful! So beautiful! I thank you for this very much!" Alex was all smiles and exclamation points as he took off the mask and carefully handed it back to me while we bobbed in the buoyant water. "I have seen programs of Jacques Cousteau when I was a boy, but for me this is the first time I see the life in the sea for myself. It is magnífico!"

Back on the shore, we sat drying on our towels when Alex said, "Do you go in the sea every day, Ana? Has the sea been good for you?"

"I almost died in it, Alex," I found myself replying. "But yes, the sea — even that experience — has been good for me. That's why I have a job here, now."

"I do not understand," Alex looked at me with confusion and concern. "What is this 'almost died,' Ana? You must tell me of this."

I told him everything that happened the morning I swam into the riptide. I explained it mostly as it happened, letting him believe that the antique coins were relics of someone I had cared for who was now gone, which was true in a sense.

I told him José had offered me a job, a job that I hadn't done yesterday because of the cloudy sea but that I must do today. I described *La Tortuga* and how I rowed out to the seagrass forest.

Alex took it all in, nodding and smiling at my rescue and job offer. "Ana, mi amiga, you are very lucky. You almost die in the sea but instead you find a job and love and a place to live."

"I guess you could see it that way," I replied slowly, taking in this truth. It felt good, too, telling someone besides José about my near-death experience, even in this slightly dishonest form. Alex was a good listener, another among his many fine attributes. I had indeed been lucky to meet him.

I was gazing down the beach toward Mazunte, thinking about my ironic good fortune, when I noticed a dark shape at the tideline. I got to my feet, grabbed my mask, and ran toward it, my bare feet making squishy footprints in the still-wet sand. Alex called after me and I motioned with my arm that he should follow me.

The sea turtle that had washed up wasn't a large one — it might weigh 25 pounds — but the unfortunate creature had a ball of translucent fishing line wrapped around its right front flipper. A few strands were also around its neck. It was not a recent encounter; I saw the line had cut into the turtle's flesh at the neck and on the outside of the flipper. The injured turtle had a short and skinny tail, the mark of a female, José had told me.

"Oh, you poor thing," I murmured to the turtle. It was upsetting to see the raw flesh, and I wished I had my jackknife. José had taught me what to do in such a situation, though, and I sprang into action. "Alex, please use the mask to get some sea water and pour it over its shell, head, and flippers while I get the tub."

I ran up to the top of the beach, looking for red, and quickly untied one of the six three-foot-diameter red, round plastic tubs with handles José and I had fastened to palm trees on strategic beaches between here and Mazunte. We had used the patrón's money to buy them at the market the same day he'd bought me my flippers, snorkel, and mask. I dragged the lightweight but sturdy tub down to the shoreline, put a bit of clean salt water in the bottom, carefully lifting the turtle from the back of its shell, and gently placing it and the tangle of fishing line in the tub.

Alex took one side, I the other. We tried our best to keep the tub level as we walked back along the track as fast as we could toward the shady overhang of Madre Hermosa's restaurant. We stopped when our arms were tired, and I used my mask as a dipper to keep the turtle's shell and skin wet. Juan Carlos, eating breakfast before his hike to school in Puerto Ángel, saw us coming, grabbed a jug from the kitchen, and ran to the water's edge to fill it with sea water. He yelled for his mother. Madre Hermosa looked up from dealing with a departing American and told Andy and Bill to run to meet us. They took the tub, keeping it level as I instructed them to do, and trotted it the remaining distance to the shady patio. Madre Hermosa pointed out the coolest spot, the tub was set down, and Juan Carlos poured his jug full of sea water into the tub. Madre looked down at the injured turtle and, retrieving a small knife from her apron, went to work on carefully cutting the fishing line from the injured animal.

Madre Hermosa looked at Alex and spoke to him rapidly in Spanish. Alex translated. "She tell me she has a sister she talks to in her head. This she has done. José will come with a boat. Do you understand? I do not." Alex looked at me, his face full of questions.

"Muchas gracias, Madre," I smiled at her. I looked at the turtle. It seemed to have settled into the tub, now that Madre had cut it free of the fishing line. "Will José come soon?"

"Más tarde, señorita Ana. Vas al mar," she replied, pointing to where the rowboats were stored on the beach. I should go out in *La Tortuga*, that was what she meant. Juan Carlos, meanwhile, had retrieved a head of lettuce from the hut under the banana tree and placed a leaf in front of the turtle. Without hesitation, the turtle grabbed it.

"This turtle is hungry. That is very good," said Juan Carlos, smiling up at me. "Tío José, he take this turtle to Mazunte. Do not worry, Cousin Ana!"

So Alex and I sat at the best-view table, drank coffee, and ate the huevos, tortillas, salsa, and black beans that Andy and Linda had made for breakfast that morning. We waited for the sun to rise higher in the sky. I told Alex how my research trips out to the seagrass forest worked and asked if he would like to come along.

"Oh yes! I never go in a boat in the sea before."

I stopped at my hut and retrieved my jackknife and my string bag as well as my usual gear. I thought I could dive down and cut fronds of grass from the forest for the sea turtle to eat while it was being relocated to the tanks in Mazunte.

I gave Alex my brown baseball cap to wear, and we headed to *La Tortuga*. Alex was impressed that I could turn the small craft over, launch it, and row with steady strokes.

"You are strong like macho hombre!" he kidded me.

"Yes, I am," I replied. "Farmgirl strong."

I saw six turtles, two of which I recognized from previous trips to the forest. I took my notes and explained to Alex that the same turtle that saved me had saved José all those years ago — and changed his life as Santa Juanita had changed mine.

"Santa Juanita, she who bring the dead back to life." Alex, like all children raised Catholic in this part of Mexico, knew the story of the miracle. "José give this turtle a good name."

Suddenly, we were startled by a loud engine noise. A sizable motorized boat had come around the bend between Zipolite and Mazunte and was fast approaching our position. As it drew nearer, I could make out José waving his straw hat at me. Behind the wheel of the boat was a large man wearing a white captain's hat. His eyes were shielded by dark sunglasses, and he wore a white shirt open at the neck and rolled at the elbows. As the boat drew closer, I could see the man's red-bronze skin had the leathery look of a white man who'd been in the sun too many years.

José was yelling above the motor. "Ana, mija, I have come with el patrón. He would like to speak with you!"

33

Zipolite

"You must come onto the big boat, Ana," José yelled, and motioned for me to bring *La Tortuga* around to the back of the larger boat. When I rowed there, José threw a line and lowered an aluminum ladder off the end. Alex and José introduced themselves to one another in Spanish as José helped him into the yacht. I was gratified to hear Alex describe himself as "Alejandro, un amigo de Oaxaca," a neutral descriptor that didn't require further explanation. Also, I noticed, he did not offer a last name.

While we got onboard, the patrón had cut the motor and lowered an anchor so the large boat wouldn't drift toward the shallow water close to shore. José motioned for us to have a seat on navy-colored cushions lining both sides of a sizable area behind the boat's steering wheel. It was covered by a navy canvas canopy, providing a needed respite after our couple of hours in the hot Mexican sun. As custom demanded, José introduced Alex to the patrón first.

"Alex," Alex corrected. "Please, el patrón, call me Alex."

"Name's Nathan Nelson, from the great city of San Antonio, Texas," he said in a pronounced drawl. "I spend so much time in Mazunte these days, though, I've almost become a native."

Nathan Nelson grinned at Alex while pumping his hand more than necessary. "Except for the Spanish thing. Never was too good at foreign languages. Oaxaca's one beautiful city, Alex. You must be proud to hail from there."

"Yes, sir, Mr. Nelson." Alex smiled his beautiful smile at my patrón. "But I am happy to visit my friend Ana here by the sea. And to learn of the important work she is doing for you." Such a good friend was Alex, using the introduction to advocate for me.

"Ah, yes, little lady." Mr. Nelson turned toward me, finally, and looked me up and down as if assessing a horse or a car. "I thought it was about time to meet the girl José found for my sea turtle project. Ana, wasn't it?" he finished, finally meeting my eyes.

I nodded. "Thank you for the opportunity to work for you, Mr. Nelson. I'm really enjoying it." I was glad I had put my skirt and pink blouse on over my swimsuit before we started back from the seagrass forest.

"José, get our guests some drinks," the patrón said as he sat down on the bench opposite where he'd indicated Alex and I should sit.

José nodded and returned with lemonade and iced tea bottled in America. It seemed odd, twisting off the cap of a plastic bottle. In Mexico, the bottles were glass, the caps the standard beer bottle metallic cap. I preferred the feel of glass on my lips and the intense fruit flavors of Mexican sodas. There was something phony tasting about the lemonade.

"I believe, y'all, that the Lord Almighty did not put us on this planet to fritter away our time or our health, so no drinking of liquor on any of my boats, nor cigarettes or cigars neither. Takes away from doing hard work. Takes away from the creative improvement of the human condition. That's what the Lord put us on this earth to do. That's why I put in the road to Mazunte. Not just so I can get to my hacienda with ease, though I admit that's a part of it. But so I can uplift the lives of the natives there. Right now, they got barely enough to keep body and soul together. But soon, there will be proper work to do, as I aim to build some tourist bungalows along a piece of my beachfront. Restaurants and such will surely follow, and soon Mazunte will be a little piece of heaven for American tourists to enjoy. And the natives will have good honest work serving the tourists."

He was obviously convinced of the rightfulness of his development project. I wasn't so sure "the natives," as he termed them, lacked work or wanted more of it. But he was my employer, so I just nodded and smiled.

"Yes," agreed José. "This is why we build the turtle hospital. For the tourists that will come to Mazunte."

"Praise the Lord, José. I nearly forgot why we took *The Redeemer* out this fine morning. José told me you rescued a beached sea turtle that needs our help. Good work, girl. Good work!"

"Thanks," I mumbled. "Madre Hermosa cut the line off her. And she's eating."

"Is she with Madre Hermosa?" José asked. "I take *La Tortuga* and go to her." With that, he walked to the back of the boat and lowered himself into the little rowboat, leaving us alone with the patrón.

Alex and I watched him go. I took an apprehensive breath. What would we talk about with this strange man? But Alex resumed his advocacy of me.

"El patrón sir, Ana showed me the intense notes she takes about the sea turtles in the forest of under-the-sea-grass. Over there." He pointed to where we had come from. "Today, she sees six turtles. Two she sees before — she knows the turtles by the shell. She is very good at this job, Mr. Nelson. She is a strong swimmer. She is a strong diver. She knows how to row the tiny boat very well. And she keeps the book of all she sees. You must be happy to keep her in this job, sir." Alex finished with an admiring look in my direction.

Mr. Nelson turned his gaze on me again and I felt myself blush. "High praise, little lady, even if he is a friend of yours." He emphasized the word friend in a way that conveyed that he thought Alex was my boyfriend. "Is he right, young lady? Are you earning your keep?"

"Yes, Mr. Nelson, I think so, sir. I'm trying my best to keep good records of the turtles that visit the Zipolite seagrass forest." I was blushing furiously. "Thank you for the mask and flippers. They help so much."

"I'll take a gander at your record-keeping when José returns with the boat and the turtle, but if you are doing what I hired you to do, I see no reason to change things for the present. You think you'll be here in Mexico for some time, eh?"

In a flash, I knew what to do to preserve this unlikely job I had landed. I gazed at Alex adoringly. "Yes, sir, Mr. Nelson. For a long while — hopefully, forever," I said in a voice that belonged to a sappy ingenue, not mine at all.

"Well, ain't that sweet," he replied. "You two make a fine-looking couple, and that's a fact."

Alex kissed me briefly on the cheek, playing along seamlessly.

"Mr. Nelson, sir, do you go fishing in this fine boat of yours?" He wisely turned the conversation away from me.

Mr. Nelson's eyes sparkled. "Indeed, I do. Sometimes, I think the Lord put me on this earth for two reasons: To make money in real estate and to create jobs to lift up poor natives like José. When I do that, the Lord rewards me with good fishing. And son, let me tell you about the fishing in these waters. It's as plentiful as the day after creation." He proceeded to describe in detail the sailfish, tuna, wahoo, and other fish he and his friends caught from this boat.

While he was regaling us with trophy fishing tales, my eyes wandered to the shore. I could see José returning to the rowboat, walking side by side with Andy, the red turtle tub in between. I watched them settle it into the bottom of the boat, and with a wave of thanks to Andy, José started rowing toward us. We weren't far from the shore, and not far from the One Rock, on the safe, Puerto Ángel side of it. José pulled up alongside us in minutes. Alex carefully climbed into the rowboat and together the two men muscled the red tub and its turtle into the larger boat.

"Ah, poor creature of God," Mr. Nelson exclaimed as he saw the raw flesh of the turtle's neck and flipper. "We'll have you fixed up right fine in no time, though. Don't you worry none. José, get that antibiotic salve we brought."

José brought the jar of salve and Mr. Nelson supervised as José spread it carefully on the turtle's wounds.

"You are correct, little lady, this is indeed a female," my patrón intoned in a knowledgeable tone. "And she's been kept properly moist throughout her trials and tribulations, I see. I'm impressed. José taught you well and you applied what you learned." Nelson looked in José's direction again. "José, get that backpack out of the rowboat. I presume that's where you keep your record book, young lady?"

He looked through it slowly, examining with interest the sighting chart and accompanying field notes that Thorpe had suggested. "These here notes look quite professional, missy. You had any training in science?"

I swallowed. "*Tread carefully, missy,*" I admonished my-self. "Ah, I was a history major. But we did study the scientific method, which can be applied to any observational situation." I didn't offer a university name and mentally crossed my fingers that he wouldn't ask.

Before he had a chance to ask further questions about my background, Alex cut into the conversation. "Now you see, sir, how Ana is very good at keeping this book. She goes every day into the sea to find the turtles and count the turtles. She likes this job very much. She does not want to ask the small favor of you, Mr. Nelson, but I will ask it. Please." he said, and took my hand, like a boyfriend would. "Can Ana come to Oaxaca with

165

me for five days only? You see, mi madre is becoming sixty a day after mañana and we make the big party. Mi madre, she loves Ana. She would be very sad if she cannot be in Oaxaca for the big party. In honor of mi madre. So, I ask you, sir, can Ana come away with me for five days only?"

José cut in. "I will visit this seagrass forest for five days. I will put the count in the book. I will do this so my friend, Ana, can go to Oaxaca to honor the madre of Alejandro."

"Well, little lady, it appears you have not one, but two advocates on this boat. I will take you at your word that you will be back in five days."

I nodded. What else was there to do? "Thank you, sir. Thank you, José. I will return in five days."

"Well now, I best be getting back to the turtle hospital with this poor creature the Lord has put in our path. José, pull up the anchor. Pleasure to meet the both of you. José will be in touch when you return, young lady." Mr. Nelson stood up to dismiss us.

We repeated our thanks and lowered ourselves into the rowboat. I tried to catch José's eye, but he would not meet mine. Did he know about my relationship with Thorpe? Had Madre Hermosa told Verónica, and she told him? Did he think I was betraying her with this handsome man? I didn't know what to say to him, and in any case, there would be no time right now to say it.

Alex had made it impossible not to go to Oaxaca.

34

Oaxaca

I couldn't be angry at Alex for arranging my time off from turtle watching. He had watched out for me at every opportunity. I did need new documents if I was to have any future. He needed a wife if he was to have a future with Luke and remain connected to his family. Alex, along with most of the rest of the world, was more worldly-wise than I was. He was convinced this was a plan that would serve both of us. It was hard to argue otherwise.

On the deserted shell beach, after a late afternoon swim, Alex got on his knee once again and formally asked me to marry him. "It is the right thing, Ana, for both of us. Please believe me," he implored, his brown eyes meeting my blue ones. Alex beamed at me. "Only one kiss and a nice party. This is all."

His argument was sound. I said yes.

The day after we met Nelson, Alex and I boarded the bus to Oaxaca. Alex explained my absence to Madre Hermosa, telling her the same tale he'd used with the patrón and José. She had given me a long look and told Alex she wouldn't rent my hut out in my absence. Margarita was at her juice stand as she always was, and we both drank "something with guava" to fortify ourselves for the panic-inducing bus ride through the mountains to Oaxaca. "I'm going to Oaxaca, Margarita. I'll be back in five days. If Thorpe calls, tell her that my friend Alex's mother is having a birthday party and he's invited me. Please tell her I will be back." I started blushing under my floppy hat. "Please tell her that I...ah...miss her. A lot," I ended, weakly.

Margarita nodded; her lips pursed in disapproval. I was sure she didn't want to lie to Thorpe for me. "Best you tell her the rest of the story yourself, Ana. So that's all I'll say. If she calls."

The bus ride was less frightening on the way up the mountain, as mostly we hugged the inside of the cliff when there was oncoming traffic and I made sure to sit on the side of the bus that faced the carved-out mountain, not the limitless ravines. Alex also kept my mind off the road as he described all the beautiful plazas y avenidas, churches and art, there was to see in Oaxaca. "The archeological site, Monte Albán, Ana, is muy interesante. It is the old city of the Zapotecs, the people of Madre Hermosa. This is where I meet my boyfriend, Fred, the American archeologist who tells me of the pink drink for the stomach." Alex was chattering on and on as the bus lurched up the mountain road and around its many hairpin turns. He was happy, I could tell, that he had finally landed a bride. He said I would stay until Tuesday so that on Monday we could go to the driver's license office and apply for my new ID in my new name. "While you were in the baño, I asked señora Margarita for her address. It is there they send your new card for driving. After this, you will be señora Ana Jiménez."

When the battered blue bus finally arrived in Oaxaca, most of Alex's family was at the plaza to greet us. I met three of his brothers, Pedro, Miguel, and Antonio, who were all sturdier, more world-weary, but still handsome versions of my soon-to-be husband. I met their wives, Maria, Juana, and Rosa. Two of them had babes in their arms and an older child clinging to their skirts. Rosa, the slimmest and youngest of the wives, told me, Alex translating, that she would be happy to loan me her vestido de novia, complete with un velo de novia, a veil, to cover my cabeza rapada — which Alex translated as "head with only skin." There followed a discussion among the women about how difficult it would be to attach the veil to my cabeza rapada. Finally, Alex told me, they would borrow the tiara from the wedding of the eldest sister-in-law, Maria, and attach the velo de novia to that. I spent these minutes nodding, smiling, and blushing when Alex told me of the women's focus on my lack of hair. "I tell them you had the bugs in the head. This is why you cut your long hair. It is okay — many people have these bugs in Mexico."

Great. Alex's relatives' first impression of me was as a lice head. But I was in this now and Alex would say what he wanted about me, us, and the marriage. Alex's uncle, the train station master, walked over to greet us as well. "When I saw you two together," he told Alex in Spanish, "I knew she would be your bride." Alex grinned and put his arm around me.

We walked in a boisterous bunch the few blocks from the plaza to the family home, where Alex's mother lived with one of her middle sons, Manuel, and his family. I tried to take in the pastel facades with wrought iron-fenced balconies that we were passing, the arched stone entrances to shopping areas, the red and yellow umbrellas put out over the busy restaurant tables that lined one side of the street. Huge tropical trees shaded a plaza we passed. Underneath their branches, women in peasant dress from the countryside sat with their handicrafts and vegetables displayed on colorful blankets, and old men played cards and smoked. The air here was pleasantly cool and dense compared to the dry heat of Zipolite. I breathed in one grateful lungful after another, in out, in out, trying to calm my jitters as our procession paused at what Alex described as "the home of my father, his father, his father father and his father father father."

"Hola, Mamá," Alex called out as he grabbed my hand and opened a solid wooden door. "Mi novia está aquí, mi novia está aquí." He sounded as excited as if we were really lovebirds on the path to our wedding day. I took off my sunglasses and hat and followed him into the cool front room, a stone floor, timbered ceilings, and bright blue stucco walls setting off heavy, dark wood furnishings that looked like they had come with the Conquistadores. Alex dipped his fingers into a small reservoir of water under the prominent crucifix just inside the door and made the Sign of the Cross. He indicated that I should do likewise. "You will be Catholic now, Ana," he whispered. Ma had been a devout Catholic, so I'd been well-schooled in the rituals and strictures of the Church. Well-schooled in the Church's catechism, such as the Fifth Commandment. I dipped my unholy hand in the water and made the Sign of the Cross.

Mamá Jiménez, for so she was addressed by the sisters-in-law, came out from a back room, drying her hands on a dish towel. Her silver hair was pulled back from her face in a braided bun, and she was the very essence of what Alex would look like thirty-five years from now — handsome, with a beautiful smile that she turned on me now.

"Welcome, Ana. I am pleased to meet you," she said slowly, in heavily accented English, to everyone's astonishment. She smiled and shrugged, and everyone laughed. She looked me in the eyes for a moment, hers a brown so deep it blended with her pupils, mine such a foreign blue they gave her a visible start. Or could she tell lying eyes from honest ones? Taking both my hands in hers, she continued to assess me, looking at me from head to toe with a cool analytical eye. Only after what felt like a long time, did she give me a kiss on both cheeks.

Alex was clearly touched by his mother's effort to learn a few words in English to welcome me. "¿No es hermosa?" he asked her, gesturing to me, the only blue-eyed blond, and recent lice head in the room.

"Sí, ella es hermosa. ¡Pero no tiene pelo!" Mamá Jiménez ran her hand over her own well-coifed head. I thought she said I was beautiful, for someone with no hair.

"Ella tenía piojos," Alex repeated the story about my fictional headlice.

"Todo el mundo tiene piojos a veces," Mamá replied, gesturing at a child standing next to her mother and one of Alex's brothers. She pointed at Alex. And smiled at me. She asked the room in general, "¿Cómo usará el velo de novia?"

The room erupted in offered opinions in rapid Spanish, flavored with laughter. I stood there, holding Alex's hand, the very picture of a blushing bride. Oh, how I hated my lying self at that moment! All these good people, first among them Alex. And me, a murdering fugitive who had recently maybe discovered she was in love with a woman. I had no right to sully this close-knit family with my presence, never mind become a relative to them. At that moment, I wanted to wrest my hand from Alex's grasp and flee back to Zipolite, not to the humble village that had so improbably nurtured me but right into the sea so the riptide could take me to my oh-so-deserved death.

Alex sensed my rising panic and interrupted the discussion, which had moved on to plans for our wedding day party. "It is time for siesta," he said to the room at large in Spanish. And to his mother, "Where will Ana sleep tonight?"

Alex's many relatives scattered after bidding me polite, "Adiós, señorita Ana, hasta luego."

Alex let go of my hand. "I go to the house of my brother, Pedro, to sleep now. I come to this house again after siesta. We have a small dinner with mi mamá, my brother Manuel, and his family who live in this house, too. Tomorrow, we go to the church to make the marriage. We go to my cousin who has a taberna, where we eat much food and have many dances. Do not be afraid, Ana. Everything is okay." He turned on his heel and followed his departing relatives.

Mamá Jiménez took me to a nun's-cell-sized room at the back of the house, sparsely furnished with a single bed and simple nightstand. I took off my dusty sandals and lay down on the narrow bed. I fell asleep immediately, but it was not a restful siesta nap. Instead, I had a dream of the blue bus driving away with Thorpe's face pressed against the window. I could hear her yelling repetitively, "Jane, why are you lying to me? Jane, why are you lying to me?" as the bus started up the mountains. In the dream, I went running after the bus, trying to catch up, trying to explain. But it was going too fast for what speed my legs could muster. As I watched it disappear up the hill, it missed the sharp turn and went hurtling over the edge of the steep road and into the bottomless ravine.

35

Oaxaca

"Reader, I married him." How often as a girl I had mouthed the words that started the concluding chapter of *Jane Eyre*, a novel I'd read obsessively during my dark teen years. Jane Eyre, like Jane Meyer, had her share of cruelty and disappointment, hardship, and heartache when she was young. But Jane Eyre found her way to happiness by finally accomplishing what all the 19th-century novels I'd read emphasized should be a woman's goal in life — marriage to a man who loved and cherished her. Jane Meyer, not so much. Alex was looking for an impersonator wife so his family would quit bothering him and not find out that he was gay. I was looking for a new identity and paperwork to prove it. Necessity, not love, drove the deal that enabled me to state, like the heroine of my youth, "Reader, I married him." The real deal for Jane Eyre; just one more lie to add to all the others for Jane Meyer.

The dress fit perfectly, though it was a tiny bit short. I hadn't considered shoes but one of the sisters-in-law had thought to bring some high-heeled white sandals that fit me. They had come over to Mamá's house in a group the morning of the wedding and began fussing over me right after the breakfast of chilaquiles verdes con huevo — a crispy tortilla with cheese, herbs, and green sauce on it with a fried egg next to it. It was so tasty that I ate it despite my stomach's butterflies. Mamá also made delectable, strong coffee, cooked on the stove like I was used to now. We sat in silence — having very few words in common — but Mamá Jiménez reached out her hand, grasped mine, and smiled twice during our breakfast.

The silence was shattered by the arrival of the sisters-in-law — las cuñadas, Alex told me they were collectively referred to as by everyone in the family. They brought the dress, the veil, the white tiara-like headdress that one of them had attached the veil to, and the sandals. They also brought nail polish to paint over my sand-encrusted toenails and my equally unkempt fingernails. The cuñada in charge of my nails — was it Josefina? — tsk-tsked at their dirt and unevenness as she hid them behind the red varnish. Next, another cuñada — was it Juana? — made up my face. All these feminine cosmetic enhancements were completely new to me — I had always sought to be as anonymous as possible as I moved through the world.

Multiple women fussing over my looks, primping, and preening to make sure my dress was arranged just so, the veil was on straight, the lipstick expertly applied, was as alien as the rest of what Mexico had been to me, done to me, thus far in my time here. My impending marriage, my going to Zipolite, my scientist job, even my romance with Thorpe — all of these had been the ideas of others. I had gone along. not resisted. The only decisions I had truly made for myself recently were to see Johnny in his office that awful night and to try to drop his Roman antiquities in the sea. In the first instance, I had murdered; in the second, almost drowned. So I sat there and let las cuñadas do what they would to me in preparation for a marriage not my own idea, to a man who was not made to be any woman's husband. When I spied myself in the mirror next to the front door, a lice head with lipstick looked back. No one I knew or had ever known.

Mamá Jiménez and I shared the back seat of eldest brother

Pedro's car, a rattletrap of a vehicle with a hole in the floor of the back seat to watch the road passing by. Exhaust poured from the tailpipe. Fortunately, it was a short trip to the church. I wouldn't be marrying into money, I deduced.

Mamá Jiménez and Pedro walked me down the aisle since, according to Alex, I was an orphan and a single child, with no parents of my own to attend the wedding, and no siblings, either. In Alex's telling, there had been a terrible car accident when I was but a girl. I had been raised by an older maiden aunt, also now deceased. Alex was better at weaving my false life story than I was. I was glad of their support, never having walked in high heels before. Alex was waiting for me at a pair of kneelers placed in front of the altar of the church, in dark pants and a white linen shirt — a guayabera — that he'd described during our bus ride as the traditional garb of the groom. We took our places. Padre Domingo — a secretly gay priest who had befriended Alex and come out to him, when, as a teenager, Alex had confessed to the reverend that he liked boys, not girls — began the Mass in which our wedding would be encased. The priest was fully complicit in our lie but justified marrying his gay friend to a near-stranger American, Alex had told me, because "it would be good for the entire Jiménez family."

The ceremony went on and on as I tried to follow Alex's cues about standing, kneeling, and praying. Finally, the time came for the vows, the rings, the presentation of a mysterious box of gold coins, and the promised "one kiss only." I tried my best to look as happy as Alex did when it came to the kiss, but a tear escaped my eye as everyone clapped for the newlyweds.

To Alex, this kiss represented a long-sought-after solution to a problem that had haunted him all his adult life. To me, it was the ultimate symbol of my failed adult life. I had run away from graduate school, ruining any chance for a decent career. I had built my new existence on a tangle of lies, and in doing so, betrayed all the people who had been kind to me, Alex and

Thorpe most of all. I had failed at romance in the most spectacular way possible — by murdering my lover. I was a failure in every conceivable way. I forced these thoughts to the back of my mind and pasted what I hoped was a believable smile on my face as we walked down the aisle to smiles and applause. I would not embarrass Alex in front of his entire family and half of Oaxaca besides.

A mariachi band stood just outside the church, and when we emerged, they began to play. "We will now march down the street to my uncle's taberna and there we will have the long party," Alex stage-whispered to me as the musicians played a cheery melody. Las cuñadas — all in flounced, brightly colored skirts — their husbands and their many children poured out of the church. My new sisters-in-law greeted me with smiles and kisses and "felicidades." Their husbands shook our hands and clapped Alex on the back. When the church had emptied, the band began a slow walk up the street with all of us following. My new sisters-in-law danced as they walked, lifting their skirts as they kicked out their legs, twirling their flounces in time with the music. I let the music and the colorful skirts distract me from my dour thoughts. I could contemplate my sorry life at leisure after this misbegotten weekend was behind me. For now, I had to act the part of Alex's bride.

I focused on putting one wobbly foot in front of the other as we walked the short distance to "Fernando's," as Alex's uncle's taberna was called. Once my eyes had adjusted to the dark interior, I saw the place had been decorated with flowers and streamers. Tables covered by white linen were piled high with a sumptuous feast. The mariachi musicians took their places on a low stage in front of which was a sizeable area for dancing. On the bus ride here, Alex had alerted me to the behavior that would be expected of us on this day. "Okay, there will be two parties, not just one," he'd admitted. "And okay, I must kiss you twice also, Ana, once at the altar and once after the first dance at la taberna de mi tío Fernando."

"In for a penny...," I said, and had to explain to Alex what that meant.

So, we did the bride and groom dance, a slow dance that I now realized Alex had practiced with me, the unknowing novice, at Madre Hermosa's a few nights ago. He had planned well for this sham marriage, no doubt of that. Still, it felt good to lean into him for a few minutes as we did our turn on the floor. I didn't mind the kiss at the end — he was a very handsome man, after all — and I hoped he didn't mind so much either. After our dance, the band picked up the tempo and others flowed onto the floor.

Alex took me to the food line and made suggestions for what foods to sample. I tried to concentrate on all the food on my plate, on all the hard work that had gone into making it, on all the kind words the many guests were bestowing on us as we filled our plates. If not for the complete fraud at the center of it all — me — it would have been a joyous and memorable occasion.

"Señora Ana Jiménez," Alex beamed at his use of my newest name, "Would my wife mind if I dance with my cousin Guadalupe? She and me — we are flamenco partners for many years."

I had to smile at his formality, though something in my gut quaked. I was a wife now, with all the unfamiliar and frightening connotations of that term, even if an imposter wife. "Of course, mi esposo," I played along and smiled back at him. "I would love to see you do the flamenco again, especially in more appropriate shoes."

Alex and Guadalupe were familiar and beloved dance partners and the crowd cheered and clapped and called out "bis, bis" which seemed to mean encore.

I ate. I smiled. I said gracias many times. I danced with Alex again.

The party went on for hours and hours, but finally, Alex said it was time to leave for la luna de miel — the honeymoon.

"What honeymoon?" I asked, almost panicking. Then I realized it was all one more part of Alex's convincing show.

"I have rented a room in a small hotel on the other side of Oaxaca," he whispered. "For tonight and tomorrow night. We will get much sleep there, nothing more. And it has two beds!" he grinned at me.

He had ordered a taxi and most of the partiers came out to wish us good night and good luck — with much elbowing and winking on the part of the men. The taxi drove off into the night with Mr. and Mrs. Jiménez.

Alex was right. I slept like a dead woman the whole of the night.

36

Oaxaca

Las cuñadas had realized how clueless I was about all of this to the extent that they had packed a basket for me for my honeymoon night. In it was a modest nightgown, a bottle-green linen shift to wear the next day, a pair of tan huaraches just my size, a collapsible straw hat, a toothbrush and toothpaste, and various mysterious cosmetics that I looked at but didn't try. We were expected at a "family only" party that evening, Alex explained, but during the day, Alex was supposed to "make the romance" with me, he said with a sweet smile. "I will show you my beautiful city and we will go to the Zapotec city of Monte Albán in a taxi," Alex explained. "Tío Fernando has given me pesos for this day, so no worries about money. We must also make the photos with this," he drew out a small camera. "Mis hermanos give me this camera and tell me I must bring back the photos of the new wife and husband..."

"Newlyweds," I supplied.

"Yes, newlyweds. We go now for coffee. We walk in the city. We eat in a restaurant. We go with a taxi to Monte Albán. After all this, we go to the family party. When we are tired, we make the eyes at each other." He grinned and made a jerking motion with his head and raised his eyebrows in an unmistakable fashion. "Everyone will clap, and we go for the second night of our honeymoon."

Alex's plan for us was executed without a hitch. We dressed in our honeymoon clothes and walked the streets of the beautiful city, with Alex asking passersby to take our photo now and again, for which we held hands and smiled at one another. We had a wonderfully prepared lunch at a restaurant neither of us could usually afford and Alex had someone take a photo of us with the chef. We took an air-conditioned taxi out to the ruins of the Zapotec city and walked around the interesting site, using a brochure in English and Spanish as a guide.

I had never been a tourist anywhere before and found myself drawn to the otherworldliness of the experience. As a tourist, I could be a carefree explorer, enjoying someone else's culture, taking in new sights and sensations without consequence. After the tense day of faking my way through what I thought of as my "lice-head wedding," it was relaxing to be following the lead of my handsome and cheerful "husband." We laughed and joked together and hammed it up for the occasional photos. I wasn't sure if I had ever felt so comfortable in my own skin. Was this what happy felt like?

Our enjoyable day helped ease me into the evening's festivities, which mostly involved eating and talking in the garden behind the Jiménez house. I thanked las cuñadas as best I could in my limited Spanish for the many ways they had helped make this occasion easier for me. I could see they were trying hard to welcome this odd, blond, American addition to their family. By the evening's end, I thought I had found some acceptance among them, though I wondered if it would matter. Would I ever see them again?

"Muchas gracias, Mamá Jiménez," I said in goodbye, looking into her eyes with what I hoped was gratitude in mine. "Mamá has estado tan amable conmigo." She had been so kind to me. I thought the least I could do was memorize a thankful phrase in her language as she had memorized a welcoming one in mine.

"No fue nada. Eres mi hija," she replied with a smile and kissed me on both cheeks.

"She say you are her daughter, now," Alex translated.

"Muchas gracias, Mamá," I said again, and brushed away tears. At that moment, no matter how impossible it was, I wished I was part of this kind, large family. Imagine having five sisters, a handsome husband, the promise of children... I shook my head in sorrow. I shook my head to banish these useless thoughts. Such a life was not for me — not with this man, not with anyone.

Early the following morning, Alex and I packed up our belongings and took the last taxi paid for by Fernando. We stopped at Mamá's to drop off the wedding dress and other borrowed items and we both hurriedly packed the small backpacks we'd come with. I kept on my green dress — best to look like you don't need it when you have to ask a public official for a favor, Alex said. Mamá Jiménez was out shopping — it was market day, Alex told me. We went to the driver's licensing office and Alex deftly took the five twenty-dollar bills I'd given him and transferred them with a handshake to the man he'd spoken with a few days ago. I filled out the paperwork, Alex produced the wedding license signed by Padre Domingo, I produced the visa he'd helped me procure in Ciudad Juárez, and the official diligently copied the other necessary information onto yet more forms. Alex made sure he had Margarita's address clipped to the paperwork.

"Dos semanas," the official muttered. Two weeks and I'd have a visa, a marriage license, and a driving license, all informing anyone who cared that I was Ana Jiménez. My new identity just might work.

"Thank you," I said to Alex when we'd left the office.

"It is good for you to be señora Ana Jiménez?" he asked with a seriousness I'd rarely seen in him.

"It is good," I nodded.

"Thank you, too, señora Ana," Alex smiled back. "You see why I ask you to be mi novia. I love mis hermanos. I love las cuñadas. Mi madre. Fernando y Guadalupe. All the little ones. It would not be good to never see them. I love them. They are mi familia."

"A good family you have, Alex. I am proud to be a member of the Jiménez family, even if it is only on paper." I found myself getting choked up as I said these words.

"We will visit them together again when I come back to México."

I nodded, too close to a sob to trust my voice.

"Now you must go to Zipolite to work in the sea. To wait for tu mujer — your lady friend, Thorpe. I go to Texas to see mi amante, Luke. We will be who we are."

The bus to Zipolite left from the other side of the plaza, out of view of his uncle the station master. Alex had a plan for avoiding his uncle as he boarded his train back to Mexico City to start the long trip to Texas. I changed into my pink blouse and my pink and blue skirt, folded my linen shift, and carefully tucked it into my backpack. I brought out my leather sandals and strapped them to my feet. No sense getting the huaraches dirty on the dusty trek back to Zipolite. I tied them to the outside of my pack instead. Alex and I looked at each other, hands grabbing hands. We collapsed into each other's arms and hugged, as if we truly were esposo y esposa about to be parted on long, separate voyages.

"I will see you again, mi esposa Ana," Alex told me with conviction. He turned and took off at a trot for the train departing for points north.

I watched until he ran around the station corner and disappeared. I got on the old blue bus that would take me back to the tiny life I had made for myself in the stick hut haven of the beach of the dead.

37

On the Bus to Puerto Ángel

My second bus trip to Puerto Ángel was less terrifying than my first had been. I knew where I was going. I wisely found a seat on the cliff-side of the bus, so staring into the abyss was infrequent. Still, I could feel the blisters rising on my palms from gripping the rusty bar welded to the seat in front of me as the bus swerved along. I was used to the black-haired Zapotecs, who, unlike the Mexicans of the city, still wore serapes around their shoulders and rope sandals on their feet. I was used to hearing incomprehensible conversations drift around me. I was used to the odors of rural Mexico — a heady mix of unwashed bodies, chilis, herbs and spices from the baskets of the women returning from the Oaxaca market, and diesel fumes from our ancient vehicle wafting into the open windows. What I wasn't used to, nor expecting, was the wave of loneliness that swept over me as we twisted our way over the mountains and down the other side to the Pacific.

As a young girl I had asked Ma why I had no brothers or sisters. Our neighboring farm couple, the Jacobsons, had five children. Many of the kids I went to school with also came from large families. Ma always said, "You were all we could afford." It was hard to argue with that, given my hand-me-down wardrobe and the ramshackle state of the farm, inside and out. As I grew older, though, I became aware that Ma had been pregnant twice since I'd been born at the start of their marriage. Both had ended in miscarriages caused by my father's brutality. The last one I remembered, because I was eleven and Ma was thirty when it happened. I was old enough to know why she had started wearing loose-fitting clothing and wise enough not to ask about it. I was afraid I'd jinx it by forcing her to tell me I had a sister or brother on the way.

There was a day she came home from work late — someone had a birthday party after her shift had ended and she'd risked staying after to sing and eat a piece of cake with the other workers at the old folks' home. She'd paid for that one with a dislocated shoulder as he'd thrown her to the floor. He'd grabbed the casserole cooling on the stove — a casserole she'd made the night before and I'd baked — and dumped it over her head. He'd placed some well-aimed kicks as she screamed and tried to protect her swelling belly to no avail. I'd watched in horror as the kitchen floor grew red with blood. I'd tried to stop him that time by jumping on his back and pummeling his face, but he backed into the nearby doorframe and slammed me into it, over and over, until I let go. He had to take her to the doctor's that time.

I was sure the emergency room nurse knew perfectly well that my mother hadn't slipped on a wet spot in the kitchen and crashed into the hot stove, but neither she nor the doctor who told her she'd miscarried inquired much about any other explanation. And Ma was too afraid to risk saying anything herself. I didn't find out the details about that night until years later, after he was dead, and I felt I could ask Ma about it. That was why I was an only child, Ma had said. There had been an earlier one too, she told me, when I was five. Ended the same way, in a pool of blood on the kitchen floor after she'd committed some infraction or other in his mind. I remembered the blood, but had been too young to realize the cause.

When I was little, Ma dropped me off at the Jacobsons for the day during the summer when school was out, but she had to work. The two boys and three girls were almost like having siblings and they were mostly nice to me, teaching me to swim and ride a bike, taking me along on their hikes into the woods behind their farm. But during my darkest teen years he'd enlarged his web of control to include me. Then it wasn't just Ma who had to be home immediately after any appointment in the outside world, who couldn't have friends or even go on a solitary walk. During those years, both of us were his prisoners.

Despite the wave of heat and humidity that washed over me as we crested the mountains and began our descent to Puerto Ángel, I shivered at those terrible memories. Ma's only surviving child, that's what I was. He hadn't beat her much during the first few years of their marriage, she'd told me that time we talked about my missing siblings. That was before he became a drunk. Before he lost the farm, and later, his job working for the new owner of the farm he'd been forced to sell. It had been Ma and me for my entire life. Not a whole lot of love to go around, though Ma tried to care for me and love me in the slivers of time we had together.

Ma! How I wished I could let her know that I was alive and okay. But surely, if I was a suspect by now — and my sudden absence and prior relationship with him made that likely — the authorities would contact Ma and question her about my whereabouts. Better that she be able to truthfully answer that she had no idea where I was. During a brief straight stretch when it felt safe to let go of the handhold, I briefly hugged myself in sorrow, in longing for the only human who I was certain loved me.

My life had been nothing like Alex's. He'd been the baby brother everyone doted on. Eventually, he'd had five sisters too, aside from his warm and loving brothers. And a mother who didn't live in fear and had herself been loved by a husband whose only major flaw was his early death. I imagined being permanently cocooned in that large and fun-loving family, as I would have been, headlice and all, had I really been Alex's wife. Tears streamed down my face as I contemplated my lonely future. No Ma. No Alex. No Jiménez family. No Thorpe. Especially no Thorpe. The other Americans I'd met since arriving in Zipolite were nice enough. Margarita was like a wise aunt I could count on for advice. Madre Hermosa and Juan Carlos were kind to me, and José had called me "mi hija." But the Americans would be leaving soon. Margarita was busy with her drink stand in Puerto Ángel and Madre and Juan Carlos were part of the hidden village of Zapotecs. José was far away in Mazunte.

The woman in the seat across from mine pointed to my wet cheeks. "¿Estas enferma?" she asked and pointed to my stomach.

"Mi esposo está en Oaxaca," I blurted miserably and pointed to my ring, which I hadn't yet removed. I didn't know how else to explain what I was feeling. Regretful? Self-pitying? Abandoned? The woman reached over and patted my knee in sympathy.

A lonely, lice-head bride cut free from her sham marriage with nowhere to go and no one who cared.

The bus rounded the last curve and there it was, the uncaring Pacific. An ocean that had nearly drowned me, and one that had nurtured me too. But both extremes were of no concern to the boundless waters. The ocean just went on as it would with no regard for the tiny life forms that lived in it or visited it. Where could I find solace in all this vastness?

The bus screeched to a halt. I took the wedding band off my finger and put it into the front pocket of my backpack along with my cash and my fake documents. I slung the backpack over my shoulder and shuffled off with the others. I walked the few steps to Margarita's, for just like the first time I'd gotten off the old blue rattletrap, I had an unslakable thirst.

Margarita looked up as I approached the bar.

"Something with guava, Ana?" She smiled at me.

38

Puerto Ángel and Zipolite

It was so unlike me, or at least unlike Jane, but when I saw Margarita, I rushed behind the bar and gave her a long hug.

She returned it, grabbed me by the shoulders, and held me at arm's length. "Have you been crying, Ana? Again? Still? Here, sit. Have some water while I make your drink. Wanna tell your bartender about it?"

I nodded sorrowfully, retreated to the customer side of the bar, and sat on my usual red barstool. I sighed. I sighed again.

"No news from Thorpe," Margarita said as she loaded the blender with guava, pineapple chunks, and coconut milk. "In case you were wondering. It's only been a few days though, so she's probably just settling in wherever it is that she went. How was the wedding?"

"Alex told his relatives that I had head lice and that's why my hair was so short," I blurted.

Margarita laughed. "Well, I guess that was better than saying you were a dyke. If you are. We do have a long hair thing in this country, especially for girls your age. His relatives would wonder. He'd have to say something."

"Funny thing was, I didn't even mind. I was such a fish out of water there. What was one more thing?" I sighed and took

187

a long drink of the boiled, chilled water Margarita kept in her blue cooler.

"It didn't go well? Didn't his mother and brothers like you?"

"I'm not sure. None of them spoke English and you know how much Spanish I speak. But they were very kind to me. Alex was very happy, and that was the whole point, so it did go well, really. It did."

"But?"

"It was nice being a part of a large, fun-loving family, even if for just a few days. I'm an only child, so I never had that before. And the wedding, the feast, the dancing, it was so... storybook. Everybody clapping and cheering for us. I felt a part of something, a family, a history, a bunch of people who cared about each other." I thought about las cuñadas and their gift of the honeymoon basket, their loans of dress, veil, and shoes, their attempts to make me into a respectable-looking bride, despite my hair. "It felt bad to be such a phony while they were so generous, so sweet to me." It was the first time I had admitted the sadness of my phony life, even to myself. And Margarita knew only a single item on my long, long list of lies.

"It was for a good cause, though, hon. Alex seemed like a nice man. Now Alex's family can be proud of him instead of shunning him. That's why you did it, wasn't it?"

"Yeah, of course. For Alex," I said a bit too quickly. Did she suspect something?

But Margarita replied, "Cheer up, Ana. You did a good deed."

I left the smoothie stand a bit later and walked to Zipolite.

Halfway there, I heard someone running behind me. I turned to look, imagining, improbably, that it was Thorpe. It was Juan Carlos, his string bag of homework clasped in his arms, his tie flying behind him, his black dress shoes covered in red-brown dust.

"Hola, prima Ana! I am happy to see you. Please tell to me about Oaxaca. It is muy hermosa, ¿no es así?

"Hola, Juan Carlos. Sí, Oaxaca es muy hermosa e interesante."

"¿Hablas español ahora?" He grinned at me, swung his string bag over his shoulder, and took my hand.

"Just what my friend Alex taught me so I could speak a little with his madre."

"Alex, who can make the dance like this." He struck a flamenco pose. "I want to be Alex, so all señoritas fall in love with me!"

Not quite, I thought, but just squeezed his hand and smiled at him. I told him about the large pastel houses lining the shady streets, about the arched stone buildings, the colorful umbrellas over the outdoor restaurant tables, the plazas with their huge trees and even grander churches. We traded words back and forth for the various sights I named. "We went to see the ancient site of the Zapotec — Monte Albán — where your people had a great city many, many years ago."

"Yes, yes! I know about this city. We learn about it in school. Someday, I will go to this place! I will take the bus to Oaxaca!"

"I am sure you will, Juan Carlos. You will have a life of adventure."

"Aventuras, yes, I hope."

"Juan Carlos, I want to ask you a question about Thorpe."

"Sí, señorita Angelina. Mi madre la ama. My mother love señorita Angelina."

"Yes, I see that. Why does your mother love her so much? And why does she call her Angelina?"

"Angelina? It is her name. You are Ana. She is Angelina." Juan Carlos seemed confused.

"To me, she is only Thorpe. But okay. But why does your mother love her?"

"Mamá tell me this thing. When señorita Angelina come to Zipolite when I was a baby, the first time she come to Zipolite, there are four bad men — gringos. They do not pay. They say bad words to mi mamá. They are — how you say — maleducado..." He paused, trying to remember the English word. "Rude. This is the word. They drink too much at night. They say mean things about mi madre. They think she is stupid. They think she does not understand. Mi madre, she understand English. Mi madre does not want these gringos in Zipolite. Angelina, she speaks español. She see mi madre is sad. She talk to mi madre. Mi mamá speaks to her about the bad men.

"Señorita Angelina, she talk to the other turistas, good people, like los señores Frank y Andy. Many American peoples go together to these bad men. They say, 'Go away and never come back.' They go away. This makes mi mamá very happy.

"But she do another thing, señorita Angelina. She tell the good turistas — you must take care of mi mamá. She work hard. She cook every day. She here every day. You must help. You must clean the dishes. You must cook the breakfast. You must not drink too much in the night. She take care of us. She is our Madre Hermosa. Señorita Angelina, she give mi mamá this name.

"The good people, they do these things. Now mi mamá, she no wake up before the sun. She no have bad men who make too much drinking. The turistas help mi madre and mi madre help them too. It is very good here now, and mi madre is happy. This señorita Angelina do. Mi madre say she is angel. Her name now is Angelina. Mi mamá name now is Madre Hermosa. This is why mi mamá love señorita Angelina. She make heaven in Zipolite."

I later confirmed this story with Linda and Andy.

"Yeah, he's right, Ana." Andy told me over a mezcalita later that evening.

"Thorpe collected us all, and we went over as a group and told those four assholes to get the hell out of Zipolite. They tried to blow us off, they tried to intimidate us, but eventually they saw that we were serious, and we weren't going away. So they left."

"But Thorpe also read us the riot act about Madre Hermosa," Linda added. "How we took her for granted. How tough her life was, taking care of us all the time. How we needed to pitch in so she would have some time off. How we needed to learn Spanish out of respect for her."

"Madre came and sat with us here at the restaurant and we spoke with her too, with Thorpe translating," Andy picked up the story. "Madre told us she would decide how much alcohol would be consumed around here and if we messed with her, we'd regret it. I think Frank told you about the hassle she gives us the next morning if we've had too much. We argued some, and this one dude and his lady who drank a lot got real surly, left, and never came back. But the rest of us eventually got it, saw that if we made things better for Madre, it would also be better for us. Thorpe changed this place that season and way for the better. And we've kept it going all these years later. All that, *and* she plays a mean hand of cards!"

Thorpe was a local hero to Madre Hermosa and to the regulars of Zipolite, too. She had become an angel.

What did that make me — the devil?

39

Zipolite

The mezcalita and my general state of exhaustion from my wedding weekend resulted in a long dreamless night. I was comforted by my hammock, my cradle-rocking rope, and the light blue blanket that Madre Hermosa had washed while I was away.

Dawn was breaking when I finally regained consciousness. The cicadas were boisterous this morning. Tiny forest birds had started to join in. There was humidity in the air today and gray clouds hung offshore. The sea was a bit choppy. I'd have to put my strength to the oars if I were to row out to the seagrass forest today.

Out of the hammock, I opened the small outer zipped pocket of my backpack and pulled out Thorpe's note. It didn't say much. Not where she was going. Not how long she'd be. But it did say, "Wait. Please?" Comfort words. Words of hope and longing? I hugged the tattered page to my chest for a moment before carefully refolding it and zipping it back into the outside pouch of my backpack.

I opened the main compartment and unpacked, straightened the bottle-green linen dress as best I could, and laid it beside the rest of my tiny wardrobe.

What had Margarita advised me to do? To wait and have faith in Thorpe. That's what she'd said.

Waiting. I was good at that. I'd spent my childhood waiting for my father to leave the farmhouse to plow, plant, or harvest so I could sneak a walk outside where he couldn't see from his perch on the tractor. I'd waited for Ma to come home from her job so I could sit at the kitchen table and do my homework while she cooked dinner. Those precious minutes were the most normal family time that ever occurred in our household. Waiting. For him to get over his bouts of anger, for him to pass out from the beer and Canadian whisky he kept by his La-Z-Boy recliner. After he started snoring, I could freely move around our small, shabby house. Waiting for the graduate school application verdict to come back in the mail. Waiting for Johnny to pay attention to me, to come over to my studio for our ritualized evenings. Waiting. Yes, I was good at that.

Faith, though, might be a problem. I hadn't had faith in anything or anyone for a long time. I'd never had faith in my father, except if you counted having faith that he'd regularly brutalize Ma and me. Ma. Oh, how I wanted to have faith in Ma. But I couldn't count on her. She had entirely subjugated herself to his violent whims, to the "until death do we part" strictures of her faith. She tried to be there for me. Sometimes, she was successful. But there was no counting on it, on her, because of him.

Then there was God. As a kid, I did have faith that there was someone listening to my fervent prayers to get bigger so I could protect her from him. God had answered that prayer by making me a substitute victim for his rapes of Ma. I started praying for my father's death, for years after my first prayer was so horrifyingly mis-answered. But God had gone deaf to my pleas. I quit praying, quit having faith in anything but the regularity of violence in our little family. My father's unexpected death hadn't restored my faith in God. God, like my father, was a cruel tormenter. Or he didn't exist. I was on my own in this world. It seemed wiser to believe that there was nothing to believe in, nothing to have faith in.

As I made my way down to the restaurant to start the beans and salsa heating and get the cups, plates, and forks out for the morning meal, I realized I did have faith in something. I had faith in nature. In the sun's rising and setting, the dramas of life and death in the natural world continuing, faith that the striving to survive that all of nature's wonders shared would go on, too. Living just a stick hut away from nature gave me faith. Not that I would have a good life or could count on anything for emotional solace. But that nature would go on, predictably doing as it did and surprising me with beauty whenever I encountered it. That, I could count on.

I decided to imagine Thorpe was part of this natural river of life, as indeed we all were. She would try to go on, as all creatures did. She would try to thrive. I might be part of her definition of what it meant to thrive. Or not. I tried to think of her like I thought of Santa Juanita — the turtle, not the Virgin. The old mother of many would go about her life. As José said, she was all about life — eating, traveling the sea, staying alive just to lay eggs and fulfill her role in the great cycle of life. Whether I would ever see her again was uncertain. But she'd be out there, doing what nature made her to do.

I was uncertain if I could think of Thorpe that way, if I could strip away the way she made me feel, strip away who she was and imagine her as merely another member of the natural world trying to stay alive. But if I thought about her as I thought about Santa Juanita, a fellow creature who may or may not grace me with her presence from time to time — and when she did, it would be a special moment in my life — perhaps I could have faith in Thorpe.

There was an ugly fact in all this thinking about faith. I might find a way to have faith in Thorpe, but any faith she had in me would be misplaced — she'd be putting her faith in a sham, a phony, a fraud. The stack of lies Ana was built on grew higher by the day. How I wanted Thorpe to love me, long for me, want to return to me. But she didn't even know me, and as the days went by, I was no longer sure there was a me behind the edifice of lies I had told her.

Why should the angel of Zipolite have faith in me?

40

Zipolite and Mazunte

I waited, and I tried to have faith. Each morning, I went for a solitary snorkel over the rocky ledge that formed one boundary of the shell beach. I looked for shells when the tide was out, choosing only perfect shells and those that were new to me. I did my share of breakfast or lunch chores, though with our drastically reduced numbers, they didn't take long. In the later morning, I rowed *La Tortuga* out to the buoy and conducted my turtle sighting routine. Clockwise around the seagrass forest I dove, noting turtles and the other sea life I spotted. I never tired of these moments I spent surrounded by the plethora of life in the seagrass forest. I jotted down the main sightings and rowed to shore. I walked the short distance back to the restaurant. Over a cold drink — guava soda if Madre had it — I filled out my notebook, using the notation protocol Thorpe had taught me. I had a little lunch if I was hungry.

I ambled up to my hut and settled into siesta in my hammock. I read *Contact*, the novel by famous astronomer Carl Sagan. It was about a woman who has an extraterrestrial experience, but no one believes her. But before that, she keeps the faith, working on scanning the heavens for extraterrestrial life that she believes is out there. After they reveal themselves to her, after she solves the puzzle of their communication, after the planet comes together to build the machine the extraterrestrials had sent instructions for, after she eventually gets to go to someplace very far away and interact with entities from another world, after she returns and no one believes her — she still keeps the faith. The extraterrestrials will return. She has faith that this is the beginning of something, not the end. If Ellie could have faith in beings from another world, it wasn't impossible that I could have faith in Thorpe.

In the late afternoons, I walked the beaches toward Mazunte, looking for injured turtles. It was sad patrolling these beaches, for each one reminded me of Thorpe and the days we spent walking them, hand in hand, talking and taking in the beauty and the salt air. I dreaded returning to the waterfall, but there came a day when I had to do my wash. At breakfast that morning, I asked Linda if she might be heading up to the falls and, if so, could I go along.

"Sure, why not? I've always got something that needs washing." Linda organized most of the rest of the remaining Americans to go along with us. I found myself in a party of seven, each with soap, towel, and dirty clothes, walking the familiar trail. When we rounded the last bend and the waterfall came into view, my heart did clench with longing, with the visceral memory of all that had transpired here. But the others kept me from dwelling too long on those paradisiacal days. It was hard to maintain the belief that they would ever come again. I did my wash. I swam in the pool. I ate fruit picked fresh from the trees and sat under the canopy and talked with the rest of them. Naked, like the rest of them. It was like the early days of my stay here. Before Thorpe.

Evenings, I ate whatever food was on the menu that night. I drank a small and weak version of whatever Madre was making that night. I listened to the music, I watched the lackluster card game if there was one, or Linda dancing around the floor with a couple other women I didn't really know or by herself. I went to bed early. I tried to sleep and sometimes succeeded. I dreamed tragedies of dreams. I was the villain and did something mean to someone. Or I was trying to communicate something to someone, but they couldn't hear me, couldn't understand me. Or I fell over a cliff or drowned. Or Alex did. Or Thorpe did. Or Madre Hermosa did. I was glad of dawn when those specters that haunted my nights faded away.

Two weeks of routine days and unsettling nights passed.

One afternoon, I went to the restaurant to have my customary drink and work on my field notes after getting back from turtle watching and there was José, sitting at the best-view table. He was staring out at the gray clouds that were frequent companions now, bringing more humidity and the promise of rain.

"Ana, hola!" José bowed his head in greeting. "The rainy season is coming," he said with a nod toward the clouds. "I have come to pay Madre for your hut and to see how it goes with the turtles. Also, I invite you to Mazunte to see the turtle hospital and the turtle you find. You be very happy to see this turtle now!"

"Hola, José, I am happy to see you. Are you well? And Verónica?" The conventions of politeness in this part of the world were almost second nature to me by now.

"We are well, thank God. Verónica invite you to have dinner this night and stay in the guest room. Please say yes, mija."

"Yes!" I smiled. "I would very much like to see the turtle hospital and the turtle I rescued. And see Verónica and enjoy her good food again."

"You come back from looking for turtles today?"

"Yes, I was about to write up my notes. Would you like to see?"

José nodded, and I gave him my notebook. He read more English than he spoke, he explained. "Because of the American sisters who teach me when I was a boy."

He finished reading. "Ana! This is very good. The patrón will be very happy! We take this book to Mazunte. We show him."

We sat and talked turtles, helping ourselves to tortillas and beans left for the few that ate lunch at the restaurant this time of year.

"I will take the siesta now, mija. After siesta, we will make the walk to Mazunte. I meet you here." And with that José made a bow of farewell and took off up the path to the waterfall, though I supposed he was headed to the spur I'd never taken, the path to the Zapotec village.

I worked on my notes for the day. When I was satisfied I had described everything I saw in sufficient detail, I went up the short path to my hut. I packed what I thought I'd need for an overnight stay into my backpack. At the last minute, I decided to carefully fold my new green shift and add it to the pack. I thought it would honor Verónica and José if "their daughter" dressed for dinner in something other than borrowed or second-hand clothes.

I saw my paltry collection of books — Brontë, Sagan, and Marcus Aurelius — on a tiny pile on the corner of the cot. I had read *Jane Eyre* on the journey here. I had recently finished *Contact*. I had not touched *Meditations* since I had unpacked it from my backpack. I thought to bring it as a touchstone to my now-ruined future as a historian of ancient Rome. But it hurt so much to think about never going to school again, I hadn't had the courage to open it. Marcus Aurelius, I knew from reading *Meditations* last fall as I'd started graduate school, was all about living a decent, noble, courageous life. The opposite of mine.

I made myself take the little volume with me to my hammock. Though the air was still and sticky, I knew siesta would not come this afternoon. I opened the book randomly and my eyes settled on this: "Accept the things to which fate binds you, and love the people with whom fate brings you together, but do so with all your heart."

Fate. I wasn't sure I believed in it. I liked to think the individual had more power over their lives than a belief in fate allowed. Now more than ever, though, I could see the appeal of fate. If growing up under the thumb of my brutal father was my fate, I didn't have to feel guilty for not fighting back more than I had. I didn't have to be angry at Ma for not leaving him — she'd merely been living out her fate. I didn't have to wonder where the rage came from that had enabled and allowed me to murder Johnny. It had just been my fate to kill him. Seemed like an easy way out. Seemed like a way to go on — to accept that fate, not you, had made your life circumstances what they had become. Easy. Easier than blaming yourself. Easier than going on feeling responsible for taking a life, even if it was a brute like Johnny. But I just couldn't get there. I didn't think it was fate that brought me to this place. I thought it was me.

The second half of the quote was easier to accept. It was probably random accident, not fate, that had Alex take the seat next to me on the bus, that had Thorpe arrive in Puerto Ángel just as I was at Margarita's, that had José walking the very beach at the very time I washed up on it. But loving the people in your life with all your heart — at least in this part of my life — seemed like sound advice. Advice I could try to take, even though love hadn't been something I had much experience with. In all my life until now, I had only loved Ma. But now I had a friend in Alex, a kindly father figure in José, a lover in Thorpe. Again, I shook my head. Had murdering Johnny been the best thing that I'd ever done? I would have never met these fine people otherwise.

I noticed some movement at the restaurant. José had come down the hill and was about to sit down. But someone was running up the track that led to Puerto Ángel and as the small form got closer, I could see it was Juan Carlos. He launched himself into José's arms. I thought I could hear, "tío José, tío José" as they clasped one another. I saw Juan Carlos gesturing up the path that led to my hut. José said something, and Juan Carlos let himself be led to the best-view table. Not another soul was at the restaurant this time of day. Juan Carlos set his pack on the table and fetched two sodas from the cooler next to the grills.

Time to go.

As I approached them, Juan Carlos came running up to meet me. "Prima Ana, I have a special letter for you! I will get it from my bag." He ran back to the table and fetched an air-mail letter. "Señora Margarita say this letter come yesterday to you from America! She say señorita Angelina send this letter." He was all smiles at delivering this news.

My hand shook as I reached for the letter. It almost slipped out of my fingers, but I grasped it tightly. The return address said only "Thorpe" in a bold script. José motioned me to sit down at the table where he was sitting. Juan Carlos scampered off to get me a soda and soon returned, removing the bottle top on the table edge and handing it to me with a smile. He sat down next to his uncle. Mail was an unusual occurrence here and both sets of eyes were lit with curiosity.

I carefully opened the envelope. Ten twenty-dollar bills flitted to the tabletop. There was also a single piece of paper. It was quite crumpled by the time I forced it out of the envelope. I unfolded it with unsteady hands.

Dear Ana,

I'm stuck up here in El Norte for now.

Can you join me here?

I sent money for airfare.

Please come. Call me when you get stateside.

I've got a place to stay.

I miss you lots. Just come, huh?

yours,

Thorpe

P.S. I'm assuming that guy on the bus was a joke, right? Right???

There was a telephone number, an address in Washington, D.C., and the name of the airport. That was all.

41

Zipolite and Mazunte

"Señorita Angelina, she is well?" José asked.

"Yes, she is well. She misses Zipolite but she cannot come back right now." I heard a quaver in my voice that threatened to become a sob.

"She will come back, I know it!" Juan Carlos nodded with a surety I didn't feel.

"It is good she does not come back today because today we go to Mazunte," José contributed.

"Yes, that's good." That was as long a sentence as I could trust myself with. My throat was closing and I felt faint. I didn't tell my tablemates about her invitation to me. José was my sort-of boss. Juan Carlos would innocently spread that news to everyone from Mazunte to Puerto Ángel. I folded the letter and quickly put it and the stack of twenties in the front zippered pocket of my backpack, along with my new wedding ring, visa, my driver's license, and marriage certificate. "Let's go." I stood. Walking might help. Leaving Zipolite might help.

José and Juan Carlos had a rapid conversation in Spanish, the gist of which seemed to be that nephew wanted to join us, but uncle said he must do his homework today and he could come on Saturday. Six weeks in Mexico had enabled me to understand some Spanish, though my speaking was still primitive. We hugged and waved goodbye and I saw Juan Carlos getting out his lesson books as we walked away from the restaurant.

I slipped off my huaraches and carried them in one hand and walked barefoot. The tide had just gone out and the cool, wet sand massaged my feet wonderfully. I tried to focus on the sensations nature brought my way — the cooling sand, the refreshing salt breeze. I tried not to think about the crumpled letter in my backpack. We walked in silence for a while.

"You love señorita Angelina?" José asked, breaking our companionable silence. "This is what Madre Hermosa tell me. That señorita Angelina love you and you love her also. Is it so?"

"Do you think that is wrong?" I asked, stalling for time. He was a devout Catholic, so the news that he had hired a sinner was probably not sitting well with him.

"The Catholic Church think this is very wrong. So, I believe it is wrong. I am a good Catholic, now. But…" He paused, trying to find words in English for what he wanted to say.

"Madre Hermosa, she is like a church, too. She welcome all people. She care for all people. She watch over all people. Sometimes, she answer prayer, too — just like Mother Church. She is wise, like Church. So, maybe this love is not wrong. She think señorita Angelina is happy now and never happy before. Madre love señorita Angelina. She want for her happiness. She think señorita Angelina love you and that is why she is happy. Madre does not know — does Ana love señorita Angelina? She think it is so. Is she right?"

I was blinking furiously but I could not stop the tears. "I don't know. I'm not sure. I have never been in love before. I wasn't expecting what happened between us. I might love her, but she shouldn't love me. She deserves better!" I spit out the one true thing I knew about our relationship.

"Why do you say this, mi hija?" José stopped, grabbed my

wrist, and made me look him in the face. "I know you are sad. But I know you are not bad."

I turned away from his inquiring look. "How do you know I am not bad?" I said softly, my face hidden under my faded floppy hat.

"I feel it, here," José replied, putting his hand over his heart. "I see how you talk with Juan Carlos. Like sister to brother. You go to the sea and count the turtles every day. You put in your book many writings. I think you love all creatures in the sea. You have many friends here, turistas, but also México people, Margarita, Alex from Oaxaca, Madre. Me too. To all people you are kind. All people you help. You are good, Ana. This I know."

I was astonished at his words. Was that how I appeared to him? I thought I was in survival mode, doing what I had to do to get on here, to survive here. Could it be that my moral core hadn't disappeared in Johnny's office that most consequential of nights? Did Thorpe, too, see what José saw when she looked at me, and not the hopelessly scarred, damaged, and criminally involved Jane?

Yes, of course she did. Because I was living Ana's life, a lie of a life. My fake self was apparently coming off as decent, at least according to José. But did that make me decent? Could someone who had done what I'd done also be decent?

"If nothing but bad happens to a person, if they also do bad, can they still start over and become good?" I found myself asking José.

José looked over at me, startled. "Mija, that is *my* story. I do many bad things. You know I kill sea turtles. But before I kill sea turtles, I do many other bad things. I do bad to many people." He paused. "If I tell you, you not like me, I think! You not...confianza...ah, trust me. You turn around. You go back to Zipolite. You say goodbye, José. I no like you now!" José looked alarmed, like he'd already said too much.

Now it was my turn to stop, take him by the arm and look him in the face. "José, you saved my life. You gave me a job and trusted me to do it. You have been nothing but good in my life. What you did in the past doesn't matter to me. I know the good man you are now."

"Muchas gracias, Ana. But..." He paused and seemed to make a decision. "You cannot know me, all of me, if I do not tell you my bad, too. I did la transformación after I am saved by Santa Juanita. I go to Confession; I tell the padre all my sins. He forgive me in the name of God. I prayed the rosary many times as the padre tell me. But it is not enough."

"Didn't you feel that God forgave you?"

"God forgive me, but many people I hurt do not know God forgive me. Especially one. I go to find him. I tell him I am sorry. I ask him if I can work for him for no money. He turn his back to me. His mother shut the door in my face and tell me to go away and never come back."

"Who was this man you needed forgiveness from?"

"When I am eighteen, I run over this man in a car I steal. He never walk again."

"What? I don't believe it."

"Sí, I did this terrible thing. I go to prison for this. I do not go to prison for many other bad things I do. The police do not know about the other bad things. But they are bad. I steal. I sell drugs."

"Why? Were you poor, hungry?"

"Mi padre y mi madre, they die of the cholera when I was fourteen. My brother Ernesto was twelve. We go to live with nuestra abuela...our grandmother. She live in another village. She feed us and she give us a bed. But there is no money. She wash clothes for many people. But she get only a few pesos for this work. No money for school. No more school for José and Ernesto. We try to find work for money. We find work, but not good work. We steal. We work for bad people and sell drugs for them. They want us to steal the automobile so they can do more business. We find one with keys. We take it. It is night. I only drive three times before. I am nervous so I go fast to the place they say to take the automobile. It is dark. I am driving very fast when I hear thump. Now I am very nervous. I do not stop. I drive to the place. The front of the automobile, it is broken. No light. We run home. One week go by. The police knock on our door, and they take me away. The men who we work for, they tell police about me. The police tell me a man is in the hospital. I hit him when I drive. My brother, he is okay because he is still a boy. He not drive the car. But me, I drive the car. I am man. So, I go to prison. Five years. It is a terrible place. Many bad men."

"Young men often make poor choices, especially when there is no money."

"Sí, many like me in the prison. But one American man. He sell drugs in Zipolite. He is in prison for five years, too, like me. We speak English together. He help me remember what the holy sisters teach me when I am a boy. This is why I speak English. Not so good, but English." José gave me a sad smile. "This is why I come here with Ernesto after prison. The American man, he tell me about the turtle factory in Puerto Escondido. They give any man a job, he tell me."

"You worked at the factory after prison?"

"Yes, for two years. I bring Ernesto. We are good workers. El jefe, boss man, he ask us if we would like a new job, catching turtles. He give us old truck to get turtles to Puerto Escondido. We are happy to work in the sun, in the good air. We do this work for many years. Until Santa Juanita save me and I see my new life is bad too, like my old life. La transformación happen, el patrón americano give me the job of saving turtles, and Verónica say she will be mi novia, all very quickly." José paused and looked over at me as we continued our beach walk.

"I lost mi padre y mi madre. I did many bad things. I almost kill a man. But I start over and now I am happy. I cleanse myself of all that is death."

My head jerked up. Again, he said the words I heard in my dream. When I heard those words in my sleep, it seemed self-evident. I needed to dump the antiquities I had taken from Johnny's office. But José seemed to imply there was more to cleansing oneself of all that is death. "Tell me about la transformación, José. What do you mean?"

"Am I a man you trust after you know this story?"

"I still think you are a good man, José. You did commit crimes, but you changed. When you changed, your life changed too. And now you can be happy."

"Because of la transformación. It is when I become a new person in the heart. This happen when I look inside, I find all my sin. I say yes, this is my sin. I make the Confession and tell the padre all. He tell me God forgive me. But he say one more thing. To be free of this sin, I must forgive me, too. And this I can do only if I make una disculpa...the apology to the man I hit with my automobile. I must try, the padre tell me, even if he does not forgive me. He did not."

"Were you able to forgive yourself?"

"Sí, because I tell Verónica everything, Madre Hermosa, too. Now, you, mi hija. It is right to confess not only to the padre but to the people I have in the heart. If they have you in the heart, they will forgive you."

"You are in my heart, José." A tear rolled down my cheek as I said this truth to the man who had saved me.

"If you do a bad thing, Ana, you must confess it. This I know."

His words hit me like a gut punch. I pitched forward and stumbled a few steps, only catching myself at the last minute. How could I confess all I had done? And to whom?

42

Mazunte

Fortunately, we came up on the outskirts of Mazunte and the modest adobe house where José lived with Verónica. I desperately needed a distraction from José's frightening prescriptions. Confess and make amends. I could easily drown in those two pieces of advice. There was no limit to the people I had to confess to. The list included everyone I had known in Mexico, and Ma and Maddie in America, too.

Confessing seemed impossibly fraught. What would I say to people I'd met in Mexico? "Sorry, but everything you know about me, including my name, is a lie?" To Maddie, I'd have to say, "Sorry, but you were mentoring and befriending a murderer." To Ma, I'd have to say, "Sorry, but all the years you spent raising and protecting me? It's all been a waste, Ma. It ended up you raised a murderer." Would that make me able to move on? Would that help the people I knew, some of whom I loved, in any way whatsoever?

Then there was the crime that started all the lying. Exactly how would I make amends for murdering Johnny? That implied contacting the surviving family members at least, didn't it? Liz, Johnny's wife, and Jenny, his daughter. I'd never met either of them, had seen Liz from a distance only once and knew Jenny only from a photo. Would it help give them peace to know who had killed their husband, their father? Or just give them someone to hate? I deserved Liz's hate. Not only had I killed her husband, but I'd been his lover, too. I remained convinced that Jenny had suffered at Johnny's hands in just the same way that I had been permanently defiled by my father. But what if I was wrong, and she had loved him and been loved by him in a proper, daughterly way instead?

"Here is my home, Ana," José interrupted these dreadful thoughts. "We say hello to Verónica and you put the backpack in your bedroom. We go to see the turtle."

"Hola, Ana," Verónica greeted me with a brief hug and backed off to look at me. "Tu cabello esta creciendo!" She stroked her own hair for emphasis. Cabello — hair. I was familiar with that word from the many times it had been mentioned by las cuñadas — my sisters-in-law. That all seemed a lifetime ago already. "¿Estás bien?" she asked, no doubt seeing in my face what my mind had been thinking about.

"¿Estoy bien, y tú?" I hoped to change the subject.

"Sí, muy bien," Verónica replied. José spoke rapidly to her. I noticed the word "tortuga" and presumed he was telling her of our plans.

Verónica motioned for me to follow her, and she pointed out the little room where I had napped the day I almost drowned. I nodded my thanks and took a few seconds to take the linen dress out of my bag and lay it on the bed.

We walked the five minutes to the turtle hospital in silence. Though I longed for conversation, I didn't want to talk about sins, confessions, and the path to redemption. It was possible for Catholic José to find peace and happiness. But I couldn't see that future for the likes of me.

Again, I wished the riptide had been successful. At the time, I hadn't thought consciously that suicide might be the result of my foray to the abalone colony. Had I been trying to off myself? I had tried to die by propane in the immediate aftermath of the murder and almost succeeded. I had escaped to

Mexico instead. Did I really wish I had died in Texas and never met Alex, never met Margarita, or Madre Hermosa, or Lily, or Andy and Linda? Never met Juan Carlos? If I had died in the riptide, I would have never met José and Verónica. Never met Thorpe. In my heart, I knew I had loved meeting all these people, loved trying on this new persona, loved feeling like I belonged somewhere. Wouldn't I lose all these tentative steps toward a normal life if I told them who I really was, what I'd really done?

There seemed no answer to my life, no way to rectify the old one, no way to live and enjoy the new one.

The path turned a corner, and we came upon an adobe building with a tin roof. *"Hospital de Tortugas Marinas"* was painted in a neat hand, green on the whitewashed adobe. José opened the door. The interior seemed strangely lit; my eyes were no longer accustomed to artificial light. Fluorescent fixtures hung from the ceiling, casting an unnatural brightness on what was below. Three large metal tanks, each the size of my hut, took up most of the large room. There were five turtles being rehabilitated or housed permanently here, José explained. Two had missing flippers from a boat accident or predator attack. They couldn't be released to the sea again as they couldn't properly swim. The other three, including the little female I'd found, would be brought back to health and released.

"Here she is, mija. See how her neck and flipper get better? New skin grow on her. We will take her back to the sea in one month — I think so! I have named her señorita Ana!" José smiled. He could see I was troubled, but he had decided to cheer me with good turtle news.

It did help to see her healing nicely and eating lettuce and seagrass eagerly from my hand. I'd done one irrefutably good thing since coming to Zipolite. I'd saved a life. "That's so sweet, José, to name the turtle Ana." I almost said "after me" but I wasn't feeling very "Ana" at that moment. Jane had resurfaced with a vengeance.

He told me his plans for a display on the life cycle of the sea turtle. About how there would be a display on the conservation of the turtle and how the numbers were increasing. About the incubator he wanted to create to hatch some babies every year. "We will put them in the sea after the tourist season is over. We will take tourists out to the seagrass forest here with a mask and they can jump into the sea and see the free turtles," José was growing excited about his plans. "We will paint new words on the outside to say, 'Sea Turtle Center of Mazunte' in English, for the americanos to read. Mr. Nelson, he say he will pay for all. He say I will be guide for tourists. I hope you will also work at this center, mi hija."

"You never know," was all I could manage. My head was swirling with all my misdeeds. Could they all just disappear into "Ana Jiménez, sea turtle tour guide?" It seemed a life that belonged to someone else.

A shadow crossed the door. When the shadow stepped into the room, I saw it was el patrón.

"Hey there José, little lady," he greeted us in Texan. "José, I aimed to ask you if you'd crew for me on the way up to Acapulco to pick up some buddies of mine who are flying in. But little lady, if you'd like, no harm in coming with us. Boat up, bus back, as my buddies and me will be heading out to do some deep-sea fishing. But if that works, you're both welcome to join me. What d'ya say?"

43

Mazunte

There was an airport in Acapulco. That was all I digested from the invitation. If I went with him, I could take a plane from there to Mexico City, and on to Washington, D.C.

"Thank you, Mr. Nelson. I'd like that very much." I noticed I was breathing in, not breathing out. Thorpe! Would I be seeing her soon?

"Sí, Mr. Nelson, I will do this. Tomorrow?"

"Yes, José, we'll leave 7 a.m. sharp. Meet at the boat. I'll bring food." He stepped inside. "That little creature of God is healing nicely, isn't she?" he said to the two of us, glancing into the tank. "I'll have one of my men feed them while you're away. One entire day on the boat, another back to the crossroads by bus. Hasta luego," Nelson waved as he left the turtle hospital. He pronounced the "h," I couldn't help but noticing.

"Oh, Ana." José was sparkling. "You love going on the boat. We see many wonderful things. You become happy, I think!"

We closed up the building housing the five turtles and walked back to his house.

Verónica was enthusiastic about José's temporary job. José looked at me. "El patrón pay me good money to work on the boat," he said by way of explanation. "Verónica tell her sister

213

Madre Hermosa that you will be away for three days. No problem."

As I changed for dinner, I thought about what I had left behind in my hut. Two pairs of jeans. My mud-encrusted sneakers, unworn since I had arrived in Puerto Ángel. My three books. The pink shirt and aqua and pink skirt. My brown baseball hat. My raincoat and the altered ice blue sweater. Everything else I owned was in the backpack I'd brought with me. All my money, all my documents, too, were in my backpack. The letter from Thorpe with airfare, directions, and a phone number. I could purchase new clothes and shoes, new copies of books when I'd returned to America.

I put on the bottle-green linen shift and huaraches, and ran my fingers through my hair. I joined my hosts in the garden.

"Te ves hermosa," Verónica said, smiling and indicating my new dress.

"Gracias, Verónica," I blushed. Beautiful. Not a word I associated with myself. I did look much better than the last time she'd seen me when I'd been half drowned.

Verónica had roasted a whole fish over coals, surrounded by peppers, tomatoes, and tomatillos. There were tortillas and beans and rice as always. For dessert, steamed sweet potatoes with evaporated milk and guava jam.

I tried to focus on the nicely prepared meal, but my mind raced ahead. Would I be leaving these lovely people the day after tomorrow? Would I be taking my first flight ever? Flying to Washington to find Thorpe?

I tried to make conversation to take my mind off my frightening future.

"José, do you have any children?" I was ashamed I had never asked him that until now. I felt so close to him, fellow riptide survivor. But I knew very little about him.

"No, I was in the prison during the time the men of México take a wife. After that, hard work killing turtles. I meet Verónica. I know she is my love. But she is very sad. One year before, she lose her husband, her only son in the sea. She tell me she never want to lose a child again. It hurt in the heart very much. So, I say, okay, no babies. It take many, many days to win her heart. It take la transformación. But after many, many days, Verónica, she say she will be my esposa." He grabbed her hand as he said this, love burning in his eyes.

Verónica smiled back, and I could see she understood what he had told me. I could see how much she loved him, too. "Él me salvó," she said. "Su amor me salvó," she said with emphasis, patting his hand and smiling at him.

"She say I am savior, my love save her," José translated. "It is true. Now she not sad."

"You not sad with señorita Angelina," it was Verónica speaking in English, her eyes fixed on mine, her hand grasping mine across the table. "Madre Hermosa say to me. This is good."

"Mi hija," José picked up her thought, "we want for you happiness. Love is happiness. This we know."

Madre Hermosa thought I was in love with Thorpe. The flutter my heart was doing at the mention of señorita Angelina indicated she might be on to something.

"Did Madre Hermosa have a husband — the father of Juan Carlos?" I asked to take the conversation somewhere besides my own happiness.

"He was also lost in the sea, the same day as the husband of Verónica, the same day as the son of Verónica. Juan Carlos was not lost because he is sick on that day, so Madre no let him go in the sea. The husbands, they were brothers, but not... twins. But they look alike, they think alike. They catch fish in the sea. But it is a big rain, high..." Here he made a gesture with his arm.

"Waves," I said. I had noticed by this time that sometimes English words deserted José when he was emotional.

"Sí, waves. The boat is small. It never come back from this storm. The men in the village, they look and look. But the boat, the husband of Madre Hermosa, the husband of Verónica and the son of Verónica, all lost in the sea."

"Oh, I am so sorry." I looked at Verónica.

"Okay, ahora," she said. "José ahora."

"And Madre Hermosa has Juan Carlos."

"Sí, he is her joy of life. He is the joy of life for his tío and tía, also." José pointed to himself and Verónica, but Juan Carlos had already taught me the words for uncle and aunt.

"He is a lucky boy," I agreed.

We sat in the little garden on the side of their house, listening to the night sounds of the jungle and the sea breeze rustling the coconut palms that fringed the beach here.

I was lucky, I reflected, to have these fine people calling me "mi hija." If they knew that I was really Jane Meyer, murderer, that would instantly be the end of that. Yet José had said that confession and an attempt at restitution was the only way to leave one's sins behind. Even mine? Even with them? It was hard to believe.

Later, I tossed and turned in my bed in the little guest room. A full day on the boat, Nelson had said. Then we'd be in Acapulco. His friends were flying in, he'd said. Therefore, there was an airport. That I could fly out of. It was whether that was what I wanted to do, had enough courage to do, that I couldn't decide.

"Ana?" It was José, softly tapping at the woven mat door. A weak dawn light was coming through the gap in the room's small, curtained window. "It is time to go to the boat."

44

The Pacific Ocean

Verónica, of course, was already at work in the tiny kitchen when I'd dressed in the outfit she'd given me, donned my sandals, and put the linen dress and huaraches back in my pack. She had already made coffee on the one-burner propane stove and offered me a tin cup full of the steamy, flavorful brew. Now, she was expertly cracking eggs into a black skillet. We downed our breakfast on the patio in silence as birds twittered in the surrounding bushes and fruit trees. Suddenly, the long hoot of a foghorn cut through the pleasant morning.

"El patrón, he want us now," said José. He got up from his blue-painted wood-and-thatch chair and grabbed the string bag in which his essentials were packed. We bid adiós to Verónica, who looked resigned to José's absence.

"Verónica not worry that I am lost in the sea," José told me as we walked toward a modern-looking boat dock. "She say that Santa Juanita mark me for luck in the sea. You, too, she say."

"Well, that's a comfort." I didn't tell him that the only Santa Juanita I believed in was a large sea turtle who had improbably saved my life.

The Redeemer, all fiberglass and chrome, gleamed in the

morning sunlight. Now that I examined it more closely, I saw it had an enclosed cabin along with the canopied deck space. Three heavy-duty fishing rods were inserted in chrome tubes affixed to the deck at the back of the boat. A Mexican woman hoisted several heavy bags of groceries onto the deck, got onboard, and disappeared into the cabin. Nelson was talking to a local man who had arrived in a small truck with fuel for our voyage.

"There you are, José, little lady...ah, what's your name again?"

"Ana," I replied. "Thanks for this, Mr. Nelson."

"Yes, Ana. Why don't you go help Lupe in the galley so we can be underway as soon as the refueling is done."

I went into the cabin and found the woman I'd seen putting cans on shelves that had guardrails on them, to keep the provisions safe in high seas. The kitchen was tiny but had a two-burner hot plate and a microwave oven. I smiled at Lupe and asked if I could help.

"Sí, señorita," she smiled back and indicated some wooden cases that needed unpacking. She picked up a string bag heavy with linens and went out of the small space, presumably to make up the beds. I emptied the wooden cases filled with bottles of soda and water into a large cooler stowed below the microwave. The cans, mostly of soup made in the U.S., I placed on the shelves as Lupe had.

Some minutes later, Lupe told me, "Gracias," and, string bag now empty, walked to the back of the boat and stepped back onto the dock. The fuel truck had also disappeared. José was busy untying ropes and looping them in neat piles on the ship's deck. Nelson was at the steering wheel, checking the radio and various gauges. Soon, he'd started the motor, and we pulled slowly away from the dock.

He motioned me to sit under the canopy on the sea side of the boat and handed me a pair of binoculars.

When I finally figured out how to use them, I looked first toward the disappearing village of Mazunte. Everywhere, I could see evidence of building, especially close to the beach. It was true. Nelson was developing Mazunte into a resort. Soon, we were too far away from shore to make out anything clearly, though I noted that we were traveling northwest along the coast. I started as José tapped me on the shoulder.

"Look, Ana, this way!" He gestured toward the open sea.

I saw a spout of water rise up from the surface. "A whale?" I yelled at José over the noise of the engine.

He nodded and pointed and sure enough, I saw the back of the large animal emerge from the water and a flap of a huge tail before it disappeared under the ocean waters again. That sighting was the first of many, I soon found out.

"Migration season," Nelson yelled at me. "Humpbacks."

As the hours went by, other wonders of the sea made their presence known too, despite the loud thrum of the engines. Once we saw a large dorsal fin poke out of the water. "Shark?"

"Mola mola," my host yelled back. "Ocean sunfish." Later, José took over driving while Nelson and I had a lunch of Cokes, bags of chips, and ham sandwiches — the first I'd had since arriving in Mexico over six weeks ago now.

"Can't stomach the food here," Nelson said, his mouth full of bread. "So I bring all my provisions from Texas." He scoured a pile of magazines he drew out of a large plastic bag he removed from a cabinet below the steering wheel. He pulled one out and flipped through the pages. "This is what we saw this morning." He pointed out a strange-looking fish that had huge vertical fins sticking out above and below its oddly truncated torso. The diver swimming next to it in the photo gave me an idea of how huge it must have been. "Mola mola. I see them on occasion, but you two are lucky to see one, given you don't go boating often."

This is my first time," I admitted to him. "Unless you count the rowboat."

"Where'd you grow up, missy, to have never been at sea before?"

"Io...Michigan," I hastily retreated to my fake bio. Iowa had almost escaped my lips, though the motor noise was so loud, and he was only half paying attention to me as he flipped through the pages, so he hadn't noticed. "In the middle of the mitten, nowhere near the Great Lakes," I clarified further.

"Landlubber," he grinned. I nodded.

José called out and pointed in front of the boat. Dolphins of the *Flipper* variety, dozens of them, were leaping out of the sea. Soon, they were swimming alongside the boat, looking for all the world like they were playing in the wake and leaping up to see what was going on under the canopy. I flashed back to the TV show about a tame dolphin that I had enjoyed so much in my childhood and the library book on a young woman who studied dolphins I had found at the tiny public library in Hutton, Iowa, where I had actually grown up. If I'd had a dream of being elsewhere when I was nine or ten, it was swimming with dolphins, like the young woman in the book I'd read. Now, here I was, nearly living that dream, just a few feet away from actual, live dolphins. I shook my head at the irony of my life.

So the day went, José and Nelson taking turns steering the boat, me watching the horizon for the occasional astonishing sight. There were places where the waves were sizable, though not worrisome. There were places where they leveled out into a small chop. I didn't get seasick, I was happy to learn. I loved the salt breeze, the occasional spray, and the feeling that we were on an adventure, even if, to my companions, it was a familiar run. José stuck a line in the water and caught a two-foot tuna for dinner. He cooked it on a small grill he'd gotten out of the hold. The hold, stern, starboard, port, berth, galley. I slowly absorbed the words of ship life as Nelson spoke them. As it got dark, I discovered the boat had headlights and a lit navigating panel, though I couldn't figure out what the dials and gauges referred to.

The ocean calmed somewhat in the dark. While Nelson

was driving, José showed me my berth in the bow of the ship. It was a snug single bed with just enough headroom not to feel claustrophobic.

The steady thrum of the engine and the rhythmic slap of waves against the ship put me to sleep almost instantly. I dreamed I was flying second seat in a primitive plane, the kind that fought and flew in World War I. My long blond hair was flying in all directions, blinding me, and I tried to capture it in my hand so I could see better. Far below, a choppy sea. Suddenly, the engine sputtered. We began falling out of the sky. "Save me, save me!" I yelled to the helmeted pilot in the front seat. The pilot turned around, an impish grin displaying the little space between her two front teeth. Thorpe said, "The only way out is through, Jane. The only way out is through." The motor died and we started spiraling into the sea.

A soft rap on the door to my sleeping space. I shot up to a sitting position and hit my head smartly on the ceiling.

"Ana," José said in as low a voice as the engine noise would permit, "The lights of Acapulco are very beautiful. Come see."

45

Acapulco

The dark sea was dead calm. Only the boat's incessant throb broke the early morning stillness. The sun hadn't risen yet, but the sky was significantly lighter than the sea below. Both were gray in the dim light. A long way out to the west, dark thunder clouds. To the northeast, the lights of Acapulco shimmered their reflections on the dark water.

"In one hour, Acapulco," José said from the captain's wheel. He had throttled down from the speed we'd been going at last night, so he didn't have to yell to make himself understood.

One hour. That's how long I had to come up with a plan for leaving Mexico.

"José, will we go with Mr. Nelson to the airport to pick up his friends?" I asked, all innocence.

"No, Ana. We will put the boat at the *Club de Yates*. El patrón will take a taxi to get his friends. El aeropuerto is far away. We will walk to la estación de autobuses. It is ten-minute walk only from the boat parking."

"Will we have long to wait for the bus to Mazunte?"

"One hour only for the bus. But bus no stop at Mazunte. Twelve hour on the bus. After this, we wait for mi amigo Diego to come in the automobile to take us to Mazunte."

This seemed more impossible by the minute. I could take my own taxi to the airport. But what if it was small and Nelson saw me? What would I say? Besides, didn't I have to get my ticket before I went to the airport? I knew there were travel agencies to help a person with such things, but I'd never been to one.

José asked me to go knock on Nelson's cabin and tell him we would be in port in 30 minutes.

The three of us shared some eggs José had scrambled last night when Nelson had the wheel, warmed up in the microwave oven. I poured the coffee José had started on the two-burner stove earlier.

The sun came up over the horizon but was still hidden behind the mountains east of the city. I could pick out individual high-rise buildings by now, most of them white, many of them just off the beach. We pulled close to the yacht club's marina. Few people seemed to be stirring, just a few workers walking to their jobs. José jumped out as we sidled next to a slot marked with "Nelson" and secured the ship with the docking ropes.

"Hope you enjoyed the trip, little lady." We stood on the pier, saying our goodbyes. Mr. Nelson had apparently forgotten my name again.

"Yes, sir. It was great to see whales and dolphins and that strange fish — the mola mola. I really enjoyed it, thanks." I hoisted my backpack on my shoulder.

"José, I threw in a bit for bus fare for the little lady, here," Nelson said as he handed José a stack of pesos. "I'll see you back at the ranch in four or five days, depending on how the fishing is and if that storm yonder holds off." He waved in the direction of the clouds I'd noticed earlier.

"Yes, sir. Muchas gracias." José gave a little bow.

With that, Nelson strode off, heading for the street on the other side of the yacht clubhouse. Looking for a taxi. Looking for a taxi that I wouldn't be taking with him. To the airport.

Why was I so committed to keeping my escape to America a secret from these two? I wasn't sure. I suppose I didn't want to burn my bridges in case my plan failed. More likely, I wanted to avoid the disappointment on José's face as he learned I would be leaving him and all the kindness he'd shown me for an uncertain future. I told myself I didn't want to hurt him, but I knew it was because I was too cowardly to tell him the truth.

José started walking to the bus station. I followed, glancing around at my surroundings, as anyone new to a city might do. The bus station was in view when I spied a low-slung building with the large words "Travel Agency" written in English on a professionally painted sign above the door. Crucially, there was a middle-aged woman coming out of the open door below the sign. She had a sandwich board sign that she set out a few feet from the door. As we walked by, I could see that it said, also in English, "Bus, Train, Plane Tickets for all destinations, national and international, sold here." I had a chance, if only one.

We went into the bus station and José bought our tickets. The bus would leave in about an hour, he explained. It was early, so the covered waiting porch had many vacant seats. We found two near the edge of the porch that had a bit of a breeze. We sat.

I waited a minute, then said, "José, I have to use the baño." I got up, my backpack still slung over my shoulder.

He nodded and pointed. Fortunately, the bathroom was in the same direction as the travel agency.

As soon as I was out of sight, I doubled my pace. The door was still open and when I got to it, I could see the single woman I had noticed before sitting behind a counter. The place had travel posters, some faded and curling at the edges — Mexico City, Lima, Los Angeles.

"Uh, hi, do you speak English?" My voice was hoarse from talking over the boat engine.

"Yes, I do, young lady. What can I help you with?" Her accent was definite, but her pronunciation made me think she was almost as bilingual as Margarita. Margarita. I suddenly flashed on her. Would I never see her again?

"Uh, I have to fly to Washington, D.C., as soon as possible. Can you help me with that?"

"Certainly. There is a flight to Mexico City leaving later this morning. From there, it's likely there's a direct flight to Washington, D.C. Let me look for you." She got out a booklet and started flipping through the pages. "Yes, it says here Pan Am has a flight this afternoon at 18:00 hours, 6 p.m. I will call Pan Am to confirm before I make out the tickets."

She dialed a number and spoke rapid Spanish to the person at the other end. I could see by her nodding that the news was all good

"Yes, señorita, there is a flight today, and it has seats available. The flight to Mexico City also has seats. Will this be one-way or round trip?"

"One way," I said, feeling a sudden clenching in my gut. It was happening!

She did some calculations on an adding machine and printed out a strip of paper with the price on it. I would have plenty of funds to get there, I saw immediately.

"The price is good, yes?" she asked, and I nodded.

"Okay, señorita. I will make out the tickets for both flights. Passport please."

"What?"

"For the international portion, I will need a passport."

"Uh, I don't have one. I lost it. Can I get to the States with this?" I fumbled with the outside zipper, intending to show her my fake driver's license.

"Are you an American citizen, miss?"

I hesitated. Jane Meyer had been a U.S. citizen. Was Ana Jiménez? "Ah, I just got married to a Mexican man," I said.

"Do you have a Mexican passport? You will need a passport to fly to the United States by plane."

Of course, I would need a passport. In all my worrying, I had failed to think about the one essential item. A passport. "Ah, I lost it in the sea," I replied finally, repeating the lie Alex had concocted to get me a driver's license.

"I could put you on a flight to Mexico City with a driver's license or other form of identification. Perhaps you could go to the embassy there. They will help you get a new passport. It will take longer than a day, though, I'm sorry to say."

"Oh. Yes, of course, the embassy. Ah, let me think about it. Thanks." I beat a hasty retreat to the street and hurried back to the bus station.

My documents indicated that I was Ana Jiménez. I had a visa coming into Mexico, showing that I had once been in the U.S. But my driver's license and marriage certificate indicated I was a Mexican, with a Mexican husband. If I went to the U.S. embassy, what would I do to prove I was an American? If I told them my real name, I supposed it might be on some list of wanted criminals by now. If I used my fake name, they would find no record of Ana Jiménez — at least a blond one — at all. Possibly, I could get a Mexican passport with the license and marriage certificate. But I was pretty sure I'd have to produce Alex to make that happen. Women weren't exactly liberated in this country. I didn't know how to contact Alex. From what he'd told me, he was in Texas with his boyfriend. All the trouble to forge a new identity was for nothing.

José, fortunately for me, was snoozing gently in his seat when I returned.

Thorpe! If I didn't come, she'd think I had made off with her money. If I didn't come, she'd think I didn't love her.

If I did come, I'd have to sneak across the border, as I heard some Mexican workers did. I had no idea how hard that might be. Even getting to the border would take five days if I returned the same way I came. Then traveling to Washington from Texas — I wasn't sure how far that was, but I knew it was a half-continent away. By land, I was a week, ten days away from Washington, even if I could manage to get there on my own.

I looked over at José, my savior, my mentor, the loving father I'd never known. How could I leave him and all the people who had been so kind to me, so unquestioningly accepting of a strange blond girl with a crewcut? In my life, there had been so little love. At this moment, it seemed there was too much pulling me in opposite directions. Leave? Or stay?

An announcement over a tinny loudspeaker roused José. "The bus." He got up and shepherded me to a bus that looked more like the Greyhounds back in the States and less like the bus to Oaxaca from Puerto Ángel. I did not resist, letting him, finally, make my decision for me. A coward's way out. We got on with a smattering of other passengers. The seats were upholstered, comfortable, and could even be reclined a bit. José told me to take the window seat, and he sat next to me. "I sleep now," he said and soon drifted off.

The bus headed off on a well-paved road next to the coast. In twenty minutes, we passed the "aeropuerto" sign, indicating the place I wouldn't be leaving from today or any day. Thorpe! Her faith in me had been misplaced. I didn't have it in me to risk it all for love. I could have flown to Mexico City on the identification I had. I could have taken the train from there to Ciudad Juárez, made the illegal border crossing like so many braver-than-me Mexicans did every day. I could have figured out how to take a bus to Washington, D.C. and called her from there. But the pathologically passive Jane Meyer had apparently resurfaced and had gone along with existing conditions, as she always had. Even my one decisive act had been driven by what I thought Jenny would have wanted me to do.

I got the navy-blue handkerchief out of my backpack and quietly wept into it while José snored in the seat next to me. I didn't know if my tears were caused by longing for Thorpe or frustration at my own fearfulness and ineptitude. At my own continued failure. I blushed in shame when I realized there was another feeling lurking among all the rest — relief.

It was easier to stay in Zipolite, among accepting people, easier to stick with my small job of sea turtle researcher. Safer, too, than going out again to face the unforeseen but certain dangers of the wider world, especially the north-of-the-border part of that world, where I was a fugitive from justice. Where the unknown terrors of romantic love would find me.

Zipolite — that's where I should stay, was meant to stay, I tried to convince myself as the comfortable bus lumbered along the increasingly bumpy coastal road.

But fate — or at least Mother Nature — had other plans.

46

On the Bus

Eventually, we turned inland from the Pacific and made our way through tropical lowlands. Eventually, I ran out of tears and tried to wash them away with a bit of water from my canteen soaked onto an end of my handkerchief. Eventually, José woke up, opened his string bag, and retrieved the tamales Verónica had sent with him for precisely this purpose. We used the corn husk wrappers as our plates. The tender chicken encased in cornmeal dough was flavored with smoky, slightly hot pepper. Chipotle. Verónica had taught me the name.

"Excuse me, Ana, but I have a question," José asked after we had returned the corn husks to his string bag. "When Mr. Nelson and myself come to get the hurt turtle, you are with Alejandro. You hold his hand like Alejandro was your boyfriend. But Madre Hermosa say, and you tell me, you love Thorpe. I am confundido...." He trailed off, not finding the right word in English.

"Confused?" I guessed.

"Sí, confused. Do you love Alejandro or Thorpe?"

"Alex — Alejandro — is my friend only. He is a man who loves other men, like Thorpe loves other women." I wasn't sure why I had used her, not me, as the parallel case.

229

"But why did you...?"

"I wanted Nelson to think I would be staying here a long time, so he would let me keep the job. If I was involved with a Mexican man, he would think I would stay in Mexico."

"Ah, entiendo, mija." He thought for a moment. "Alex stands by your side. But Thorpe, she is in your heart."

I nodded and smiled. I guess that was one way of expressing the essential difference between a friend and a lover.

"Now, I rest again, but with no worry," José smiled over at me.

The day's light waned, but still the interminable bus ride continued. All day, I had focused on the lush scenery under an increasingly overcast sky, willing myself not to think about the failure that had led me to get on the bus instead of rushing to Thorpe. Now that the light's distraction had abandoned me, I found myself reaching into the backpack stowed under my seat and retrieving her second letter, the one with the unused twenty-dollar bills in it.

P.S. I'm assuming that guy on the bus was a joke, right? Right???

She'd chosen to have faith in me, with those few words, with the money she had sent. I'd repaid her faith by marrying Alex. The money she'd sent was sitting uselessly in my backpack. She'd understand Alex's desire to marry me. But Margarita was right. My reasons to marry Alex — he'd helped me out on the way to Zipolite and I hadn't been seeing anyone else — seemed woefully inadequate. I doubted Margarita had believed it. She had instead decided it was none of her business. But if Thorpe and I were a couple, as Margarita thought we might be, it was Thorpe's business. If I told her I needed a new name, new documents, she'd wonder why. If I told her I couldn't return to the U.S. — ever — she would rightfully demand to know why. The words she had spoken to me the last time I had dreamed about her came back to me suddenly — "Jane, the only way out is through," she'd said, pilot of our plane in the dream, as she surely was in our relationship's reality. But, in my dream, our plane had fallen out of the sky into the cold depths of the Pacific. Ending us definitively, as any truth-telling on my part would be bound to do. What kind of person would continue to love someone who revealed what I had to tell?

José suddenly started awake. "¿Dónde estamos?"

The bus driver heard him and answered in rapid Spanish.

"Okay, he say we are ten kilometers from where one road cross another and we must get off the bus. He say he not forget what I tell him before."

Soon thereafter, the bus stopped at the side of the road and disgorged the two of us. Down the road a bit, I could hear music and see dim lights.

"We go there to make the teléfono, have a drink, and wait for Diego."

It was a shabby little space with a dirt floor. I was the only woman present and all the brown male eyes in the place examined me closely as we entered. José noticed the looks, though he seemed familiar with the men. "Mija," he said and put his arm around me in a protective way.

Guffaws and what I took to be rude remarks flew in our direction from the handful of men sitting at tables behind their beers. I thought I even heard the word piojos — lice — flung in my direction. José fended off the comments, insisting I was his daughter. The guitarist, who had been playing a sad melody, had stopped and put his instrument down when we entered. Now he got up to greet José with a bear hug and an, "Hola, amigo."

He went behind the crude bar and out came a black rotary phone, two small glasses, and a bottle of mezcal. He poured while the two rapidly exchanged the news — I heard mention of Verónica, el patrón, and Juan Carlos. José dialed the phone, spoke into it briefly, and smiled.

"Diego will come to get us in the Jeep," he said to me. To

his friend, he said, "Por favor, toca más de música, Marco."

What followed was one achingly beautiful song after another. Marco sang with some of them in a soft, husky, rich voice. I saw to my astonishment that some of the rough-looking men in the little bar were openly weeping, and José, too, had tears in his eyes.

"When we hurt in the heart, we come to Marco," José said, surveying the scene.

Guess I was in the right place.

The music mesmerized me. Visions of Thorpe and me at the waterfall rose in my mind. I stared into my still-full drink so the men couldn't see the tears welling in my eyes.

All too soon, Diego arrived, and Marco got up to greet him as well. The spell was broken. He was offered, and refused, a mezcal. "El coche del jefe," he said, by way of explanation.

I sat in the rear seat of the Jeep on the drive back to Mazunte, head lolling from the tiring travel, ready for my little bed at José and Verónica's.

She had put a tall glass of cool water and an orange on the tiny table next to the bed.

In the morning, Verónica fed us a hearty breakfast. As I said my goodbyes and got ready to walk the road back to Zipolite before it got too hot, she grabbed me by the shoulders, looked at me seriously, and said, in her heavily accented English, "It come, mija, but be no afraid. Go to Madre Hermosa."

I had no idea what she meant.

47

Zipolite

For the first time since my arrival in Mexico, the sky was gray and there were dark clouds massing on the horizon. There was a humidity to the air and a chop to the sea. There were no frigates flying above me, no small birds twittering in the trees that lined the beach.

Stranger still, when I came up from walking the beaches to the rough road into Zipolite, the town seemed to be deserted. No one at the shell beach. No one at the restaurant, though it seemed as though it was still coffee hour. Finally, I spotted some humanity beneath the small stand of coconut palms where *La Tortuga* rested. I hurried toward them. Andy, Steven, Bill, and Dylan were gesturing at Zapotec men, who were discussing something among themselves. As I approached close enough to hear, one of the Zapotecs approached Andy, and the two exchanged some words. Andy was nodding and pointing and the Zapotec man was nodding and speaking to his comrades in the other language of Zipolite, the language of the Zapotecs.

There were seven boats, including my little rowboat, normally kept on the spit of sand under the coconut palms when they weren't being used. Most were a bit bigger than mine. All were propelled by rowing.

"Hi guys, what's up?" I asked those who understood English as I approached.

"Hey, Ana. We're discussing how and when to move the boats," Dylan answered.

"Huh?"

"Cuz of the hurricane coming."

"Some nasty dark clouds out there." Bill pointed at the darkening horizon. "And you can feel the barometer dropping."

"But it's going to be a hurricane, not just a storm?"

"That's what Madre Hermosa is predicting," Bill said. "She had one of the village men go out and look in the seagrass forest for turtles early this morning. Zero. No rays either. The men say they go out into the deep before a hurricane, so they don't get caught up in the surf when it comes."

The Zapotec men gathered around the largest of the rowboats and gestured for the Americans to lend a hand. The one who spoke Spanish told Andy to form a party for the second, somewhat smaller boat.

They would carry the boats across the road to where there was a crevasse in the hillside. They'd done it before, Andy said.

"We had one in August '77, the one and only year I stayed during the summer. There were only five boats that year. We stashed them in that slit in the hillside there, and they survived the storm just fine. Weird to be having a hurricane in May, so early in the season, but it happens now and again.

"Ana, why don't you start carrying the oars and buckets across the way?" Andy continued. The Zapotec men had walked the boat halfway toward the slit in the rock. The Americans and two Zapotec men gathered around the second boat and started hauling it to the crevasse, too.

I did what Andy suggested. First, I untied and flipped the remaining boats. I gathered three pairs of oars and walked as quickly as possible to the destination, setting the oars in the middle of where they would put the first boat. I ran back twice and took as many oars and buckets as I could. A Zapotec man saw what I intended — that we use the first boat to shelter the equipment — and he quickly collected the remaining gear. By the time we had placed the equipment in as tight a pile as we could manage, the Zapotecs arrived with the largest boat. Together, they flipped it over the top of the equipment. Andy and his crew arrived with their boat, which was flipped and placed in such a way that it began to form a wedge, fixing the boats into the crevasse. The other boats were hauled similarly and cleverly wedged into the slit in the hillside so that they were tight against both walls. Lastly, I took a side, and we carried *La Tortuga* across the track and into the crevasse. The men fit my small boat snug against a wall of the crevasse and another boat. Our work looked so solid that I wondered how we would ever get them extricated from being wedged into the narrow crevasse. Surely, they would be safe, so far from the beach. I couldn't imagine any storm being strong enough to come so far inland.

"Our last lunch here," Linda said later, and she scooped the usual onto her tin plate.

"What do you mean?"

"Madre said we would move inland before dinnertime and have dinner up there. We've been scrambling eggs and making tamales for the last couple of days, as it might be hard to cook for a while. And carting stuff up to the shelter."

"There's a shelter?"

"Wait until you see it, Ana. Interesting. Pack your bag and bring your blanket with you. We'll leave before the rain starts."

After lunch, I helped Linda, Andy, and Bill move the tables and benches under the shore side of the platform the restaurant rested on. Placed sideways, they could be wedged under one side of the plank platform we'd eaten on and danced on these past two months. The grills were closed and roped to the rough log pillars that held up the roof. The pots and pans were moved into Madre's small hut across the track under the banana trees. A portion of the tin plates, cups, and utensils were packed in baskets to take along to the shelter.

When the restaurant had been secured as much as possible, I went to my hut. I was still packed from my two-day trip to Acapulco, so all I did was add my books to my backpack and dig up the $40 I still had buried under the nightstand. At the last minute, I took one of my two pairs of jeans, thinking I could use them for a pillow. I left my snorkel and mask, fins, sneakers, raincoat, sweater, and the other pair of jeans. I couldn't imagine needing any of them. As Linda had instructed, I draped my blue blanket over my shoulders.

I heard a small commotion outside my door. It was Juan Carlos, still in his school uniform, and out of breath from running up the hill to my hut. "Hola, Ana, I am glad to see you," he said in his accented but well-enunciated English. "I have a message from señora Margarita. She say señorita Angelina call you yesterday on the telephone. She say she will call again, not tomorrow but the day after tomorrow at two o'clock. Señora Margarita say you come to her before this time, and she will take you to the house of her father. The telephone is there. Not tomorrow. The day after tomorrow."

"Muchas gracias, Juan Carlos. But will the storm be over by the day after tomorrow?"

"Only God knows this, my cousin." He smiled shyly at me. "But all will be good in the cueva. You will come, señor Andy, all the americanos, and my people, too. I go to help my mother now!" He scampered off down the hill.

Cueva? I didn't know that word in Spanish.

I stood in front of my hut, looking out to sea. The Pacific Ocean had grown dark, the sky above even darker. The wind was up — my empty hammock swayed and the thatch above me fluttered noisily. I saw Linda and Andy heading down the hill. I touched the door of my hut as if to strengthen its resolve and started down the path to join them. Our small group of Americans, only thirteen of us now, gathered in front of the closed-up restaurant. Madre Hermosa emerged from her hut under the banana trees, chaining her door shut as we had done and clicking on the combination lock. Right behind her was Juan Carlos.

"You stay with my people. Come," she spoke the longest English sentence I'd heard her use. She raised her arm to indicate we should follow her. We started up the path to the waterfall. But where it forked, she went right, not left to the falls. We were headed to the village in the jungle Lily had told me about.

48

With the Zapotecs

It was a longer walk than to the falls, and all uphill. That might be better though, farther from the hurricane's power. I expected a modest cluster of thatched huts, but when the jungle gave way to a clearing, I saw that the Zapotecs of Zipolite lived amid a half-grown-over ancient city that had some of the same features as the ruins of Monte Albán that I'd seen with Alex in Oaxaca. There was evidence of a high cut-stone pyramid structure, with the top cut off. Along its ground-level perimeter, an intricate design carved into the stone wall was still visible where the jungle hadn't covered it. In front of the ancient structure, there was a large area cleared of trees. Though it didn't have rows like in the Midwest, I saw immediately that it was a vegetable garden. One that had been recently harvested, by the looks of it. Behind this structure were other ruins of more modest dimensions. Current dwellings had been remade with a mix of ancient stone and recent adobe. Carved, intricate geometric designs decorated the outsides of several of them. Some of the entrances had wooden doors; others had colorful textiles hanging from ancient wooden lintels.

Madre led us around the back of the ruined pyramid. As she passed, she called out in the language of the Zapotecs.

Grandmothers carrying infants, mothers and fathers laden with baskets filled with provisions, girls and boys holding their younger siblings by the hand, emerged from their homes and walked behind Madre. There was a hush of serious purpose; not even the babies or the several small dogs that accompanied us made a sound. Their homes looked sturdy enough to survive a storm, but, evidently, we were sheltering elsewhere. Madre entered the jungle on the far side of the village, and we fell into single file behind her on the narrow path. A five-minute walk and we came upon a cliff edge overlooking a lush ravine.

Madre pointed to the left. Amid the trees and ferns, I made out a dark hole — the entrance to a cave, five feet high and similarly wide. Cueva, that must mean cave. Some rough-hewn steps had been cut into the sandstone in front of the hole. Madre took a flashlight from her apron pocket and climbed the stairs. "Cabeza, cabeza," she said, pointing to the low overhang, and we tall Americans ducked as we entered. The hole opened to a small room. We turned on our flashlights and Dylan mumbled, "We're not going to all fit in here." After making sure none of us hit our cabeza on the low entrance, Madre walked to the front of our group and continued toward a pitch-black slit in the cave wall. It was barely wide enough for a single person to pass through; my backpack got stuck in the narrow passage twice and Bill, who was behind me, had to wrestle it free. The passage was twenty or so footfalls long and, suddenly, we were in an immense room. The ceiling was covered in stalactites drip drip dripping their mineral water onto the cave floor, where it made red-streaked white flowstone, stalagmites, and columns. I flashed back to why I knew what I was seeing, back to the Time/Life book in the Hutton library, *Life of the Cave*. I had devoured that book as a child, entranced by the blind albino salamanders and fish, the mineral formations that had grown for thousands of years. But until this moment, I had never been inside of one. A long aaaahhh of wonder escaped my throat as I took in the ceiling adorned with crystalline icicles. The mostly level floor had plenty of space for villagers and Americans alike. Most astonishingly, there was a sizable pond in one corner of the vast room, and it bathed the cave in a ghostly blue.

"Agua fresca para beber," Madre pointed to the pond.

"Think we'll start glowing if we drink that stuff?" Bill commented.

Madre started organizing the nearly 100 people, giving each family or couple a spot on the floor to call their own. Another area was set aside for our provisions. I saw that many baskets of food had been brought here prior to our evacuation. Madre pointed to another crevasse behind the pond. "Baño," she said, shrugging her shoulders.

I took out my blanket and spread it on an unoccupied spot, and took my folded jeans out of my backpack to use for a pillow. I now wished I had brought my sweater. The cave was cooler than I thought any place could be in this hot part of the world. I got up and walked over to the provisions area, intending to help the women organize the food they had carried here, but they shooed me away with a smile. One young woman with a small boy at her side insisted I take the serape she offered. I was already feeling a chill, so I accepted the loan gratefully. I went back to my spot.

"Wanna play cards?" It was Linda, with another woman, Alice, who I hadn't really gotten to know these past months.

"Ah, I don't know how."

"We'll teach ya, not to worry," said Alice, with a strong Minnesota accent. "How about Hearts?" The two women got their blankets, and we formed a circle. Soon, a second Zapotec woman approached and offered Linda and Alice serapes as well, which they also accepted. The men had started a poker game a small distance away from us.

"I was here for the last big one," Linda said. "But I still forgot how cold a cave is. Nice place to wait out the storm, though, especially with that glow-in-the-dark cave plankton providing light. And yes, ladies, you can drink it."

We played cards for a time. The Zapotec women lit candles in terracotta holders like the one I'd left in my hut and distributed them around the room. They organized and delivered our picnic dinner, tamales with a squash and beans filling. We filled our canteens in the blue pool. The water was a bit salty but palatable enough. In the evening, one of the Zapotec men played guitar and others in the group sang along. One of the Zapotec men had gone to the entrance and returned with a tale of wild wilds and sideways rains. But we were safe here in the cave.

"How long will the hurricane last?"

"A day, 36 hours, two days at the outside. Madre said they brought food enough for two days." Andy had come over to retrieve Linda. "Let's see if we can get some sleep, hon," he told her.

"'Night, ladies," Linda nodded at Alice and me and headed to a close-by spot in the cave. Alice soon retreated to her spot with her boyfriend or husband — Kevin, I thought his name was. Leaving me alone to think about the phone call.

Not tomorrow, but the day after tomorrow. According to Andy, the storm would likely be over. Thorpe would be expecting me to be at Margarita's parents' house to talk with her. And what would I say?

I tried a practice call in my mind. The pleasantries, a bit about the storm on my end, a bit about her research on her end. I'd say, "Thanks for the money, Thorpe, that was so kind of you. But I can't come back to the States." She'd say, "What do you mean, Ana, you can't come back? Is it your turtle job keeping you there?" And I'd say, "No, I don't have a passport and I can't get one." She'd say, "What? Why not?" That's when I'd have to say, "Because if I tried to apply for one, I'd be arrested." She'd say, "Arrested? You? For what?" I'd say, "Thorpe, I'm a murderer, and my name's not even Ana — it's Jane." She'd either hang up or wish me eternal damnation and then hang up.

Could I possibly have a conversation with her without giving my reason for not coming back? I could say, "I'm committed to staying here, Thorpe. I'll try to get the money back to you." But she'd think I didn't care about her. Or I could try, "I love you, Thorpe, but I can't go back to the States, ever. Don't ask why. Could you come back here?" But then she'd know that I had a major secret. She'd come back here if she could, if she really did care about me as much as Margarita and Madre Hermosa thought she did. But how long would we be together before she would rightfully demand to know why her girlfriend was so geographically limited? We'd be back to the essential conundrum: If I was honest, she'd learn I had murdered; if I had murdered, how could she love me? If I didn't tell her, how could she love me, because she wouldn't know the real me? It all led to the same place. Thorpe couldn't love me, couldn't love the real me. She was in love with a lie. I didn't want to hurt her, but it would be better to just break it off now, before we got any deeper into this. I couldn't be Thorpe's love, or anyone else's either. I was permanently, inextricably tainted.

49

Zipolite

The storm had passed. The man who had been assigned to assess the weather told Madre, who told Andy in Spanish, who told us in English.

We gathered up our belongings. We tourists went to help carry the now mostly empty food baskets back to the village, and this time our offer of help was accepted. Andy and Bill volunteered to clean up the baño area by taking buckets of water from the pool and sloshing them into the crevasse where we had reluctantly gone to do what we had to do. "It's the least we could do," Bill said. "They sheltered us, they fed us, and they introduced us to this glorious cave. That's worth a lot to me." Andy nodded his agreement.

When we squeezed through to the small front cave, I found myself at the rear of the group of tourists. I saw that it was here that the villagers had brought the donkey that carried our soda and beer from Puerto Ángel, recognizable because one of her ears didn't stand up straight. Six black pigs snorted noisily, and an assortment of chickens squawked in terror as we walked by. The Zapotecs behind me began basketing the chickens as they caught them. The pigs were leashed with braided fiber ropes around their necks and prodded toward the entrance. One of the boys grabbed our donkey's bridle and talked quietly to her as he pulled her forward.

Our group walked back on the path leading to the village. It was strewn with leaves and small twigs, but no worse than the thunderstorms I'd been through in the Midwest had produced. The village, too, when we came upon it, seemed quite intact. One large tree had fallen, but it had not landed on a house. The place was filled with leaves, some of them plastered to the outside of the houses, but again, nothing that would take more than a couple of hours to put right. Madre Hermosa spoke rapidly to a few of the village women, gesturing at us to wait. Soon, Madre in the lead, we started down the path toward the sea and our little enclave, Linda, Alice, and I, waving goodbye to the Zapotec women who had fed us and loaned us their serapes. The closer we got to the beach, the more of a beating the jungle had taken. Some of the trees had lost nearly all their leaves. We had to pick our way through a tangle of upended foliage, or sometimes scramble over fallen trees.

"¡Ay Dios mío, ay Dios mío!" I could hear Madre Hermosa exclaiming from my place behind the rest of the tourists on what was left of the narrow path. As the others emptied out of the path and on to the beach, I saw what nature had wrought. Looking toward the Pacific, it looked beautiful; deep blue waters and an expanse of pristine caramel-colored sand under a cerulean sky. I realized I was looking at the spot where the restaurant used to be. It was completely gone. The track leading to Puerto Ángel was now a part of the beach, all the ruts of the rugged road filled in with newly deposited sand. A few palm stalks were still standing, though not a one had any fronds. I looked toward the place where Madre Hermosa's welcome and storage hut had been. The hut and the lush grove of banana trees around it had been reduced to a tangle of refuse, some of it identifiable as part of what had been the restaurant. I spied one of the tin drums we used as the bottom of our cooking grill, battered and twisted, half-buried in the sand and 50 feet from where it had been. A few tin plates were visible in the tangle of brush. Almost nothing else was recognizable. I looked at my companions of these last weeks. Some were slack-jawed, staring at the entirely new landscape. Others, including several of the men, were openly weeping.

I willed myself to look up the hill toward our cluster of huts. The entire cliff had been scoured out. The terraces where our huts had been built had been obliterated. Along the far edge of the massive hole the storm had made, I saw the pile of debris that contained what remained of our huts. Roped stick bits that had once been hut walls were piled up haphazardly. Bits of color in the pile of broken huts proved to be the remnants of hammocks or clothing we tourists had left behind. I noticed a light blue bit and walked over to the ten-foot-high stack of refuse. Tangled in among the sticks and parts of trees, but whole and salvageable, was the sky-blue sweater I had worn the night I killed Johnny. I gently disentangled it from the pile of sticks and rope.

Everything else — my refuge, my home these past two months — was no more.

Zipolite was gone.

I'm not sure how long I stood there, apart from the others, staring at absence. I felt shock so profound that it drained all emotion from me, like the hurricane had washed everything I was or had been in Zipolite away, just as the might of the storm had washed away all humans had made.

I felt a hand seek out mine. "Oh, mi prima Ana," Juan Carlos looked at me with fear and sadness in his eyes, "How will we live now?"

That snapped me out of my fugue state. The Zapotecs depended on our modest payments to pay fees for their children to attend the Catholic school in Puerto Ángel. Juan Carlos had told me that, though Madre Hermosa ran our little tourist enclave and collected the money, proceeds were shared among the Zapotec villagers. The village men fished for our dinner and one of them drove the donkey cart to Puerto Ángel for our beverages every few days. But the Zapotecs lived communally, sharing what they caught, what they grew, what funds came their way from the turistas they allowed to live in Zipolite. Without us, the twenty or so school-aged children, including my cousin here, would no longer be able to go to school.

"Let's go see if the boats made it," I said, mostly to give the both of us a project to focus on. We walked the few minutes to the crevasse where we had stashed the boats in silence. The sand was a bit damp but not wet, so the walking was easy. As we approached the crevasse, my heart sank. The boats were not visible, as palm tree parts and other former jungle plants were stacked in front of the opening. Juan Carlos saw a way to scramble up the twisted branches and get a better view of the crevasse. He looked for a long time before carefully picking his way back to the ground.

"I could not see them very well, Ana. Too many trees are on them. I could not see *La Tortuga*." His face was full of pain.

That was when the tears over all this loss began to roll down my cheeks.

We walked back to where the others were assessing the devastation and trying to find useful items from our previous life here. Juan Carlos told his mother the uncertain news about the boats.

Linda and Alice had started scavenging the area where Madre's hut had been. Plates, tin cups, and even the occasional fork or spoon started to appear. I pitched in, glad to have something useful to do. Andy and Bill emerged from the forest. We let them have a moment to take in the extent of the damage.

"Someone's got to walk to Puerto Ángel today," Andy said soberly. "And see how bad they got it."

"We will," said Bill and Kevin, who set off immediately. They were gone most of the day and returned nearly empty-handed. The villagers had given them a string bag of candles, dry matches, and a bucksaw. But that was all.

"The part of Puerto Ángel near the water, where the grocery store used to be, where Margarita's and the bank used to be, was leveled," Bill reported. "Señor Mendez, his wife, the kids — they're all missing." We were all silent for a moment, absorbing that news about the grocer and his family.

"They got nothing left but big debris piles, just like us." Bill continued. "Some buildings on the mountain road made it. But they have no electricity. More importantly, the bus to Oaxaca got seawater in its engine and is probably ruined. And the worst news is that a couple of guys with gas and a working car tried to go over the mountains. The road at the first hairpin fell right into the ravine. Not even enough of a ledge left for a person to pass through on foot. We are totally cut off."

50

Zipolite

It had been late morning by the time we'd gotten to the beach. While the men went to Puerto Ángel, all but a few of us relocated to the crevasse where the boats were located and started trying to dismantle the tangle of vegetation. We had no gloves, no saws. Most of us didn't even have proper footwear. It was slow-going. After a couple of hours of painstaking work by nine of us, the pile of debris looked little different than it had before.

Madre Hermosa and Juan Carlos had taken Linda and Alice back up to the village to bring food and help. Just as we were too famished to continue, the four of them returned, followed by two Zapotec women and eight Zapotec men. The women carried plantains and bananas and a large clay pot of beans. The men brought water, rope, and most importantly, a bucksaw. We stopped to fill our stomachs and thank our benefactors, and went right back to work, with new help from the village men. Even with so many hands, the work was frustratingly, grindingly slow. We worked until it grew dim, and stumbled up the path to the village, where Madre said we would stay for now. For dinner, the villagers and the Americans shared a kind of corn mush with a flavorful squash mixed in. We were shown to a sizable airy room with half-walls, poles made of raw tree trunks and a partially damaged thatch roof. It looked like a gathering space in need of repair from the storm. We all still had our Madre-provided blankets, and most of us stretched out on them and fell immediately to sleep, so exhausted by the day's exertions and emotions were we.

I had a better pillow than most, what with my blue sweater adding to the jeans pillow I'd had during my nights in the cave. Yet sleep eluded me. Tomorrow was the day I was supposed to speak with Thorpe. But Puerto Ángel had no electricity, no phone service. Margarita's fruit drink stand was gone. What about Margarita herself? When would I even be able to find out her fate? A sudden thought had me on my feet, flashlight at the ready, searching for the way out of the pavilion.

"You okay?" It was Linda, her voice groggy with sleep.

"Yeah, thanks. Just have to check on something."

I left the building and went toward the sounds of people speaking in low voices. A dozen Zapotecs, the community's elders, I saw in the flickering of the small fire they sat around. Though she wasn't an elder, Madre Hermosa was there, too. The group fell silent as I approached.

I went directly to Madre Hermosa.

"Por favor, Madre Hermosa. ¿Verónica y José — ellos están bien?" I couldn't believe I hadn't asked if they were okay, hadn't thought of them before. Surely the twin sisters would have felt each other's minds during this trauma.

Madre Hermosa looked up at me from the low stool she was sitting on. "Sí, señorita Ana. Ellos están bien. Se escondieron en el hospital de tortugas. El hospital de tortugas es muy fuerte." And she made fists with both hands and raised them to her shoulders. They had sheltered in the turtle hospital. It had survived, and so had they. I was sure that's what she was telling me. "Acuestate ahora." She said with a smile and waved me back toward our sleeping area. "Mañana, Mazunte."

"Muchas gracias, Madre. Muchas gracias!" At least they

were safe. I was depending on some telepathic connection between the two identical sisters for this information, but whether because I'd seen it work before or because I suddenly couldn't bear not knowing if they were okay, I believed Madre Hermosa. When I crawled back onto my blanket in the pavilion, exhaustion, both physical and mental, finally overcame me and I fell into a deep, dreamless sleep.

We did not walk to Mazunte in the morning. The rutted track on that side of what used to be Zipolite was buried in sand, too, just as the piece of the road near our now-disappeared enclave had been. Juan Carlos and I, the two designated to go to Mazunte, tried to walk the beach route, as I had so often in recent days, looking for injured turtles and, before that, hand in hand with Thorpe. We didn't get far. About a twenty-minute walk toward Mazunte, Juan Carlos and I came upon a massive landslide that extended from what had been a familiar cliff all the way into the sea. It, like everything now, had a huge pile of tangled tree limbs and palm fronds on the side facing us that would have to be climbed over before we could start our way up the massive hill of sand and rock. Nothing looked stable enough to climb on. Juan Carlos thought we should swim around the part of the landslide that was in the water. We might have tried, but the sea was still windblown from the storm, with sizable waves. Not knowing what awaited on the other side of the slide, I hesitated to attempt it. What if this was the first of many slides and we got trapped between them, too tired to swim back? Better to help the others unbury our small fleet of boats today and make the attempt in a boat tomorrow.

"Is there enough food in the village to feed us all?" I asked as we made our disappointed way back to the salvage operations the others were attempting.

"Yes, Ana. We have much corn, much beans in our village.

We can eat for many days, I think! And the chickens, they still lay the eggs."

When we returned with our dismal news, we saw that a fire had been built, and a metal pot brought from the village was set among the embers. A battered tin plate was next to it with a half dozen eggs. "Boiled," Linda explained as we approached. "The hens just started laying again. They were traumatized by the storm, too, I guess." In the large pot was more of the corn mush we had for dinner last night. A bowl of corn mush and a half an egg was our lunch that day.

Appreciable progress was evident when we later went to help with the boat debris pile. By the end of the day, we could see that all our efforts were for naught. The boats were there, all right, but every one of the seven small crafts had sustained catastrophic damage. *La Tortuga* had been reduced to a pile of boards, I saw with horror. My little rowboat was no more, as was my job counting turtles in Zipolite.

The Zapotec men discussed the situation for some time before one who spoke Spanish came to relate their thinking to Andy, our best Spanish speaker.

"He said they would try to use the pieces to make new boats, but that would take several days at least. There are a few oars that made it, though, and even a bit of fishing gear. But it looks like it's corn mush and eggs until we can get something seaworthy. There won't be anything to catch from shore this soon after the storm. Everything that can goes to the deep water to ride it out. And the sea's still too rough for diving."

We continued to dismantle the debris pile, and by sunset, we were removing parts of boats from the crevasse and hauling them to an empty spot on the beach where the Zapotec men would work. Tomorrow, the village men told us, they would come with saws, hammers, drills, screws, and nails. In a day or two, at least one of the boats would be seaworthy.

Again, we climbed the trail to the village. Other Zapotecs had cleared the major obstacles from the path, and it was quite navigable.

Again, we had corn mush for dinner, though the women had also cooked some beans and rice.

"Who would have ever thought I'd consider frijoles y arroz a luxury item?" said Andy sardonically, and I agreed. Best tasting beans and rice ever.

Again, we laid on the blankets that were our only remaining link to our heavenly hammock nights, when we had used our cradle-rocking ropes to sway through the night while a gentle breeze kept the mosquitos away. Here in the village, smoking bundles of herbs and corn husks did the job. But it was nowhere near as pleasant as our hut nights had been.

Again, sleep eluded me. I had well and truly missed my phone call with Thorpe by now. I wasn't sure what the phone on her end did when it connected with Margarita's out-of-service phone. Was there just silence on the other end of the line — or did it ring and ring with nobody picking up? Did she know that there had been a major storm here? That seemed unlikely. The weather news on television was mostly local and Thorpe didn't seem like the type that watched TV in any case. She would think I didn't care enough to be there, or worse, that I didn't want to talk with her.

I had failed to leave Zipolite when I'd had the chance. Even if I had made my way to the border, without a passport, I would have had to wade across the Rio Grande in the dark of night and wend my way through the Texas desert like the migrant workers did. There were always stories in the newspaper about people dying in the desert who had attempted that. Still, I could have at least tried. Those weeks with Thorpe — had there only been two? — had been the happiest of my life. Why didn't I try harder to continue them?

I was afraid I wouldn't be able to keep my facade intact. That was part of it. The closer we'd become, the more it had started to slip. It was as if I was on stage, play-acting someone else's life twenty-four hours a day. It was tiring, daunting, especially when the other party was trying to get to know me, trying to get closer. Rather than simply experiencing love and longing, my feelings were all mixed up with guilt for deceiving her and fear that she'd find me out and reject me, as would be her right.

There was a deeper level to the fear. It wasn't all about being found out. I knew I also feared that, eventually, whether it was Ana or Jane, I would be revealed as unworthy of Thorpe's, of anyone's, love. Not knowing if that was definitively true was why I could go on, damaged as I was. If I got too close to someone, if they knew the real me, it would kill that little glimmer of hope that lived inside me. The one that promised that, despite everything, I was capable of being loved, when every fiber of my being said otherwise. Lying Ana or truthful Jane, either way I was despicable, damaged beyond repair. Somewhere deep down, I didn't want Thorpe to be the one to prove to me beyond doubt that I was permanently broken, forever unlovable. That promised to be pain beyond anything I could bear.

I guess I fell asleep despite these thoughts, because the next thing I was conscious of was Linda poking my foot with hers as she stood above me.

"Time for another day in paradise, Ana," she sighed.

The chickens had started laying at normal rates again so we had scrambled eggs today and corn mush again, though the portions seemed slightly smaller than the day before. The Zapotec women waved away our offer of clean-up help, so we Americans left for the beach to see if we could help with the boat rebuilding or if there was any more to salvage from the restaurant or storage hut.

As we came out of the leafless jungle and onto the sand, we all cocked our heads in unison. "Do you hear it?" Linda whispered, only half-believing what her ears were telling her. I nodded. The sound grew louder, and the source of the noise came into view. Madre Hermosa dropped the load of driftwood she'd been gathering and ran toward the beach, waving her arms wildly.

Above the noise of the boat, I heard her screaming, "Veróni-ca! Verónica!"

I squinted to see and there was Madre Hermosa's twin waving frantically from the boat, there was José in the straw hat I'd never forget waving too. Behind the wheel, a big white guy, leather-burned from years of sun, was steering the boat closer to the shore. *The Redeemer* had come to save us.

51

Zipolite

There were a couple of other people in the boat, but the full weight of my attention was on José putting the anchor out, José unclipping the little dinghy *The Redeemer* was dragging and bringing it alongside the bigger boat, José helping Verónica and Mr. Nelson into the tiny rowboat and José making toward the shore with all the strength he could put to the oars. Verónica leapt from the craft while the water was still above her knees and ran through the water and onto the beach as fast as the wet sand allowed. When the sisters met, they clasped each other tightly for a long while, leaned back to look the other in the identical face, then clasped again. Juan Carlos practically threw himself into his uncle's arms and I could see José smiling and wiping the tears from his eyes, tussling Juan Carlos' black hair, hugging him again. I started running toward them, too, tears streaming down my face at the sight of José, the man who had twice saved me now.

"Mija, mija," was all that José was able to say for quite some time as we held each other. "With my own eyes," he said next, looking me in the face. "I must see mi hija with my own eyes." Verónica and Madre Hermosa came to where Juan Carlos, José, and I were standing, and Verónica let go of her sister for a moment while she gave me a hug and a tear-stained smile.

"We do the talk," she said, nodding in the direction of her sister. "I know. Is okay. But..." she hugged me again. I had the strangest feeling, an emotion that caused copious tears to roll down my face. These people, who looked nothing like me, who came from cultures I hardly understood, were nevertheless family to me. I cared about them as I had no one else in my life, except Ma. I loved them. And as improbable as it was, it seemed they loved me too. Not señorita Ana, the liar. Not Jane Meyer, the profoundly damaged killer. But the real me, the girl that had retreated to some deep place long ago, that had been locked up there all these years. Somehow, they had seen through my disguise, had recognized the core of me. And found value there, had found worthiness there.

"I know you are sad," José had said to me half a lifetime or just a short number of days ago. "But you are not bad." For this moment, I felt the truth of his words in my very bones.

Madre and Verónica were making the rounds of the Zapotecs, Verónica hugging her friends and relatives from the village. She looked around at the extent of the devastation and shook her head in sorrow.

"I must go back to the boat," José said suddenly, disentangling one arm from around my shoulder and the other from around Juan Carlos. "There are other people who wish to come to the shore."

As I looked at José walking to where the dinghy had been pulled up on the beach, I felt a hand on my shoulder.

"Well, there, little lady, I am *shore* glad to see that you are well. And all the other Americans here, too. That long-haired feller over there" — he pointed over to where Andy was speaking with the Spanish-speaking Zapotec man I had learned was named Pedro — "told me all about how the Indians sheltered you up in the cave yonder and fed and housed you — that was mighty Christian of them. Don't you worry none, though. I've got provisions on *The Redeemer* for the Indians. You Americans, I'll evacuate to Mazunte later today." Mr. Nelson had it all worked out.

"Did the road survive there?" I asked, just to have something to say.

"The Lord works in mysterious ways, little lady. Mazunte got some wind, some rain, too. But it just wasn't as exposed as Zipolite here. Most of the town is back from the shore a piece, just like my place. We had some trees down, some thatch ruined. But, thanks to yours truly, we had a good road in, and it survived intact, more or less. Just a few places need patching. We are still connected to the rest of the world."

"That's good news," I said. "I tried to get there yesterday, but there was a big landslide..."

"Yessiree, I saw that on the way over here. Nothing that some decent road-building equipment couldn't handle in a couple of days. As I said, the Lord works in mysterious ways. I was waiting for an opportune moment to press the government on the idea that the road to Mazunte needs to go all the way to Puerto Ángel if they ever want to see a decent passel of American tourist dollars coming their way. This is that moment. If we put in a good road through Zipolite here, I will commit to rebuilding the whole place. Not like it was, of course, but with decent tourist bungalows, restaurants, the whole nine yards. The hurricane taking out those shacks you lived in was the best thing to ever happen to Zipolite, of that you can be sure."

I tried to smile and nod my head, but my insides were clenching, and I thought I might start crying again. I excused myself to use the makeshift baño — just a hole with a couple of pieces of hut remnants around it on the beach side to offer a bit of privacy. I did what I had come to do, picked up the bar of soap someone had put in a scallop shell, and poured a bit of water from the bucket there over my hands. Zipolite! My refuge, my solace, the community I'd come to treasure, was well and truly dead now and would be no more. I couldn't imagine how Linda and Andy, how Frank and Kathy, how Lily, how Thorpe would feel when they found out about the destruction of the hurricane and Nelson's development plans. Some of the people I'd met here had built their lives around this place. What would they do without it? What would Madre do without it? For that matter, what would I do without it?

"Ana! Are you in there?" It was Juan Carlos. "You must come right now!" The voice was insistent.

I emerged from the screen just as Juan Carlos was about to break in on my privacy.

"What is it?"

"Shut your eyes, shut your eyes!" He commanded and grabbed my hand. He walked me a few paces and let my hand go. "Bye, bye!" he cried, and I heard him running across the sand back to where the others were talking.

I opened my eyes.

"Hey, Ana. You didn't think I'd fold just cuz of a little hurricane, did you?"

Thorpe wrapped me in her arms and kissed me deeply and with such relief and longing and tenderness that I knew Margarita had been right — I was in love.

52

Zipolite

Our kiss, our embrace, went on and on. I never wanted to let go. I never wanted to be out of those strong arms again, never wanted to stop pressing my lips on Thorpe's. Finally, she released her arms, put her hands on my shoulders, and backed up a foot so she could look me in my teary eyes.

"Guess ya missed me a little, huh, Ana?" She smiled, and I remembered how much I loved the little gap between her two front teeth. "Wasn't sure after that strange display with the guy off the bus and you not hopping on the next flight when I sent you funds. But I thought, 'I betcha she's scared.' And when Margarita's phone went down, and I called my buddy at NOAA and he told me about the early hurricane here, I was the one who was scared. So, damn what's happening in the States. I had to come right away and find out. I had to come and find you, Ana." Thorpe was tearing up herself now. "You okay, truly?"

I nodded. "But how...?" I couldn't trust my voice.

Thorpe shook her head, trying to get control. She swallowed a couple of times and looked out toward the Pacific. Not looking at me helped her to regain her composure. She took off the navy baseball cap she'd been wearing, visor backward, and her hair, a bit more unruly than when I'd seen her last, swirled around her face a bit, reminding me of the first time I'd sat with her at the best-view table. When I'd given her my hat to wear.

"That first day, when you and I and José walked to Zipolite? I know I seemed exhausted, but I was paying attention. I remembered the name of the Texan José said you both were working for — Nathan Nelson. Such a good ol' boy sounding name, it stuck. So, when I couldn't get Margarita or you on the phone, I thought, 'How can I find out what is happening down there?' Nelson's name came back to me. About umpteen hours later, I found how to connect to his number. He wasn't home, but one of his staff answered the phone. Fortunately, he was in Acapulco with his boat and the guy at his house — Diego — knew how to contact the Yacht Club. I called there, arranged to speak with him finally, and told him my tale. The guy loves to play the hero, I could tell that right away. So he said he'd wait if I caught the next flight out. So, on to Mexico City, then Acapulco. Met him at the Yacht Club and we started off right away. We stopped to pick up José and his lovely wife, Verónica, who I am predisposed to love because she looks just like Madre Hermosa. They were so worried about you, Ana! Verónica and Madre have this telepathic link somehow, so Verónica was sure her sister had survived. And of course, Verónica grew up in the Zapotec village, so she knew everyone would shelter in the cave. She kept saying on the way here, that of course Madre would take the turistas with her to the cave, that you all were safe. She kept saying, 'I do not sense any death in Zipolite.' But seeing is believing." Thorpe turned to look at me. "I think she and José were worried that you would be traumatized by the storm. How are you, Ana, with Zipolite wiped off the map and all?"

"I don't think I really believe it," I said, looking to the scoured-out cliff where our huts used to be. "I keep thinking I'm hallucinating, that if I blink a few more times, it will be as it was." Then I said the most truthful thing I'd said to Thorpe about my past. "Strange as this sounds, Zipolite was the first place that felt like home I've known in a long time." I guess I *was* traumatized. Zipolite had been the safest spot I'd ever fallen asleep in. But how must Thorpe feel? "You, and Linda and Andy, all the old timers — you all must be devastated, huh?"

"It's tough seeing for myself that it's all gone. If I hadn't come, I could pretend it was still there, and I just hadn't gone there in a while. All the way here, Nelson had to go on and on about how it was a blessing in disguise, how now it could be rebuilt the American way, by him, of course. And all the 'Indians,' as he called them, could get decent work waiting on a better class of tourist. If he hadn't been the only reason I was able to get here so quickly, I would have decked him and thrown him overboard as shark bait."

"Yeah, he told me about his plans. It's all so sad." I was threatening to well-up again.

"You know, though, Ana, I've been living outside most of the past ten years. Nature does change things up unexpectedly and life must adapt. And does. That is the most important thing I learned doing the work I've been doing. We have to look at this like that. The time has come to adapt to our new circumstances."

"I hope the waterfall is okay. I haven't been up there since it happened." As I said this, I started to blush.

"We'll go there later. Best that we see what's up with the waterfall together, huh?" At this, Thorpe kissed me tenderly again and my body quaked with an aliveness I hadn't felt since she'd left. "But now, Ana, let's go find the friend I brought along. You'll like her, I think, and she was a real pal when I was freaking out over the phone about how I couldn't get ahold of you. She told me, 'Well, Thorpe, let's go find her.' And she dropped everything and came with me."

We walked to where most of the others were still chatting. I could see a small figure speaking with Nelson. My body suddenly turned to ice. I started trailing, but Thorpe grabbed my hand and walked up to where the others were gathered in an uneven circle.

"Here she is, finally." Thorpe was saying. "I'd like you to meet..."

"Jane?" Maddie said and moved toward where I was trying to cower behind Thorpe. "Jane, is it you?"

53

Zipolite

Maddie. Maddie Haystead. Professor Maddie Haystead, who, until six or seven weeks ago, had been my teacher, my mentor, even a bit of a friend during my suddenly truncated graduate school career. Even in sunglasses and a baseball hat, it was undoubtedly Maddie. Her slight frame was clothed in a t-shirt, shorts, and sneakers. Her distinctive brown curls were twitching in the wind despite her headgear. Most damning of all, her maroon hat had my former university's logo on it. It was undeniably Maddie, and she had undeniably recognized the woman formerly known as Jane Meyer. Me.

"No, Maddie, this is..." Thorpe was trying to interject, but Maddie and I, sunglasses off, stared at each other for a long moment.

Busted. I unclasped my hand from Thorpe's. I didn't dare break the lock Maddie had on my eyes to look at the woman I loved. I suddenly felt exhausted, like my shoulders had borne a huge weight for an eternity. I started sinking to the sand, hoping, willing myself to lose consciousness. But my farmgirl toughness would have none of the wiles of a damsel in distress. I didn't faint. I opened my mouth, closed it. What could I possibly say to either of them? The conversation around us had died until all that was left was the hush of anticipation and the lap, lap, lap of the water hitting the shore a few feet away. The small cluster of people Maddie had been standing among included most of those I had come to love since arriving in this improbable place. They wanted to know what was going on.

"Sorry," Maddie said, finally breaking the alarming silence. "You look a lot like someone I used to know." Her eyes, though, revealed that she absolutely knew I was Jane Meyer.

"How strange," Thorpe said as if from a great distance, though she was standing right beside me. "Maddie, this is Ana; Ana, Maddie." She looked from Maddie to me, her face a question.

Maddie stuck out her hand. "Nice to meet you...Ana." She nodded her head in a way that made me understand she knew perfectly well that Ana was not my name.

I couldn't find enough breath in me to have a voice, so I took her offered hand, gave it a brief shake. My head may have nodded. I felt strangely disconnected from it.

José, who had been observing this odd scene, sensed that I and this woman new to him had something we needed to talk about. "Señorita Angelina, please, let us go to the big boat and make the start to bring food to the people." He extended his arm to the now-empty fishing boat.

Thorpe wrested her eyes away from her friend and her lover. "Yeah, sure, let's do that, José." The two walked down toward the dinghy.

"Shall we stroll a bit, Ana?" Maddie said in the authoritative voice I remembered so well from the methods class I had taken with her only weeks ago. She started walking toward Mazunte, away from the clusters of people discussing how our rescue would proceed. I somehow got my wooden limbs unstuck from the sand and caught up with her a few yards on.

The first thing she said to me was astonishing.

"Do you love her?" She looked over at me, sunglasses back on, hat brim hiding most of her face.

Tears rolled down my cheeks, but all I could do was nod. Somehow, my breath wasn't sufficient to make words.

She nodded in acknowledgment. "There's that to consider."

We walked on the damp sand toward Mazunte in silence for a few steps.

"You came here because of me, didn't you?" she asked as we walked out of earshot. "Because of that story I told you about coming here when I was in graduate school."

I sighed audibly. I wasn't sure she heard it, or if the sound was washed away with the waves.

Maddie continued. "That makes me somewhat responsible for what's happened — between you and Thorpe, I mean."

"What?" I found enough voice for that. "No. This has nothing to do with you."

Up ahead, I could see the massive pile of debris, rocks, and dirt that now blocked the way to Mazunte. Maybe I'd try swimming. Maybe I wouldn't get there. Maybe that would be fine. Surely better than the situation I found myself in. We walked a bit closer to it in silence.

"How'd you find out about Jenny?" She asked another shocking question in a conversational tone, as if we were not discussing matters of death and betrayal. "I hadn't seen her in years, since she was a young teen. But I did see her at the funeral. I got a good look at her as she and her mom, Liz, were following the casket down the chapel aisle. I almost had a heart attack when I saw her face; she looked just like you."

My legs suddenly did betray me, and I sank to the sand. Maddie stopped walking, came to where I miserably huddled, trying to disappear into myself, and sat down next to me. Maddie spent a few moments straightening her hat and sunglasses. A few more looking out to sea. I spent that time hyperventilating until fainting was a distinct possibility. Maddie stared at the icy sapphire Pacific, waiting for an answer.

"He left his wallet in my chair cushion one night and I looked through it. There was a photo..." I couldn't go on.

"Jane," she said, deciding to call me by the name familiar to her. "I saw that you tried to call it off. I saw you avoiding him. I saw him moping around. It's a small department. Not much goes unnoticed. But what happened?"

This weight on my shoulders was too much to bear. I suddenly thought of that dream I had on the boat, the dream where Thorpe was piloting our plane for two, the dream where she turned to me and said, "Jane, the only way out is through," right before the plane went into a nosedive and crashed into the ocean with both of us aboard. The only way out is through. I had no idea what she had intended with those words. But now I saw what she meant, and the Thorpe in my dream was right. I'd been trying, desperately trying these past two months, to run from what I'd done. I'd run away from the scene of the crime, but also from myself. Tried to make Jane, Ana. And in so doing, I'd lied to everyone who had shown me kindness, been a phony with everyone who loved and trusted me. It was a hopeless approach. The only way out is through.

If I were ever to get rid of this burden, if I wanted to go on instead of ending it in the alluring cold of the Pacific, I would have to tell someone the truth about me, the whole truth. Here sat the perfect confessor. She knew Johnny, Jenny, Thorpe, and most especially, she knew me. At least a little.

I decided to start there. "You know, Maddie," I said, my voice finding strength as I decided to use it to tell the truth for once. "The night I saw the photo, I had a dream that Jenny and I not only looked alike, but we were also alike in a crucial life-altering way."

"What way, Jane? Tell me."

"That for both of us, it was our fathers who first did to us what men do to girls…" I faltered. I looked at Maddie, imploring her to understand.

She did. "You mean rape, Jane? Is that what you mean? That your father raped you? That Johnny raped Jenny? Father-daughter incest, is that what you mean? It was a habit with the two of them, your father and Jenny's?" Her voice had an anger to it, a horror to it, that I'd never heard anyone sound like before. There was a pause. "You'll forgive me if I tell you I'm not surprised. In either case."

"What?" Not surprised? I reveal my deepest, darkest secret and Maddie wasn't even surprised? She wasn't surprised that her colleague engaged in such things?

"Jane, I could tell you were deeply traumatized by something — or someone — from the first moment I met you. I'm sorry, but it was obvious to anyone who truly looked at you, who truly saw you. I didn't know by what, of course, but the hair covering your face, the loose clothes, your palpable embarrassment at taking up space, never mind speaking up, well, it suggested a sexual trauma of some sort.

"And Jenny, — well, that makes a whole lot of sense, now that I know Johnny's despicable backstory."

"Sense?" I wasn't making sense of this at all. How could she say that what Johnny had done to Jenny made sense? But before I could find the words to ask, she said the most astonishing thing of all.

"I wish I had had the courage to do it myself, that fucking bastard."

54

Zipolite

"It's not like I think murder is a good way to solve problems. I'm basically a peacenik — I went to every damn Vietnam war protest I could. But..." Maddie paused for a long while, nodding to herself, like she'd come to a decision. "I have a story to tell you that only a few other people know. But first, what happened, Jane? How'd Johnny wind up dead and you on the lam?" She asked so matter-of-factly, as if it was a what-did-you-do-last-weekend kind of question.

I shook my head at my utter stupidity, thinking Johnny would be a safe pick for a relationship. It was embarrassing to admit, especially to someone I admired, as I did Maddie. But I knew I had to get it all out now or I never would. I drew a deep breath and looked ahead at the endless blue while I spoke. "I never had a date, Maddie, never had anything with a man except..." I paused and sucked in a fear-filled breath as a sudden flashback of one of my father's attacks came rushing back. I girded myself and continued. "I thought it might be better to see a married man. It would be sort of a low-risk test run — to see if I could stand being with a man...that way...after what had happened to me. And he wanted me so much. I didn't know why at the time, of course. It was nice to feel wanted, surprisingly nice. He seemed like an unstoppable force. And he was my advisor, so I was afraid to say no. But really, I didn't want to say no. I thought it would be low-key enough for me to handle..."

"I wish you had confided in me, Jane. It's never a good idea to sleep with your graduate advisor — that's what I would have counseled. But I can't blame you for not doing that — we hardly knew one another. Last fall, I knew Johnny to be a narcissist and blowhard. Annoying, but tolerable. I had no idea..." She let out a long sigh. "So, when did you find the wallet?"

"Three months ago or so. He came over to my place and it must have fallen out of his back pocket when he was sitting in my reading chair. I found it after he left for the evening. I returned it the next day. But the plastic photo folder fell out and got stuck in the chair cushion. I found that days later. I couldn't help but look at it. If I hadn't, I suppose I'd still be a graduate student now. Oh, Maddie, it hurts so much not to be in school!" I shut my mouth quickly, but not before a sob escaped. I paused to take a deep breath, another. I fought for control, found it, and continued.

"As soon as I saw the photo, I knew, I knew it was his daughter. And there was a photo of the three of them, so I knew for sure. I took it out of the plastic shield and the back was signed. That's how I learned her name. I decided right away to stop seeing him. It was horrifying to think he was attracted to me because I looked like his daughter. I felt so... dirty...for what I had done. It made me feel so small, learning that it wasn't me he was interested in at all. I thought it was just a dirty old man's fantasy — him wanting to..." I hesitated but spit out the word I was thinking "...fuck someone because she looked like his daughter. But that night I had a dream that her eyes were the same as mine, held the same secrets as mine. I still believe that — I know, it's based on nothing but a dream, but..."

"Hmmm, not very scientific, Jane, but I might have a piece

269

of evidence to suggest you are on to something. Later though. Continue, please."

"I tried to avoid him, and for a couple of weeks I was successful. I thought I would stick it out for the rest of the semester and try to transfer somewhere else. But his wife Liz went to visit Jenny at college for the weekend. Ironically, that was what enabled him to stake out my apartment and accost me when I came out to do some shopping. He looked so miserable in the pouring rain that I agreed to meet him later at his office. Why, oh why did I agree to that?" Tears were streaming down my face as I contemplated the many errors that had led to now.

"So, you met him Saturday night..." Maddie prompted. When I looked at her for how she knew that, she said, "Coroner's report. The details got all over campus. It took them a lot longer than it took me to finger you for it, mostly because they had a hard time believing a 'young girl of medium build' could possibly have had the strength to do what you did. They did interview me about you, but all I said was that you were shy, and I hadn't known you very well — true enough."

"I kept the photo of Jenny. I brought it with me when I went to his office. I confronted him with the photo. He could tell I thought he was only interested in me because I looked like his daughter. He had always insisted on calling me Janey and I finally realized how much that sounded like Jenny in his Texan accent. I think he was worried I'd blow his cover and tell his wife or Jenny herself or the entire department, though actually I was too ashamed to ever admit how stupid, how gullible I'd been to anyone. But he was nervous that I would tell, I think. He tried to insist that no, it was me that he loved. He tried to show just how much he loved me by trying to conduct our sordid business right in the office..."

"Wait, he tried to force himself on you? Jesus."

"Maddie, Jenny was deep inside me by that point. It felt like she and I were one and the same person, sharing a body.

So, when he tried to violate me, us, I couldn't let that happen to her, to me, to us. The pair of scissors was right behind me on the desk he had me up against and I..." The nightmarish scene came back to me in all its bloody detail, and I couldn't go on.

Maddie put her arm around me and we sat there in the sand, she, holding me tight, me sobbing and gasping. I'm not sure how long we sat there, rocking back and forth a bit, Maddie offering a protective arm.

"Jane, you killed a vile rapist. Johnny's a rapist and has been since he was fourteen years old. I live with the proof of that every day."

55

Zipolite

Maddie's strange claim shook me out of the memory of that night, the memory of all that blood, the memory of the shocked look on his face in the seconds before his lifeforce bled away. "What proof do you live with every day, Maddie?" My voice came out in a croak, but it was audible over the lapping of the waves. The bright blue sky still filled our view, the black silhouette of a frigate soared high above. The indigo Pacific still spread out in its endless way to the horizon, unknowing and uncaring that it had caused a few humans to lose their treasured community.

"Roz," was what Maddie said next, confusing me further. She continued. "Jane, I'm out to very few people because Texas is not a friendly place for people like me. Gay people. Lesbians. That's what I am and have been for as long as I've known what a lesbian was. Roz is my partner in this life — we've been together for more than ten years now and I hope to be her love until the day I pass into the great beyond. Last summer, Roz left me. She had found out something about herself that she thought I couldn't understand and shouldn't be burdened with. So she left. It wasn't until months later that she came back and told me what she had found out."

I wondered what this had to do with anything we had been talking about before. But Maddie was determined to tell her truth, too.

"It's complicated. It's fraught with our peculiar history in the United States. Our history of slavery, I mean. Roz is Black. Her ancestors were enslaved in Texas before the Civil War. Her brother Jerry, who is a lawyer with the NAACP, had done some research and found out something quite startling. Roz's people had been 'owned'" — she said this with a venom that made the word a curse — "by none other than Johnny Wharton's people."

"Wow, that is strange..." I began, but Maddie cut me off.

"Way more awful than merely strange, Jane. Some of Roz's cousins still worked at the old plantation house where Johnny grew up, taking care of the grounds and Johnny's grandfather, who raised Johnny and still lived there. When Roz's mom — her name is Grace — was a girl, she would go and stay with the cousins for a few weeks as a sort of vacation. The summer she was fourteen, the same age as Johnny — there's no easy way to say this — Johnny raped her. Worse, it was part of some sick ritual that all the Wharton men participated in when they were fourteen — raping a Black girl. In slavery times, it was a kind of enforcement and continuity ritual — a demonstration that the 'Young Master' could do as he liked with the people he 'owned' just as his daddy before him had done. Our country comes with a totally immoral history, Jane. No other way to parse it."

A lightbulb went on inside my head and I knew where this was heading. "Roz?" I asked.

"...is Johnny's daughter via the rape of Roz's mother. The love of my life not only is the child of a rape, but a rape committed by the same man you killed. We both found out who her father was a few short months ago. So, you can understand why I said I wished I had had the courage to do it myself. Excuse my French, Jane, but the world is a better place without that sick fuck in it."

This was not at all the reaction I had imagined from Maddie, or anyone else, to my admission. It seemed like Maddie might think my act almost deserved congratulations. "Taking someone's life can never be acceptable, can it?" I asked my mentor.

"Nah, you're right, Jane. Murder is a terrible thing 100 percent of the time. In the abstract, at least. It's funny how one's core commitments can get washed away when confronted with a specific case. Both things can be true at once, though. Homicide can be wrong 100 percent of the time, but still justified in a specific case. The rapist was raping you, Jane. I'd call it justifiable homicide. But only the goddess knows if a Texas jury could be convinced to see it that way. There's a big difference between philosophizing about good and evil and the letter of the law in a place as backwards as Texas. Not sure I'd turn myself in if I were you."

"Has Roz been able to adjust to learning about where she came from?" I was looking for a profile in courage.

"Surprisingly, these past few months have been good for her. Grace and Roz got even closer than they'd been before Grace told her. Once Roz told me all about it, we were able to get back on track too, even though she's right — in some deep sense I can never really understand how it must feel to be Roz. But I can still support her, still love her — that's what I told her. Roz decided to tell her mom about our relationship, but it turned out that Grace had already seen that we were more than just friends and accepted us. That was such a relief for both of us. So, yeah, I think Roz has been able to deal with it, because knowing the truth and everyone sharing the truth has led to all of us feeling closer than ever."

"The only way out is through," I couldn't help but say the words Thorpe had said to me in my dream.

"Ain't that the truth," Maddie replied. "True in the historical sense and the personal sense. We've got to come clean about where we've been if we are ever to move on."

"Oh, Maddie, how am I ever going to come clean with Thorpe? She'll hate me."

"No," Maddie said. "She won't. She's got a big heart. She already knows something's not right with you. When we were discussing you, she said to me, 'She's so sad about something, Maddie. Traumatized by something. I hope she'll come to trust me enough to tell me someday.' Literally, that's what she said to me. You've got to tell her, Jane, and now's the moment. Tell her."

The sound of a woman clearing her throat made us look up.

"Am I interrupting something, ladies?" Thorpe smiled her gap-tooth smile, but her face couldn't hide her concern. "You know each other, don't you?"

56

Zipolite

Surprisingly, I was the one who answered. Courage — or was it desperation to salvage something from these past two months? — had given me a voice. "Yes, I knew Maddie from before I came here. I came here because Maddie told me Zipolite was a paradise. Which it was." I looked down the beach. In the distance was a sandy gouge where my protective village of huts used to be. My lip quavered, and tears threatened, but I shook my head to ward them off and continued. "There's a lot you don't know about me, Thorpe, a lot I've kept hidden from you. No more." I let out a deep breath, and it seemed as if my shoulders weren't bearing such a heavy weight any longer. "Maddie, I'm going to take Thorpe up to the waterfall. I hope you don't mind staying here on your own for a bit." I looked at my former professor, who was nodding in affirmation.

"That's the ticket, Ja...Ana. I'll go see what's up with the others and let them know you will be a while." Just like that, Maddie got up and walked off, leaving the two of us alone.

"I'm carrying this canteen, Ana. Let's go right now before Nelson decides to evacuate us. I have to see if the waterfall and pool survived. Besides, I gotta, gotta know what's up with you two."

I stood and the two of us walked back to the recently cleared trail. Until we came to the fork, it was easy walking. No one had yet been to the waterfall. The trail was cluttered with leaves and branches and an occasional tree trunk, as if the hurricane had just occurred. We silently picked our way up the trail, clearing small branches, crawling over the few larger barriers in our way. By the time we got to the ledge with the trickle of spring water, the going had gotten easier. The trail was sheltered by a cliff on one side nearer the pool, and it had provided shelter from the storm. By the time we reached the last bend in the trail before the waterfall became visible, I was confident this piece of our Eden had survived intact. I was not disappointed. There were leaves in the pool that wouldn't have been there otherwise, but not a tree was down. Even our purple blanket canopy was still standing. The water cascaded like before, but with more volume from the rain the hurricane had deposited. I turned to Thorpe, who had atypically followed me up the trail. Tears were streaming down her face.

"I know I said I try to take nature's changes as they come. But I don't know if I could have survived if this place had been taken by the storm, too," she said softly. "It's taken on so much meaning for me recently."

No mistaking her meaning — or her look. I reached out my hand and gently brushed her tears away. I began a lingering, tender kiss, possibly a last kiss, with this good woman.

A long moment later, she broke away, took my hand, and we walked around the pool and over to the canopy. It was shady and cooled by droplets from the falls, but it was far enough away from the noise of falling water that we could talk in normal tones. She sat crossed-legged, patting the woven mat next to her, indicating I should sit, too.

"So, tell me, beautiful woman, what the hell is going on?" She smiled an encouraging gap-tooth smile. I could see in her look of love that she was confident that whatever I was about to tell her would not change what we had together. A feeling I did not share.

I wondered where to start and realized it probably didn't matter much. So, I said, "Almost everything I've told you about myself is a lie, including my name. It's Jane. I'm on the run, Thorpe. I've done a terrible thing, and I came to Mexico to hide out. If I go back to the States, it's quite likely I'll be arrested."

There was a silence on Thorpe's end as she contemplated my words. "What kind of terrible thing?"

Here goes. "I killed a man."

"Whew. Seriously? Who?"

"He was my graduate school advisor — at the same university Maddie's at. I was a student in her department. She was my professor. So was he. That's how she knows me."

"Why? There's gotta be a good reason, right? What was it?" There was a bit of panic in her voice now.

"I never planned to kill anyone. But I had to stop him from hurting Jenny again. It had to stop." If there had been any reason at all why I murdered, I knew it was wrapped up inextricably with a woman I'd never met, but who shared my face. Though weeks had gone by since I'd had the dream that convinced me that Johnny had done to Jenny what my father had done to me, I still believed it. I was sure of it.

"Ana...Jane...whatever your name is, you're not making any sense. Who's Jenny? How was this jerk hurting her?"

I took a moment to collect my thoughts, to let the rational part of my brain resurface. "If you cut it down to the essentials," I said slowly, feeling my way back to the origins of all this mess, "it's all about incest — father-daughter incest." I had never uttered those words before, never even dared to think them.

Thorpe reached for my hand and cradled it in both of hers. "I knew there was something like that in your life."

"I grew up in Iowa, Thorpe, not Michigan. On a farm though, like I told you. Only child. My father was a failed farmer...."

"That's no excuse," Thorpe interrupted.

"I know, but that's what started him drinking and beating — and raping — my mother. I turned twelve just when he had the ultimate work disappointment. The day he got fired was the first time he attacked — no..." I was fighting for control now, fighting to not fall off a cliff into a ravine of darkness, "...the first time he raped me. But it wasn't the last. He came at me regularly for almost five years until I came home from school one day and found him dead. I was seventeen. I never told Ma what he'd done. Her life was tough enough. I had no friends; he didn't allow either of us friends. So, I never told anyone anything about this until this morning. This morning, I told Maddie. And now, you." I felt both lighter and more exhausted than I'd ever felt in my life at this admission.

Thorpe gave my hand a little squeeze. "So sorry, kid, so sorry.

"I thought if I left Iowa, I could leave it all behind. So I applied for graduate school in Texas. And met Johnny. The man I killed." I braced myself for the next part; somehow it was harder to admit this to Thorpe than to admit murder. "He wanted to have an affair with me. I said yes, even though I knew he was married. I thought it would be a good way to see if I could be with a man...that way...despite what my father had done." I paused, seeing Johnny's eager face when I'd said yes to his proposal of an affair. To think I'd been flattered. But I had been, and I wasn't about to shrink from that fact now. "Pretty dumb, huh?" I risked a glance at her.

"No. It sounds like a survival strategy to me."

"Hmmm, never thought about it that way, but you could be right. I was trying to ease into what I thought could be a pseudo-normal life for myself — you know, career, lover, a future. What a stupid plan!"

"Don't keep knocking yourself. What happened to you when you were a girl wasn't your fault."

"It's easy to say that, but damn, it's hard to believe it." I realized the truth of my words as I said them. Deep inside, I did feel it was my fault. I wanted to press on, so I pushed that thought aside for now.

"Johnny accidentally left his wallet at my house one night. I opened it. It had a picture of his daughter in it. Her name was Jenny. She looked like my twin."

"Whoa, that's heavy. What a bastard. Getting his rocks off on a look-alike instead of his...wait..." Thorpe trailed off. "Where was Jenny at this point? How old was she?" Thorpe was figuring it out.

"She had left home for college in Madison the year before. I guess he got lonely."

"You're saying he raped Jenny just like your old man raped you?"

"He insisted on calling me 'Janey' — which sounds a lot like 'Jenny' in Texan. I only have a dream as evidence that that was what was going on. But to this day, I believe I'm right. There was something in her eyes, even in the photograph, that convinced me."

"Damn. But you said you didn't plan it. I would have — what a slimy bastard. What did happen?"

I told her what I had told Maddie a few hours — or was it centuries? — earlier. About my confronting him with the photo of Jenny. About his attempt to force himself on me. About me reaching for the red-handled pair of scissors. About going back to my studio apartment, the one with the gas heater, intending to end it. About Jenny coming to me in a vision telling me to get up out of the gas fumes that were about to overwhelm me, to get up and get the hell out of there and run away to Mexico. "There's more I have to tell you," I concluded, "but that's pathetic Jane Meyer's life in a nutshell."

"I'm going to call you Ana," Thorpe said. "Ditch Jane. Start over. Be Ana," she advised.

The way she said it, it sounded like she thought we'd know each other in the future, and she'd have occasion to call me by name. A frisson of pleasure and heart-clenching pain drove me straight out of my memories into the present. I heard the rush of water as it tumbled into the pool. I heard birds twittering in the branches around us. I felt the moisture on my face, not from tears but from the sheltering canopy above us, keeping us cool in the midday heat.

Suddenly, she dropped my hand, put both of hers on my shoulders, and looked me straight in the eyes. "Wait. What did you say that jerk's name was again? Was it Johnny? Was it the same Johnny that raped my dear friend Roz's mom all those years ago when she was a fourteen-year-old girl? Maddie told me all about it on the way here."

I nodded. "I just found that part out this morning from Maddie."

"That's where he got the taste for fourteen-year-olds, I'll bet," Thorpe concluded. "First Roz's mom, later, his own damn daughter. After she fled, he tried to legitimize it — in a fashion at least — with a daughter lookalike that was at least over the age of consent." She paused, still looking me straight in the eyes. I didn't — I didn't want to — look away. "Guess I get why you didn't hop the first plane when I sent you that money, Ana." Then she said the strangest, most wonderful thing of all. "You can stop running, now, Ana. You're with me."

57

Zipolite

"With you?" I looked at her, wondering if she had developed a sick sense of humor during our weeks apart. "Thorpe, didn't you get what I said? I'm a murderer — and a fugitive from justice, too."

"Justice." She was still looking right at me from an arm's length away. "Let's just say I have a rather jaundiced view of that concept. He was trying to rape you. Arguably, that's all he ever did to you. It's not like you would have consented to the relationship had he told you why you appealed to him."

"True enough," I admitted.

"So, he's a rapist at least three times over. He raped Roz's mom. He raped his own daughter, for god's sake. Probably for years. More recently, he raped you. So, the guy's a serial rapist. He should have been locked up long ago. But that hardly ever happens. Men just do what they want and go on their merry way to the next victim. I don't generally believe in the death penalty, even for rape. But as I see it, you did mete out a sort of cosmic justice. Possibly, it would have been better if you had just cut off his balls with that pair of scissors. Or his dick. But, in the heat of the moment, you didn't think of those distinctions."

"It's still murder."

"In self-defense. Yeah, thou shalt not kill. I get it. Still, in my book, it was justified unpremeditated homicide. That's the way I see it. I don't see you as a murderer, Ana. I see you as a woman who stood up for herself, and Jenny, in a moment of crisis. Too bad that jerk is dead, but if he had respected women, none of this would have happened."

"You...you...don't...hate...me?" I was blubbering, gasping, tears pouring out like I'd never cried before.

She stared at me. "I love you, Ana. Don't you get that by now? I came back for *you* — no other reason. Your past was a horror show — all of it, until you showed up here. But that's the past. We live in the now, the future. To me, that's what matters."

"How...how can we have a future? I can't go back. You...you can't even visit me here because there *is* no here anymore!" I was choking, almost yelling.

Thorpe looked at me, her face calm to my hysterics. "I got some ideas about that. But first, let's have a swim." She stood, stripped, and dove into the pond.

I stared at the ripples spreading out from where she'd disappeared. Halfway across, she surfaced, turned her head back towards me, and said, "You coming, or what?"

Suddenly, I could think of nothing I'd rather do than strip off my clothes and follow her into the welcoming cool of the pool. As I disrobed, I noticed a lightness to my body, as if the clothes had been made of lead and being freed from them had returned me to my original weight. I dove in and let the cool water wash the tears from my face, the fears from my mind. She loved me. She loved me. I repeated the mantra with each stroke I took toward her.

No matter what my future, I would hold the next hours close to my heart always. Our longing for one another had only grown with time and with my confession. I could tell, as Thorpe and I made love under the purple canopy, amid the mist from the nearby waterfall, that there was no hesitation about touching me, life-taker though I was. For my part, there was the deliciousness of her knowing who I was and still loving me. There was an incredible lightness to my body now — every physical movement came to me with grace and ease now that I had unburdened myself to someone at long last. And the someone still said she loved me, still showed she loved me. Our little spot of Eden here above our ruined village had not merely been reclaimed — it had been made anew as if two new lovers had discovered it. I cherished, I relished, every moment, every touch. In the back of my mind, I knew we'd have to part soon. In the back of my mind, I knew I had yet to tell her about Alex.

Many minutes later, we untangled our limbs. Gazing at each other, we kissed tears of relief from each other's faces. We were still connected, only now it was clean and true. She knew me. Yet still loved me. It seemed a miracle. A profound sense of joy and well-being suffused my body, my heart, my mind. I'd been a child the last time I'd felt those feelings.

"Let's go see what's going on at the beach. I almost feel guilty for spending so much time up here." Thorpe kissed me. "Nah, I don't." She smiled.

She got up, dressed, and offered me a hand. "Come on, my beautiful Ana, back to the world with us." We gave the waterfall a last quiet look before heading down the trail.

Juan Carlos was sitting on a log at the place where the waterfall path met up with the one to the Zapotec village. He was reading an English-language comic book with Superman on the cover and smiling to himself.

"Hola, señorita Angelina. Hola, prima Ana. Madre, she tells me to wait for you here. You will stay with us in the village tonight. Tomorrow, señor Nelson, he will come back with his boat and bring more of everything for our village. He will take you to Mazunte with him tomorrow. He takes the other tourists today."

We ate dinner with the Zapotec villagers. Thorpe spoke emphatically with Madre Hermosa, Pedro, and the smattering of other adults who spoke Spanish. The children listened in. It was evident they all understood Spanish. I could tell they were speaking of the schoolchildren, and how they would pay for Catholic school now that there would be no tourists. Thorpe was reassuring them that señor Nelson would pay for several of the men to work for him in the coming months. She had spoken to him about it on the way here from Mazunte yesterday. Madre Hermosa left the gathering and soon returned with a small clay pot with a tight-fitting lid. When she pried it off, she reached her hand into the jar and withdrew a sizable stack of American dollars. These she counted in front of the gathering. "Okay, money for school," she said to Thorpe in English. "No problema."

More talking ensued and during a time when Madre was translating the conversation for those who spoke only the Zapotec language, Thorpe translated for me. "They have more than enough for the remainder of the school year and for about half of the kids for the fall. Nelson will gladly pay the rest in wages for some of the men here to help him build new tourist bungalows. He told me he already owns the land — that when he inquired, the government said 'nobody' owned it, and he was able to get legal title to the whole swath for 'a song,' he told me. Which I bet translates to a bribe. He hopes to have a new Zipolite built by December, when the winter tourists start to return."

"Don't the Zapotecs own Zipolite?" Something about this didn't seem at all right.

"I suppose no one from the village ever asked the government about it. They've been here for centuries. They probably think it is their land to use and live on. It's only in Juan Carlos' generation that the Zapotecs will become educated enough about the way Mexican government works to protect themselves. And by that time, it will mostly be too late." Thorpe was shaking her head sadly. "I did talk to Nelson about this on the way here. He promised he'd never kick them out of the village and that he would give them jobs in his newly planned tourist enclave. Sadly, that's probably the best deal they'll get — working for a gringo patrón as some sort of indentured servants. The modern world sucks, Ana."

That night, we slept in the pavilion that we'd been meeting in earlier in the evening. Since all the other Americans had departed with Nelson, we had the place to ourselves. It was time I brought up the other subject I'd been afraid to speak with Thorpe about: Alex.

"You know that guy you saw getting off the bus the day you left Puerto Ángel?" I asked, my voice soft, blending in with the chirpings of the night creatures. A lit stub of a candle gave our sleeping area a soft glow.

"You mean the one who proposed to my girlfriend in front of a busload of locals? So you do know that guy? I was hoping he was just some sort of comedian, using you as his foil."

"His name is Alex Jiménez, and I met him on the way down here. He could tell, somehow, that I was on the run, though I've never told him any bit of it, even now. But he was so helpful to me." I told her about the visa he got me from his cousin at the border, about being my companion all the way to Oaxaca, about how he got me on the bus to Puerto Ángel and even came to visit me in Zipolite. "Thorpe, you're not going to like this, but when I told Margarita about it, she said you'd be okay with it. I hope she was right." I took a deep breath. "Alex is gay. His family was harassing him about not getting married. So he was looking for a bride of convenience that he could take home and show off to his family, so they'd get off his back. Alex could see I was looking to start over, so he asked me to be that bride. His family would stop pestering him and I'd get a new name. So my name is Ana Jiménez now and on paper, I'm married to Alex. He even got me a Mexican driver's license in that name."

Thorpe was silent for a long moment. "I noticed he was a handsome guy, Ana. You sure there's nothing more to it?"

"He's a dear friend, nothing more. He's got an American boyfriend, so it's mutual — that we're just friends, I mean."

"That was nice of you. I bet you were a beautiful bride." I could hear the smile in her voice.

"I was a lice-head bride." I told her about Alex's excuse for my short hair and how the sisters-in-law had to strategize how to get the veil to stay on my shorn head. She started laughing as I told her all my adventures as a weekend bride. Soon, I was laughing at myself along with her. It was the first time I had laughed at myself, in the whole of my life. Nothing about me had been funny before.

"Who could be mad at a lice-head bride?" Thorpe cuffed me softly on the head and shook imaginary lice off her hand in mock disgust. "Where is he now?"

"We parted in Oaxaca. He told me he'd call Margarita when he got back to Oaxaca in a few months and we'd go visit his family there. I have his mother's phone number and address. But I don't know where he is exactly in the States, though he's probably in Pine Hill Station. I think that's where Luke, his boyfriend, lives. I'm not sure when I'll see him now, though. The road to Oaxaca is out."

We decided to walk to Puerto Ángel the next morning to see if we could find Margarita. Snuggled in each other's arms in the coolness of the tropical evening, we both fell into dreamless sleep. Right before I fell asleep, I thought of the final chapter of *Jane Eyre* once again. Like Jane, I'd returned to find the only place I'd ever felt at home had been destroyed. But like Jane, I also realized that home was not a physical place. Home was being with the one I loved, who miraculously still loved and wanted me. As we lay on a borrowed grass mat covered by a borrowed blanket in an open-air pavilion belonging to a culture utterly unknown to me a few weeks ago, I knew I'd come home.

When we walked through the jungle trail to the beach the next morning, Nelson's boat was just coming into view.

We could see Nelson, Maddie, José, and one other person aboard. As the boat drew closer, I drew in my breath.

"Mi amiga Ana, I have come to save you!" Alex called out to the shore.

58

Zipolite

"That him?" Thorpe thumbed in his direction. I nodded. "He's very good looking. Just a friend, though? A friend you happen to be married to? Nothing to be jealous about?"

"He's a great dancer, too," I said with exaggeration. "Kind, thoughtful, charming. He'd make a great husband. Except for one thing. He likes men!"

"Two things," Thorpe rejoined. "You like women."

"Nope. I like woman." I found myself giving her a flirtatious look, like I was someone else. Joking, flirting, laughing at myself. Like I was 'that fun-loving woman with the short blond hair, Ana Jiménez' I had imagined I had the power to become all those weeks ago when I had first arrived. For a moment, that Ana of my imagination — all of her — seemed to fit me, be me.

By this time, José had gotten Alex in the dinghy and was rowing him ashore. He was barefoot, with sandals and a baseball cap in one hand. His pants were rolled up, and he jumped out of the boat as it reached the shore. José gave a little wave, but Alex pushed the rowboat back into the water and José turned the small craft around and rowed back to the bigger boat, to get the other passengers.

"Ana, I am so happy to see you are well. When mi mamá calls to tell me that there is a hurricane, I tell the lady at the dance studio I must leave and come to México right away. A long bus to Acapulco, a long bus to the X in the road, a long walk to Mazunte. I find Mr. Nelson and I tell him he must, he must take me to you." He was smiling, hugging me. Finally, he noticed Thorpe. He looked at me and turned to her. "Ah, you are Thorpe, are you not? Ana told me of you. You are correct, mi amiga, she is muy hermosa. And I see I am too late. You are already saved by the beautiful Thorpe." He bowed, took her hand, and pressed his lips to it, as if he were meeting the queen.

"He *is* charming." Thorpe smiled at me and Alex. "Hi Alex. Ana has told me all sorts of things about you, too. Most of them good." She gave him a big hug. "Very cool of you to come."

Alex was looking around and shaking his head. "Oh, this is terrible. The restaurant, the tiny huts, everything is gone. I am so sorry you lose your home, Ana. Where did you hide during the hurricane?"

I invited him to sit on the sand with me above the tide line, where it was dry, and I told him our survival story. Thorpe walked down to the shore and met the rowboat as it brought Maddie, Nelson, and José.

"Good to see you this fine morning, Dr. Thorpe," Nelson intoned at the edge of my hearing. I could see him pumping Thorpe's hand. No 'little lady' for Thorpe, I noted. She must have insisted he call her by her formal title from the moment they met. "I came to meet with someone from the government about my new property here."

As he spoke, I heard the faint sound of a boat motor coming from the direction of Puerto Ángel.

Alex was talking. "...so I stay in Mazunte with José and Verónica."

I tried to focus on Alex. "Will you stay with them tonight, too?"

"Yes, but I will sleep in the hammock in the garden. You will sleep in the bed."

"Alex, I have many more things to tell you. Could we go somewhere and talk?"

"Yes, of course. But now, we help to empty the boat. Mr. Nelson buys everything in the food store in Mazunte. But the man who owns the store says no problema. The food truck from Puerto Escondido is coming today, so he is happy to allow Mr. Nelson to buy all the food. He wants to make the people of Zipolite happy with him, so they will work for him when he builds the tourist bungalows."

"Not sure they want this development," I said. "But I think they are going to get it anyways."

The boat was pulling close to where Nelson had docked offshore. I saw José run to where the dinghy was up on the shore, drag it around, push it off the beach, and hop in for one more ferrying trip. He hurried toward the now idling speed boat. One of the men on it was putting out an anchor. There were two other people on the boat, and one of them was a woman. Could it be?

Alex was looking out to the boat, too. He stood and waved.

"Margarita!" we said at the same time and headed toward the shore to welcome her.

There was a small crowd of people waiting to greet Margarita. She didn't know who to hug first. Madre Hermosa came to the front of our group and grabbed her hand, kissed her on both cheeks, and brought her to Thorpe.

"What a sight for sore eyes!" Thorpe gave Margarita a big hug.

"Damn, Thorpe. How'd you even get here?" Thorpe indicated *The Redeemer* anchored next to the government boat.

"Hi Ana, glad you're safe." She gave me a hug, too. "Alex? What are you doing here?"

"I come to save mi amiga Ana, but she is already saved." He indicated Thorpe.

"You all sheltered up at the cave, huh?" Margarita said. Madre Hermosa asked about her parents and her fruit stand, and Margarita answered in Spanish. I gleaned that her parents were fine and that a friend of hers had helped her pack up the furniture and blenders from the juice stand and move it to her parents' house a mile inland before the storm. While the stand itself had disappeared in the storm, rebuilding wouldn't be as onerous as many of us had worried it would be.

"In a month, I'll be back up and running," she finished in English. "They got big plans, I heard, on the way over here." She indicated where Nelson and the government official were chatting and pointing at the gouge in the cliff where our huts used to be. "If they put a decent road in to Zipolite, there's no telling how many tourists will come. I might have to open a second fruit stand in Zipolite."

"Progress sucks sometimes, though," Thorpe put in.

"Yeah, but change is the way of the world. It was just a matter of time before this piece of paradise would be washed away. On the way over here, I made sure that government guy knew that we wouldn't put up with them taking the Zapotec's ancestral lands and leaving them with nothing. Surprisingly, he's on their side. He and Nelson are talking about an arrangement where the Zapotecs have veto power over any of Nelson's plans. And continued access to their beachfront. Their village is going to be declared some sort of living heritage site — with no development allowed, except that decided by the Zapotecs. So, it may turn out all right for everyone but the Americans who spent their winters here."

José suggested that he row Alex and me out to *The Redeemer* to start loading the rowboat with the goods for the Zapotecs. We worked awhile at stacking cases in the small boat. José stayed in the rowboat, making sure it was weighted evenly. He rowed to shore and a couple of Zapotec men unstacked the small boat. A third man had brought the donkey to the beach, and he loaded up her two woven saddlebags for the walk up to the village. Sacks of corn flour for making tortillas, dried corn and beans, crates of tomatoes and onions, and other provisions gradually made their way from the large boat, into the small boat, and eventually up to the village.

While we waited for José to return and start another round, I told Alex my story. "You knew right away that I was on the run, didn't you?"

"This is true, but I also know you are a good person. In my heart, I feel it."

Alex thought the fact that I had killed a man was very sad. "I know you would not do this unless there was no other way to save yourself, Ana."

I wasn't so confident that was the case, but his look of brotherly love and the way he squeezed my hand in support made tears of gratitude come to my eyes. Why had I been so afraid to tell my love and my friends all my secrets?

Eventually, we emptied the larger boat of goods and José came back to *The Redeemer*. "You will stay with me this night, mi hija," he said. "I believe we will talk about the past and talk about the future."

The future. It wasn't something I had thought about these last few days. When I wasn't spilling my guts about my past, I had lived in the moment, feeling incredible sorrow over the loss of Zipolite. And incredible joy because of Thorpe, but also because it felt so good to live in honesty, finally. I stood up straighter, held my head higher, let people see more of my face than ever before in my adult life.

All that was about to change when we left the remnants of Zipolite for good. The future. I couldn't see my way to feeling joy about that. It promised only separation from Thorpe with ever-present fear of arrest for the rest of my days. If not prison.

But again, I had underestimated my friends. And quite possibly myself.

59

Mazunte

We returned to shore and sat cross-legged on the sand for a lunch of squash, beans, and tortillas brought from the village, made by Madre and two other Zapotec women. We visited with Margarita for a time, and I was glad she felt hopeful about her business future. Nelson called us to board *The Redeemer* and make our way to Mazunte. Maddie and Thorpe — or Professor Haystead and Dr. Thorpe, as Nelson called them — would stay up at his house in the hills. He had invited me too, but I politely turned him down and instead accepted José's invitation to stay with him and Verónica and Alex.

It was a quick and loud ride. I sat on the bow bench, letting the breeze ruffle my still-short hair. The future. I focused on it keenly now, because it had started to rush up to snatch me from this place. Thorpe said she had some ideas. When I focused on what I wanted, I realized I did too.

After we'd docked and José had tied the boat securely, our party split in two. Maddie, Thorpe, and Nelson turned to begin the walk up to his house on the hill. "Verónica has invited us for breakfast, so we will see you tomorrow," Thorpe said as she and Maddie waved goodbye. I looked after them with longing in my heart for Thorpe, but with resolution — I had to tell Verónica and José my story.

José turned to Alex and me. "Come and see the small turtle you saved."

Mazunte was surprisingly intact, I saw as I looked around. A bit of wind damage here and there, but all the buildings were still standing, and the jungle surrounding them also looked undamaged. There was a streetlight next to the dock, and it had recently gone on as the sun lowered to the horizon. The village hadn't even lost electricity in the storm.

José unlocked the door of the well-made turtle hospital. I silently thanked Nelson or Providence, or the hospital builders for making a strong building for the injured turtles — one that protected Verónica and José as well. We went to the tank where my rescued female had been put. She was gliding leisurely from one side of the tank to the other and looked at us when we approached her quarters. José tore open a crate of lettuce sitting near the tank and handed me a head. She came over and took the leaf I offered from my hand, unafraid. I could see her wounds had substantially healed and she could soon be released to the wild.

"In two weeks, the sea is flat again and all turtles, they come home to Mazunte. In two weeks, we take this turtle and put her in the sea."

Alex asked, "What do you mean, the turtles will come home?"

"When the hurricane comes, all the life of the sea that can move go to the deep water. Turtles do this, rays, sharks, many fish. In two weeks, all come back. The Zapotec men fix the boats. The fish come back close to the land. All is well in two weeks. This is when we take the turtle home, too."

I had the strangest feeling at these words. My heart, my mind, felt totally aligned. More than anything, I wanted to help José release this turtle. I wanted to dive in the seagrass forest again and search for turtles. I said nothing. I had no boat, nowhere to stay. My job was over.

We walked to the little adobe house. Verónica was in the

outdoor kitchen putting the finishing touches on a stew filled with vegetables and beans. There were stacks of tortillas to fill with queso and avocado. For dessert, she had made an egg custard with a caramel topping. We slaked our thirst with fresh-squeezed limeade. As we sat at the table finishing our dessert, I cleared my throat.

"José, Verónica, I must tell you of my past now. But before I do, I want to let you know how much I appreciate how kind, how welcoming, you have been to me."

"It is nothing, mija. We are happy to know you."

"That's the problem, José. You don't know me." With that introduction, I told the story of why I had come here for the fourth time.

"We are of the same soul, mija," was José's response to my tale. "When we are young, we do a very bad thing. But we learn how to save our soul by speaking of this bad thing to all the good people around us." He pointed to Alex and Verónica. "They make our hurt better. They make us better. We make the promise before God to be good people. Then, no longer do we have the..." He made a fist and mimicked a stab to his chest.

"Wound," I suggested. I tried to ignore the irony in his choice of metaphors.

"Sí. No longer do we have the wound to the heart from the bad thing. I know this. It is my life." José had grabbed my hand as he spoke, his voice quivering with emotion. "Mi hija, it will be the same for you. This I know!"

My daughter. After all this truth-telling, José had used those precious words in relation to me, the murdering liar. It seemed impossible. "I am still your... mija? After what I have done?"

Now Verónica took my other hand. "Si, nuestra hija, siempre." She looked at me and I thought I saw...love...there.

José said, "We have the bond. We are saved in the sea by Santa Juanita. I find you. Verónica and me, we have no children. But I find my child on the sand. Santa Juanita send us a child from the sea. You, Ana. Esto es un milagro — a miracle."

Alex had been silent for some time, looking from one of us to the other. "Did I not tell you, Ana, that you were lucky? You almost die in the sea but instead you find a father and a mother. This is very lucky."

José nodded and smiled at Alex's conclusion. "I have a surprise for you, mija. Tomorrow. Now it is time for sleeping."

The sky was pink, and the sun still hidden by the mountains when José knocked softly at my door. "Come. I show you the surprise."

I dressed quickly and followed José out the front door. We walked the short path from José's house, past the sea turtle hospital to the dock where Nelson's boat was tied. On the other side of the dock from *The Redeemer* were two small boats. One, I recognized as the rowboat José used to go to the seagrass forest in Mazunte. The other was a red rowboat, a bit bigger than my destroyed little craft. It had oars, but it also had a small motor on the back. When I drew closer, I could see that *La Tortuga II* was painted in neat black letters on the bow.

José smiled and pointed to the name. "El patrón has given this boat and this motor for the turtle project. When it is time, I will go to the seagrass forest in my rowboat. You will go to the Zipolite forest with the help of *La Tortuga II* and the motor on the back."

"Me? Do you mean...? But where...?"

"Mija, for now, you will live here with Verónica and me. When el patrón builds the tourist bungalows in Zipolite, one small one will be for you. This is your boat. Get in the boat and I will teach you about the motor. It is not difficult."

When we got back to shore, I was confident I could operate the motor on my own. We walked quietly toward the small house. As we approached, I could smell coffee brewing and eggs cooking. I could hear conversation in Spanish and English.

"Good morning, my love. How'd you like José's little surprise?" Thorpe pecked me on the cheek and handed me a tin cup filled with steaming black coffee.

She and Maddie were sitting at the garden table with Alex, a large pot filled with coffee between them. "You sure, Alex?" That was Maddie. She gave a little wave and indicated I should sit. "We are having a meeting about you, Ja...Ana. We are concocting a plan."

"What kind of a plan?" I sat and took a long swallow of Verónica's aromatic brew. It seemed José wasn't the only one who had figured out my future.

"I haven't told you about this yet, Ana," Thorpe said, "but the reason I had to go back to the States is because the company I work for is suing me. So I had to arrange for a lawyer and get my case together."

"Suing you? Why? For what? Could you go to prison?" I had a thought of both of us in orange jumpsuits in cells down the hall from one another.

"Nah, it will be fine. It's about that item I found in Costa Rica. I can fill you in on the details some other time. The reason I mentioned it is because of Phyl — Phyllis, my lawyer. She's a bona fide member of the Lavender Menace." At my alarmed look, Thorpe laughed. "It's a group of lesbian lawyers. She does corporate law, but I know for a fact that some of the other members do criminal law." At my continued puzzled features, she added, "Like for instance, defending people who are charged with homicide."

The lightbulb went on. I found myself speaking in a clear, decisive voice — a voice I didn't realize I had in me.

"I want to stay here in Mazunte and study turtles with José."

"For now, that's a good idea," Thorpe replied, though there was disappointment in her eyes. "It will take a while to get everything in order."

"My job will be to help with the pre-trial research," Maddie said. "I know most of the pertinent background facts, and others I can ferret out quietly."

"I came here without a passport. I flushed my U.S. driver's license back in Ciudad Juárez. All I have is a visa for my stay in Mexico, a marriage certificate, and a Mexican driver's license, all in my alias — Ana Jiménez. How could I ever come back to the States? And why would I want to be arrested and take my chances with a jury in Texas?"

"When you want to go to America, I can get you across," Alex contributed. "I have many friends on the American side of the border. They will not care if I bring a gringa with blond hair who has lost her passport across with me."

"Thanks," I said to Alex, to Maddie, and especially to Thorpe. "I appreciate all the work you put into this plan. But I'm staying here with José and Verónica."

Thorpe stared at me for a while. She said, "Life is long, Ana. You may feel this is the best decision right now, and it probably is. But you will never be free, never be able to have a larger life, never be able to travel with me — something I was really hoping you'd want to do someday. The only way to get this out of your life is to confront it head on. The only way out is through."

The words she'd spoken in my dream. The advice that had made the heavy load I'd been bearing disappear from my shoulders these past few days. But I couldn't, I didn't want to. I wasn't brave enough to cross that border and take the consequences.

"Listen." It was Maddie, always a voice of reason. "It's clear you're not ready, and we aren't, either. It'll take months to find the right lawyer, quietly collect the evidence, plan a strategy, and get it ready to spring. There's no sense in making her decide now, Thorpe. Let her be. She's been through a lot."

"Yeah, I know. I just want to be with you, Ana. But I have to go back to the States for this damn case. Maddie's right. You might as well stay here for now."

That was the way we left it.

Thorpe and I took a walk on the beach, and when we were out of sight of the village, she took my hand and we stopped and kissed, over and over and over. We would have a future, she assured me, whatever it took.

My love and my two dear friends left for Acapulco later that day.

60

Zipolite

Two weeks after Thorpe, Maddie, and Alex had departed for their lives in the States, I set out in my new boat with José and the now-healed turtle in her tub of water for the seagrass forest of Zipolite. We made a mark on her shell in the shape of an "A" so we could identify her easily if we ever saw her again.

It was a beautiful, if humid, day, the first week of June. There were rain clouds off to the west that would bring showers this afternoon, as I was learning was typical of the summer weather in this part of Mexico. There was a bit of a breeze to cool us as we headed around the bend where the debris from the hurricane was still piled high. As we approached Zipolite, I heard the distinctive sounds of heavy machinery. When we drew closer, I saw that the huge yellow machines used to build roads had arrived in Zipolite. Nothing much had happened there yet, but the implications for the future were clear. There would someday be a road that reached from Puerto Escondido through Mazunte, through Zipolite, to Puerto Ángel. This spot of paradise that had protected and nurtured me would be forever changed.

When we arrived at the buoy atop the seagrass forest, I carefully lowered the throttle and cut the motor. As we glided by, José reached out and grabbed the buoy and threaded our bow rope through its ring. I retrieved my new mask and flippers from the bottom of the boat, stripped to my swimsuit, and fell backward into the welcoming sea. I put on my fins, adjusted my facemask, and got ready to follow our turtle as José gently took her from the tub she'd traveled here in and put her in the sea alongside me.

She hesitated only long enough to take a breath, and dove, heading right for the seagrass forest. I followed, keeping a respectful distance. As we approached the forest and I could distinguish the fronds waving in the sea currents, I saw that José was correct. The life of the forest had returned. I came up for a breath and called to José that I would do my usual clockwise rotation around the perimeter of the patch of green. When I dove again, I saw our little turtle munching seagrass contentedly. I saw a ray moving its sleek body over the top of the forest. I saw that the grouper had returned and was sitting on the bottom in its usual spot. Two medium-large turtles were enjoying the seagrass forest along with our little rescue, and smaller fish too were darting among its protective foliage.

I had made my way around the perimeter and counted four turtles in addition to the one we had released. One more dive and I would get back into the boat and take notes on my sightings as José maneuvered *La Tortuga II* back to the dock at Mazunte. I took a deep breath and dove down until I was nearly touching the tops of the fronds of waving grass. I was watching a school of jack mackerels shimmering past me when a large sea turtle approached. I had no doubts about her identity. She swam toward me, looking at me with her baleful eyes, letting me know that she had survived the storm, assuring herself that her rescued human had, too.

Santa Juanita turned and swam off into the deep blue of the Pacific.

Epilogue

Pine Hill Station, Texas
October 1986

I had a hard time convincing the officer on duty that I was presenting myself as the perpetrator of the most widely covered murder in recent Pine Hill Station history. "You sure you want to do this, girl?" he asked, surprisingly. But I nodded and put out my wrists to be cuffed.

I was held without bail on a charge of manslaughter, a felony of the second degree, since I'd turned myself in. I couldn't argue — I was a proven runner from justice, and I had killed Johnny. Life in the county jail, in its simplicity at least, wasn't so dissimilar from the life I'd lived in Zipolite, though the view and the food were substantially worse. I spent my days in three activities: reading Thorpe's gift of a replacement copy of *Meditations* by Marcus Aurelius; meeting with Chelsea, the Lavender Menace criminal attorney Thorpe had hired for me; and being shunted, ankle-chains clanking, between the unvaried and hyper-controlled routines of prison life for an admitted murderer. Sporadically, Thorpe would visit, ten minutes maximum, facing each other and speaking on closed circuit phones, a plastic barrier between us.

When the trial began, my routine grew to include sitting

in my orange prison jumpsuit, cuffed and chained, next to Chelsea on the defense side of the courtroom. I felt strangely detached from the proceedings, as if this was happening to a character in a courtroom drama I was watching on a small black-and-white TV.

Finally, the last day of taking witness testimony in my defense arrived. Thorpe was hopeful — there were some surprise witnesses she thought I'd appreciate. I thought it best to believe I would be convicted — less disappointment involved. But I didn't tell Thorpe that. Instead, I repeated one of the most famous Aurelius quotes to myself and tried to believe it: "Never let the future disturb you. You will meet it, if you have to, with the same weapons of reason which today arm you against the present."

Thanks to Thorpe, Maddie, and the Lavender Menace, my case received maximum publicity. It was a daily front-page story in the local paper, Thorpe reported. Women's rights groups showed up with placards: "Attempted Rape is a Crime;" "Women Have the Right to Defend Themselves." The court had been jammed every day since the trial started.

"Murder is murder," was the essential argument of the prosecutor. As I'd admitted I'd done it, the jury should convict. I didn't pay much attention to what they said about me. I focused instead on the women who crowded the courtroom — young and old, mothers and college students, Black, white, and Hispanic women. They were on my side, my lawyer Chelsea told me, and juries did pay attention to that, even though they weren't supposed to.

The character of the deceased was not supposed to be evidence in a murder trial, the prosecution argued. But Chelsea convinced the judge that it was pertinent in this case because, if Johnny had been known to rape, it would help demonstrate that I had reason to resort to the ultimate in self-defense. And they had witnesses to that effect, Chelsea argued. Eventually, the judge relented.

Maddie, Thorpe, and Alex had attended the entire trial. I noticed that today, the day the last witnesses for the defense would be deposed, there was a good-looking tall Black man seated next to Alex; when he caught my eye, he pointed and mouthed the word, "Luke." They made an extremely handsome pair. The other new attendee was Ma, who must have taken the bus from Iowa for this last big day of the defense. She had probably spent the last of her paltry savings and used her few vacation days to be here, just to see her daughter convicted of homicide. I smiled weakly at her, and she wiped a tear away with her handkerchief. No doubt it was scented with lavender, just like always. Ma — would I ever be able to visit her in Iowa again?

When the "surprise" witnesses (surprise to me, at least) filed into the courtroom, I watched them from my chair next to Chelsea. My jaw may well have been hanging on the floor — I was too shocked to notice. First came a Black woman with graying hair in a wheelchair. The chair was pushed by a tall Black woman. Both smiled and waved at Maddie as they took their places. Roz, it must be Roz. And her mother? The next witness I recognized with a start. It was Liz Wharton, Johnny's wife, whom I had seen once from a distance about a year ago. There was no mistaking her diminutive frame and her perfectly coifed silvery blond hair. She took a seat next to Roz, and the two started chatting as if they knew one another. Another pair walked in, a slim, attractive Black woman with a short Afro followed by a shorter white woman. I gasped as I saw this young blond woman take her place at the end of the row. It was me, as I had looked six months ago. It was Jenny.

Jenny. Jenny had come to my defense, as I thought I had come to hers on that terrible night. Nothing else mattered to me. Jenny was here.

"He raped me when I was a fourteen-year-old girl and he

305

a fourteen-year-old boy," Roz's mom — Grace Gaines — said from her wheelchair after taking the witness oath to tell the whole truth and nothing but the truth. "It was back in 1951."

"I am the daughter born of that rape," said Roz, when she took the stand.

"We have the laboratory scientist ready to testify about the results of the paternity test that this witness allowed to be done," said Chelsea a bit later.

"My husband raped our daughter for five years while I was at my evening job," Liz testified. "I didn't know about it at the time, but now I do. Johnny was a good provider, an able historian. But he raped my daughter, and he raped Grace Gaines. About our sexual relations, I have no comment." There was a bitterness in her voice, a horror, that made any other statement unnecessary.

"He raped me for five years, from the time I was thirteen and mom took that night job, until I left for college. I went to college a thousand miles away to escape him. I hated my mother because I thought she knew. He encouraged that belief. I almost lost my mother because of him!" Jenny choked with emotion. "The defendant and I look a lot alike."

Yes. Her eyes were my eyes; I had seen that truth when I'd first glimpsed her high school photo. No. I was not surprised to hear my dream's conclusions transformed into the barefaced truth of a courtroom testimony. Her eyes were my eyes.

Chelsea introduced my graduate school ID photo at this point in the trial. When the image of my six-months-ago self — Jane Meyer — was projected on a large screen for all to see, an audible gasp arose from the courtroom audience.

"He's a rapist, and he's been a rapist since he started as a teenager by raping Grace Gaines. My client had every reason to believe he meant to grievously harm her that night, just as he grievously harmed these women. Indeed, Jane Meyer became his substitute victim when the rape of his daughter was no longer possible. I ask you to acquit my client on the grounds of self-defense," she concluded.

Once the trial ended, it didn't take long for the jury to reach its verdict.

"Innocent on account of justified self-defense," was the verdict the judge read after the jury foreman, a glasses-wearing older Black woman, had handed him a written declaration of what the jury had concluded. "The defendant is cleared of all charges and free to go," the judge announced. A cheer went up from the crowded courtroom.

My minder clicked open the ankle chains and handcuffs I had been wearing. I knew where I wanted to go. Although there were many, many people I needed to thank, there was one I needed to approach right now.

"Hi, Jenny. It is so good to meet you. I used to be Jane Meyer, but I have become Ana Jiménez now."

I looked at Jenny with my identical blue eyes. Hers were calm and looked at me with friendship. They were no longer haunted.

"I'm so glad to meet you, Ana Jiménez."

Acknowledgments

I am indebted to several people for this part of my novelist's journey. First and foremost, I thank Maggie Shopen Thompson for providing the question that sent me to the beach of the dead in search of an answer. I thank my editor and reader, Miciah Bay Gault, and readers Judith Hinds, Maggie Shopen Thompson, and Therese Mageau, whose insight and encouragement kept me believing in my project. The members of the North Branch Writers group must be acknowledged for their cogent suggestions and constant encouragement. Kristen Plylar-Moore helped me visualize a main character and my brother Bob Bogard is the very embodiment of another. I thank Noemi Rodriguez for her extremely helpful comments on Mexican culture and language and Carolyn Siegel for her feedback on my Spanish. Laurie Broome deserves special mention; she undertook a close reading of my attempts at Mexican Spanish and English as a second language and gave me detailed feedback on how to do better. That said, all remaining errors are mine and only mine. I thank Kyle McCord, who gave me a second Atmosphere Press contract, Alex Kale and Megan Turner, my editors at Atmosphere, and Jessica Lack, proofreader extraordinaire. Ronaldo Alves and Kevin Stone produced a wonderful cover, and Cassandra Felten and Emma Riva designed a lovely interior. Finally, I thank my spouse, Michael Strebe, for his constant encouragement and unwavering support.

About Atmosphere Press

Atmosphere Press is an independent, full-service publisher for excellent books in all genres and for all audiences. Learn more about what we do at atmospherepress.com.

We encourage you to check out some of Atmosphere's latest releases, which are available at Amazon.com and via order from your local bookstore:

Icarus Never Flew 'Round Here, by Matt Edwards

COMFREY, WYOMING: Maiden Voyage, by Daphne Birkmeyer

The Chimera Wolf, by P.A. Power

Umbilical, by Jane Kay

The Two-Blood Lion, by Nick Westfield

Shogun of the Heavens: The Fall of Immortals, by I.D.G. Curry

Hot Air Rising, by Matthew Taylor

30 Summers, by A.S. Randall

Delilah Recovered, by Amelia Estelle Dellos

A Prophecy in Ash, by Julie Zantopoulos

The Killer Half, by JB Blake

Ocean Lessons, by Karen Lethlean

Unrealized Fantasies, by Marilyn Whitehorse

The Mayari Chronicles: Initium, by Karen McClain

Squeeze Plays, by Jeffrey Marshall

JADA: Just Another Dead Animal, by James Morris

Hart Street and Main: Metamorphosis, by Tabitha Sprunger

Karma One, by Colleen Hollis

Ndalla's World, by Beth Franz

Adonai, by Arman Isayan

About the Author

CYNTHIA J. BOGARD has reinvented herself as a novelist after a successful career as a Professor of Sociology and Women's Studies at Hofstra University in New York. Born and raised in rural Wisconsin she's lived in Kuwait, Greece, Mexico, New York, Texas, Vermont, and in Madison, Wisconsin.

World traveler, longtime feminist and environmentalist, Greece, mid-century jazz, and Mother Nature are all close to her heart. These days, Cynthia lives with her spouse and two rescue dogs in Montpelier, Vermont.

Visit www.CynthiaJBogard.com for news about Cynthia and her works.

Also by Cynthia J. Bogard

A History of Silence, Book One of the Heartland Trilogy

Milton Keynes UK
Ingram Content Group UK Ltd.
UKHW041844090224
437425UK00006B/162